tales a look at the world of, as one character puts it, 'amulets, rabbit feet, you name it' . . . a police procedural with paranormal activity at its black heart."
—Shelf Awareness

"[A] rich, intensely suspenseful thriller. Seeck's debut is dark and intricate—the moments of revelation are as vividly cinematic and impactful every time. Seeck has an uncanny ability to unspool reveals at just the right pace to get the reader's heart pounding as they make the connection at the same moment as the detective on page. His expertise with pacing, his careful plotting, and his choice to use short, quick chapters all combine to create a vivid, robust thriller."
—*Booklist* (starred review)

"One twist follows another, baffling the police and readers alike. Seeck imbues this riveting procedural with a deliciously creepy undertone. Readers will be excited to see what Seeck does next."
—*Publishers Weekly* (starred review)

"Seeck's riveting, multilayered debut, blending masterful police procedural with a chilling exploration of the occult, kept me up all night, devouring it in one amazing gulp, and checking under the bed."
—#1 international bestselling author Sara Blaedel

"*The Witch Hunter* is everything I wish for in a thriller: exceptional story, exceptional characters, exceptional writing, and shocking twists— exceptional everything. I loved this book, and you will too."
—Chris Mooney, author of *Blood World*

"One of the best books I have read. Ever. Absolutely thrilling, well written, and oh so hard to put down."
—Emelie Schepp, author of *Slowly We Die*

BERKLEY TITLES BY MAX SEECK

THE WITCH HUNTER

THE ICE COVEN

THE LAST GRUDGE

THE
LAST
GRUDGE

A GHOSTS OF THE PAST NOVEL

MAX SEECK

TRANSLATION BY
Kristian London

BERKLEY
New York

BERKLEY
An imprint of Penguin Random House LLC
penguinrandomhouse.com

Copyright © 2021 by Max Seeck
Translation copyright © 2023 by Kristian London
Readers Guide copyright © 2023 by Penguin Random House LLC
Penguin Random House supports copyright. Copyright fuels creativity,
encourages diverse voices, promotes free speech, and creates a vibrant
culture. Thank you for buying an authorized edition of this book and for
complying with copyright laws by not reproducing, scanning, or
distributing any part of it in any form without permission. You are
supporting writers and allowing Penguin Random House to continue to
publish books for every reader.

BERKLEY and the BERKLEY & B colophon are registered trademarks of
Penguin Random House LLC.

Originally published in Finnish as *Kauna* by Tammi Publishers, Helsinki, 2021.

Library of Congress Cataloging-in-Publication Data

Names: Seeck, Max, 1985- author. | London, Kristian, translator.
Title: The last grudge : a ghosts of the past novel / Max Seeck ;
translation by Kristian London.
Other titles: Kauna. English
Description: First U.S. edition. | New York : Berkley, 2023. | Originally
published in Finnish as Kauna by Tammi Publishers, 2021.
Identifiers: LCCN 2022032631 (print) | LCCN 2022032632 (ebook) |
ISBN 9780593438848 (trade paperback) | ISBN 9780593438855 (ebook)
Subjects: LCGFT: Detective and mystery fiction. | Novels.
Classification: LCC PH356.S44 K3813 2023 (print) | LCC PH356.S44 (ebook) |
DDC 894/.54134--dc23/eng/20220708
LC record available at https://lccn.loc.gov/2022032631
LC ebook record available at https://lccn.loc.gov/2022032632

First U.S. Edition: February 2023

Printed in the United States of America
1st Printing

Book design by Katy Riegel

To William & Lionel

THE LAST GRUDGE

Prologue

L'ÉTRANGER OPENS THE door, allows his gaze to circle the room, and smiles. The three-star hotel is ascetic, but the room is perfect for his needs. He inserts the key card into the electricity slot, and a dim light comes on.

He lowers his Louis Vuitton duffel bag to the floor and feels the weight drop from his shoulder. He hasn't let the duffel out of his grip since he disembarked from the vessel: his fingers have clutched the leather handle of his toolbox from the passenger bridge at the terminal into the taxi and across the hotel lobby.

He walks lazily to the large window overlooking a square. From the hotel's top story, the people swarming down below look like tin soldiers. And in a way that's what they are: the soldiers of their own lives, marching toward their own trivial battles. *The lemmings.*

A protest is taking place at the square's edge, outside a granite-faced office building: dozens of people swathed in overcoats carry large placards. Two police vehicles are present, and the officers who emerged from them monitor the situation passively.

L'Étranger laughs to himself. He has never participated in a demonstration. Why would he? He has always preferred to fade into the crowd rather than be the center of attention. Besides, permanent change is not achieved by gathering at some stupid square with a few dozen other losers. It's a nice idea, maybe; nothing more.

It's in the presence of crowds that he sometimes feels it, the utter detachment and alienation that has marked him since adolescence. But the sensation has never depressed him. Just the opposite: it's the result of an enlightenment he experienced during his youth. He grasps something the vast majority of ordinary people refuse to acknowledge: ultimately nothing we do or leave undone matters.

A new day dawns. And then another. And they will continue dawning until they dawn no more. That goes for him, for his neighbor, and for the entire world.

L'Étranger closes the curtains. He hoists the duffel bag onto the bed, pulls out a laptop, and opens it. The computer hums for a moment before a Tor-network messaging service opens.

His fingers lower to the keypad and conjure up a brief message: Here. Waiting.

Then he closes the email window and opens a text file. He stares at the page that appears on the screen: Existential Nihilism in the Works of Albert Camus. His dissertation topic is bold, sure to spark controversy among the academic community. Existential nihilism is generally associated with the works of Sartre, due to Sartre's atheistic worldview, but L'Étranger believes Camus—despite his agnosticism—deals with the exact same themes in his works, if from a more humane perspective.

I'll show you, you sheep. If anyone knows the meaninglessness of existence, it's me.

L'Étranger reaches into his pocket for a handkerchief and wipes away a fingerprint that has made its way to the screen. One chapter of his life is coming to a close. He needs to finish this one last job, and then he can concentrate on his academic career. Maybe he will find a position at a university. Maybe not. In the end, it makes no difference. But that doesn't mean he's going to do anything without proper compensation. As the Joker says in the film *The Dark Knight*: *If you're good at something, never do it for free.*

He pulls a book about the life of Søren Aabye Kierkegaard from his bag. Two photographs have been slipped between its pages: those of the two people who are going to pay for the completion of his studies. They will pay for it with their lives.

1

THE CAR OF the old elevator thunks between floors. The cable hums at the ceiling.

Greedy old shit.

Eliel Zetterborg catches a whiff of his bodyguard's powerful aftershave and turns up his nose. He thinks about the words painted on the placards he saw through the Maybach's tinted windows an hour ago.

He clenches and unclenches his fists; his hands feel weak. *Those ungrateful idiots don't know what they're talking about.*

Eliel steps out of the elevator and crosses the short distance to his front door, key in hand. Joonas shuts the elevator gate behind him. Eliel feels a pang of nostalgia when he hears the metal clank. The sound reminds him of the mechanical equipment of days gone by, iron and metal parts that smelled of lubricant and were powered by springs, steam, or mere gravity to perform work on people's behalf. In contrast, present-day technology is completely odorless and tasteless. Machines you could touch with your hand have turned into a series of elegant algorithms and mechanisms whose functioning is guided by principles so abstract that advertising and marketing professionals have to create beautiful stories around them to inject the tiniest hint of life. Even then, customers have only the faintest idea of how they work. No matter what these millennials say, things were better in the old days.

You killed this town, Zetterborg.

When Eliel Zetterborg founded EZEM Pipes Co. with Eetu Monto fifty years ago to the day, the name of a company still communicated its primary business. Back then, no one fiddled with computers at the machine works in the Herttoniemi industrial area; they hammered and turned parts used to build something real, something tangible. Not circuits or transistors, but industry that reeked of blood and sweat. Heavy industry—in its most literal sense.

Eliel shuts his eyes and imagines the sweet smell of red-hot metal, hears the splatter of welding at the rear of the manufacturing hall on the south side of Puusepänkatu.

"Will you be all right?" Joonas says with a discreet glance around the stairwell.

Joonas Lamberg is Eliel's long-term driver and bodyguard and is escorting his employer to his front door on this evening as on every other. He will then wait at the wheel of the Maybach down on the street until Eliel is ready. Then Joonas will drive Eliel to tonight's dinner venue, a restaurant located only a block from the latter's apartment. Joonas would typically be heading home at this point, but the times are exceptional: so many members of the general public hate Eliel Zetterborg and the board of RealEst from the bottom of their hearts that it's best to keep Joonas close at hand all evening.

"Yes, thank you. I'll see you downstairs in a minute," Eliel says, then opens the door to his apartment and taps the code into the alarm system.

Joonas gives a curt nod, peers up to the top floor, then starts descending the stairs. He does so every evening because he wants to make sure no one who doesn't belong there has snuck into the stairwell. Joonas is loyal and conscientious. He's a former SWAT unit officer and still dangerous, despite being almost fifty and unarmed.

Eliel Zetterborg knocks his shoes against the mat in the entryway and takes off his coat, the shoulders damp from the walk between the car and the building entrance. The apartment smells like a new fabric softener he asked the cleaner to buy. It masks the cloying, stale odor of antiques and upholstery dating from the war, as the scent has recently begun to repel Eliel. It reminds him that he is old and that he—just like everyone else on the planet—is condemned to die sooner or later. In his case sooner, no doubt. Ever since Anne-Marie passed, his days have felt like a slow slide toward death; it's as if his heart is beating less and less frequently, until one night it will stop and release him from his pain.

Eliel's eyes strike on a yellow plastic bag on the floor of the entryway. The cleaner was supposed to return the books to the Rikhardinkatu Library that morning and pick up the new ones he had reserved.

Hell's bells. That woman is getting careless.

Eliel steps into the living room, stands there with his hands in his pockets, and lets out a deep sigh. The company's anniversary has put him in a nostalgic mood.

Half a century. Over that time, RealEst has grown into a global corporation, and it's difficult these days to find any similarities to the small machine shop he and Eetu founded fifty years before.

The year 1970 was like a different reality in every respect: under the Finlandization policies of President Urho Kekkonen, the country was a very different place from what it is today, for better and for worse. In his parents' view, no doubt the latter. Eliel Zetterborg's father covered politics for Finland's largest daily, *Helsingin Sanomat*, and was a huge champion of freedom of the press. His mother enjoyed a prominent career as a playwright. The artistic, liberal Zetterborgs experienced the postwar atmosphere as oppressive and regressive, perhaps partly because their only son, Eliel, actively opposed the self-censorship the Finnish government practiced when it came to the Soviet Union. On the other hand, EZEM Pipes Co.—which became RealEst, Ltd., through a merger and IPO that took place in the spring of 1990—benefited greatly, especially in the 1980s, from bilateral trade between Finland and its eastern neighbor, a development that shaped Eliel's views of the Soviet Union in a significantly more positive way. As long as Finland's neighbor to the east was satisfied, business was good.

Opportunistic traitor.

Eliel knows he is a prime example of how ideology is cast aside in hopes of the fast profits offered by capitalism. Over the years, he has been accused of selling out his principles so many times by so many people that he doesn't let it get to him anymore. Besides, the accusations are true—even if decades have passed since then. But he regrets nothing, not for a second. His decisions made it possible for Anne-Marie and him to live a life of extreme privilege, and for Axel to be raised—unlike Eliel—in a wealthy, luxurious home. Sometimes Eliel wonders if rockier soil would have produced a different sort of son. Is their relationship difficult because their lives started out in such dissimilar circumstances?

Eliel pauses at the large mirror and gazes at the furrowed face hidden behind the white beard. His phone is flashing on top of the console, but Eliel doesn't intend to answer. His phone has been ringing off the hook today. Journalists, well-wishers, professional and amateur politicians, almost-friends, backstabbers. *Parasites.* It's a big day for Finnish industry and RealEst: at this very moment, the company's middle management is celebrating in a massive tent erected at Hietalahti Square, complete with a program and entertainment. The upper management and board of directors, on the other hand, are gathering for dinner with their spouses in the private dining room at Saslik, the venerable Russian restaurant right around the corner, in honor of the day.

Job killer.

Eliel closes his eyes and tries to forget.

He can still see them, the white placards reflecting the bright sunshine. There are dozens of them, and they are being held by hundreds of hands. Every insult in the world has been scrawled on them in large letters. Thousands of people have amassed outside the factory, and none of them are there to celebrate the company's fifty-year success story. The din raised by the angry throng is earsplitting, and the union man at the front is conducting this racket with a megaphone.

Eliel opens his eyes and feels his heart hammering. *The ingrates.* Of course it's a radical measure, but it was not taken lightly. If the factory could have been spared, it would have been. The board's decision to shut down the Kouvola unit had nothing to do with saving production costs; plumbing-material operations are being ramped down for the simple reason that they're not profitable. The factory, which employs nearly three thousand people, has been a money pit for a decade now, and the positive results in the other divisions are not sufficient justification to continue keeping it on life support into the hazy future. Presumably a bigger problem than the closing of the factory is that those who lose their jobs will be nearly impossible to place in the company's other divisions. That's how significantly RealEst, Ltd.'s operations have changed over the last ten years. Even if the company pays for costly training, there is no way a fifty-year-old metalworker is going to learn how to produce a single line of code. At least not fast enough.

Get out of Finland, you capitalist pig.

Eliel sighs. He reads the text message he received fifteen minutes ago. It's from Axel.

On my way to the restaurant. Please don't be late.

He considers his son. The boy's fine features and unique voice, which is surprisingly high. It has a tinge of jazzy whisky bass, just like that of Anne-Marie, from whom the boy also inherited his beautiful face and his birdlike build.

The curious heartburn that troubled Eliel throughout the drive has started again. The visit to Kouvola was not, he will admit, particularly pleasant. He knows he will not be serving as chair of the RealEst board for even a year, which is the precise reason he was prepared to take this bullet. The condemnation of the entire nation. His successor will start from a clean slate and perhaps even have the backing of the labor unions. That will make it possible to steer RealEst on to future success.

Eliel considers his reply, then settles for tapping an OK into the text field.

Just then he feels a sharp pain in his chest. For a moment he feels as if he can't breathe. He collapses onto the stool in the entryway.

Damn it.

Eliel is in splendid physical condition for a seventy-four-year-old—he recently ran a half-marathon in the senior division in two hours and fourteen minutes—but the idea of long restaurant dinners with ten-course menus and the accompanying wines wearies him body and soul. He probably ought to have his heart checked again, but Eliel looks askance at doctor visits and avoids them to the last. *Damn it all to hell.* If it weren't the company's fiftieth anniversary today, he would sink to the couch with a glass of whisky and watch *Emmerdale.*

Eliel advances slowly down the entry hall and into the living room. The long floor planks, stained brown, creak under his merino wool socks. He touches the light switch and the chandelier hanging from the ceiling comes to life. He undoes his cuff links and lets his sleeves dangle over his hands.

The needle of the record player lowers to the black disc. Johann Sebastian Bach: *Siciliano, Concerto in D minor, Bach-Werke-Verzeichnis 596.* Eliel thinks it the most beautiful piece of music ever composed. Listening to it feels almost masochistic—that's how wistful and melancholy it makes him. The concerto brings him back to Anne-Marie's funeral, when Axel's cousin played it on the piano at the beginning of the memorial service, here in this very room three or so years ago. More than a thousand long days and nights have passed since then, but the apartment still smells of Anne-Marie. In the end, it makes no difference what brand of fabric softener the cleaner buys.

Anne-Marie.

He ought to wear something tonight that reminds him of Anne-Marie.

Eliel walks past the grand piano to the sofa set and pauses in front of the oil painting that hangs there. The depiction of a capercaillie hinges outward to reveal a safe embedded in the wall. Eliel taps in the code, and the safe beeps and opens.

He takes from the top shelf what is perhaps his most prized possession: a Vacheron Constantin Genève with an eighteen-karat gold casing. The watch probably has little monetary worth, but it has all the more sentimental value: Anne-Marie gave it to him as a wedding present in 1969.

Eliel senses the weight of the watch on his wrist; it feels foreign yet familiar. He returns to the grand piano and gazes at the spacious living room: the Persian carpets covering the floor, the furniture fashioned by hand long ago, the large oil paintings ensconced in decorative gilt frames.

Eliel has no interest in attending the party tonight. Not without his wife.

And then he hears something above the music.

He has stopped at the liquor cabinet next to the piano, but the floor is still creaking. As if there were a second-long lag between his footfalls and the sound they produced.

He holds his breath. Suddenly he's sure he's not alone in the apartment. He glances back, but the arch leading into the kitchen is empty. The kitchen is dark; the only glimmer comes from the windows facing the Russian embassy. Eliel shakes his head. It's just the Jugendstil building; old structures live a life of their own.

J. S. Bach is playing in the background as beautifully as it does every night.

My mind is playing tricks on me. It's been a long day.

Eliel opens the bar, reaches for the masculine, broad-shouldered bottle of Macallan Reflexion. If the sensation in his chest grows unbearable, he'll cancel his attendance at tonight's dinner. That's one good thing about growing old: there's always an acceptable excuse for getting out of doing things one would prefer not to do. Age itself. No one can have anything to say about that.

The brown liquor burbles to the bottom of the glass like water from a pure tundra stream.

And the wooden floor is creaking again, this time more distinctly. He tosses back the contents of the glass, and the plummy whisky burns his throat.

"Hello?" Eliel says forcefully, despite knowing there will be no reply. The last time he did so, Anne-Marie was still alive. On a night he came home and wasn't sure if his wife was there or out.

Eliel lowers the tumbler to the liquor cabinet and coughs into his fist.

Of course he's home alone. The alarm was on when he stepped in, and he would have heard the front door open.

"Hello?" he hears himself say again. He knows he wouldn't if he were a hundred percent certain there was no one else in the apartment. The doubt is like a rapier at his breast. "Who's there?"

This time the creak comes from the other side of the wall, from the kitchen. A dragging sound that ends in an abrupt clunk. *A kitchen drawer.*

Eliel feels a shiver surge up his spine to his neck.

He reaches for his phone, brings up Joonas' number on speed dial.

The footfalls are more pronounced now. And then he sees it: a shadowy figure emerging calmly from the darkness of the kitchen.

The phone slips from Eliel's grasp and drops to the floor at his feet.

2

JOONAS LAMBERG OPENS the car door and steps out. The drizzle mists his shaved head, and his cotton blazer offers little protection against the biting wind. He's on the verge of pulling on his overcoat but rejects the impulse, and instead shuts the door of the gleaming, freshly waxed Maybach. After all, he's a former member of police special forces who he has dived into frigid water in full tactical gear and lain for eight hours on a metal roof, rigid from the subzero temperatures, staring through the sights of a sniper rifle without moving a muscle. He has shot to kill more than once and has been shot at just as often. One of the bullets—propelled by a 9mm belonging to a Swedish-speaking bank robber in November 1998—left a permanent scar above his knee and started the countdown to the end of his SWAT days, which forced him to switch to the private sector. Over the course of his long career, knives and bicycle chains have been wielded against him, but he has usually walked away from such encounters the victor. Although he has a firearm at home, he hasn't carried one since his law-enforcement days. No, he puts his faith in the Israeli self-defense system Krav Maga, in which he has forty years of experience and a black belt, second Dan.

So there's no question he can puff on a cigarette without an overcoat, even if the wind blowing off the sea tonight is downright murderous. The temperature is slightly above freezing, but he feels like he's standing in an air-conditioned freezer chest.

Lamberg places a cigarette between his lips, lights it with a butane torch, and scratches the scar tissue at his neck, which itches in the cold. The tinkle of a wind chime carries from the direction of nearby buildings.

He takes a drag and glances up at his boss' windows. The boss, who seems to have aged ten years over the past three. Since his wife's death, Zetterborg's step has gradually grown slower, and it has become harder than ever to establish any sort of contact with the old man.

Lamberg's thoughts turn to his mother, who is a year younger than Zetterborg and lives in an assisted-living facility. Alzheimer's has tightened its grip on her during the past few months, plunging her more recent memories into oblivion. Her future isn't looking too bright, and sometimes he wonders if he ought to snatch her away and take her off to live out the rest of her days somewhere where the sky blows a soft Mediterranean breeze instead of this icy drizzle.

Lamberg exhales the smoke from his lungs, and it flees instantly with a gust of wind.

He glances at his watch again, as if to check how long the cigarette has been burning. He takes a few sharp drags, drops the butt to the ground, and as he does, he notices his phone on the Maybach's passenger seat is ringing.

Lamberg climbs into the car and picks up the phone. The name flashing on the screen is `Prince Charles`. An inappropriate joke, of which the elder Zetterborg would no doubt disapprove if he were aware of the nickname Lamberg has bestowed upon Axel. In his interactions with the family, Lamberg is always polite but never fawning or officious. The boss man himself wanted it this way.

"This is Joonas."

Axel Zetterborg's voice is agitated: "Hi, Joonas. . . . I'm just calling because . . ."

Lamberg does what he does best: waits patiently.

"Are you with Dad?" Axel finally spits out.

"Your father is at home. I'm downstairs, in the car."

"I thought you were supposed to come straight to the restaurant."

"Your father wanted to stop by the apartment."

"OK . . . Dad is expected here at the restaurant, and he knows it."

Lamberg leans forward to look up at the corner windows of Zetterborg's apartment. They glow with a faint light.

"He's not picking up. He almost always answers." Now Axel sounds concerned. "I wouldn't call you, but he was complaining earlier today about not feeling well."

"I'm sure he'll be—"

"Go up and check on him."

"But—"

"Do as I say, Joonas."

"Certainly. I'll go upstairs."

Lamberg opens his car door and pushes himself out. In all likelihood there's nothing to worry about, but under no circumstances can more than a couple seconds pass between the tiniest suspicion and action. That would be unprofessional.

Lamberg strides to the front door of the building and pulls the key from his pocket. The call is still connected as he bounds up the stairs: six floors in under thirty seconds. His kneecap is working just fine, even though Lamberg knows it looks appalling in X-rays and could give out at any moment.

"I'm at the door. I can't hear anything inside . . . ," Lamberg says into the phone, slightly out of breath. He presses the doorbell.

"That's not what I was thinking, but . . ." Axel lets the sentence trail off, presumably because he hopes to hear his father's crotchety voice: *Coming, darn it. Hold your horses.*

But he doesn't hear it, and the door doesn't open.

Lamberg stands there outside the door with the phone at his ear, staring at the nameplate that reads ZETTERBORG in white letters against a black base. Then he bangs a few sharp raps against the door. The seconds follow one another until he's sure over a minute has passed.

"Joonas?" Axel says, and now Lamberg can hear the uneasiness in his voice.

Lamberg lets himself in with his key.

"Axel," he says upon reaching the living room, "you're right. Something is really wrong."

3

Detective Sergeant Jessica Niemi watches a squirrel scamper across the road in its self-grown winter coat, then climb a fat tree trunk with surprising speed. Nature's little miracles, like the agility of the gravity-defying rodent, have never ceased to amaze her. With the passing years, she seems to yearn for nature more and more, perhaps to create distance between herself and the tragedies and horrific fates she encounters on the job.

However, her love of nature isn't the reason Jessica has ventured into Helsinki's Central Park on this gloomy January evening.

The squirrel disappears, but Jessica can hear its tiny claws scrabble against the bark and see branches sway high up in the tree.

The path running through the dense forest is dark, and the icy drizzle has kept all but a few fitness enthusiasts inside. Jessica brought a flashlight, but so far she has managed with the lamps spaced sparsely at intervals along the path.

She zips up her windbreaker with the fingers of her left hand. Her right arm still dangles in a sling—not because it's necessary in terms of recovery, but because her arm muscles throb every time the wrist she injured in mid-December isn't supported.

A little over a month ago, a sledgehammer wielded by a young woman did a number not only on Jessica's wrist, but on the base of her thumb. It crushed the trapezium, and it was only the virtuosic performance of the operating surgeon that ensured the thumb had even a moderate chance of functioning again someday. Despite the successful surgery, Jessica is facing a patience-trying rehabilitative process that will continue for some time. A conservative guess puts Jessica wrapping her hand around a firearm at the police shooting range in summer at the earliest, maybe even autumn.

If she wants to go back, that is. Right now there's no guarantee.

The idea of taking a leave of absence caught Jessica off guard: she and her boss, Hellu, had agreed she could continue at the unit as long as she left the fieldwork, which requires a functioning hand, to others. And for a while Jessica felt like she wanted to get back. Despite everything Hellu had learned about Jessica and her past, Jessica had been given a second chance. Hellu had thrown her a life preserver, and for a fleeting moment, Jessica had clung to it. But then . . .

Jessica stops abruptly and gazes at the soaked sawdust on the surface of the path. The puddles there haven't frozen yet, and the wind is setting the water skittering.

This is where it happened, in this exact spot: last November, a drunk assaulted Jessica. After knocking her to the ground, he repeated a phrase in her ear, over and over: *Christmas Eve.*

And only fifty yards from the path, in the middle of the woods, the charred body of a man was discovered on Christmas Eve.

A gust of wind sets the leafless branches swinging in the darkness.

Jessica is roused from her reverie when she hears someone approaching rapidly. A few seconds later, a cyclist in Lycra zooms past and vanishes as quickly as she appeared.

A cold wave washes over Jessica. She doesn't believe in coincidence. She knows something is going on. Something she needs to get to the bottom of—alone.

She remembers looking out her apartment window on Christmas Eve.

She remembers what she saw. Horned figures. Witches. All a part of that insane cabal that murdered numerous people a year ago and ultimately threatened her life too.

But even so, she cannot completely trust her perceptions. It's perfectly possible her mind has mingled two worlds, only one of which is real.

This is why she must dig into the matter alone; otherwise she will never be at peace.

Jessica brings up her phone's camera, turns on her flashlight, and steps off the path, making for the place where a burned body was found on Christmas Eve.

4

DETECTIVE SERGEANT YUSUF Pepple of the Helsinki Police Violent Crimes Unit parks at the intersection of Vuorimiehenkatu and Muukalaiskatu, where blue-and-white police tape has been unrolled across the street. Fella Nalle's "Karhukirje" is blasting from the car's speakers; the jump of the bass can undoubtedly be heard at the front door of the building nearby.

Finnish rap is Yusuf's lifeline; he's been tanking up on it since early adolescence, when he first heard *Punainen tiili*, *Renesanssi*, and *Hampuusin päiväkirja*—all the classic albums of the genre—being played at house parties in Söderkulla.

He turns off the ignition, grabs his pack of Marlboro Lights, and climbs out of the car. January or not, the temperature is a few degrees above freezing, but the brisk wind coming off the sea a few blocks away makes the air frigid.

Yusuf hears the side door of the nearby van slide back, and a blond woman steps out with a duffel bag over her shoulder. Yusuf and the woman nod at each other in a discreet greeting.

"The Flatiron Building," she says as Yusuf lights a cigarette.

"Huh?"

The woman points at the triangular white building standing before them. "That. Copied from Manhattan."

Yusuf casts a look of feigned surprise at the woman. Her name is Tanja, and she is a crime scene investigator—a very cute one. Yusuf danced a slow dance with her at last year's Christmas party, and it ended in a kiss but it went no further, and Yusuf can't exactly remember why. Maybe the split with Anna was too still too fresh; maybe Yusuf thought fooling around with Tanja would permanently exclude the possibility of him and Anna reconciling. In retrospect, and although he wasn't fully conscious of it at the time, he spent last autumn still wrapped up in his previous life. In any case, the intimate dance at the Christmas party had remained a one-off, which was also a bit strange. As if two complete strangers had met for the length of one magical kiss, then gone their separate ways before the carriage turned back into a pumpkin. Or something like that.

"What are you talking about?" Yusuf says.

Tanja looks at him with exaggerated disappointment. "The architect Max Frelander visited New York and fell in love with the Flatiron Building, this iconic triangular skyscraper on Fifth Avenue. Frelander wanted to bring a cosmopolitan vibe back to Helsinki, and this is the result."

"Flatiron? So this guy built his own version of a building shaped like an appliance?"

"Not exactly. He modified a building that already stood on the lot, added stories, and rounded the end. I think it was around 1930 or so."

Yusuf eyes the eight-story example of functionalist architecture and takes a long drag of his cigarette. The clank of a tram carrying passengers from Tehtaankatu sounds like the start of an earthquake.

"A cosmopolitan vibe? I'm not sure I'm convinced."

"That's not surprising. The original Flatiron Building is three times taller."

"So Flanders' version is a runt."

"Frelander's."

Yusuf shoots Tanja an amused look and points the fingers holding his cigarette at her. "Frelander. Of course. And you know all this because . . ."

"Didn't I tell you last time? Or did we just dance?"

"Is that what we did? Dance?"

"Mostly." Tanja smiles and slips the hair falling out from under her beanie behind her ear. "I'm this close to being a licensed architect."

Yusuf's mouth turns up in a smile, revealing flawless teeth. "Wow. How the heck did someone who's about to start designing buildings become a forensic investigator who hangs around blood-soaked crime scenes?"

"You can still make a U-turn after you've arrived, Yusuf. It's even easier before you get there."

"I guess," Yusuf says, bringing the flirtatious conversation to a close. He starts walking toward the building. He and Tanja might be able to pick up where they left off at the Christmas party sometime, but it seems inappropriate to make a date or even fantasize about one at a crime scene where the body's still warm.

Three vans and an ambulance stand in the street lined with parked cars. For Yusuf, the blue flicker bouncing off the building's facade is such a familiar sight, he could describe it with his eyes closed. It's a message telegraphed to the surroundings that is never well received. As if death has scrawled its name in the guest book.

"It looks like we'll be working with a high-profile client today," Yusuf says, dropping the cigarette butt to the ground. He kills the burning end with the tip of his shoe.

"I've always figured it was only a matter of time before something like this happened," Tanja says. "You'd think the top dogs at RealEst would have arranged for extra-robust security for the time being."

"Tell me about it." Yusuf looks on as two officers in uniform talk to a man sitting on the steps leading to the door. The man is wearing dress trousers and a long black overcoat. *That must be the driver-slash-bodyguard Hellu mentioned on the phone.*

"See you inside. I'm going to put on my space suit," Tanja says, and heads back to the van.

Yusuf waves good-bye and directs his feet to the street door of the triangular building. He scooches under the cordon, then presents his ID for his uniformed colleagues' inspection. Yusuf has been trudging around crime scenes for six years now, but he's still stopped on occasion when entering a police cordon. Apparently his casual civilian clothes and dark skin still don't match the description of a detective in Finland, even in the 2020s. As the only person of color in the unit, Yusuf is used to having to deal with lingering gazes and blurted comments when meeting new colleagues or customers. But this time he's greeted by officers he knows.

"How's it going?" Yusuf says as he approaches one of the officers, hands in his pockets. The officer's name is Hallvik, and he's a tough cop Yusuf has bumped into at crime scenes before.

"The superintendent's inside," Hallvik says as the other officer continues questioning the driver.

Yusuf nods, then shoots a quizzical look over Hallvik's shoulder.

"The chauffeur," Hallvik says in a low voice. "He's the one who called it in."

"Did he see anything?"

"Doesn't seem like it." Hallvik hawks up a loogie and spits it to the ground. "The victim's son was also in the apartment when we arrived. Axel Zetterborg. Apparently he rushed over from a nearby restaurant where the victim was supposed to be having dinner tonight."

Yusuf appears to take a moment to digest Hallvik's words. "Where's Axel Zetterborg now?"

Hallvik nods at one of the vehicles. "In the van. He was a wreck. We had to be pretty forceful in insisting he leave the apartment. But at least so far there don't appear to be any contradictions between the two stories."

Yusuf glances over at the van where the younger Zetterborg is waiting for news. They should get his interrogation out of the way so he can go home. Unless there's reason to suspect he's mixed up in his father's death.

Yusuf turns back to Hallvik. "You two were the first to arrive?"

Hallvik nods.

"So what exactly happened in there?"

"It's a pretty sad sight. I'd say, go see for yourself, if you can enter the apartment without contaminating the scene. . . . There are a few CSIs in there already, and I guess more are on their way. . . ."

"OK."

Yusuf enters the building through the open door. He pulls the blue protectors Hallvik handed him over his shoes, a mask over his face, and white gloves over his hands.

The irreverent rap music continues ringing in his ears, completely incongruent with the ornamental lobby he just stepped into.

5

A WOMAN WITH short bleached, black-rooted hair stands on the sixth-floor landing. Hellu—officially Superintendent Helena Lappi—is wearing a black overcoat and the appropriate protective gear. Yusuf can't see Hellu's mouth, but her eyes look tired and a little irritated. Actually, that's how Hellu always looks.

"Hi," Yusuf says.

Hellu doesn't reply. She turns to look through the open apartment door, and a blinding flash goes off at the end of the long entry hall. The subject of the photography shoot is no doubt Finland's most prominent industrial magnate, if for reasons other than one might assume on the company's fiftieth anniversary.

Yusuf waits near the elevator, hands on his hips. He glances at the name on the apartment door. "Zetterborg," he says softly.

"Just figuring that out now?" Hellu says wearily but not unkindly.

"Well, yeah, I got that, but—"

"This is a massive case, Yusuf. The biggest of both our careers to date." She turns to Yusuf and removes her mask. "Eliel Zetterborg was stabbed right in the heart with a big knife."

"Jesus Christ," Yusuf says. "Do we have any—"

"Joonas Lamberg, driver and bodyguard. You may have seen him downstairs."

Yusuf nods. There's a faint clang followed by a low hum as the elevator shudders into motion and slowly disappears down the shaft. Male voices carry up from somewhere below.

"Questioning Lamberg is the most acute item on the agenda," Hellu says. "Evidently he escorted Zetterborg to his apartment door and said he heard Zetterborg deactivate the alarm. So logically there couldn't have been anyone inside the apartment waiting for him."

"The killer waited in the stairwell?" Yusuf suggests.

Hellu shakes her head. "Lamberg came down the stairs and checked every floor on the way. Says he does it every night."

"What about the top floor?" Yusuf asks.

Hellu nods.

"And no one entered through the door to the street?"

"At least Lamberg didn't see anything. He seems pretty sharp, so I'd give his words some credence," Hellu says.

"Well, what the hell, then? Did the killer come from one of the other apartments?"

"The officers knocked on every door in this stairwell with the super. There was someone home in every apartment but no one saw anything." Hellu points at the door across from Zetterborg's flat. "The woman who lives there said she might have heard a faint shout around the time of the killing, but she wasn't sure and couldn't provide any further details."

"Yeah, you'd think the victim had time to do a little shouting," Yusuf says.

"So how the perp magically appeared in Zetterborg's apartment is a mystery for now. The lock on the door hasn't been touched. Zetterborg must have opened the door for the killer himself."

Yusuf can't help thinking about his friend Jessica Niemi's palatial flat in Töölö. "What about the back door?" he says quietly.

"Uncompromised."

The elevator gate closes down below and the car lurches into motion again.

Yusuf opens his mouth to continue asking questions, but Hellu raises a forefinger and brings her silently ringing phone to her ear.

"This is Superintendent Lappi. Hi. Yes . . . exactly."

She disappears into the entry hall of Zetterborg's apartment, leaving Yusuf in the stairwell.

At that moment, the elevator car stops at the floor, and out steps a bearded man, about fifty, who looks as if he's just seen a ghost. His black hoodie reads MAKKONEN MAINTENANCE in big letters across the chest.

Yusuf glances at Hellu, who has appeared at his side with the phone lowered to her chest.

"The super," she says, then continues her call.

"Evening," Yusuf says.

The man shuts the elevator door and parks himself in front of the door opposite from Zetterborg's, arms akimbo. "Hi there. I'm Jari Makkonen, the super—"

"Yusuf Pepple, police." Yusuf flashes the ID hanging around his neck. "You and the officers knocked on all the doors in this stairwell?"

"Yes, all twelve." Makkonen puts his hands in the pockets of his black jeans, presumably because he can't think of where else to put them. His upper teeth are stained from snuff, and his breath smells of spicy food.

"Where does the back door lead?" Yusuf asks.

"It has access to the attic and down to the courtyard."

"Is there an elevator there?"

Makkonen shakes his head.

"Is it possible to access the other stairwells from the attic?"

"No."

Yusuf looks at Makkonen's graying beard. The tip is tied off in a little knot. "Did you go up to the attic with the officers?"

Makkonen nods.

"And from the courtyard you can access the street through the vehicle ramp. . . ."

"Exactly," says Makkonen. "And stairwells B and C too. There's

also an entrance on the other side of the building, on Vuorimiehenkatu."

"Does the same key work for all entrances?"

"No, the keys are cut so you can't use them to open the doors of the
other entrances."

"How far is the vehicle ramp from entrance A?"

"Fifty feet," Makkonen replies, and Yusuf pictures the tall trees on
Muukalaiskatu, whose leafless branches provide shelter for passing
pedestrians. Someone could have easily slipped in through the gate
without Zetterborg's bodyguard noticing. And if the killer knew or
noticed the bodyguard was waiting on the street, he no doubt used the
Vuorimiehenkatu entrance.

"Do you live in the building?" Yusuf says after a brief silence.

Makkonen's expression is incredulous, as if the idea is preposter-
ous. "No. I live over on Pietarinkatu. I handle maintenance for other
buildings too."

Yusuf shoots another glance at Hellu, who has her back to him and
is muttering into the phone. As the person ultimately responsible for
the investigation, Hellu is juggling a lot of balls right now, but it would
be nice if she could handle the political hobnobbing from, say, the car
on her way back to the station. Oh well, that's Hellu for you, and she's
unlikely to change.

"Are there any cameras or anything else in the building that might
be of use? Electronic locks, digital access systems, anything like that?"

Makkonen shakes his head again.

Hellu finally ends the call and steps out into the stairwell to join
Yusuf and Makkonen. She regards the agitated-looking super coldly,
as if she smells his fear and takes strength from it. "We need to be able
to reach you over the next few hours . . . and days."

"Sure, of course," Makkonen replies, peering over Hellu's shoulder.
He is presumably hoping to catch a glimpse of what's going on in Zetterborg's apartment.

"Detective Pepple will be in touch," Hellu says.

She stares pointedly at Makkonen until he takes the hint, steps back into the elevator, and presses the button for the ground floor. Yusuf watches his terrified face disappear between the floors.

Then Hellu nods at the apartment. Showtime.

6

AXEL ZETTERBORG HEARS voices outside the car but can't make out the conversation between the police officers. He looks at his hands; they have finally stopped shaking.

Blue lights flash from the roofs of the vehicles stopped on Muukalaiskatu. It's like something out of a B action movie.

Axel lets out an agitated sigh.

Dad is dead. It's hard to believe it's real.

Yet at the same time, everything is plain as day.

Dad is somewhere that hopefully isn't much better than hell, and good riddance.

Axel clenches his fists.

He has given his all to the firm, skipped vacations year after year despite his wife's wishes, turned down the tempting job offers that have rained down from as far away as across the Atlantic. His private life might be colorful, but even so, the firm's interests have always come first. *That wasn't enough for Dad. Fuck.* RealEst's success even took precedence over his wife's desire for children. Or perhaps the reason for their childless state ultimately lies in the fact Axel doesn't want children: he has finally convinced Alise to give up the fertility treatments that have dragged on for years and proven incredibly expensive. Axel's sperm isn't the issue; that's been made clear once already.

Axel's hand feels the pocket of his dress trousers, but it's empty. The police confiscated his phone. Evidently he'll get it back as soon as one of the detectives has finished questioning him.

Axel buries his face in his hands. This evening could have gone so differently, in the best case. He would have drunk himself into a safe state of inebriation in the private dining room at Saslik, boosted his invincibility with a few lines of coke, and left the celebration in plenty of time to hit the VIP area at Teatteri and the strip club on Uuden-maankatu. The company's anniversary was supposed to come to an unforgettable end: he had booked the Mannerheim Suite at the Hotel Kämp, where he'd meant to release the stresses cf the week with Shirley or some other whore from the late-night bar. Maybe he would have taken two of them, screwed the brainless bimbos for hours on end, and ordered a heap of burgers.

Now he can only dream about it.

Dad is dead.

How could everything have turned from golden to shit so fast?

Axel punches his fist into the window of the police van.

YUSUF STEPS INTO the apartment, which smells like a museum. Next to the front door is a stack of books with covers protected by clear plastic. He squats to take a closer look. "Zetterborg liked to read, I guess?"

"Just don't touch them," Hellu quickly says in a maternal tone. "They might be relevant to the case."

But Yusuf has already picked up one of the books in his gloved hand. James Joyce—*A Portrait of the Artist as a Young Man*. A classic Yusuf skipped during his high school years. A stamp from the Helsinki City Library adorns the book's flyleaf.

"That's why I always use protection," Yusuf says, wiggling his fingers.

He dodges Hellu's murderous glance, sets the book back down, and follows his superintendent into the living room.

Eliel Zetterborg is lying on his back on the floor between the grand piano and the liquor cabinet. His dress shirt, revealed by the sleeves to have been white at one point, has been stained red.

"The weapon?" Yusuf points at the long bloodstained kitchen knife jutting out of the floor planks only three feet from the victim. The tagged piece of evidence looks like it was stabbed into the floor.

"The first breakthrough in the case," Hellu quips, stepping around a suited-up CSI who is standing in the doorway with a box of supplies. "It was taken from the knife rack in the kitchen drawer."

Someone walks in, and a moment later Yusuf hears tech investigators chatting in the kitchen. He recognizes Tanja's voice.

"Weird," Yusuf says softly.

"What?"

"That the killer chose something as random as a knife from the kitchen as the murder weapon. If someone broke in here intending to murder Zetterborg, you'd assume they were already armed."

"Maybe the trespasser didn't mean to kill Zetterborg," Hellu suggests.

Yusuf shakes his head. "The killer stabbed the victim with a knife, then pulled the blade out of the chest. They had to have known that meant the victim would be more likely to die and die faster." He frowns at Hellu. "That doesn't sound very spontaneous, even if the murder weapon was sourced from the kitchen."

Hellu grunts drily. "On the other hand, it's been seen before: raging, long-term violence might have played a role in a completely heat-of-the-moment act. Maybe someone was in the apartment meaning to rob the place and Zetterborg showed up unexpectedly. They had to kill him so there wouldn't be any eyewitnesses."

"I guess. . . . I just think it's maybe a little naive to presume the perp was here to rob the place, considering the man lying dead here is one of the most hated men in Finland right now. The fact that the perp, in some incomprehensible way, managed to deactivate the alarm system and, on top of that, slip out unnoticed indicates forethought. A seasoned security professional was out front, and I doubt he was reading comic books. . . ."

Hellu shakes her head barely perceptibly. "Slow down, Yusuf. If the break-in was planned, it wouldn't necessarily mean the homicide was." She glances around.

Yusuf sighs behind his protective mask, wondering why his boss is so committed to the idea of the killing being a spur-of-the-moment act, even if a knife taken from the victim's kitchen was used as the murder weapon. He takes a few steps toward the body. "Well, at least we can count out suicide."

Hellu's phone rings again, and she vanishes into the hallway.

"Superintendent Lappi. Not yet . . . Of course, of course . . ."

Yusuf glances at his watch: seventy twenty-five p.m. The wind is sending the icy drizzle pattering against the windows. The sound of a tram carries up from the street. The clatter calls to mind an image of a medieval wagon coming to fetch the old man's corpse and cart it off through the fog.

Yusuf looks around and tries to form some sort of overall impression of the situation. Is it possible that the killer had a key to the apartment, that they were there the whole time? Yusuf thinks back to the witch case from a year before: he and Jessica had entered a luxurious waterfront home in Kulosaari and found a dead woman in a black evening gown sitting at a table, surprisingly erect. That time, the murderer had still been hiding at the scene and slipped away disguised as a crime scene investigator. The case was utterly unlike anything they had ever seen before, and Yusuf was not going to make the same mistake twice. Since Kulosaari, all crime scenes have been investigated meticulously, at times even with thermal imaging. Despite this, Yusuf is overcome by the nagging sensation the first officers to arrive on the scene missed something in this spacious flat.

"Yusuf," Hellu says. She's off the phone and standing, hands on hips, in the doorway between the kitchen and the living room. "In the first place, the bodyguard didn't call it in; Eliel Zetterborg did himself. Lamberg entered a little later and continued the call and requested an ambulance."

"OK, but does that change things somehow?"

"I don't know. You figure it out. Secondly, I have to head to Pasila."

"Press conference?"

Hellu nods. "You're lead investigator now."

Yusuf feels his stomach lurch. This is a bombshell he didn't expect. "Huh?"

"Huh? Huh?" Hellu mimics Yusuf's look of surprise. "Harjula is still on the road, heading back from Tampere. We can take another look later if it feels like too much pressure."

Yusuf nods. The unexpected responsibility is making his palms sweat. He has investigated dozens of crimes but has never led an investigation.

"But if you feel—," Hellu says.

Yusuf quickly shakes his head. "No," he says with a hint of a smile. The initial shock has quickly transformed into pumped enthusiasm. "I'll handle this, Hellu. Thanks for your confidence."

8

THE DEAD BRANCHES on the frosty moss snap under Jessica's shoes as she advances through the trees.

She curses under her breath when a whip of a twig evades her raised left hand and scratches her cheek painfully. The wail of emergency vehicles carries from Ruskeasuo. The air feels damper and colder in the woods than it did on the asphalt surrounding the apartment buildings on Mannerheimintie.

Jessica trudges deeper into the woods, until the trees give way to bare granite.

She unlocks her phone and sees Yusuf has sent two text messages. She decides not to read them. She needs to concentrate now. She browses the series of photographs of a charred corpse on her phone and compares them to the dark landscape opening before her.

This is the same place. There isn't the slightest doubt, even though the murder by fire left no traces on the rocks. The circle of small stones visible in the photographs has lost its shape; some were presumably collected for analysis.

Jessica squats and picks up one of the stones. It's an ordinary rock the size of her thumb tip, presumably brought to the site from somewhere in the vicinity.

It appears to be the scene of a ritual murder.

Jessica read the report; it included the detail that the unidentified victim was missing his two front teeth. Jessica instinctively glances at her slinged right arm. Her fist broke the front teeth of the drunk who assaulted her.

She hears a rustling and looks in the direction of her approach. The wind is tossing the crowns of the immature spruces growing at the edge of the granite.

There's no sign of anyone.

Jessica is overcome by the unpleasant sensation that she ought not be alone here in this exposed place. Not now.

Maybe someone is waiting for her out there in the darkness. Maybe she has walked into a trap.

You're fine. Concentrate, Jessica.

She shakes her head, takes a few photographs of the spot where the victim was found, and drops a pin on her map app. Then she puts her phone back in her pocket and briskly retraces her footsteps.

More rustling.

And now she hears it clearly: movement in the darkness behind her. She picks up her pace and glances back.

When she sees the antlers rising beyond the young spruces, she roars in terror.

Just then the ground gives beneath the ball of her foot, and she falls face-first between two pines. She howls in pain as her slinged arm is trapped beneath her.

She throws herself onto her back and aims her flashlight at the saplings growing a stone's throw away.

The antlered head rises until it is fully visible.

And then four slender legs carry the creature off.

A deer. Holy hell.

Jessica catches her breath and drags herself to her feet.

The path is only a few dozen meters away, and the lights of the riding stables glow beyond.

She hears the whinnying of horses and faint voices she can't understand.

9

Nina Ruska moans faintly. Her knees are starting to sting; they've been chafing against the sheet so long, she's sure she'll have burn marks. She already came twice and is ready to call it a night, but for some reason Tom, the guy firmly gripping her buttocks, hasn't come at all yet.

"Can we switch positions?" Nina gasps as Tom thrusts inside her over and over. For a second Nina thinks he hasn't heard. He doesn't stop; his fingers dig into her lower back, and she can feel his stomach against her butt. Then he puts his mouth right up to Nina's ear and lets out a deep groan.

"Sorry," he says, and collapses, spent, at Nina's side.

Nina rolls onto her back and snuggles up under his arm. "For what?"

"That it took so long. Rocketman was having trouble launching."

Nina laughs and touches her knees. They feel like they've been rubbed with sandpaper. "Are you stressed?"

"I don't think so."

Tom sweeps back the hair pasted to his brow, and Nina catches a whiff of strong deodorant that smells somehow quintessentially Finnish: fresh forest and tar shampoo.

"I think your phone just rang," he continues.

"I silenced it."

"Yeah, but it keeps flashing over there on the table. Yusuf."

"Is that what was bothering you?"

"I wouldn't care otherwise, but his face kept flashing on the screen."

Nina laughs heartily. "Who told you to look at Yusuf's face while you're screwing me?"

"Who is he?"

Nina rolls away from Tom and reaches for her phone. "Are you jealous?"

"Come on, if he calls you twice during one fuck, I think I'm allowed to ask who he is."

Nina can tell from Tom's tone he's only half joking. "One really long fuck . . . Look at my knees."

"I said I was sorry." Tom stretches over to the nightstand for his watch. "Besides, having some male stamina probably isn't the worst crime in the world."

Nina runs her fingers across his cheek, activates her phone, and sees Hellu has tried to reach her too. Did something happen?

"Yusuf is a colleague." Nina lifts the phone to her ear; she has decided to call him first.

"A police officer?"

"Yup," Nina replies as the phone starts ringing at the other end.

"Did someone get whacked?"

"Apparently."

Just then Nina hears Yusuf's voice on the phone. She listens in silence for a moment before replying, *OK, I'll be right there.*

She hangs up and sits there staring at the screen, lost in thought.

"What is it?" Tom says, snapping his Submariner to his wrist.

"I have to go."

"What happened?"

"Turn on the TV," Nina says, and she feels Tom's rough fingertips slide down her lower back as she rises from the bed.

10

YUSUF WATCHES FROM the window as Helena Lappi climbs in at the wheel of her Toyota Prius and soundlessly speeds off. It's unlikely the rumble of any engine would penetrate the closed windows and the noise from the street, but Yusuf knows Hellu's always-charged hybrid doesn't make a peep when it starts up. The thought that his crotchety superintendent has just left the scene powered by an electric motor strikes him as comical for some reason. Then again, Hellu is pretty comical, if unintentionally so.

But what happened just a moment ago in Eliel Zetterborg's apartment isn't the least bit amusing. Yusuf spins on his heels and scans the spacious living room. The industry magnate's body, which lies at the left edge of the enormous Persian carpet, is bathed in the glow of a spotlight. A black grand piano and a well-stocked liquor cabinet stand nearby.

The motive for the homicide is almost grotesquely plain, and it shouldn't require much guessing for anyone who pays the slightest attention to the news. Just a few days ago, one of the biggest companies in the country announced it would close its decades-old factory in Kouvola and begin layoff negotiations involving thousands of employees. The board of directors has unambiguously indicated it gave the management free rein in the decision. The incident has been processed in headlines and current affairs shows nonstop for days now: the decision has been commented on and criticized by not only the labor unions but dozens of MPs and the president of the Republic. Even the Confederation of Finnish Industries has indirectly messaged that the decision is head spinning, considering the company's healthy profits, and wondered about its social responsibility. Nevertheless, the decision was not rescinded: at today's press conference, Eliel Zetterborg appeared boldly, perfunctorily, and without the slightest hesitation. Nevertheless, the notion of undertaking such radical action on the cusp of the company's fiftieth anniversary has sent the media into a tizzy—as has Eliel Zetterborg's firm desire to publicly claim the role of ax-wielding executioner. He truly took one for the team. Especially when viewed in light of tonight's tragedy.

"Quite the bombshell."

Yusuf hears the female voice and turns to see Tanja, who has appeared behind him surprisingly silently.

"Tell me about it."

"Did Lappi hand you the reins?"

Yusuf nods and smiles tentatively.

Tanja nudges Yusuf's shoulder. "Congratulations."

"Did you guys find anything out of the ordinary?" Yusuf says, clearing his throat. The cigarette he smoked outside left a bitter taste in his mouth. "What about those books in the entryway? The place is so tidy; it's funny they were on the floor like that."

Tanja shrugs and points at the piano, where a crystal tumbler stands on the lid. There are a few ounces of whisky at the bottom. "I don't know about them, but if I were you, I'd give some thought to that whisky glass." Tanja steps past Yusuf and crouches close to the victim. "Because the glass this gentleman drank from himself is presumably this one," she continues, pointing at an identical glass lying on its side on the floor. It probably fell from the victim's hand to the carpet without shattering. There's a dark stain on the carpet where the tawny liquid was absorbed not long before.

"Two glasses?" Yusuf says, intrigued, as he squats near the stain.

"We'll have to wait for analysis, but at first glance it looks as if the only fingerprints on both glasses are the victim's."

"Weird," Yusuf says, rubbing his bald head. "What else?"

Tanja shrugs. "So far we've looked for only fingerprints and fibers. . . . At least that was wiped carefully." Tanja points at the large kitchen knife jutting up from the floor. "It's going to take a while, but there's not a whole lot to see here. No picked locks or broken windows. No signs of a struggle or muddy footprints."

Yusuf looks up from Zetterborg's corpse and glances around. "I heard the victim's son mentioned a wall safe."

Tanja stands and nods toward the sofa set. "Yeah, we took a look behind that painting. The safe is really solid. And locked. And it's going to stay that way if our friend here didn't remember to leave the code to anyone in his will."

"We ought to have the victim's son come in and have a look around to see if there's anything out of place. Or missing,"

"Do you really think this could be a robbery?"

"No. But Hellu seemed to think it was a possibility."

"But I understood the son was specifically told to leave the apartment—"

"Right." Yusuf sighs. "Axel Zetterborg is waiting in a van downstairs. I'll bring him up as soon as we get Zetterborg's body out of here."

"I understand." Tanja points at the doorway at the far end of the living room with her thumb. "The place is incredibly tidy; there's not a speck of dust anywhere. I'm guessing the cleaner was just here. . . . Probably today, because Zetterborg's bed is made too."

"Unless the big man made it himself," Yusuf says. "In any case, we need to look into it. The cleaner—if there is one—probably has a key to the place and the code for the alarm."

"So if someone got to the cleaner, it would have been easy for them to take the key and pressure her into giving them the code."

Yusuf nods and looks at the friendly bright green eyes twinkling above the mask. They're trying to communicate something, a question or maybe an insight Tanja hasn't dared express yet.

"What?" Yusuf says.

Suddenly he remembers how Tanja looked in her red dress when they pressed up against each other as the DJ played the first notes to Chicago's "If You Leave Me Now."

"There is one thing," Tanja eventually says as if catching hold of a memory. She gestures for Yusuf to follow her. "All the rooms are spanking clean, but . . ."

Yusuf at her heels, she crosses the living room to a room with a huge bookcase, a globe, a fireplace, and two leather armchairs facing a coffee table. A half dozen framed vintage movie posters hang on the walls. The scene could be out of some old Agatha Christie screen adaptation, even though there's no fire in the hearth and the body was discovered in the next room.

"Look." Tanja points at the coffee table. Now Yusuf sees a mountain of tiny cardboard pieces on its glass surface. "That mess stuck out to me in these surroundings."

"You're right," Yusuf mutters. He takes a few steps closer and sees a heap of puzzle pieces the size of a fingertip have been dumped on the glass tabletop.

"A puzzle," Tanja says.

"This hasn't even been started."

Yusuf looks up at the bookcase. The cardboard box that contained the puzzle pieces must be here somewhere: the box that would show what the completed puzzle looks like. But there's no sign of one. Only hundreds of old books in six neat rows.

Yusuf pulls his protective glove tighter and takes one of the pieces, raises it to eye level. On its own, the piece is such a minute fragment of the whole that it doesn't give the smallest shred of information regarding the completed picture.

"I'll have to ask Axel Zetterborg," Yusuf says.

"Ask him what?"

"If his late father liked solving puzzles."

11

SUPERINTENDENT HELENA LAPPI of the Helsinki PD Violent Crimes Unit turns onto Laivasillankatu and watches the wind shake the trees' leafless branches and send their crowns swinging against the dark sky. The Silja Line passenger ferry is docked at the Olympia Terminal, apparently delayed by the storm. With its bright lights, it looks like a skyscraper tipped on its side in the sea.

Hellu can't shake the thought of the corpse lying on the Persian carpet, its open eyes staring at the ornamental chandelier. The panicked look on the industry magnate's face is seared onto her retinas, and when she momentarily closes her eyes as she approaches the empty traffic circle, the image grows stronger.

Irrespective of whether Zetterborg's death was a spontaneous killing or a planned murder, they must not let the perpetrator escape. Such high-profile homicides are rare in Finland: this case is no doubt going to receive as much media attention as the still-unsolved 1986 murder of Prime Minister Olof Palme across the border in Sweden. There is going to be immense pressure to solve the murder of Eliel Zetterborg, and there is no doubt going to be a meeting with the National Bureau of Investigation this evening. Which is why Hellu is suddenly regretting her decision to make Yusuf lead investigator. Yusuf is a sharp guy, no doubt about it. But does he have sufficient credibility in the eyes of Hellu's superiors? Until now he has been at most a spectacular Watson, whereas Sherlock Holmes—

An infernal ringing rouses Hellu from her thoughts.

Damn it! She hears the tram's insistent warning bell, sees the headlights out of the corner of her eye, and steps on the gas. It's the right reaction. Her car barely makes it into the traffic circle. She glances at the tram in the rearview mirror as it crawls on toward Kaivopuisto; then she lets out a deep sigh. *Fuck. I have got to focus.*

Hellu accelerates and passes the Makasiini Terminal and a moment later the old market hall. A semi is parked outside, and goods are being rolled into the building.

Just then Yusuf's name appears on the small screen on her dash. *Can't the kid do anything without me holding his hand?*

Hellu presses the green button. "Well, what is it?" She can hear the clank of an old elevator in the background.

"Something turned up in the apartment that we need to take a closer look at, but I'm not sure exactly what resources to use. I was wondering if I should call Rasse . . . or who."

"What turned up?"

"A puzzle."

Hellu feels a combination of irritation and surprise. "A puzzle? What the hell are you talking about?"

"I don't think Zetterborg was a puzzle guy, and his son agrees. Axel Zetterborg has never heard of or seen his father putting a puzzle together."

Hellu presses her fingers to her forehead. "Yusuf."

"What?"

"Do you have any idea how angry this call is making me right now . . . ?"

There's a moment of silence on the line, but Hellu's annoyance has clearly done little to discourage Yusuf.

"I'm guessing there are thousands of pieces. . . . It's going to take a full day to put it together, if not more."

For a split second, Hellu has the urge to berate Yusuf, order him to focus on what's important. But if there's something she's learned over these past few months of arm wrestling with Jessica Niemi, it's that she needs to make room for her subordinates' thoughts. *Don't shoot down a single idea, no matter how idiotic it might seem at the time.*

"You're lead investigator now," Hellu eventually says as she pulls up to the red light at the *Havis Amanda* statue. "So if you think the puzzle needs to be put together, delegate it to someone who doesn't have anything better to do. Plain and simple. Although it's pretty hard to imagine anyone has much spare time right now—"

"OK."

After you give them the carrot, Hellu, you have to show them the stick.

"But listen to me, Yusuf. If it turns out you've dedicated resources to . . . putting together this puzzle or playing Monopoly for no reason, I'll make sure to turn the reins over to Harjula and you'll be spending a month pounding the pavement with the patrols."

The line goes silent. The light turns green, and Hellu's car nudges forward.

"All right, boss. Thanks."

Yusuf ends the call, and Hellu's fingers with their painted nails grip the steering wheel.

Yusuf had better be right.

She has to do her best with the material she has. There are plenty of talented investigators on the team: Nina Ruska, Rasmus Susikoski, Jami Harjula . . . not to mention the reinforcements she will no doubt receive from other departments and the NBI. But she can't help but reflect—and the fact that she is having these thoughts drives her crazy—that Jessica Niemi's absence from the ranks is a huge loss to the team. In December, Hellu swallowed her pride, put the well-being of the team before her own ambitions, and allowed Niemi to rejoin the group. And at first, everything seemed to go perfectly well. Some sort of budding respect had even developed between the two of them, and the atmosphere was nowhere near as toxic as it had been after the disappearance of the bloggers and the investigation of the human traffickers. But then, completely out of the blue, Jessica had blindsided Hellu by requesting sick leave. And now that Hellu needs Jessica and her incomparable knack for problem-solving, the detective has chosen to be absent from the investigation.

Goddamn it, I never should have trusted that girl.

12

Jessica lets her fingers slide along the tall wooden fence as she makes her way down the path. The surrounding silence feels as if some malevolent force has fallen still, only to erupt from the depths of the darkness at any moment. The tension fills Jessica's body as if she is steeling herself for an attack.

Jessica approaches the corral and sees a young woman walking a white horse with a blanket over its back. Jessica stops at the edge of the path and leans against the wooden fence with her good hand.

"Excuse me," she says calmly so as not to pointlessly startle the woman or—even worse—the haltered horse at the end of the lead.

But her words are drowned out by a gust of wind, and she repeats herself a little more loudly.

Now the woman turns toward Jessica.

"Sorry. I didn't mean to scare you." Jessica pulls her police ID from her coat pocket. Technically she shouldn't do so; she's on leave from the force.

"Yes?" The woman steps away from the horse and warily approaches the fence.

"I'm with the police."

"So I see," the woman says indifferently. Maybe she's not as young as Jessica thought—more like Jessica's age, if not older. With her long, slim legs and small backside, she is the prototypical equestrian. "What can I do for you?"

"Do you work here?"

"Yes. I'm in charge of the stables."

"OK." Jessica nods at the thicket from which she just stepped onto the path. "I came to have a look at the site."

"So horrible," the woman says. "I wasn't able to sleep for a week after Christmas."

Jessica nods and returns her ID to her coat pocket.

"Someone already came around asking questions when it . . . when he was found," the woman says, brushing the front of her coat with her palm.

Jessica swallows the lump in her throat. Her heart is still galloping from the fright she just had.

She knows the Violent Crimes Unit had its hands full at Christmastime, and not many resources had been dedicated to investigating the man found burned in the woods, which is a good thing: Jessica is terrified where the case will eventually lead, and she doesn't understand why.

"But you didn't see or hear anything out of the ordinary?" she asks.

The woman shakes her head.

"Are there any security cameras here at the stables?"

"There's one. But it's aimed south, that way."

Jessica turns in the direction indicated by the woman. "It covers the path, though?"

"Yes." Suspicion flickers in the woman's eyes. "But I already gave copies to one of the detectives in December."

Jessica knows she's treading on thin ice. "Of course. So you did."

"Don't you and your colleagues communicate with each other?"

Jessica acknowledges the question with a smile meant to appear relaxed. "I hate to admit it, but sometimes pretty poorly. We have the same problems as every workplace." She laughs. "Could we go take a second look?"

13

THE WIND SEEMS to have picked up, and the intermittent gusts lash at Yusuf's bare neck. He watches Tanja place a clear plastic bag in the back of the van and pull the sliding door shut. The bag and the thousands of puzzle pieces it contains will be transported to Pasila, where Rasmus Susikoski is already headed. Yusuf grunts as he thinks about his colleague. Rasmus is a hopeless nerd who avoids eye contact and smells of sweat but is perhaps one of the most important cogs in the team's investigative machinery. He serves as the unit's data security and IT expert but knows a surprising amount about just about everything, actually. Maybe that's why delegating the puzzle to him seems like a waste of resources. On the other hand, there don't seem to be any other leads to start with. Eliel Zetterborg's home was clean as a whistle otherwise, not counting the patch of living room where all hell broke loose a couple of hours ago. Yusuf is going to have to trust his own intuition now, believe the task he is assigning Rasse is significant in some way.

There are plenty of things requiring his attention: the investigative team has a ton of questioning to do, and Rasse would be of no use there. He's gifted in just about everything except human interaction, which some might call the curse of creative introversion.

Yusuf watches the wind toss a lone plastic bag that must have escaped from the tech van a moment before. Hopefully it was empty.

Then he starts walking toward the nose of one of the police vans, where Hallvik leans, tapping at his phone.

"Is Joonas Lamberg in there?" Yusuf asks.

Hallvik nods.

The sound of a foghorn carries from the harbor.

Yusuf opens the door to the van, climbs in the back seat, and looks at the powerful man sitting across from him. The guy's jaw is enormous. If what Yusuf has heard at the gym is true—if the size of the jaw truly correlates with the amount of testosterone surging through the body during the growth years—Joonas Lamberg must have been a real hormone Hercules as a teen.

Yusuf flashes his ID, but Lamberg doesn't bother even glancing at it.

"You used to be on the force too," Yusuf says to lighten the mood.

Lamberg eyes the floor, then lifts his head to look at Yusuf and straightens his coat collar. "I did. I could just never figure out what to do with all the money I earned as a cop, so I switched over to private sector," he says drily.

Yusuf can tell from Lamberg's tone that he's not so much trying to be clever as to bring a bit of levity to a moment of paralyzing pain. "You and I need to have a little talk."

"So let's talk," Lamberg says flatly.

"How long have you worked as Eliel Zetterborg's personal bodyguard?"

The instant Yusuf says the words "personal bodyguard," something in Lamberg's eyes goes out. The guy is understandably upset: first over the death of his boss—maybe the two of them had grown close—but presumably especially because he failed at his most important job: keeping Zetterborg alive.

"Ten years," Lamberg says. "Actually pretty exactly. I started working for him around the company's fortieth anniversary."

Lamberg's voice is low and hoarse as if he took a blow to the larynx at some point. Yusuf discreetly eyes the powerful neck, where the mottled skin looks as if something of the sort truly might have happened, but decides he doesn't need to learn more about that right now.

"I'm sorry," Yusuf says, looking down at his notes. "To my understanding, you've done your work as conscientiously as anybody could hope for. It's clear that a one-man security team can't work miracles. That's why the US president is guarded by thirty-two hundred special agents."

"That many, huh?" Lamberg says wearily as if he might be more interested in the topic under different circumstances.

"Yup," Yusuf says. "A fuck ton."

"I can't say that's a whole lot of comfort," Lamberg says. "I had one job to do."

Yusuf doesn't immediately reply. At first glance the idea of tears streaming down Lamberg's stern, stony face seems impossible, but Yusuf sees the other man wipe the corner of his eye.

He gives Lamberg a moment to pull himself together, then says: "There are a couple things we need to go over now."

"Sure." Lamberg pinches his lips together so firmly, they turn from pink to bright white.

"You said earlier that you didn't see anyone enter the building. Or come out. I have to ask you this, Joonas. Is it . . ."

"Possible I was looking the other way? Is that what you have to ask?"

Yusuf nods and calmly continues. "No one assumes your eyes stay on the door the whole time. You must have glanced in the rearview mirror, at other vehicles. . . ."

"Observing or watching something doesn't mean you stare at it nonstop. Just the opposite, actually," Lamberg says seriously. "I'm sure as a police officer you understand."

Yusuf glances out the van's rear windows and sighs. Questioning this former SWAT officer is no walk in the park. "Meet me halfway, Joonas. You know exactly why I'm asking these questions."

Lamberg eyes Yusuf probingly. But then his gaze softens as if the devil on his shoulder has ceded the floor to the angel. "I went up with Zeta, listened to him turn off the alarm, and came down the stairs.

That's what I always do to make sure there's no one in the stairwell. And I also look up to the top floor just in case."

"You went down the stairs. What happened next?"

"I sat in the car to wait and stepped out for one smoke."

"What time?"

At first Lamberg looks as if there's no way he's going to be able to remember, but then he pulls his phone from his coat pocket.

"A little before Axel called," he says, and taps at his phone. "Six twenty-eight p.m."

"What did Axel say?"

"He said he was worried because Eliel hadn't shown up at the restaurant and wasn't answering his phone. And above all, I guess, because his father had said something about not feeling well earlier in the day."

"And at that point you went to check on him?"

"Yes."

"Apparently Eliel Zetterborg was dead by that time."

"Yeah, I guess. . . . I ran up. I opened the door—"

"You have a key?"

"For safety reasons," Lamberg says as if the matter is self-evident. "And I found the boss on the floor. I saw a bloody knife, open eyes. . . . I felt his pulse. I could tell right away that he was dead and there was nothing to be done."

"Did you call emergency services?"

Lamberg stops and stares. He looks annoyed, because he knows the question is a trap, that Yusuf wants to know if he's telling the truth. "No. Emergency dispatch was already on the line. The phone was lying on the floor next to the body. Apparently the boss hadn't been able to give the operator his location before he died. I picked up the phone and told them what had happened. Not much later the ambulance arrived, and a second after that, the first patrol."

"OK," Yusuf says. "And then of course the most important thing: do you have any idea who could have committed this crime?"

Lamberg uses the fingers of his right hand to rub his left ring finger at the spot where a lot of people wear their wedding band. Lamberg doesn't have one. "As you know, there's no shortage of people who'd like to kill Zeta right now. A lot of folks are going to be out of a job—"

"But do any names come to mind? Had Zetterborg received any threats? Calls, texts . . ."

Lamberg shakes his head. "No, no threats per se."

"Per se?"

"Yeah, well . . . there's one guy who's been acting a little strange lately. Made angry calls to Zeta . . . Not that I eavesdropped, but—"

"Who?"

"Niklas Fischer. VP of Strategy."

Yusuf writes down the name, but for some reason, it doesn't feel significant. It seems truly implausible that a corporate executive responsible for strategy would sink a kitchen knife into his boss' chest, no matter what sort of disagreements the two men had.

"You ought to ask Axel," Lamberg continues.

"I will," Yusuf says. "Does anything else in particular come to mind?"

Lamberg initially shakes his head, but the movement stops abruptly.

"What?"

"Well, if there's anything else worth mentioning . . . ," Joonas continues. He has trained his thoughtful gaze on the little park climbing the hill and the pedestrian path that splits it.

"What?"

"When Zeta and I pulled up here at Muukalaiskatu . . . ," Lamberg says, then momentarily falls silent again. "I heard someone shouting really loudly just as I opened the back door for Zeta."

"Shouting?"

"Yeah, it was some guy yelling at his dog. It seemed odd to me that someone would shout at a pet that way in the middle of Ullanlinna. . . ."

"Tell me more."

"I don't really know how to describe it any better than that. He just made this weird yelp. . . . Maybe the dog had slipped the leash and the guy was calling it back to him," Lamberg says. "But he shouted really loudly."

"Did you hear what he shouted?"

Lamberg shakes his head. "It was more of a squawk . . . nothing intelligible. It could have even been a foreign language. Or the dog's name. Maybe it was one of the Russian diplomats who live in the area."

Yusuf chews his lip gravely. In all likelihood, this is nothing but a completely random dog walker and, judging by the exclamation, crazy or drunk. Maybe the dog tried to do something repulsive, like eat shit out of the bushes. Yusuf remembers how his Lapponian herder used to do that when he was a kid. Ate shit, animal or human—anything went. And rotting bird carcasses and all sorts of other disgusting stuff. And then came back inside to lick the kids' faces. *Peppi, give me a kiss. I love you, Peppi.*

Yusuf is on the verge of thanking Lamberg but then remembers he's the lead investigator. *Stay sharp, Yusuf.* When investigating a serious crime, no detail is too minor to ignore.

"Can you describe the man? Or even the dog? We need all the information we can get right now," Yusuf says, pulling his cigarettes from his pocket.

"He was wearing a red coat . . . and the dog was beige and extraordinarily large. Not a retriever or a shepherd or any other breed I could name off the top of my head," Lamberg says. "I don't actually like dogs, so I can't say."

Yusuf nods, writes down what Lamberg said, and stares at the page of the notebook. For some reason, his thoughts turn to Jessica. If only she were there on this dark night, on which the black asphalt has sucked all light from the world.

14

Rasmus Susikoski watches the woman from Crime Scene Investigation lower a transparent bag to the table in the small conference room. Apparently her name is Tanja, and she is, with her sparkling eyes and laugh crinkles, incredibly beautiful. Rasmus wasn't at the Christmas party, but he heard Yusuf and Tanja were kissing on the dance floor. No, Rasmus was nowhere near the dance floor that night; he was alone, sweating between his sheets with a 102-degree fever. His mother had carried orange soda and chicken soup upstairs to his man cave and spooned liquid pain reliever into his mouth. After the fact, Rasmus wondered why his mother had syringe-administered paracetamol in her medicine cabinet—wasn't it meant for kids? Or maybe cats, which would, he supposes, explain it, since three of the creatures live in the home. Maybe they could have called in a veterinarian just as well.

"You're going to need some help with this," Tanja says, taking a seat across from Rasmus.

Rasmus shoots her a furtive glance and gulps almost audibly. *Say something, Rasmus. Anything normal.* Why does he find it so hard to talk to members of the opposite sex? Or to anyone, for that matter?

"I'm Tanja, from the lab. Tanja Kettu," Tanja says, tying her hair back in a ponytail.

"Rasmus . . . Rasmus Susikoski."

Tanja laughs. "Look at that. *Susi* and *kettu*. The wolf and the fox."

Rasmus can feel himself turning red. The worst thing about blushing isn't the color that blazes up on his cheeks or the searing heat, but the sweat that instantly drips from his scalp, sparking a furious urge to scratch it. This happens anytime Rasmus is forced out of his comfort zone, which appears to be a tiny patch of turf in the middle of a soccer pitch. In other words, Rasmus is easily embarrassed, and there is no doubt the physical consequences are evident to others.

"Right . . . You can just call me Rasse." Rasmus strokes his scalp as discreetly as he can, but the itching doesn't ease.

"All right, Rasse. I can see you need a little help with this."

"Yusuf did say that if I needed it, I could ask—"

"I don't have anything going on right now." Tanja glances at her black digital watch, which looks enormous on her slender wrist. "At least for the next hour."

Rasmus opens his mouth to say something but can't think of anything sensible, let alone clever. The second hand on the wall clock has never been so loud. He tugs on a pair of latex gloves, takes the bag, and calmly dumps the contents on the table. The pieces form a tidy mound, just as in the photograph taken at the scene, which Tanja has set down in front of him.

"Have you ever done anything like this before?" Tanja asks, pulling on a pair of latex gloves as well. It's more than possible that when complete, the puzzle will contain fingerprints or something else useful.

"Put together a puzzle at work?" Rasmus says quietly, and shakes his head. "No. I don't think anyone else has either. In the entire history of the police force. At times like this, I find it hard to take my job seriously."

To Rasmus' surprise, Tanja bursts out in heartfelt laughter. For once he actually said something funny. Or maybe she's laughing at him? That would be the more familiar story.

"Don't say that. Yusuf thinks this is important," Tanja says as Rasmus spreads out the puzzle pieces.

They gaze at the sea of bits of dark gray cardboard and suddenly the task before them seems impossible. They don't even know what the finished image is supposed to look like.

"What do you think? How many pieces are there in this puzzle?"

"I happen to have a little experience with puzzles. There are a lot of pieces here. . . . I'd say this is a two-thousand-piece puzzle."

"Jesus. How long does it take to finish one of these?"

"Depending on the picture, anywhere from a few hours to a full day." Rasmus sighs. "But since we don't have a reference image to help us put the pieces in place . . ."

"Yeah?"

"It might take a few weeks."

Tanja leans back in her chair and folds her arms across her chest.

There they are again, those sluggish seconds.

"Which doesn't mean I'm giving up right away."

Rasmus starts flipping pieces so they're all right side up. Tanja stares at him for a few moments, then pitches in. They work in silence; Rasmus can hear the big hand on the clock tick to half past.

After a while, Tanja asks: "How well do you know Yusuf?"

Rasmus feels a pang in his gut. It's a familiar sensation that reminds him beautiful women never talk to him without an agenda. And that agenda never benefits Rasmus in any way.

He thinks back to a memory of himself carrying a love letter across the schoolyard. It was put in his hands by the most beautiful girl in the class, who smelled of fresh soap and whose cheeks were bright red. *Rasse, can you give this to Karri? And find out if he's going with anyone? Thanks, Rasse. You're so sweet.*

"I know Yusuf pretty well," Rasmus says, trying to conceal his disappointment. "Why?"

Tanja doesn't immediately reply, but there's no mistaking the coy curve of her smile. The rumors about the Christmas party appear to be true.

"No particular reason. I was just wondering. Seems like a nice guy," Tanja says.

In his mind's eye, Rasmus sees himself approaching the group of boys. They were all wearing black coats, FUBU or MicMac jeans, and

FILA or Caterpillar footwear. The air smelled of menthol cigarettes and something Rasmus only later came to identify as marijuana. The boys looked at the hunched, cowering messenger with suspicion.

What do you want, faggot?

The letter transfered from shaking hand to confident fingers.

Oh, it's from Henni? Tell her I'm down and to come to the Alepa at Kurvi at five today. And tell her to wear those high boots. And don't you dare fucking touch her or I'll drop you tomorrow.

"Yusuf's a nice guy," Rasmus says, eyeing the pieces spread on the table.

And for the first time in ages, Rasmus feels himself boiling with rage: as if it isn't humiliating enough that he's been given the task of putting together a puzzle in some dark dungeon while everyone else is investigating a murder, he is also being asked to serve as the sounding board for the romantic feelings of an attractive woman. The word "overqualified" is, in this instance, more than an understatement: Rasmus graduated from law school at the top of his class and has since participated in internal police trainings whenever he has been able to. He deserves better but is never going to find the courage to demand it. To demand anything from anyone. And that's exactly why he's never going to be the hero, just the goofy sidekick who, if he's lucky, will be played by Jonah Hill in a bald cap.

"If you have to go . . . I can handle this on my own," he says. Right now he'd rather be alone.

"No, I can still help for a little while. . . ."

Rasmus scratches his scalp, flips one more piece over, and as he does, he catches something on the back. A black edge. He holds it up to his eyes, studies it carefully, and feels his senses heighten. Could it be . . . ?

Tanja notices the change in him. "What do you have there, Rasse?"

"There's something here. . . . It looks like marker." Rasmus sets the piece on the table and begins raking his fingers through the pile. There have to be more, and if there are . . . "Look," he says, fishing out two more pieces. "These have black marker on the back too."

And now that they take another look at the pieces on the table, black marker turns up here and there. The backs of some pieces are totally black.

"Are you saying . . . something was written on the back of the puzzle?"

Rasmus nods eagerly. "Yusuf's right," he says almost breathlessly. "We need to finish this puzzle and fast."

15

YUSUF SUCKS DOWN a few last drags from his cigarette and flicks the butt to the roots of the leafless trees planted outside the building. The police vans are parked thirty feet apart from each other. He watches the one with Joonas Lamberg in the back start off. The bodyguard will provide an official statement at the station, and after that, he'll be free to go. At the moment, there's no reason to doubt the stories of Lamberg, who discovered the body, or Axel Zetterborg, who appeared on the scene a moment later.

Yusuf takes off his hood and opens the back door to the second van.

Axel Zetterborg stares at him intently, eyes wide and bloodshot.

"My condolences," Yusuf says as he steps into the vehicle and shuts the door. "And apologies for the wait."

Axel doesn't reply, just looks at Yusuf the way many civilians and colleagues do on the job.

Yusuf flashes his ID. "Yusuf Pepple, police. Lead investigator on the case."

"Zetterborg. The younger one," Axel says, and the voice catches Yusuf off guard.

It's a tad soft and phonetically nuanced, and has a jazzy ring to it. The younger Zetterborg's appearance is stylishly understated: a black suit and tie are visible beneath the wool coat and scarf. His black hair is curly, and the shine is more likely from strong gel than the icy drizzle outside. The face is narrow and delicate and in good conscience could be called beautiful. The word has been used in reference to Yusuf's own face more than once.

"I know this is tough," Yusuf says, pulling a notepad from his pocket, "but I have a couple questions for you."

Axel buries his face in his hands and appears to nod.

"Do you have any idea who could have done this to your father?"

Axel doesn't immediately reply, just stares at the van floor. Eventually he looks up and shakes his head. "I guess it must have something to do with the factory closure. I don't know."

"Is there anyone in your circle your father had any disagreements with recently?"

Zetterborg scratches his head. "In my circle?"

"Yes, for instance, at the company? We have to consider all possibilities."

"I have a really hard time believing—" Axel abruptly stops talking, as if he wants to shake off a thought that just occurred to him.

"Go ahead," Yusuf says encouragingly.

"Friction between Dad and the VP of Strategy has caused some turbulence in the management team. Niklas was opposed to closing the factory from the start."

"Niklas?" Yusuf reflects that the VP of Strategy's name is gradually becoming more interesting.

Axel sighs. "Niklas Fischer. Dad more or less ignored the strategy Niklas had devised when he decided to bring in external consultants on the Kouvola factory decision. The consultants were strongly in favor of its closure."

"In your experience, is it normal for the VP of Strategy to cause a stink about the board's decisions?"

"Absolutely not. We were all pretty surprised, even though everyone knew Niklas was opposed to the factory closure just to maintain good relations with the labor unions. That opposition no doubt led to Fischer's name being dropped from discussions of who would be the next CEO."

"Are you saying there's going to be a change in CEO in the near future?" Yusuf asks.

Axel nods. "The current one is retiring at the end of the year."

Yusuf fiddles with the ballpoint pen between his fingers. "And plenty of people have put themselves forward?"

"Of course."

"So, what about you? Was your father considering making you CEO?"

Something flickers in Axel Zetterborg's eyes during the few seconds of ensuing silence. "Absolutely. I've dedicated my entire life to the company. And I believe the time was right. Both of us did."

Axel lowers his head, and Yusuf glances out the van window. One of the crime scene investigators is carrying something to the van.

"Could you tell me what happened in your own words?"

Axel looks at Yusuf, stunned. "How would I know? I wasn't there."

"So where were you, then?"

Axel's look of protest releases Yusuf and circles the interior of the vehicle. "I was on my way to Saslik."

"Did you make it all the way to the restaurant?"

Yusuf knows Zetterborg understands why he's asking. *Do you have an alibi?*

"No. I got there pretty early. I drove. My car is still parked around the corner up there, in front of the restaurant." Axel points toward Saslik. "I figured I'd wait in the car until Dad showed up. I didn't feel like going inside to socialize. I'm really fucking exhausted, to be honest."

Yusuf listens to Axel's words and writes down, *No alibi.* Axel's expression reveals that he clearly understands the conclusion Yusuf has drawn.

"So, what happened next?"

"It was getting pretty late, so I tried to call Dad. Twice. Somehow I felt like something was off. Dad was never late for anything, and then with this slightly volatile situation . . ."

"Go ahead."

"I had a bad feeling. I called Lamberg, and when he went upstairs and said something had happened to Dad, I ran here as fast as I could."

Suddenly Axel bursts into soundless tears.

"Lamberg said your father mentioned something earlier about not feeling well. Do you know anything about that?" Yusuf asks.

"That's one of the reasons I was so worried. But I never expected anything like this."

"All right. Can you tell me if Niklas Fischer was present at dinner?"

"As I said, I didn't go inside the restaurant. But he was invited. I assume he would have been there on time, as usual."

"OK."

Yusuf slips the notepad into his pocket and lowers a hand to Zetterborg's shoulder. But the gesture feels corny, and he quickly pulls his hand back.

16

JESSICA PAUSES THE recording, rubs her eyes, and listens to the wooden window frame creak in the storm. The small flat-screen television mounted to the wall is showing muted ads and casting a restless glow over the kitchen.

She has fast-forwarded through the recording she received from the stable, and now the time stamp reads 5:55 P.M. According to the forensic pathologists' estimate, the man was set on fire around seven p.m., so if there's anything of significance on the recording, it will appear on her screen any moment now.

Jessica shuts her eyes, and when she finally opens them, she doesn't want to watch the rest of the tape after all. Not now. The truth feels too frightening.

She reaches for her cup and feels the warmth of the steaming rose hip tea against her fingertips.

She raises the cup to her lips, and her tongue savors the unique taste of her favorite beverage. She remembers Dad's story of how, during World War II, British schoolchildren were sent out to collect rose hips when there was a shortage of oranges. A vitamin C–rich syrup was produced from the roses' fruit. It was one of Dad's many stories that were not particularly interesting when she heard them as a child but stuck with her nonetheless. That was Dad, a natural storyteller. And then he died, twenty years ago on a sunny day in Los Angeles, when her mother steered their car into an oncoming semi. Jessica has seen the photographs of the scene taken by the authorities, studied the wrinkled raisin of black metal: a hopeless death trap in which the only survivable location proved to be the right back seat, where Jessica was sitting. Toffe, who'd been sitting on the left, hadn't had a chance: in the blink of an eye, her beloved little brother became part of the mass of the crumpled car.

Toffe didn't feel any pain.

Jessica sips her tea, and the intro graphics of the ten o'clock news appear on the TV.

Tonight, the newscasters' faces look more serious than usual. The white letters against the red base quickly reveal why. Jessica feels her senses sharpen. *What on earth?*

She lowers her cup to the table and unmutes the television.

. . . the Minister of the Interior condemns the killing and offers her condolences to Eliel Zetterborg's family.

Jessica watches the video footage shot at Muukalaiskatu, its wet asphalt dyed blue by the lights of the emergency vehicles. A photograph of the prominent industry magnate flashes across the screen and is then replaced by someone Jessica knows.

Superintendent Helena Lappi from the Helsinki Police Violent Crimes Unit, could you . . .

The reporter's question is drowned out by the surrounding hubbub, and Jessica turns up the volume. Besieged by microphones, Hellu is planted between two of her bosses dressed to the nines in brass blues. She looks stressed, and it's no wonder.

At this point, we cannot provide any information regarding the cause of death, but I can confirm it was a homicide.

Is this incident in any way related to the recent news about RealEst?

The motive isn't clear yet, but all resources at our disposal have been dedicated to solving the crime.

Have the police made any arrests?

We are looking at all possibilities and are confident the case will be solved quickly.

Are the lives of any other RealEst figures in danger?

I can't speak to that until we have a better understanding of the motive.

Suddenly Jessica remembers the text messages Yusuf sent her earlier, flips open the cover of her silenced phone, and sees a third message has arrived in the meantime.

7:01 PM Eliel Zetterborg was killed

7:01 PM Come back to work

7:26 PM Holy fuck. Hellu made me lead!!

Jessica stares at the messages as the nails she filed earlier that day tap the side of the porcelain cup. She locks her phone and turns back to the television.

An expert Jessica remembers meeting a few times has thrown on a blazer and an ill-fitting dress shirt and has appeared in the studio.

. . . it is extremely rare for a prominent business figure to be targeted by violence of any sort, let alone the victim of a homicide. Such incidents can have an impact on general impressions of Finland, which is generally considered a very safe place to do business. Nevertheless, the government has long been prepared for such eventualities. Despite the fact the police are very successful at preventing the majority of crimes . . .

Jessica lowers her cup to the table and reflects on the expert's words.

Crimes can be prevented only if they are truly premeditated. Who knows? Maybe the person who took Eliel Zetterborg's life acted on a whim. Jessica thinks back to the example used during an internal security training: in 1982, Michael Fagan succeeded in sneaking into Buckingham Palace and the royal family's private apartments in the middle of the night, and not just once, but twice. The second time, Fagan made it all the way to the queen's bedroom. To Elizabeth II's good fortune, he wasn't violent. But he never would have made it that far had his act not been spontaneous. If Fagan had planned his trespassing at length or told someone about it, in all likelihood it would have been preventable.

Turn it off.

Jessica feels shivers run up her neck as someone steps into the room.

Turn off the television. You're not part of that. Not anymore.

Jessica looks at the remote on the table and is on the verge of reaching for it. Then she shakes her head, shuts her eyes so tightly that her cheeks burn. She holds her breath and concentrates on the darkness spreading across her retinas: it's like a curtain that, if drawn back, will reveal yet one more tragic scene from her past.

When Jessica finally opens her eyes, the room is empty. No cold touch at her shoulder, no bony forefinger wrapping around her black hair.

Her mother has stopped speaking.

But her mother has no need for words. Jessica knows what she was about to say.

Watch the rest of the tape.

17

NINA RUSKA WALKS down the paved pedestrian path cutting through Ullanpuistikko. She passes the park's austere playground with two red horses on springs and a small sandbox where plastic pails and shovels are frozen in the sand. Nina has always wondered about the whole notion: playgrounds where children in rain suits are forced to play irrespective of the weather. It's hard to imagine children being taken out to play as diligently anywhere else in the world, rain or snow notwithstanding. Children don't usually get cold while they're playing, but adults do all the more. Nina has ended up standing around similar playgrounds with her godchild over the past couple of years, and the experience has in many ways confirmed her decision to never get pregnant. She likes children but hasn't ever seen herself as a mother.

Nina shifts her gaze to the intersection of Muukalaiskatu and Ullankatu and the half dozen vehicles parked pell-mell there. Even from a distance, and even with their lights no longer flashing, it's easy to spot the cavalry. A little farther off, toward Tehtaankatu, a group of gawkers stands with a camera crew from one of the TV stations. Yusuf is smoking outside one of the white vans, staring at her.

"That's a pretty intense look," Nina says when Yusuf can hear her. "Do I look guilty or something?"

Yusuf drops his cigarette butt down the sewer grate. Then he raises a finger in the direction Nina just arrived from.

"Where you came from, Tähtitorninmäki . . . Zetterborg's bodyguard, Joonas Lamberg, says he saw a guy in a red coat standing near those bushes, shouting something at his dog. When he and Zetterborg drove up."

Nina glances backward and shrugs. "There are plenty of people who walk their dogs around here, even after dark."

Yusuf looks thoughtful. "Lamberg says there was something weird about the way he was shouting."

"Weird in what way?"

"I never really figured that out. Maybe he was drunk or something."

"The bodyguard?"

Yusuf chuckles drily. "No, the guy walking the dog."

For a moment it looks as if Yusuf is going to continue, but he shakes his head. He seems atypically solemn and reflective. Responsibility eats away at one's spirits. For the first time in his life, Yusuf is the lead investigator, and he has neither the time nor the desire right now to toss around his renowned black humor.

"What's wrong with you?" he asks.

Nina grunts. "What are you talking about?"

"You look different somehow. . . . Happy."

Nina puts on a neutral expression. She feels her stomach tingle warmly when she thinks back to her intimate moment with Tom. A successful date, never mind the fact she had to sacrifice her knee skin to it.

But she has no intention of discussing it with Yusuf. Not now, and not ever.

"Do we know anything yet?" she says, gazing at the windows of the apartments surrounding the little park.

Yusuf's mouth turns up in a barely perceptible smile. Then he starts walking toward the entrance of Zetterborg's building.

"The guy was killed with a kitchen knife. The weapon was found next to the body," Yusuf says. "Go have a look at the photos if you want; they're in the tech van."

"I'm good with your account at this point," Nina says, following Yusuf. "What do you want me to do?"

THE LAST GRUDGE 71

"The most acute task is finding Zetterborg's cleaner, who, judging by all signs, was in the apartment today."

"Is the cleaner a suspect?"

Yusuf stops, hands on his hips. "That's a good question. I don't think so. But she's one of the few people who has a key to the apartment and an access fob so she can activate and deactivate the alarm."

"Who else does?"

"Eliel Zetterborg himself, the bodyguard Joonas Lamberg, and the victim's son, Axel Zetterborg."

"And you think the perp had to have both?"

"Yup."

Yusuf pulls a pack of cigarettes out of his pocket. He's smoking more and more every year. The chain-smoking reminds him of some B Western. Or their former boss, Erne, who fell victim to lung cancer the previous spring.

"But there is one thing," he says, cupping his palm around the lighter flame. Eventually the cigarette burns, and Yusuf rewards himself with a long drag.

"What?"

"We might have to initially assume the perp isn't Joonas Lamberg."

Nina frowns. "OK."

"Technically speaking, it would have been easiest for him to carry out the crime, but it's hard to come up with a motive. So at this point, I guess we'll have to trust Lamberg's account of the chain of events or what he says he saw and heard."

"What exactly did he see and hear?"

Yusuf sets the cigarette between his lips and pulls his lightweight black beanie over his ears. "Lamberg says he escorted his boss to the front door and heard the alarm start beeping when the door opened. Then Zetterborg tapped in the code to deactivate the alarm and closed the door behind him."

"So the apartment must have been empty at that point?" Nina asks.

Yusuf shakes his head. "Lamberg has worked in private security for a long time and knows alarm systems. Contemporary alarm systems have a so-called perimeter mode, which the resident can turn on even if they're at home. In that case, the motion sensors inside the apartment aren't activated, just the magnetic sensors at the doors. In other words, the alarm will go off if someone tries to enter while the resident is asleep or whatever."

"OK, so you're saying that . . ."

"It's possible the perp unlocked the door with a key, deactivated the alarm, and turned on the perimeter mode. And Lamberg heard the system beeping and assumed the apartment was safe."

"Can we retrieve access logs for the alarm system?"

Yusuf nods. "Rasmus promised to contact the security company. They can tell whose fob was used and the alarm system status at any given time."

"All right."

Nina pulls her phone from her pocket, and Yusuf hands her a slip of paper.

"What's this?"

"The cleaner's phone number and address. Find out where she is and talk to her. Bring a patrol just in case."

"So you think she's mixed up in this after all?"

"We can't exclude the possibility. A fob was needed to commit the murder. Unless . . ."

"Unless what?"

"Unless the answer is the simplest one: Joonas Lamberg is lying through his teeth." Yusuf stares intently at the glowing tip of his cigarette before it drops to the wet asphalt. "Or Zetterborg's son. No one can confirm Axel Zetterborg was sitting in his car at the time of the murder. In theory he could have entered the apartment with his own key, manipulated the alarm system, killed his father, exited the building through the back entrance on Vuorimiehenkatu, called both his father and Lamberg, and then returned a moment later, shocked."

"What about the base station data?" Nina says.

"It all happened on the same block. There's no way the positioning information is going to be detailed enough."

"But why would the son have wanted to kill his father?"

"I don't know."

In that instant, Yusuf's phone rings. Nina catches Rasmus' name on the screen before Yusuf lifts the phone to his ear.

18

RASMUS SOUNDS LIKE he's out of breath, which is generally a sign the elevator at headquarters is broken or he's made significant progress in some aspect of an investigation. This time it appears to be the latter.

"The image on the front of the puzzle," Rasmus says, then draws a breath, "doesn't necessarily matter. There's something written on the back."

"Something? What?" Yusuf asks, then immediately understands it's a stupid question. "And we don't know the answer to that yet, do we, Rasse? Not until the puzzle has been put together."

"Exactly. The good news is the text is going to help us finish faster than I thought. There are more unique pieces now."

Yusuf feels a weight drop from his shoulders. The puzzle is worth closer examination, and Hellu's probably not going to have any reason to lose her cool.

"Good. Knock it out." Yusuf glances up at Nina, who's standing in front of him, arms folded across her chest. Rasse's agitated breathing is still carrying down the line. "You got something else, Rasse?"

"I talked to the guy from Securitas and found out the following: according to the information fetched from the log for Zetterborg's alarm system, the alarm was activated at seven twelve a.m. with key number one, which is Eliel Zetterborg's personal fob. Then at nine oh one a.m. it was deactivated with key two—the cleaner's fob. This fob was used to activate it again at twelve oh two p.m. And then almost six hours later, at five fifty-one p.m., the system was deactivated again with the same fob. And just as you guessed, perimeter or so-called home mode was activated with a code, but not until six oh nine p.m., or just a few minutes before Eliel Zetterborg walked in through his front door."

"Which means the trespasser must have been standing at the window and seen the car pull up outside the building, with Lamberg at the wheel. Why didn't they activate home mode the second they entered the apartment?"

"Hard to say. The delay option had been selected for the system in any event, which means the alarm doesn't go off the second someone opens the door; it starts beeping and gives you thirty seconds to deactivate the alarm," Rasmus says. "That moment, six fifteen p.m., is the final entry in the alarm's log. At that point, Zetterborg opened the door, deactivated the perimeter mode, and assumed he was stepping into an empty apartment."

"Yeesh," Yusuf says, lowers the phone to his chest, and locks eyes with Nina.

"Nina," he says emphatically, "it looks like we're going to have a SWAT team lead the way."

19

NINA RUSKA'S GAZE shifts between the navigator on her mobile phone and the glistening black road. The prevailing conditions are perilous in the extreme: without a reflector, a pedestrian who steps out of the darkness and into a crosswalk is for all practical purposes invisible. Nina is well aware her driving habits—keeping an eye on the traffic out of her peripheral vision and checking the directions from the phone in her lap—are dangerous, unbefitting a police officer, and unforgivable in every other way as well. But the present investigation has her running in overdrive.

She glances in the rearview mirror and sees the police van follow her as she turns onto Ahjokuja. *Looks like Steniuksentie is the next right. . . .* Nina can feel her fingertips tingling with suspense. The thought still makes her shudder: two hours earlier, Eliel Zetterborg thought he was entering an empty home, but in reality a killer had been waiting inside for the unsuspecting victim. And now they might come face-to-face with said killer.

The cleaner Sanni Karppinen is about fifty and lives alone on the third floor, in apartment six.

Nina flicks the turn signal and muses on the possibility that the woman who has cleaned Eliel Zetterborg's home for several years is the murderer they're looking for. It doesn't seem likely: Rasmus checked the woman's background, and nothing seems to suggest her culpability. Except of course the fact that the perpetrator used her keys to enter the apartment.

Yusuf has just gone over the security company report on the fobs for Zetterborg's apartment. A total of four keys exist, and numbers three and four are in the possession of Joonas Lamberg and the victim's son, Axel Zetterborg. According to Rasmus, neither one has been used to activate or deactivate the alarm system in months. In light of this information, it's apparent the killer is someone who got their hands on the cleaner's keys one way or another.

Nina steers up the gently rising Steniuksentie and pulls over about a hundred yards from the building the cleaner is known to live in.

The black SWAT van is parked on the hill at a similar distance from the building in the other direction. Hellu has reacted quickly and effectively to the information received from the security company; kudos to her for that. No one wants to take any pointless chances right now—if the perpetrator is inside the apartment, he or she is no doubt dangerous. At first glance, Eliel Zetterborg's murder appeared spontaneous, but the way the apartment was broken into was anything but.

The radio crackles softly.

SWAT One to Delta.

This is Delta.

Secure the building.

Six SWAT officers armed to the teeth spill out of the back of the van. They head toward the three-story concrete building with surprising speed.

The time is eight thirty-four p.m. The snow is falling so lightly, it's visible only in the streetlamps' yellow glow.

Nina watches as two of the SWAT officers circle around to the back of the building and one remains posted out front.

A moment later, the door opens from inside, and the remaining three men rush in.

Nina opens her car door, grabs her radio, and unsnaps her holster.

She has been on the force for fourteen years but has never fired a shot outside the firing range. Not that she's unusual among her colleagues in this regard—there is a total of about seven thousand police officers in Finland, but only about ten shots are fired in the line of duty during an ordinary year, which in international comparisons is an unbelievably low rate.

Nina feels a lump in her throat as she thinks back to the last time she felt so tense. The memories thrust into her consciousness, and she shuts her eyes to force them to disappear.

She climbs out of the car and starts walking toward the building, the uniformed officers at her heels. Her heart is throbbing in her chest. No, Nina has never used her weapon in live situations, and there's no need for her to do so today either. As a matter of fact, since she started in the unit, Nina has rarely seen any sort of real action. Her role has settled into perusing evidence and questioning parties of interest and suspects. Even though her muscular, ultratrained body might give a different impression, her work almost never involves dangerous situations. She is a bull terrier dozing near the fire.

A crackle breaks the silence.

Target is not reacting to the doorbell.

Nina lifts the radio to her lips. "Go in."

Roger that.

Nina and the officers stop in front of the door.

She doesn't want to remember but she can't help her thoughts.

The last time Nina was sent into the field, things went badly for her. She still has nightmares about it: she's lying on a cold stone floor, only a sheet of some sort covering her, while a group of robed figures is standing around her.

But just like Jessica and Yusuf, she survived that night.

Waiting for the command.

Even though the wind picks up just then, down on the street Nina can hear Sanni Karppinen's front door smash in and the SWAT team crash into her apartment, accompanied by a loud racket and lots of shouting.

20

Nina rushes up the gray granite stairs. Her fingers fly over the steel railing. On the second floor, the doors to both apartments are open, and surprised faces peer through the cracks. Nina points at the ID dangling from her neck. *Police! Get back inside! Shut your doors!*

She has just received information via radio that the apartment is secure and that the target is alone and alive.

When she makes it to the third floor, she finds two SWAT officers in balaclavas at the door to the apartment, semiautomatic rifles equipped with optic scopes at their shoulders. The sweet smell of sawdust wafts through the air. The floor is littered with shards of wood from the broken doorframe.

"Where is she?" Nina says, panting, and one of the officers mumbles a response Nina interprets to mean the bedroom.

She strides briskly through the compact entryway, which has white IKEA dressers jammed in on either side. The apartment is not messy, per se, but not particularly tidy either. It looks like there's too much stuff. A cooking show is playing on the television in the living room; the judges are tasting a stewed-berry dessert.

"In here," one of the SWAT officers says. His fingers are on the trigger guard of his dangling weapon as if anything at all might still happen.

Nina turns into the bedroom. A thin woman is sitting up on the bed with the help of one of the officers. Her hands and feet are bound with zip ties, and she is alternately licking her lips and coughing up phlegm.

Nina shoots a questioning look at the officer she knows is in command of the SWAT operation. "She was tied to the bed," he says, pointing at the scarf on the bed. "And gagged."

Nina turns to the woman. "Sanni Karppinen?"

"Yes! Yes! I already said so," the woman says tearfully. "Cut me out of these zip ties, goddamn it. . . ."

Nina looks at the woman, who is trying to wrench her slender wrists free. Nina leans closer and sees the woman's lower lip is swollen and the skin around her eye is turning a nasty blue.

She nods at the SWAT officer, who conjures a Leatherman from his gear belt and severs the zip ties around Karppinen's wrists.

"You don't have to worry anymore, Sanni. You're safe," Nina says, kneeling so that her eyes are level with the other woman's. "Who did this to you?"

For a moment, Karppinen just stares back. Then the tears start gushing down her cheeks. Maybe they're tears of relief.

"You're OK," Nina reassures her again. "I need you to tell me what happened. Where is he?"

"I don't know. . . . He rang the doorbell and . . . I opened it because I had no idea—"

"Who rang the doorbell?"

"A man."

"What did he look like?"

"I don't know. . . . He was wearing a mask . . . sort of like theirs," Karppinen says, eyeing the armed officer standing between the bed and the window.

"A ski mask?" Nina suggests, and the other woman nods. "What happened?"

"He forced his way in and dragged me to the bed. Tied me up."

"Why? What did he want?"

Karppinen sobs and says, "The keys to Zetterborg's apartment."

Nina slowly picks herself up and looks around. There's a small desk in front of the window, and the walls are hung with photographs of toddlers one could presume are Karppinen's grandchildren. The blinds are shut and the curtains drawn across them, just as Nina was informed they were a moment ago via radio.

The room looks normal in other respects; it wasn't a major struggle for the man to tie the petite woman to the bed.

"How long have you been lying here?" Nina says, immediately following up with: "What time did all this happen?"

"When I came home . . . between eleven and two."

Sanni Karppinen wipes her eyes while the police officer standing next to her snips off the zip tie pulled around her ankles. A quick glance over Nina's shoulder reveals the other SWAT officer is still holding his semiautomatic rifle at the ready. Relentless suspicion is the most critical attribute for these officers; they cannot afford to lower their guard in this apartment. It's unlikely Sanni Karppinen caused the injuries to her own face, then tied her hands and feet with zip ties, but it's by no means impossible. Nina eyes the chafing at her wrists and ankles: the abrasions clearly took some time to produce.

"You gave the man your keys?" Nina says.

"He took them from my coat pocket. Then he made sure the zip ties were tight, shoved the scarf in my mouth, and taped it shut."

"And then?"

"And then he left."

"What did his voice sound like?" Nina asks.

"I don't know."

"Did he say anything the whole time?"

"He must have. . . . I can't remember at all. He attacked me as soon as I opened the door."

"Can you describe him otherwise? What was he wearing? Was he tall or especially big?"

"A black hoodie, if I remember right . . . maybe some band on it . . . Metallica? Pretty normal sized . . ."

"OK. If you didn't hear him say anything . . . is it possible it was a woman?"

"I don't think so. He must have said something. Or grunted. I'm sure it was a man."

Nina stood in front of the woman, hands on her hips, and is suddenly overwhelmed with sympathy and some sort of shame that this woman, who has been tied up in her bedroom all day, is being forced through the wringer the instant she's freed, and that the body language of the heavily armed officers suggests she might be something other than a victim.

Sanni Karppinen's eye makeup has dried in thick streaks on her cheeks.

"OK. I'm sorry, but I need you to come with me to the station to give us a statement," Nina says, helping Karppinen up from the bed.

21

THE FRONT DOOR of the apartment building shuts behind Nina. She watches as the set just erected for the incredibly suspenseful scene is broken down as if this is a location for some action movie. The officers from the SWAT team pack their gear back into the van, the sliding doors shut, and helmets are removed. Farther away on the hill stand a few gawkers with phone cameras in their hands.

"Ruska, right?"

Nina turns toward the low male voice. A brawny guy with his ski mask lifted to his forehead is approaching. The round chin is covered in stubble, the cheeks are pitted with acne scars, and the eyes are anything but friendly.

"Yes."

"Roni Kerman, squad commander," he says, extending a hand.

"Nice work," Nina replies, because nothing else comes to mind. The reality is the assignment that just ended was a piece of cake for the hard-boiled team.

"Pretty wild, that Zetterborg case," Kerman says, jamming a tin of snuff into his breast pocket. Then he looks through the glass doors into the stairwell, where Sanni Karppinen is waiting for someone to escort her to one of the vehicles. "Someone went to a lot of trouble to get inside the boss man's house."

Nina shrugs, despite knowing doing so is certain to aggravate Kerman. But he appears to accept the fact she isn't going to discuss the details of the investigation with him.

"Well, it's not really my business," Kerman says with a laugh, and

Nina glimpses a clump of brown snuff at his gums. "Even so, I have something that might give you some food for thought."

"What?"

"Wasn't Zetterborg murdered while his security waited outside the building? The bodyguard?"

Nina nods. *A little information swap among colleagues probably isn't going to hurt anyone.* "What about it?"

Kerman scratches the side of his nose and appears to drop the macho routine for a moment.

"I happen to know Joonas Lamberg. I've been on the SWAT team for almost twenty years now and I remember Joonas from the days when he was still on board."

"OK," Nina says, wondering where the conversation is heading.

"Don't take this the wrong way, but he's an unusual guy. I recommend you question him carefully."

"What do you mean?"

"He always talks about how he was forced to quit because he took a bullet to the knee, but that's not exactly how it went. Sure, it was kind of a slog to get his knee working again, but by the end, it was perfectly functional. He was forced out for different reasons, even though I'm not sure that was ever officially the case."

"What reasons?"

Kerman adjusts his Kevlar vest. "He's a problematic guy. Jumpy trigger finger. I was along on his last gig when he shot an unarmed crook sitting in a red leather armchair during an arrest."

Nina looks at Kerman intensely and can't help but think that the red leather armchair strikes her as a strange detail in an otherwise so loosely given account.

"Actually it wasn't the first time something like that had happened. It felt like he shot whenever he had the chance. And that's why they couldn't keep him in the SWAT unit anymore. Or on the force at all. He left after our commander at the time sat him down for a long chat."

Kerman draws his mouth up into his distinctively cruel smile. "What's the word for it again . . . 'ironic'? It's almost ironic that a guy like that became someone's private bodyguard."

Nina frowns. "Am I understanding correctly that the SWAT unit has been covering up a murder committed by a police officer and you're just spontaneously blurting it out to me?"

Kerman's expression grows grim. "It wasn't a secret. The incident was thoroughly reviewed, according to protocol. An internal audit found the criminal had a gun and had pointed it at Lamberg. So Lamberg acted in accordance with the guidelines."

"But you just said the guy was . . ."

"Unarmed? Listen up, Ruska. If you've been in the field doing this stuff for a while, you start noticing if some things on the battlefield just don't add up once the firing is finished and the dust has settled. It's all the same to me what happened to that criminal in the end or if he really pointed a gun at Joonas."

"Who was the guy?"

"A slimeball called Kangaroo. He had kidnapped a seven-year-old girl and was blackmailing the parents. The girl was returned in one piece, but the NBI located the guy, and the next day, a SWAT raid was made on the place. In a way, Kangaroo got what he deserved. But as a group we still made sure Joonas Lamberg lost permission to carry a weapon."

"Are you saying Lamberg somehow staged—"

"I'm not saying anything. I've already talked too much. It's all speculation. And like I said, the internal audit found Lamberg's use of force wasn't excessive. But if I were you, I'd talk to him some more. The guy is a loose cannon, plain and simple. And on top of everything else, a really shitty team player."

22

JESSICA LOWERS THE cup to the table and pauses the recording.

The butterflies swarming in her stomach stop flitting about; instead, she is overcome by a vague sense of precariousness.

Jessica rewinds the tape fifteen seconds.

The image is grainy and dark, but the person approaching from the south is clearly visible in the pale light of the path-side lamp.

It's a woman.

Jessica checks the time stamp.

DECEMBER 24, 2019, 6:50 P.M.

The woman's face is impossible to make out, but Jessica sees white running shoes, black running tights, and a white Gore-Tex jacket. A ponytail is swinging at the neck, and the black ballcap is emblazoned with a Yankees logo.

Suddenly Jessica feels like she can't breathe.

No, it can't be.

The woman's arm is in a sling, and she is striding briskly and purposefully down the path.

Jessica's heart hammers in her chest as she takes her phone and thumbs to her Sports Tracker app, then swipes furiously with her forefinger to check the workouts saved the previous month.

December 24, 2019—walk.

The hand holding the phone starts quivering. Her heart is galloping wildly.

There's no way she could have been at that place at that time; if she had been, she'd remember. She taps her phone, and a map appears on the screen.

She drops the phone to the table and clenches her left fist to stop her fingers from shaking.

Jessica thinks back to Venice, to the rough fingertips, to the tongue on her throat. She has killed before and would, she presumes, be capable of killing again. If she only had good cause.

She shuts her eyes, lets out a trembling sigh, but even the safe darkness provided by her lowered lids can't help her make sense of what happened.

23

THE HANDS ON the clock are pointing directly upward, marking midnight. Yusuf and Nina step into the conference room, where Rasmus, Hellu, and Jami Harjula already wait at the long wooden table. The brown paper bags have been opened, and the cardamom rolls have made their way to the white paper plates. The Thermos coffee dispenser gives off the aroma of scorched hot plate coffee.

"All right," Hellu begins in her typical fashion, then licks her fingers.

All right. These two little words introduce almost every conference and one-on-one confab with Hellu. They are literally the beginning of everything, good and bad, and even the tone in which they're uttered never reveals anything about the meeting's agenda. They could presage anything from the start of the Winter War to the Interim Peace.

"We're off to a pretty brisk start here," Hellu says. "Yusuf, you've done a superb job."

Yusuf seats himself at the table, thrown by his boss' praise. He shoots a quick look at Harjula, who is sitting to Hellu's right and looks annoyed, as if the superintendent's compliment has been flayed from his back. Maybe Harjula is one of those guys who's willing to pay a hundred euros to make sure his neighbor doesn't get fifty.

"Thanks," Yusuf says, hoping the flush he feels spreading across his cheeks isn't outwardly visible.

Nina reaches for a plate and fishes a cardamom roll out of one of the bags. This maneuver seems to attract the attention of everyone in the room: after all, it's not every day Nina is seen with a sweet roll in her mouth, especially the dry, marked-down supermarket variety probably baked the day before. A sworn fitness enthusiast, she is very particular about what she puts in her mouth. The sinewy Nina eats plenty but usually very deliberately, and she's known for weighing her food in the springtime.

"Correct me if I'm wrong, Yusuf, but I believe we have a few concrete bits of information now." Hellu grabs her pen and studies her chaotic notes. "According to the cleaner's statement, we are looking for a solidly built man, approximately forty to fifty years of age. We can say with certainty the perpetrator is neither Joonas Lamberg nor Axel Zetterborg. This conclusion is based not only on the description, but also the fact that both were confirmed as present in Kouvola at the time the trespasser forced his way into the cleaner's home. In other words, we know how and when the suspect entered Eliel Zetterborg's apartment. And as far as the puzzle goes . . ."

Hellu turns to Rasmus, who is staring lustfully at the bag of cardamom rolls, and loudly clears her throat to rouse him from his musings.

Then she continues: ". . . you will be able to finish it or at least have it in a sufficient state of completion . . . tonight?"

"Right," Rasmus says, sitting up straighter. "Four people are working on it right now. Whatever's written there on the back in marker, we'll know within a few hours."

"You'd think there'd be a computer program for that," Harjula grumbles, revealing a generous glob of masticated cardamom roll in the process.

Rasmus shifts his perplexed gaze from Hellu to Harjula. "A computer program?"

"Yeah. Some kind of software. It seems pretty weird someone has to do it by hand. Seems so eighties."

"And what's the alternative?" Rasmus says with surprising assertiveness. "I mean, sure, it's weird no Professor Propellerhead has decided to invent a machine where you dump the pieces in a blender and crank the shaft and out pops the finished puzzle—"

Yusuf bursts into laughter before Harjula even realizes Rasmus is being sarcastic. Yusuf glances at Nina, and she smiles proudly. Rasmus Susikoski has always been their very own nerd, a warrior whose deodorant fails him every day, whose bald crown bobbing in a lifesaver of hair sheds mountains of dandruff to his black sweaters. At times it almost seems Rasmus goes out of his way to give people reasons to bully him at the workplace. But no one really wants to be mean to Rasse, not even Harjula or Hellu. For all his quirks, Rasmus is a lovable guy. The overgrown adolescent squirming awkwardly inside his bachelor body is not only a genius with computers; he's a walking computer himself.

Even so, it's clear that over the course of his life Rasmus has taken his share of figurative and literal licks, the latter primarily during his school years. Which is why it's so refreshing to see him for once put Harjula in his place with this sarcastic retort. Way to go, Rasse!

Harjula folds his hands across his chest. "Huh? That's not what I mean."

"Theoretically the pieces could be spread right side up on a white surface and an algorithm could be coded that scans the shapes and arranges them into as complete a configuration as possible," Rasmus says, perhaps a little conciliatorily. "But I believe we'll be able to finish it faster using traditional methods."

"Moving on," Hellu says quickly. "What's your view of the case, Yusuf?"

"Umm . . . what do you mean?"

"What's our man like?"

Yusuf is on the verge of opening his mouth but decides to extend the artistic pause by pumping himself a half cup of coffee from the Thermos. He lifts the coffee to his lips and savors its flavor in his mouth, and a craving for a cigarette instantly infects every cell in his body. *If only it were 1995, goddamn it, when you could still smoke in the conference room.*

"I have mixed feelings," Yusuf says, mouth hidden behind his paper cup. "Think about it. He sinks a knife into the heart, forcefully, through the breastbone. And then just to be sure, yanks it from the wound so the victim bleeds out from the severed veins. A deliberate, efficient killing, no unnecessary fuss."

"So why the mixed feelings?"

"Because the motive is a mystery."

"Was anything taken from the apartment?" Hellu asks.

"Doesn't seem to have been. According to Axel Zetterborg, the son, there was nothing of value in the apartment other than the paintings on the walls and the contents of the safe. But the art seemed to be in place, and the safe is locked."

Harjula eyes his fingernails. "What's inside the safe?"

"I don't know. Like I said, it's locked. According to Axel, random valuables and presumably cash. But the last time he got a peek inside was years ago, and no one knows the combination other than Eliel Zetterborg himself."

"OK. So it wasn't a robbery; it was a murder committed by some damn lunatic," Harjula says.

Yusuf gives Harjula a disappointed look. "This so-called lunatic was very methodical in every respect."

"What do you mean?"

"In the first place, he left a puzzle for us to find that, by all indications, contains some sort of clue. In addition, the perp has gone to the trouble of figuring out who cleans Zetterborg's apartment, where she lives, and when she's home."

"I don't necessarily disagree with you, Yusuf," Nina says, rubbing pearls of sugar from her palms to her paper plate. "But he could have just stalked Karppinen and waited for the right moment to snatch the keys."

"Sure," Yusuf replies. "But right now I can't think of any better place to take the keys than Karppinen's own apartment. That's where the perpetrator could make sure she wouldn't be able to report what happened to anyone, right? Sure, it's possible—if really damn risky—to snatch a bag or a backpack in a public place, even during the day. But in that case Zetterborg and his bodyguard would have probably learned about it and changed the locks right away. And Zetterborg's security would have been ratcheted up immediately."

"That's true too," Nina says.

"Are we sure the cleaner is a victim and not the perpetrator? Could she have killed Zetterborg, returned home, tied herself with zip ties, and come up with a story of a man who broke into her apartment? Theoretically the bruises on her face could have been self-inflected," Hellu says.

"The medic who examined Karppinen said that judging by the chafing at her wrists and ankles, she had been bound for several hours," Nina says. "I'd say Sanni Karppinen's story is credible."

Yusuf lifts his hands behind his head and stretches his triceps. "Which leads us to two other factors that don't support the theory the killer acted on a whim."

"Let's hear them," Hellu says.

"The first has to do with the perimeter mode."

Yusuf looks at everyone in the room in turn. Only Hellu looks as if she's not familiar with the concept. Even so, Yusuf decides to direct his gaze to Harjula instead of Hellu as he launches into his explanation.

"Home mode is typically kept on when you're asleep, in case someone tries to break in at night. And according to the logs, that's exactly what Zetterborg did. Joonas Lamberg encouraged his boss to do so." At this, Yusuf sees Nina look up from the table.

"OK. You learn something new every day," Hellu says, not even trying to hide her ignorance. Good for you, Hellu.

"The alarm system logs indicate the perpetrator activated home mode. That's how he fooled not only the victim but also Joonas Lamberg, who walked the victim to the door, into thinking there was no one in the apartment."

"Meaning?"

Yusuf drains his coffee and crumples up the cup in his fist. "You don't have to be some Rasmus Susikoski to know how to pull off a stunt like that, but it demands a little knowledge of how alarm systems work and the different possibilities they offer. So much for the lunatic theory."

Although Yusuf didn't intend to put Harjula on the spot, the tall detective looks sheepish. Yusuf is the lead investigator on the case, which means that for the first time in his life, he is responsible not only for solving the case, but also for the psychological and physical well-being of the officers tackling it. The unnecessary chest thumping and jabs have to be kept to a minimum; he has to look out for the team's internal dynamics.

"I get your point, Harjula," he says in a conciliatory tone. "A knife in the chest and some goddamn message on the back of a puzzle . . . it sounds crazy."

Harjula nods. And with that, an unspoken truce is reached before the volatility level rises.

"Activating home mode also gave the killer the advantage of surprise. He wanted Lamberg to return to the car," Yusuf says. "He didn't think he'd be able *to take* the bodyguard, because he didn't have a weapon. The weapon turned out to be a knife he found in the kitchen."

"Which indicates a lack of premeditation," Hellu points out.

Yusuf takes a deep breath and nods. "I know. When it comes to the weapon, the act seems spontaneous."

"But you had one more argument against this line of reasoning?" Hellu says.

"Yup." Yusuf looks down at the crumpled cup in his fist, then continues: "I think it's strange that a person who plunged a huge knife into someone's chest didn't go any further than tying his other victim by the wrists and ankles to her bed earlier the same day. The contrast between the way these two victims were treated is pretty distinct, considering that leaving the cleaner alive was relatively risky in terms of the plan's successful execution. In theory, Karppinen could have wriggled free or beaten her head against the window or the door and alerted her neighbors. If that had happened, Zetterborg's security arrangements would have been instantly boosted to head-of-state spheres."

"So yet again . . . ," Nina says.

"The fact that the perpetrator didn't harm Karppinen is a good thing, of course, but it's a little strange, because the perpetrator is clearly more than capable of taking a human life." And then Yusuf nods emphatically, signaling he has reached the conclusion of his analysis.

"Doesn't that suggest the perpetrator has some personal grudge against Zetterborg?" Hellu says. "The one and only person he wanted dead was Eliel Zetterborg. That's why the cleaner got to live."

"So it would seem."

"Shit," Harjula says. Yusuf shoots Harjula a quizzical look, and Harjula laughs. "This guy sure isn't making it easy on us. If this is about some personal grudge, we need the alibis of every single male worker from the Kouvola factory. About two thousand of them."

Silence falls over the room.

"What about the books in the entryway?" Yusuf says, suddenly aware this detail is becoming an obsession for him.

"Classics: Joyce, Harper Lee, John Williams," Nina says. "Zetterborg was an avid library user. I looked into it: he checked out a few books a month from the Rikhardinkatu Library."

"Can't a guy that rich buy his own books?" Harjula says, but his quip falls flat.

"Let's ask Karppinen if the books were in the entryway when she left the apartment earlier that day," Yusuf says. Nina nods and makes herself a note.

There's a knock at the door, and a handsome young man peers into the room.

"What is it, Lionel?" Yusuf asks.

Lionel sounds apologetic: "You asked me to find out who was waiting at the restaurant when Zetterborg was murdered."

"And?"

"The board of directors were all there, as was upper management, with the exception of three people."

"Who was missing?"

"The victim, of course, and his son, Axel Zetterborg . . ."

"We already knew that."

". . . and Niklas Fischer, who said he'd come down with the flu and would be staying in."

Yusuf feels a tingling in his fingertips. "Thank you, Lionel." He turns back to the team as the door behind him closes.

Hellu looks at Yusuf, intrigued.

"Harjula, could you find this guy and bring him in for questioning? Let's see how bad his flu really is."

Harjula gives a curt nod and writes down the name.

"Who is he?" Hellu asks.

"A VP of Strategy who needs an alibi. He and Zetterborg have been beefing lately."

Hellu doesn't look convinced. "Watch your step, Yusuf. Don't go around busting any more kneecaps than necessary. Powerful people can make life tough for an ordinary police officer really fast."

Yusuf looks at her incredulously.

"But at the same time," she continues, "no one is above the law."

"OK, let's get to work . . . ," Yusuf says in relief.

But Nina has raised her hand. "There's something we need to take a closer look at."

"What's that?"

"It's about Joonas Lamberg."

24

THE DRIVE FROM police headquarters in Pasila to the forensic medicine lab on Kytösuontie takes a mere seven minutes on the deserted streets. The parking lot is almost empty, and Yusuf speeds across it to the spaces at the foot of the concrete stairs.

He turns down the music to discern whether the knocking he heard a moment ago is coming from the innards of the Golf, which has seen better days. But there's nothing; maybe he imagined it.

This car is breaking down from exhaustion too.

Yusuf jumps out of the vehicle and sticks a smoke in his mouth, but at the same instant sees forensic pathologist Sissi Sarvilinna waiting for him at the doors.

"*Damn it,*" Yusuf curses under his breath, and raises a hand in greeting.

It receives no response. "Where's Niemi?" Sarvilinna asks as Yusuf slips into the brightly lit lobby.

"She's not working right now," Yusuf replies, taking off his beanie.

"Peculiar. Such a high-profile case."

Sarvilinna leads Yusuf toward the dim stairwell instead of the elevator.

"She's on leave," Yusuf mumbles.

He is trying to keep up. The tall Sarvilinna glides down the stark corridor surprisingly swiftly in her high-heeled sandals, like a six-foot-four ghost with incredibly erect bearing.

At the end of the corridor, Yusuf sees the yawning doorway he has passed through on many occasions before. Far too many. He's grown accustomed to seeing the dead being hacked up, but it's probably too much to ask for him to learn to like it. In the end, Yusuf might be too sensitive to react to death with the sufficient pragmatism.

"Well, before you start complaining about what a rough shift you've had, I'll tell you about my day," Sarvilinna says, barking out a dry laugh. "A fishing vessel sank in the Gulf of Finland on Thursday. Perhaps you read about it?"

"Yup. Six passengers—"

"For some reason or other, the boat caught fire and went down. Really ugly case. Five of the six who were missing were recovered by divers only today. Do you know how hard it is to identify totally or partially burned bodies that have been bobbing in cold water for almost a week? Well, I'll tell you. It's really darn hard. The water turns the skin to mush—you know what I'm talking about if you've ever sat in the bath for an hour. Our fingerprinting technology here at the unit isn't advanced enough, so I had to saw off the hands of all five bodies, number them, pack them in ice, and send them to the lab at Otaniemi." Sarvilinna walks into the room and clicks on the bright halogen lights.

Yusuf shudders. "What's going to happen to the hands?"

"When they've taken the fingerprints, they'll return them to me and I'll sew them back on the bodies. As a matter of fact, I'm trying to get the mortuary to do it for me, because I've got my hands full here, as you well know."

Yusuf sighs deeply and decides he won't be asking any further questions on the subject.

He scans the brightly lit room. It looks like an industrial kitchen. Unlike in Hollywood movies, real autopsy surgeries are rarely in windowless basements. Even so, the lateness of the season and the hour ensures the artificial light is surrounded by an eerie darkness.

Yusuf sees the figure lying on the chrome table. The white sheet laid over it looks like a protective tarp wrapped around a boat dry-docked for winter.

"I understand the superintendent will not be joining us," Sarvilinna says from the corner of the room, where her fleet feet have already carried her. She glances over her shoulder. "Would you like some honey?"

Yusuf shakes his head, bewildered.

"I can't work without it," Sarvilinna says, stretching out the final words in an odd manner, "as you perhaps remember."

"Yes. I'm fine. Thanks. You go ahead."

"I certainly shall," Sarvilinna says. A steaming cup has appeared from somewhere in the grip of her long fingers.

"And no. I mean, no . . . Superintendent Lappi is not coming," Yusuf says.

"Well, it's enough to have someone from HQ here."

Sarvilinna pulls back the sheet, revealing the body as if it is some lottery prize. Yusuf sees a naked old man lying peacefully on the table, hands at his sides.

"The obduction technician will arrive soon to remove the other organs, but as far as I'm concerned, we can get a head start and take a look at the spot all arrows are pointing to: the heart."

"The heart," Yusuf repeats emphatically, studying Zetterborg's gray face and the tidy white beard surrounding the mouth.

Sarvilinna pulls on her gloves and reaches for one of her sharp instruments, talking all the while, but Yusuf hears only every other word. His attention is focused on the lifeless man, whom all of Finland knows as the embodiment of capitalism. The man who hasn't been able to take a single cent of his earthly property into the hereafter, not that Yusuf believes in the existence of one.

"Pepple?" Sarvilinna says, and Yusuf isn't sure if she's had to repeat his name or how many times.

"Yes?"

"Are you awake?" Sarvilinna asks, turning on her small recorder.

"Yes," Yusuf says.

Without his noticing, the victim's torso has been cut open, and the loose chest muscles are flipped to the sides, like the covers of a big book. For some reason, the macabre sight makes him sad.

"I performed an external examination on this gentleman prior to your arrival. There's a contusion at the back of the skull, which could have been caused by a blunt object, but I believe it resulted when the victim fell to the floor. Weren't the floors wood?"

"Yes."

"Good. I don't think there's any more of a mystery to that, then."

"OK."

Sarvilinna seems to be evaluating the durability of Yusuf's stomach. But he isn't nauseous. A mutilated corpse is par for the course in the work of a homicide detective.

"The entrance to the wound channel is visible two centimeters below and four centimeters to the left of the nipple," Sarvilinna says, and Yusuf notices that she's directing her words not at him, but to the recorder resting in its stand. "The edges of the wound channel are clean, and the incision is three and a half centimeters wide at its widest. The incision tapers toward the ends. The incision is pointed toward the nipple, forming a line between seven o'clock and one o'clock from the body's meridian. The wound channel is oriented from the left side of the sternum between ribs five and six and continues approximately two centimeters to the left of the heart's apex."

Sarvilinna moves her scalpel around in the wound. Then she nonchalantly takes hold of the heart and lifts it out of Eliel Zetterborg's chest like a little puppy.

"The trabeculae carneae in the left ventricle have been severed," she says after studying the organ for a moment. "The ventricle is otherwise undamaged. The wound in the wall of the left ventricle is about a centimeter wide and jagged at the edges. No trace of the wound channel is visible in the other areas of the heart."

Sarvilinna glances at Yusuf.

"And the width and jaggedness of the wound channel are what tell us the knife was withdrawn from the heart immediately after its insertion."

"OK," Yusuf says as Sarvilinna reaches for her mug of hot honey water with her bloody glove.

After a couple of lingering swigs, she continues her attack on the heart. A few silent moments pass, during which Yusuf concentrates on listening to the monotonous hum of the ventilation system.

"Fascinating," Sarvilinna eventually says. "The walls of all coronary arteries in the heart show signs of severe atherosclerosis. The left anterior descending artery is almost completely blocked, and there we see a blood clot that formed when the subject was still alive. At the corresponding location on the wall of the heart's left ventricle, there is a plethoric change consistent with a recent infarction."

"You mean, Eliel Zetterborg suffered a heart attack recently?"

"If not multiple. But there's no doubt as to the cause of death. It was caused by the kitchen knife in the chest."

"I see." Yusuf scratches his forehead. "He told his son he wasn't feeling well earlier that day."

"Chest pain?"

"He just said he wasn't feeling well."

"It's possible there were a series of smaller infarctions. They wouldn't necessarily knock him to the ground but would certainly cause discomfort. He should have sought care immediately."

"Right. That way he could have avoided getting stabbed too," Yusuf says, and Sarvilinna laughs. Evidently Yusuf has accidentally struck her drier-than-dry funny bone.

"I understood the victim called the emergency number himself."

"Correct."

Sarvilinna looks reflective.

"Is that odd?" Yusuf continues.

"It depends. Based on these wounds, I would have assumed death followed so quickly, he wouldn't have had time to call anywhere. Is the recording from emergency services available for review?"

"I'll be getting it soon."

"Anything's possible, of course. I know cases where people have survived for hours with wounds one would presume to be fatal in seconds."

Yusuf rocks back and forth on the balls of his feet and glances restlessly at his watch. It's quarter past one in the morning.

"I happen to have such a case in the cooler there. . . . I never would have believed he would have held on and made it to the emergency room in the condition—"

"Thanks. I have to get going," Yusuf says when he sees Sarvilinna heading toward the cooler, eyes burning with excitement.

"Fine," Sarvilinna says. Disappointment flashes across her thin face but disappears just as quickly and is replaced by the familiar cold impartiality. "I'll send along the report when I'm finished. But I doubt I'm going to find anything earth-shattering here."

25

RASMUS SUSIKOSKI GLANCES at the text message he received earlier that evening. It's from his mother, who can't get the new cable box to work. It's probably just an incorrectly configured connection or a button his parents haven't figured out they need to press on the remote. He will have a look when he gets home. Right now he is otherwise occupied.

He sits down at the table in the small, dark cubbyhole turned over to the puzzle-solving team. The space was presumably once part of a bigger conference room that was divided into two or more parts.

Rasmus is alone. The trio from Crime Scene Investigations, two women and one man, exited a moment ago for a well-deserved ten-minute break.

The door opens, and Tanja steps in. She stands in the doorway for a moment, looking around in confusion, then turns on the banks of fluorescent lights with the switch.

"Are you sitting here in the dark on purpose?"

"Oh . . . no. I just got here. My guess is those bright lights were giving the team a headache," Rasmus says.

Tanja nods. The team has been creative in coming up with the best possible setup for solving the two-sided puzzle. Four unopened tubes of snuff tins have been placed on the table, and a thin sheet of glass found somewhere has been laid over them. This has made it relatively easy for them to monitor the formation of the text written on the underside of the puzzle.

"It's starting to come together." Tanja sits down across from Rasmus. The air current from the ventilation system sets the blinds rustling.

Rasmus looks at the puzzle. The left half is significantly more complete than the right. "The picture seems to be of some creature lying on a black base. But the image is blurry; my guess is it's been blown up from some low-quality photograph. As you can tell, the figure itself is almost white, and dark stripes are visible in the background."

Tanja nods, then sticks her head under the jury-rigged glass surface to see the puzzle's reverse.

"Were you right about the text?" she asks, standing up straight again.

Rasmus nods. "Something's written on the back in marker. They used a ruler."

"To mask the handwriting."

"Exactly."

Tanja bends down to take another look at the text. "'Fa . . . teles . . .'"

"Yeah, we're close, but that doesn't mean anything yet."

"On two lines . . ." Tanja mutters. "It doesn't sound like Finnish. More like . . . Greek or something."

Rasmus rakes up a few loose pieces from the corner of the table. "Let's wait until it's finished."

Just then, the door opens and Superintendent Helena Lappi peers in. "How much longer?" she asks as if she has poked her head into the room merely to pick up the conversation where it left off in the team meeting not too long ago.

Rasmus glances at the time: 2:03 a.m.

"We're almost halfway there, and it's getting easier and easier. My guess is we'll be done sooner than we expected."

"I need a time, Rasse. An estimate," Hellu says wearily and a little peevishly.

But Rasmus doesn't take his boss' behavior personally. No one can be expected to be very chipper at the end of an eighteen-hour workday, especially when they're the one ultimately responsible for solving the case.

"I'd say between six and seven in the morning."

"Good." Hellu shuts the door, but quickly opens it again. "And, Rasse . . ."

"Yes?"

"Thank you. Excellent work."

26

A JACKDAW IS hopping outside the door, pecking at a hamburger wrapper that escaped from the cigarette-butt-littered trash receptacle. Yusuf doesn't know much about birds; he just remembers his grandfather telling him most jackdaws fly south for the winter, but some are simply too fond of the Finnish winters to exchange them for the warmth of Málaga. Yusuf sticks a cigarette in his mouth and for a moment pictures himself as a jackdaw: a black bird that ought to be in some sunnier place right now.

He lights the cigarette, takes a long drag, and sees a judgmental look shimmering through the white smoke. Nina has appeared in the smoking area.

"You really ought to quit," she says, folding her arms across her chest as the door shuts behind her.

"No one's perfect," Yusuf quips as he pulls on his gloves. "Not even Zlatan Ibrahimović or Yusuf Pepple."

"I just had another word with Sanni Karppinen. She said picking up books from the library for Zetterborg was part of the job. He gave her a list of books to check out every month, and she would return the previous ones at the same time. She was supposed to go to the library today, but she forgot the bag in the entryway."

"The bag? There was no bag. All there was were those fucking books," Yusuf snaps. He catches himself sounding just like Erne. Like the Erne from those final years, who had a tendency to genial grouchiness.

Nina looks at Yusuf as if he's lost his mind. "Maybe the cleaner misremembered. But I don't think the books have anything to do with the case."

Yusuf exhales a cloud of smoke from his nostrils and then blows it away. "OK. So, you think we ought to take a closer look at Lamberg?"

Nina nudges the thin film of ice that has formed on a puddle with the tip of her shoe, then looks enigmatically over Yusuf's shoulder. "That guy from SWAT. Roni Kerman. Apparently he knew Lamberg well. For better and for worse. Mostly worse."

"I thought Lamberg seemed a little unstable too," Yusuf says. "But Eliel Zetterborg trusted him for years. A prominent guy like that must have conducted a thorough background check on Lamberg before hiring him as a bodyguard."

"I could still do a little digging around," Nina says. "If that much dirt turns up on him without us even looking, I'm pretty sure we've just scratched the surface."

"We have to remember Lamberg has a ninety-five-percent alibi," Yusuf says, releasing a tiny puff of smoke from his nostrils. The thunder of a large engine carries from the street, and the jackdaw flaps off.

"How so?"

Nina rubs her arms. She looks like she's cold. Yusuf on the other hand is fine in nothing but a hoodie, as if the tobacco generates extra body heat.

"Eliel Zetterborg called emergency dispatch at six twenty-seven p.m.," Yusuf says. "The victim's son, Axel, called Lamberg a few minutes later and said he was worried about his dad. At that point Lamberg started climbing the stairs to check on his boss."

"How do you know Lamberg wasn't already in the apartment—"

"I just got this," Yusuf says, pulling his phone from his jeans pocket. "The recording from emergency services." He searches his phone for the right file, glances around to make sure there isn't anyone nearby listening, and hands the phone to Nina. "Press Play."

Nina does.

What is your emergency, please?

Unintelligible mumbling.

Hello? What is your emergency? Can you hear me?

My chest . . . My chest . . .

OK, stay calm. Can you give me your location?

A groan echoes from the phone.

The classical piano music in the background lends an eeriness to the call.

"That's all Eliel Zetterborg was able to say," Yusuf says, the cigarette dangling from the corner of his mouth. "Dispatch tries to get him to give them his location, but apparently he loses consciousness at this point. The dispatcher decides it's a heart attack and sends an ambulance to the corner of Tehtaankatu and Muukalaiskatu based on base station positioning."

Yusuf lowers his finger to the screen of the phone and fast-forwards a few minutes through the recording.

But in order to get you help, we need an exact address, an apartment number and floor. . . .

The doorbell can be heard ringing. Then insistent knocking.

"Lamberg's at the door?" Nina's eyes are perhaps tinged with disappointment.

Yusuf nods and twiddles the cigarette between his forefinger and thumb.

Before long, they hear Lamberg open the door and call Eliel by name.

If there's someone else there, hand them the phone.

Zeta. Zeta?

Maybe thirty seconds pass. Lamberg seems to be walking around the apartment.

Kianto . . .

"Was that Zetterborg? *Kianto?* What the hell does that mean?" Nina says, pulling her coat more tightly around her.

Yusuf shrugs.

Then there's a faint rustling as Lamberg presumably takes the phone from Zetterborg's hand.

Hello?

This is emergency services. We need an exact address.

Hell . . .

"Then Lamberg gives the address and his name and asks them to send an ambulance, fast," Yusuf says.

"Does dispatch still think it's a heart attack?" Nina asks.

Yusuf nods.

Can you feel a pulse?

No . . .

Do you know how to perform CPR?

Yes, but it's not going to help at this point. . . .

Does the patient have any other injuries?

Any other injuries?

Yes, can you assess—

Lamberg raises his voice in agitation: *No, it's pretty clear he's been stabbed in the chest with a steel blade. . . .*

With a steel blade?

Yes! There's blood everywhere. . . .

Yusuf pauses the recording.

"Lamberg stays on the line until the ambulance arrives," Yusuf says. "Axel Zetterborg also shows up."

Nina chews her bottom lip thoughtfully. "What about what Zetterborg said? Kianto?"

"Damn good question. The only thing that came up when I Googled was Ilmari Kianto, a Finnish author from the 1900s. Died in 1970. No idea why Zetterborg would say his name right before he died."

Nina stares at the phone as if it is hexed. Then she sighs deeply. "You said Lamberg has a ninety-five-percent alibi?"

Yusuf nods emphatically. "I think the recording supports Lamberg's account perfectly. Of course it's theoretically possible Lamberg stabbed his boss, left the apartment, then came back in a moment later."

"But you think that theory is only worth five percent?"

"Yup. The biggest problem with the scenario is whether Lamberg would have been able to: (a) sneak out so quietly, it wouldn't be audible in the background of the call and (b) be sure Zetterborg, who was still alive at the beginning of the call, wouldn't reveal to emergency services who stabbed him in the chest with a knife."

"Sounds pretty tricky, I agree."

"And (c) Lamberg entered the apartment only because Axel Zetterborg called him and asked him to. And that happened just a few minutes before we hear Lamberg enter with his own key." Yusuf extinguishes the cigarette by rolling it against the lid of the trash can. "And then of course (d) Lamberg spent all day with his boss. So he couldn't have taken the key from the cleaner, snuck into his boss' apartment, or left the puzzle. The perpetrator simply has to be someone else. That's also indicated by the description given by the cleaner."

"You're probably right," Nina says, reaching for the door handle.

"But . . . ," Yusuf says, stopping Nina midmovement, "that five percent. We need to be able to exclude it."

"How?"

"Hellu has submitted a request to the Russian embassy. Their cameras cover that big lot twenty-four/seven, and would have caught Lamberg's Maybach on Muukalaiskatu too. If we see Lamberg sitting in his car on those recordings until Axel Zetterborg calls, we can forget that five percent."

"OK," Nina says. "What did Sarvilinna have to say?"

"The autopsy revealed Zetterborg suffered a heart attack recently. One or more. Which could explain why he said he wasn't feeling well earlier in the day."

"Wouldn't a heart attack cause severe chest pain?"

"Not necessarily. A lot of the time, but Sarvilinna said it can also manifest as sudden nausea."

"OK. But is the heart attack he had earlier that day relevant in terms of the murder or even the cause of death?"

Yusuf shakes his head reflectively. "I don't know. No. Maybe. Fuck. In any case, the cause of death is the knife plunged into his heart."

"Evidently," Nina says. "What do we do now?"

"Go home and get some sleep. I'll stay here to keep an eye on things," Yusuf says, and opens the door for Nina.

At that same moment, his phone rings, and upon answering, he learns from Harjula that Niklas Fischer has been found and brought in.

27

Yusuf rubs his forehead. His exhaustion has taken the form of pressure at his cheekbones. The air in the interrogation room is stuffy, and the breath of the individual being questioned, which reeks of alcohol fumes, isn't helping matters.

Across from Yusuf sits a man whose round red face and enormous nose make for a memorable appearance. The short beard is carefully trimmed around the chin, and there's no sign of stubble on the throat. Niklas Fischer left home voluntarily with Jami Harjula an hour earlier and seems not so much fluish as intoxicated.

"Thanks for coming in spite of the hour," Yusuf says, pushing his chair closer to the edge of the table.

Fischer grins, and his shoulders shudder from the force of his silent laughter. "Did I have a choice?"

"You didn't participate in the anniversary dinner tonight," Yusuf says quickly.

"I'm guessing no one did in the end," Fischer says, cracking his fat knuckles one at a time.

"You said you were indisposed and that's why you couldn't attend."

"Well, I'm not. I just didn't want to go."

"And you did what instead?"

Fischer unzips the zipper of his black sweater a little and takes a swig of water from the disposable cup in front of him. "I stayed home and had a few drinks."

"Would you like to reveal why you weren't in the mood to celebrate?"

"What?"

"Wasn't today an anniversary, a big night?"

"I'm sure you guys already know. Otherwise I wouldn't be sitting here," Fischer says, and raises his forefinger at Yusuf as if he is poking him from a distance. "So, since I'm giving you my time—despite the hour being what it is—I expect you to ask smart questions, not stupid ones."

Yusuf feels rage wash over him. Fischer is a pompous ass who doesn't seem to think he's at any risk of losing his freedom.

"Is there anyone who can confirm you were home all evening?"

"No. But I'm sure you have your ways of finding out. Check my phone's cell tower info or something."

"You can be sure we will." Yusuf shuts his heavy eyelids for a moment and realizes how exhausted he is. "I'd like to hear about the disagreement between you and Eliel Zetterborg."

Fischer smiles faintly. "Regarding Kouvola? That would be a pretty long conversation."

"Why don't you give me the short version for now?"

"Have you seen the YouTube clip where Steve Jobs tells Bill Gates a joke? In it, Steve Jobs is the captain of a ship. There's a hole in the hull, and it's Jobs' job to steer the ship in the right direction," Fischer says, and his shoulders jiggle in time to the snorting that resembles laughter.

Yusuf reflects that anyone who laughs at such a bad joke is either a billionaire nerd or a VP of Strategy.

"Do you get it?" Fischer says.

"Zetterborg wasn't prepared to fix the company's problems and instead just stubbornly charged ahead to new challenges."

"Exactly. And those problems were very fundamental in nature. They still are. Zetterborg's death didn't change anything."

"Couldn't an unprofitable factory be a hole in the bottom of the boat?" Yusuf folds his hands behind his neck. The stretch feels delicious in his fatigued upper-back muscles.

"You could see it that way. But the factory wasn't closed so the company would finally start accumulating cash reserves it badly needed. No, he wanted to use the savings to fund something totally unfathomable: buying a component manufacturer from Gothenburg. Didn't you hear about this? Do the police even read the *Business Times*?"

Yusuf ignores the jab and responds with an intent stare that Fischer dodges a moment later. "Maybe over in white-collar crime. Around here we just read *Alibi*."

"In any case, it's like a middle-class family putting down a beloved dog so it can use the savings to buy a gold-plated toilet. The plan was idiotic: in the right hands, the Swedish component company might have been a gold mine, but our hands are definitely not the right ones. By any measure RealEst is a dinosaur that Silicon Valley is going to hunt to extinction over the next decade."

"So you were thinking purely about what was best for the company when you publicly opposed the strategy?"

"Of course."

"You're known for having friends in the labor unions."

"So?"

"Did you see yourself as the CEO of RealEst? Did you think you would need the support of labor unions in the future?"

"Horseshit," Fischer says, staring at his cup of water with disdain. The consequences of his fading intoxication must be sinking in, body and soul. "That's a hell of a fanciful conspiracy theory."

"Answer the question." Yusuf glances at his watch. It's ten to three in the morning.

Fischer scratches his clean-shaven neck and looks a little worried. The corners of his mouth have drooped, and there is less belligerence in his eyes.

"Yes, the disagreement led to friction between us and to my name no longer being mentioned in discussions of who would lead the company in the future. But no, I didn't kill him over that. And yes, I've already started looking for a new job. There are plenty of takers."

Yusuf taps his fingers against the tabletop and eyes Fischer probingly. Could this be the same man who broke into Sanni Karppinen's home, then snuck into Zetterborg's apartment and sank a kitchen knife into the old man's chest the evening before?

"You've sent Zetterborg some nasty text messages." Yusuf unfolds a printout on the table and reads out loud:

You're destroying everything the rest of us have built.
Why don't you just shoot yourself, damn it!
A heart attack would do you good, Zeta.

Fischer blanches. "Those are private messages—"

"Which look pretty bad for you in light of what happened."

"Aw hell, so I was blowing off a little steam. But those are just words."

"Shoot yourself?"

Fischer gulps. "Come on, I wouldn't have sent those if I'd meant to do something, would I?" It's undeniable he is taking the situation more seriously than before.

"We need to verify your alibi." Yusuf stands and strides past the thunderstruck VP of Strategy toward the door of the interrogation room.

"What the hell? Are you just going to leave me here?"

"Yes," Yusuf replies laconically, then remembers what Hellu said: don't go out of your way to annoy the powerful. "There's coffee. Unfortunately I can only offer you black. We're out of milk," he says, shutting the door behind him.

28

YUSUF SETTLES INTO the dark gray sofa in the break room; he's slept there on plenty of occasions, even if more than a year has passed since the last time. Recently he's started going home to sleep at the end of overlong workdays, despite the drive time resulting in even less precious rest. But now it feels important to be present at the command center; he is, after all, lead investigator. He needs to be reachable around the clock as long as the investigation lasts.

Thanks to the text message exchange discovered on Eliel Zetterborg's phone, they can hold Niklas Fischer until they can come up with a reasonable alibi for him. Maybe they won't be able to, and the case will start to unravel of its own accord. Initially the VP of Strategy seemed like he would cause a stink about the way he was being treated, but as he sobered up and realized the hopelessness of his circumstances, he seemed to accept his lot.

Is the solution to the mystery genuinely this simple?

Sometimes it is. Sometimes it isn't.

Fischer didn't admit to knowing anything about the mysterious puzzle, the cleaner's keys, or Zetterborg's alarm system. Base station data indicated Fischer's mobile phone hadn't left his home on Lauttasaari since morning, but on the other hand only an idiot would bring along a GPS-equipped electronic device on the way to commit a crime.

Yusuf fluffs the couch cushion under his head and glances at the time: his watch reads three fifteen a.m. If there are no major middle-of-the-night developments, he might be able to catch a few hours of sleep before the next agonizingly long workday begins.

Yusuf shuts his eyes, smacks his lips, and tastes the cigarette smoke

ingrained in his mouth's mucous membranes, then starts the breathing exercises he's gotten in the habit of doing at night. Six seconds in,
six seconds out. The trick to help him fall sleep originated with Erne,
but Yusuf has started making use of it only recently. As he counts the
seconds, he can't help but think how ironic it is that he has taken health
advice from a man who smoked and drank himself to death.

   Text message.

   Yusuf swears silently and pulls his phone from his pocket.

   When he sees the name on his screen, his heart starts hammering.
It's from Anna.

   Yusuf hasn't heard a peep from her in months. Their long relationship ended amicably, and the aftereffects of the split have followed the
usual formula: they're sad but determined; they promised to stay in
touch and be friends. *Don't be a stranger,* etc., etc. See each other on
occasion, go for coffee or lunch: it's a concept that's both therapeutic
and nerve-racking. Come to the joint conclusion that things are better
this way and promise to be happy for the other party, no matter what
happens. And it all goes smoothly until new complications and part-
ners enter the picture: storm clouds gather over the now-fraught relationship. And then everything safe and familiar disintegrates like sugar
dissolving in water.

   Anna hasn't mentioned anything about seeing anyone, but the sudden lack of contact implies as much. And now she just texted him in
the middle of the night.

   Hey! Can you call me in the morning?

   Yusuf taps out a reply.

   I can call now, everything OK?

   For a moment Yusuf watches the arrows that have turned blue at the edge of the screen. Anna doesn't immediately reply. She is clearly considering the offer.

Morning is better. I'm fine.

Yusuf presses the phone to his chest, where an enormous lump has formed.

His imagination is off and galloping: Anna's new man probably isn't a police officer or some other average Joe but something totally different. Yusuf pictures a rich, handsome Swedish-speaking banker who's a bull in the sheets and has the balls to match. When he's not making love to Anna, he plays polo, saves dolphins, and volunteers his free time to work with disabled children.

Six seconds in, hold, six seconds out.

29

JESSICA OPENS HER eyes.

She isn't sure if she's slept at all, but she doesn't feel the least bit tired.

She lowers her feet to the floor and checks her phone for the time. Text message from Yusuf.

OK if I come by in the morning? Headed to the scene around
seven

Jessica considers the request for a moment, then reluctantly taps in two letters: OK.

She cautiously stands and pumps her full body weight on the balls of her feet to make sure her legs will carry her. There's no guarantee. Jessica has never been able to rely on her body, trust that the neural pathways holding it together won't launch into a painful protest without warning, won't short-circuit in an agonizing paralysis that drops her to the floor like an empty sack. But this time everything seems to be functioning.

Come with me, sweetheart.

Jessica catches a whiff of smoke. She walks slowly out of her bedroom and into the upstairs hallway. The wind hums in the rafters of the hundred-year-old building.

The night is calling to her. She knows she oughtn't answer the call, but the darkness is like an injectable drug Jessica craves even though she knows it's bad for her.

It's not finished, Jessica.

Jessica shuts her eyes, and when she opens them, she sees a gaunt woman facing the other way at the top of the stairs. Bones protrude beneath the black fabric of the gown; the shoulders are fleshless. The black hair falls to the shoulder blades, gleaming and smooth.

You can sleep when you're dead.

Her mother doesn't look at her. Luckily, because just the thought of her mother's rotted face gives her goose bumps.

Instead, her mother takes hold of the railing and starts descending the spiral staircase.

Come now, Jessie.

Jessica clenches her fists and realizes her right arm isn't in its sling. She doesn't hurt anywhere.

Come.

And Jessica follows. Her mother's movements are stiff, awkward. Her bare fingerbones clack against the brass rail.

The varnished treads feel nice beneath Jessica's bare toes. Her feet float as if of their own volition from one stair to the next. When she reaches the bottom, she falls in behind her mother, who has stopped to wait.

Jessica feels uneasy. She is standing far too close to her mother— she can smell the sweet perfume and her freshly shampooed hair, but also the peaty scent of wet soil mingled with the stench of rotting meat. Jessica hears the wet grubbing of thousands of maggots as they devour their way through her mother's flesh.

Turn on the television.

Jessica takes the last few steps and continues past her mother to the couch and the television on the console in front of it. She sits and presses the red button on the remote.

The black screen comes to life, and at first Jessica isn't sure what she's looking at.

The blurry darkness is split by crackling brilliant white fire. Jessica hears an agonized scream and instantly understands she is looking at a figure writhing on bare rock, being greedily licked by tall flames.

You filmed this, Jessica.

Jessica wails in horror and turns off the television.

Her mother has returned to the staircase, starts climbing it slowly. Jessica dashes after her.

Her mother abruptly stops moving. And then she does what Jessica has subconsciously feared this whole time: she slowly turns around.

Jessica would like to remember her mother as beautiful, not the way she appears to Jessica at night. But the truth is, Theresa von Hellens hasn't been beautiful for a very long time. Her mother's face has been shredded tissue, crushed bones, and blue, blood-smeared skin for years.

But now when she turns around, all Jessica sees where the face should be is white bone.

For the first time, her mother doesn't look like she died recently, but long, long ago.

And Jessica understands the circle is truly closing.

Something final is happening.

All things come to an end. But only if you take the path to its completion, darling.

Suddenly Jessica's phone rings on the coffee table downstairs. In a flash, it all disappears: her mother and the macabre yet familiar magic that the presence of this mangled body has brought into the room.

For a moment, Jessica's mind wobbles between two worlds—the real and the imagined—as she descends the stairs and walks over to the couch.

She picks up her phone. Blocked number.

Something deep inside Jessica forbids her from answering, tells her nothing good will come of it. She is not even an officer of the law anymore.

"Hello?" Jessica says although she can't remember having made the decision to pick up.

She hears a heavy, raspy sigh as if the caller finds breathing particularly laborious.

"Hello?" she says again.

The line goes dead. It is impossible to hear what a smile sounds like, but for some reason, Jessica has the sense that is exactly what the caller did.

Smiled.

30

YUSUF PARKS IN an empty space at the intersection where Töölönkatu meets Museokatu before continuing past Jaska's Grill and Manala toward Parliament Park. He's used to pulling over on Töölönkatu to pick up or drop off Jessica, since her fifth-floor studio apartment is located on that side of her old Jugendstil building. But this time Jessica isn't jumping in the car, at least not without a little coaxing.

Despite the darkness hovering over the city, Helsinki has woken to a new morning. People hurrying to work make their way gingerly down the slippery sidewalks, which the sanding trucks with their flashing yellow lights are trying to make pedestrian friendly.

Yusuf climbs out of the car and pulls a pack of cigarettes from his pocket. A black hearse slowly gliding past makes him consider whether this ought to be the first tobacco-free day of the rest of his life. Yusuf doesn't believe in omens, but even so shoves the Marlboro Lights back in his jacket pocket.

After watching the hearse's taillights for a moment, he crosses the street. On the other side rises the ornamental entrance to Jessica's apartment building, entrance A, which Yusuf has passed through only once. On that occasion, Jessica revealed to him the secret she so carefully guards: that she is downright filthy rich, and the studio apartment accessed from entrance B is just a facade she has erected for the world. In reality, Jessica never spends her nights in the studio, but in a sumptuous two-story palace with a view over the rooftops of central Helsinki. As he followed Jessica from room to room on that December evening, Yusuf reflected that whereas everyone else is busy creating a sleeker impression of their everyday reality—especially on social media—Jessica does the exact opposite. She goes to an incredible amount of trouble to appear as unremarkable as possible.

Why has Jessica insisted on lying to Yusuf and her other colleagues? Would the way they look at her really change if they knew the truth? And did Jessica request a leave of absence for the same reason she told Yusuf about the vast fortune she inherited from her long-dead mother? Might it be better for all parties if Yusuf never learned about it in the first place?

Not likely. Jessica has always been Jessica, and nothing will change that. Yusuf can still remember his first day at the unit, Erne's gentle handshake and, standing behind Erne, the beautiful black-haired woman whose face didn't emanate suspicion as so many other faces did that day, but a warm, sisterly empathy. *Welcome to the team, Yusuf. Hang with me these first few weeks and I'll show you how things work on this floor.*

That was six years ago. Erne's tobacco-permeated figure lives only in memory now, but Jessica is still here at his side. At least in theory.

Yusuf glances at the time on his phone and remembers the message he received from Anna last night. As he walks, he brings up her number and listens to the monotone sound of the phone ringing for a moment.

Hi. This is Anna Laine. I can't come to the phone right now, but leave me a message and I'll get back to you.

Yusuf ends the call and sighs restlessly. Judging by the message, whatever Anna needed wasn't urgent. Even so, Yusuf can't help but wonder why she texted him in the middle of the night as if something had been keeping her awake. *I wonder if something happened to Papa.*

Yusuf stops outside the dark wood-and-glass door and presses the button that reads VON HELLENS. This is Jessica's real last name. Or at least the one she had at birth.

When he hears the buzzer, Yusuf tugs on the handle and finds irritation slinking into his mind, although he's not completely sure why. Because Jessica didn't trust him enough to tell him the truth earlier? Or because Jessica has left him to solve the Zetterborg murder on his own? Or could it be, Yusuf muses as he opens the decorative gate to the old-fashioned elevator at the end of the hall, as Jessica had originally predicted? Is Yusuf bothered by what Jessica kept hidden from her colleagues? Is he envious?

UP IN HER apartment, Jessica pulls on her black stretch pants with one hand and takes a quick look in the entryway mirror. She barely got any sleep.

You filmed this, Jessica.

She shakes the words from her mind, opens the door, and realizes she has never opened it for anyone before. She guarded her secret so carefully that she herself always entered through the studio apartment accessed from the other side of the building, which is separated from this huge apartment by a narrow stairwell.

Behind the door she finds Yusuf's friendly face, beautiful in its masculine way, but radiating nearly hopeless exhaustion.

"Jesus, haven't you slept at all?" Jessica says, gesturing for Yusuf to come in.

Yusuf sighs, takes off his shoes, and follows Jessica down the entry hall into the living room. Jessica sits on the couch and folds her legs beneath her. Yusuf glances around and seems just as blown away by what he sees as he was a couple of months ago, the first time Jessica showed him her home.

"How's it going, Jessie?" he says, flopping down listlessly at the other end of the couch.

"Good."

"Where have you been? And where are you now?"

Jessica smiles and points at the steaming red coffee mug on the table in front of Yusuf. He nods and takes hold of it without further ado.

"What do you mean?"

"Everything was supposed to be fine. Between you and Hellu . . . and then you stop showing up at work."

Jessica looks at Yusuf as he tilts the coffee mug to his lips.

"I needed some time for myself."

"Time for what? You promised to explain when we saw each other."

"I did promise."

"Well, now we're seeing each other. What's up, Jessie?"

Yusuf waits a second for Jessica to answer, and when it doesn't happen, he sighs and lowers his coffee back to the table. The dishwasher burbling in the kitchen breaks the silence.

"Lead investigator—is that right?" Jessica says although she knows Yusuf hates jumping from topic to topic.

Yusuf looks at her, hurt, and settles for a nod. "And I guess the thanks for that goes to you, since you decided to take leave."

"Congratulations, Yusuf. You never forget your first time," Jessica says. "How is the case coming?"

"So you're interested after all?"

"Of course I'm interested. Come on, I'm still Jessie from the block."

Yusuf grunts and taps the sofa's armrest restlessly. "We have something."

"What?"

"A puzzle."

"A puzzle?"

Yusuf smiles enigmatically. "I'll explain when I see you."

"Stuff it, Yusuf," Jessica says, discreetly adjusting her sling.

"I'll explain it all in the car. We'll have plenty of time to go through the case during the drive to Muukalaiskatu."

"What the hell are you talking about?"

"Come with me to the crime scene."

Jessica looks at Yusuf, stunned. "A two-month *leave of absence*, Yusuf. Do we not understand that term the same way?"

Yusuf smiles again and rubs his tired eyes. "Please."

"No."

"I'm asking you as a friend. We'll go there, and you'll tell me what you see. I know I'll manage on my own too, but no one has a head like yours. You see things the *CSI: Miami* team wouldn't pick up on."

"And what would Hellu say about it?"

"Hellu would piss honey if she got to have you on the case for even an hour."

"Flattery is cheap," Jessica says.

Then she awkwardly hauls herself up from the couch, and for a second, Yusuf looks as if he means to rush over and help. Luckily the impulse remains a thought, because Jessica can't stand being fussed over, and he knows it.

The shrill yapping of a little dog echoes from the stairwell.

Jessica walks to the arch leading to the kitchen and stops. "Have you told anyone?"

It takes Yusuf a moment to grasp her meaning. "About this apartment?"

"Yes. And . . . everything."

"Of course not."

"And you wouldn't tell about anything else either?"

Jessica goes into the kitchen and switches on the lights.

"About what, Jessica? What the fuck are you talking about?"

Jessica lowers her eyes to the kitchen table and feels a lump in her throat. "OK. Come look."

Yusuf appears in the kitchen, which is now swimming in the glare of bright halogen lights.

The kitchen table is littered with printouts and a laptop. The television on the wall is playing some morning talk show with the sound off.

Jessica chews her left thumbnail as Yusuf bends over to study the papers strewn across the table.

"What are these?"

Jessica draws a quick breath. The air in her lungs feels heavy. "Do you remember when that creep attacked me while I was jogging? At the end of November?"

Yusuf nods calmly even though he looks like he has no idea where this story is headed.

"At first I thought it was some random drunk or junkie. . . . But even at the time, I was struck by how single-mindedly he kept repeating something in my ear."

"What?"

"He said 'Christmas Eve.' Over and over. 'Christmas Eve.'"

"OK."

"Then we had the Lisa Yamamoto case to deal with and other stuff and I forgot about it. But a body was found burned in Central Park on Christmas Eve. The guy was so charred, they weren't able to ID him. The only detail of interest in the autopsy was that the victim was missing his two top front teeth." Jessica picks up a printout of a photo of a burned body. "The guy who assaulted me . . . I punched him and knocked out two of his front teeth. I vividly remember them breaking. My knuckles were sore for weeks."

"So you think that guy is the same one who was found in the woods . . ."

"At almost exactly the same spot where I ran into him."

"On Christmas Eve?"

"On Christmas Eve, just like he kept saying in my ear."

Yusuf nods, does his best to conceal his surprise. "OK, I admit that's a strange coincidence, but what does it have to do with you except the fact that he happened to attack you specifically?"

"*Happened* to attack." Jessica sighs and wets her lips with the tip of her tongue.

Yusuf turns to Jessica and rubs his neck. "Do you have any reason to suspect he was stalking you?"

Jessica tries to speak, but her voice fails her.

It takes Yusuf only a second to realize something is wrong. "Jessie, what is it?"

"I don't know if I'm going crazy, Yusuf . . . and that's why I need to investigate this alone."

Yusuf looks at her probingly. He knows one of Jessica's biggest secrets: that in reality she is incredibly wealthy and lives in this extravagant home in the heart of Helsinki. But Yusuf is blissfully ignorant about the rest of it: what Erne learned long ago. And what Hellu received some hints about from a medical report that showed up on her desk. Jessica's mind is more complex and problematic than Yusuf's. Or that of anyone else who works at police headquarters.

"What did Hellu say about the teeth?" Yusuf decides to ask.

Jessica looks at him apologetically. "Hellu doesn't know about that."

"Doesn't know? What the hell, Jessica—"

"And she can't find out yet either, OK? I need some time to figure this out on my own. Concentrate on this. It reminds me too much of all of that . . ."

Yusuf appears to grasp what she's driving at. "You mean the witch gang."

Jessica nods.

"The whole thing felt so personal all of a sudden. And no one knows Camilla Adlerkreutz's whereabouts."

"There's an international arrest warrant out for her, Jessica. She can't just pop up and start terrorizing you without getting caught."

"But that's exactly what she's doing." Jessica gulps. She walks over to the counter, rips a paper towel from the roll, and blows her nose.

Yusuf steps closer and takes Jessica tentatively by the shoulders. When she doesn't resist, he squeezes her tightly against him, being mindful of her right arm and the sling. They stand there for a long moment, bodies touching, without saying a word.

"I'm not used to being afraid, Yusuf," Jessica says, and feels the tears soak into the chest of Yusuf's hoodie.

"We'll sort this out together, Jessie. Everything's going to be fine."

31

JESSICA STUDIES HERSELF in the car's vanity mirror and lets out a deep sigh. Luckily her face shows no signs of the creeping angst she experienced at home a moment before.

Yusuf pulls up to a red light at the Lasipalatsi building, and Jessica eyes the enormous banner hanging from the Forum shopping center: the rapper Kex Mace poses there, advertising his upcoming stadium concert tour that summer.

Jessica is one of the few people who know there isn't going to be any concert. The rapper is up to his ears in a sadistic human-trafficking ring, and the information will leak to the media as soon as the case is turned over to the prosecutor. His rocketlike career is about to come to a wretched end.

"All right, put on some music," Yusuf says. They've been listening to nothing but the hum of the engine and the rumble of the traffic carrying in from the street.

"You ought to learn to sit in silence," Jessica says. "Try meditating or something."

"I don't enjoy my own company enough," Yusuf says, pointing insistently at the radio.

Jessica has agreed to join Yusuf on the condition she gets to choose the music today. After bouncing around the radio stations for a moment, she comes to a rest on the news instead of music.

Jessica shuts her tired eyes for just a moment and then turns to Yusuf. "Well?"

"What?"

"You said you'd give me the specs during the drive. We're almost there."

Yusuf purses his lips, but instead of whistling, he lets out a thin sigh. "You've been watching the news?"

"Yup."

"What about before yesterday? So you know there are a lot of people with plenty of reasons to hate Eliel Zetterborg."

"They've been calling him the Axman."

"Yes. And now the Axman has been executed. He was stabbed straight in the heart with a big kitchen knife," Yusuf says. "They probably didn't report that on the news."

Jessica shakes her head.

"According to an eyewitness, our suspect is a middle-aged man on the stocky side."

"Who's the eyewitness?"

"Sanni Karppinen, the cleaner whose keys the suspect took yesterday around noon. He forced his way into her home, took the keys, and tied her to her bed. Then he made his way to Muukalaiskatu and bypassed the alarm with the fob on the key ring."

"Then what?"

"Then nothing. No one saw anything. The weapon was taken from the kitchen."

"Sounds spontaneous," Jessica says.

"Yup. Except the intrusion was deliberate and carefully planned."

"That is weird."

"One other thing occurred to me." Yusuf turns off the radio before continuing: "Not much time passed between RealEst announcing the layoffs and the homicide. But the perp must have started following the cleaner's movements weeks ago. It could just be coincidence the killing occurred the night of the company's fiftieth anniversary. When the celebration was at its highest."

"Which would mean the killing doesn't have anything to do with the factory closing?"

"Or else it does, but the perpetrator must have had a strategy in place long before it was announced," Yusuf says, and Jessica nods. "Some member of the inner circle who was deeply infuriated by the decision."

"OK," Jessica says after a brief silence. "When did the company announce the factory closure?"

"Monday. RealEst said layoff negotiations would begin for the three thousand employees at the same time."

"What about before that? Who knew about it?"

"The RealEst board. The management team . . . probably no one else."

"But the members of those bodies participated in that decision. It doesn't make any sense that some top executive would take a decision like that personally enough to break into the chair's apartment and stab him with a knife."

"No. But maybe someone leaked the information. For instance the VP of Strategy, Niklas Fischer, who has publicly opposed the closing of the factory."

"I don't know."

"Fuck . . . me either." Yusuf leans on the horn after waiting a few seconds for the taxi in front of them to shoot through the green light.

"Take it easy," Jessica says. "Let's see what the apartment reveals. If nothing else, I can at least do a little sparring with you."

32

———

JESSICA WATCHES CLOSELY as Yusuf breaks the gray seal affixed to the door and the jamb and uses a key to unlock the apartment. In the dim light, with the shadows cast by the large furnishings, the entry hall looks eerie, like an abandoned house from a horror movie.

"Your place is nicer, if you ask me," Yusuf says as Jessica walks past him, hands deep in her coat pockets. The hardwood floor creaks under their feet.

The apartment smells the way old people's homes stuffed with antiques and paintings usually smell. Neither the odor nor anything else in the entryway offers any indication the flat's owner was murdered in the middle of the living room the night before. A black overcoat hangs at the coatrack, with a tag from CSI rubber-banded around it.

Laundry service from the beyond, Jessica thinks to herself.

"It's quiet in here," Yusuf says.

Jessica listens for a moment and realizes it's true. At her place in Töölö, the thundering traffic on nearby Mannerheimintie ensures there's always some sort of noise: the faint honks of horns, the wails of emergency vehicles' sirens, the tireless clanks of trams. Eliel Zetterborg's home is, in contrast, totally silent, which makes the atmosphere ghostlier than ever.

"I'm betting things were a little livelier here last night," Jessica says as she pulls on the blue shoe protectors Yusuf handed her in the elevator. The apartment has already been meticulously combed, but as the investigation progresses, the forensic team could return to the crime scene if necessary. That's why protective gear still needs to be worn.

"Come here," Yusuf says as he passes Jessica in the narrow entry hall.

They walk down the hall single file and step through an arched doorway into the living room. Yusuf points at the spot where blood has stained the carpet red. Then he pulls a stack of photographs from his coat's breast pocket and passes them to Jessica.

"Holy shit," Jessica whispers as she flips through the pictures.

"Right in the heart," Yusuf says. "A long knife, used decisively and cleanly."

Jessica hands the photos back. She looks around, eventually casting a questioning glance at Yusuf.

"What?"

"In a way I'm flattered that you felt like you needed me. . . ."

"But?"

"But I don't know what I'm going to find here that ten investigators didn't spot last night."

Yusuf eyes Jessica, hands on his hips, and for a moment, it seems like he's going to give in. Then his expression brightens, and he hurries past Jessica to another arched doorway, at the far side of the room.

"Come here," Yusuf says.

Jessica follows him into a cozy library that reminds her of the quintessential British detective novel. She focuses her attention on the old movie posters hanging on the wall. *Silver from Across the Border. Under Your Skin. The Lapua Bride.* Every one reads *Director: Mikko Niskanen.* Zetterborg was clearly an ardent fan of the Finnish filmmaker.

"We found a puzzle on this table yesterday," Yusuf says, rousing Jessica from her thoughts. "Everything else in the apartment was neat as a pin, and as Zetterborg's son, Axel, told us, his father was almost neurotic when it came to tidiness and order."

"And?"

"The pieces of the puzzle had been dumped on the table in a big heap. Tanja immediately realized—"

"Tanja?"

"Yes, Tanja from tech."

"Oh, you mean the Tanja from tech you were making out with at the Christmas party?"

Yusuf shoots Jessica a disappointed look, and she decides to ease off. "Tanja immediately realized the puzzle was left there to be found."

"And for Zetterborg to solve?"

"No," Yusuf says, rolling his eyes pointedly. "Zetterborg is at the morgue."

"So the police, then?"

"Exactly. Hellu authorized me to assign some resources to putting it together . . . a five-person team led by Rasse. And it paid off." Yusuf draws two more photos from his pocket. He stands next to Jessica and lowers a forefinger to the one on top. "This is the solved puzzle."

Jessica eyes the photo. It takes her brain a moment to arrange the mishmash of black and white into a whole that remotely resembles a living being. Jessica feels a shudder as she realizes the image is a blurry magnification of an ultrasound. "Is it a fetus?"

Yusuf nods. "The digital time stamp is visible in the upper-left corner. It was probably even hard to make out in the original. According to the typography expert, the numbers are presumably 15-04-90, but she said we can't be absolutely sure."

"April 1990? So that's a picture of a fetus that got its start thirty years ago," Jessica muses more to herself than to Yusuf.

"And this," Yusuf says a moment later, as he points at the second photo. "On the back of the puzzle, there's text written in black marker against the white background."

Faust and Mephistopheles.

Jessica looks at the names, and though they look vaguely familiar, she can't for the life of her remember what they refer to. Perhaps her illness is finally affecting her memory.

"We had to read Goethe's *Faust* in high school," Yusuf says. "Not that I did. But Rasse knew without having to look it up that the characters appear in some anonymous German work from the 1500s, and that work served as the basis for a whole bunch of adaptations. Goethe's version from the 1800s is probably the best known. In any case, the story goes pretty much that Faust sells his soul to the devil and is given all these amazing things in return. Later, he starts to regret the deal, but by then it's too late."

"And Mephistopheles is the devil from the story?" Jessica asks.

"That's what I thought too. But apparently he's the devil's agent, the one Faust deals with."

Jessica stares at the images for a moment longer, then hands them back to Yusuf. Somewhere in the apartment, a clock chimes to note the hour, prompting both of them to turn in the direction of the sound. Then the silence returns.

"So the perp knows their literature," Jessica says.

"That's what it looks like. At least Zetterborg was a big reader. It's bothered me from the start that there was a stack of books on the hall floor. Nothing out of the ordinary was found in them, but they must be connected to all this somehow."

"Might the murderer have left the books in the entryway?"

Yusuf shakes his head. "The cleaner confirmed that she checked them out of the library for Zetterborg. And that she was supposed to return them to Rikhardinkatu yesterday but she forgot them in the entryway."

"Well, then, there's probably nothing to them—"

"Oh yeah," Yusuf says enthusiastically. "And then there's the bag. The cleaner said she left them in the entryway in a yellow plastic shopping bag. But fuck, there wasn't any bag there, just the books."

"Maybe Eliel came home and picked it up from the floor? A guy who is particular about aesthetics might not want to look at a yellow bag on the floor. I bet the kitchen cupboard is full of yellow bags," Jessica says. "Or else the cleaner simply misremembered."

Yusuf shoots Jessica a murderous look. He appears unconvinced. He shakes his head quickly as if to rid himself of a thought and shuts his eyes. "Anyway, Jessie, what comes to mind from this Faust thing?"

"Hmm. So, the murderer left a message for the police," Jessica says. "From which we can draw the conclusion that the relationship between the victim and the perpetrator involved the same sort of dynamic as in Goethe's story?"

"Yup, that seems obvious." Yusuf rustles around in his coat pocket and tosses a surprising number of pieces of gum in his mouth.

"But which was which?" Jessica says.

"What do you mean?"

"Was Eliel Zetterborg the agent of the devil . . . or was he the one who sold his soul and is now paying a steep price for it?"

Yusuf's jaws chew his gum ferociously, but a moment later, his face twists up in a smile.

"That's the reason I wanted you here with me, Jessie."

"I guess it doesn't take much to earn an MVP around here."

Jessica walks down the short hallway to the bedroom. Yusuf follows her, leaving a gap of a few feet as if he wants to make room for Jessica's thoughts to breathe.

"How carefully was the apartment searched?" Jessica says after scanning the sizable bedroom.

The king-sized bed is neatly made and, with its taut bedspread, calls to mind a five-star hotel. The walls are covered in white wallpaper with delicate blue lines depicting steadily crashing waves. Strangely enough, Jessica finds the room's decor soothing.

"Just superficially," Yusuf says. "We showed the cleaner photographs of the apartment, and she didn't notice differences from when she left. Except of course the puzzle in the library. And also . . ."

"Also what?"

"The photograph of Zetterborg's deceased wife, which had been moved from one windowsill to another. The cleaner spotted it immediately, because the wife's picture has always been in the same spot, in front of the windows facing the Russian embassy, and she has dusted it hundreds of times."

"Show me the window," Jessica says, following Yusuf back into the living room, to the scene of the bloodletting. Jessica picks up the framed photograph of a woman with just-graying hair in a blue gown. The face is mild and good-natured. The eyes radiate an unusual warmth—the sort that is hard to fake in pictures and, therefore, must be genuine.

Just then, the wind grabs at the building's structures and gutters, and the eerie silence momentarily turns to a ghostly hum.

"Anne-Marie Sofia. When did she die?" Jessica says, turning over the photo.

"About three years ago."

Jessica flips open the metal clips holding the backing in place and pulls the photograph out. She has the presence of mind to hope she won't find anything relevant to the case underneath, because Yusuf might take it as somehow humiliating. But there's nothing there. The backing is pure white, and the frame doesn't conceal any secrets within. Jessica feels a mild sense of relief. She puts the frame back together— out of respect for the dead, she supposes—and sets it back down on the windowsill in exactly the same spot it stood in a moment ago.

"It's odd that the photograph moves from one windowsill to another on the night her widowed husband dies," Jessica mutters. She stares at the photograph, then the empty windowsill, and back again. "Why did the killer move it?"

"Right?"

Jessica heads back to the library, with Yusuf at her heels. They stand near the bookcase with their backs to the window and scan the room from this new perspective.

"Have you considered the possibility that the puzzle has nothing to do with the case?" Jessica asks.

Yusuf looks agitated until he remembers Jessica is doing exactly what he hoped she would: questioning the conclusions drawn during the investigation. "Well," he says, scratching his neck, "no matter how hard I try, I just can't think of a reason it wouldn't. Like I said, the puzzle wasn't piled on the table when the cleaner left the apartment at twelve oh two p.m. It appeared there later."

"Fair enough," Jessica says. "But the answer can be hidden anywhere, including in assumptions like that."

"The place is going to be turned upside down. The crime scene investigators are coming here later today with Zetterborg's son to see if they can find anything else that would lead us to the killer."

Jessica turns to look at Yusuf. "Zetterborg's son?"

"Axel Zetterborg."

"OK. Can we one hundred percent exclude the possibility that Axel Zetterborg is guilty of his father's murder?"

Yusuf looks frustrated again.

"What?" Jessica huffs. And when Yusuf still doesn't answer, she continues: "Because otherwise it's probably not a very good idea to let him in here to contaminate the scene, is it?"

"Of course not. But the suspect entered using keys taken from the cleaner. And the man who took the keys wasn't Axel Zetterborg."

"But that man could have given the keys to someone. For example, Axel Zetterborg."

"Of course. But at the point when the cleaner's keys were used to open the front door here, Axel Zetterborg was still at home in Kulosaari," Yusuf says. "So what would have been really damn unlikely is basically impossible."

"OK, OK," Jessica says. "I'm just trying to help, Yusuf."

"I know."

Jessica smiles as a gesture of goodwill. "Responsibility breeds hypersensitivity. Have you noticed?"

"I guess," Yusuf says, turning up the lights with a dimmer switch.

"I have plenty of experience with that. You start taking totally nor-

THE LAST GRUDGE 141

mal questions personally, as if every idea or thought is automatically a jab at you, especially if it's something you haven't thought of yet," Jessica says. "You're going to find out, for instance, that Jami Harjula is going to press your buttons for as long as the investigation continues. He's really damn good at it, and maybe it's unintentional, maybe not. Where Hellu's going to make you feel small, guys like Harjula make a big production of themselves by saying obvious things out loud. It makes no difference if it's relevant as long as they're the first one to say it."

"Kind of like school. Easy points from the teacher."

Jessica turns to him and laughs: "Yusuf, a grade-school classroom is a picnic compared to our conference room at HQ. Our morning briefings should have taught you that by now."

Yusuf laughs and shoves his hands into the pockets of his jeans.

Jessica pushes a white door open and turns on the lights in the large bathroom, which has been remodeled in a more contemporary style than the rest of the apartment. She eyes the room from floor to ceiling, then opens the medicine cabinet over the sink and takes out a bottle on the bottom shelf.

"What is it?"

"Aspirin," Jessica says, returning the bottle to its place.

"I read somewhere that you shouldn't use it for pain, too many harmful side effects."

"So I heard." Jessica shuts the cabinet. "But the appearance of a knife in your chest probably can't be considered one of them."

They walk calmly through the apartment and peer into every room without saying a word. But the longer Jessica looks around the home of the deceased industry magnate, the more certain she is there's nothing to find there. Even so, an unpleasant feeling washes over her: Eliel Zetterborg's home reminds her of her own, despite the significant trouble she has gone to to give her place a more youthful vibe.

She pauses at the door to the kitchen. The heart of the home clearly hasn't been updated in decades. The cork floor is well past its prime, and the walls are covered in basic tiles in a floral pattern. Pretty musty for her tastes, but the apartment belonged to a man in his seventies.

"You said the murder weapon was taken from here?"

Yusuf nods and hustles over to open the unusual drawer: first the drawer has to be opened all the way, and then the knife stand appears. The slot at the edge is empty.

"Weird place for a knife," Jessica says. "I don't know if I'd have known to look for a knife in that drawer if it were my first time at the rodeo, especially since the knives aren't necessarily visible even if you happen to open the drawer."

"What can you deduce from that, do you think?" Yusuf says.

Jessica crosses the kitchen, brushes her fingertips across the marble surface of a little table, and stops at Yusuf's side. "That the perp knew where to look for it," she says.

Yusuf's face darkens. "Damn. So the killer had been in the kitchen before."

Jessica nods. "Unless the knife was already out."

"Nothing else in the kitchen indicates Eliel intended to cook. Everything is clean as a whistle. Besides, he was about to head out to dinner at a restaurant."

"Exactly," Jessica replies as Yusuf scribbles a note to himself.

Jessica looks at the round metal hatch above the counter. It has a handle and a homemade label that reads: *Not in Use.*

"A garbage chute," Jessica says, and grunts to herself. Trash chutes are a rare, if not impossible, sight in these old Helsinki buildings. They've been by and large removed from use, presumably because of the smell and the constant blockage. The dumping of all refuse in the same dumpster isn't how things are done anymore anyway. And speaking of trash . . .

Jessica opens the cabinet under the sink and sees a bundle of neatly folded yellow plastic bags. "Presto," she says, eliciting a smile from Yusuf.

She turns to Yusuf and leans against the counter. "Sorry, Yusuf. It's the best I can do."

The faint disappointment radiating from Yusuf's face makes him look younger than his years. "Yeah. No worries. I'll give you a case file to take home with you in case you want to take a peek."

Jessica sighs and is on the verge of saying something emphatic in protest when Yusuf's phone rings. And now Jessica realizes it's an out-and-out miracle it hasn't rung a single time yet during the hour they've spent together.

Yusuf turns his back to Jessica and takes a few steps over toward the window.

"OK, great. Thanks. Good fucking work, Rasse."

He ends the call and turns back to Jessica. There is no sign of the dejection that just marked his demeanor; it has been replaced by enthusiasm.

"The puzzle was custom-made; someone had it made from their own photograph. There aren't a ton of places that do that, and Rasse managed to track down a store where the puzzle was potentially ordered: Hobby Sammy, in Kamppi."

Yusuf starts tapping furiously at his phone.

"I can't go with you there," Jessica says, picking up on the disappointment in her own voice.

"No, you can't. Unless you want to call Hellu and cancel your leave," Yusuf says.

When Jessica shakes her head, he lifts the phone to his ear.

"Who are you calling?" Jessica asks.

"Nina."

THE DIM STAIRWELL smells of candle.

Jessica watches Yusuf fiddle the seal on Eliel Zetterborg's front door back into place. Her finger is about to press the elevator button when her eyes wander to the door opposite Zetterborg's. *Salo.* She catches the murmur of speech on the other side.

"Who talked to the neighbors?" Jessica asks as Yusuf finishes up.

"Hellu assigned the first patrol on the scene to go around to all the apartments. There are only two on every floor, so it didn't take too long."

"And no one saw or heard anything?"

"Well, the woman who lives in that apartment right there thought she heard shouting at the time of the killing. But she couldn't describe the voice in any detail. She was a little agitated by all the fuss." Yusuf pulls out his notepad. "Rea Salo."

Jessica presses her doorbell button.

"What are you doing?"

"What wouldn't I do for you, Yusuf?" Jessica says, flashing a wry smile.

Just as Yusuf is about to respond, the door opens and a beautiful woman of about fifty peers out. She looks a little frightened, and the door is chained.

"We're with the police."

Jessica fishes her wallet out of her pocket and shows her ID. She knows posing as a police officer is gross malfeasance, but for some reason, she isn't the least bit concerned about that right now.

"Yusuf Pepple, Helsinki Police." Yusuf flashes his own ID. "I'm the lead investigator of the homicide that took place across the hall from you."

"I see. Just a moment."

The woman shuts the door, and during the few seconds it takes her to remove the chain and reopen the door, Yusuf shoots Jessica a murderous look.

"Jessie, what are you—"

"Let me handle this."

The door opens, and the woman takes a couple of steps backward into the entryway.

"Rea Salo?" Jessica says.

"Yes," Salo replies, gesturing for Jessica and Yusuf to enter. "We have just a few questions."

Jessica shuts the door behind her. The candle scent has intensified, and Jessica sees fat table candles burning on the console in the small entryway. Few people know that stearin candles, as mood setting as they are, ought not to be burned in confined spaces; numerous studies have shown the detrimental effects of the microparticles they emit to be comparable to those of smoking.

"It's such a terrible thing." Salo leans against the wall, arms folded across her chest. "Eliel Zetterborg was such a nice man . . ."

As Jessica waits for Salo to finish her sentence, she studies the woman's manicured appearance. For a woman in her fifties, Rea Salo is a downright stunning apparition, with her plump lips and presumably enhanced breasts. In all likelihood, the blond tresses also conceal scars indicative of face tightening.

"Did you know Eliel Zetterborg well?"

Salo shakes her head firmly. "We chatted a couple of times when we ran into each other in the stairwell. . . . But for something so awful to have happened right next door . . . ," she continues, delicately raising her hand to her mouth.

Jessica abruptly understands this woman is not so much shocked by her neighbor's death, but by the fact that the deceased was her next-door neighbor. That's human nature for you: the closer things are, the more awful they seem.

"You told the police officers you were at home yesterday between six and seven p.m."

Salo nods, red nails still covering the full lips.

"And apparently you heard something?"

"A shout . . . ," Salo blurts, then nods nervously. "Would you care to come in . . . ?"

Jessica shakes her head and smiles. "Thanks. We just have a few quick questions. How long did the shout last?"

"It was a short, agonized . . . cry, very faint. . . . At first I didn't pay any attention to it. The television was on, and it didn't occur to me that it could have come from next door. . . . I had just started watching a movie."

"What time did you hear this shout?"

"I'm not sure. . . . Quarter past six, I guess?"

"You didn't happen to look out the peephole?"

Salo shakes her head. "No," she says under her breath. "Then sometime later I heard noises in the stairwell, and before long the doorbell rang and it was the police."

"I see."

Jessica glances at Yusuf, but her colleague doesn't appear to have any further questions.

She is just about to thank Salo for her answers when she catches motion by the kitchen, and she and Yusuf hear the soft creak of footsteps against the wooden floor.

"You have guests?" Jessica asks.

Suddenly Salo looks frightened. "It's . . . my son, Felix." She leans in to Jessica and Yusuf and lowers her voice to a near whisper. "He's not in the best shape. . . . He's autistic, and I don't want to shock him right now any more than necessary."

Jessica sighs. "We'd like to ask him a few questions."

"Why?"

"Where was your son yesterday?"

The woman looks accusingly at Jessica. "You're not suggesting—"

Yusuf folds his arms across his chest. "Could you please answer the question?"

"With me . . . here at home."

At that instant, the door at the far end of the entryway opens fully, and a thin thirty-year-old man steps through. His uncombed black hair, pale skin, and the enormous black circles under his eyes make him look like the drummer of a punk band. He is dressed in sweatpants and a black hoodie and looks exhausted.

"What's wrong, Mom?"

34

THE DARK CURTAIN of clouds grazes the roofs of the apartment buildings surrounding the little park. The morning sky looks so gloomy that it's doubtful even the sun, which is due to rise soon, will be able to cast any light over the city.

Jessica and Yusuf walk toward the car parked on Vuorimiehenkatu.

"It goes without saying that you need to look into the backgrounds of all the neighbors," Jessica says as she reaches for the door handle.

Yusuf shoots Jessica a pointed look from the other side of the Volkswagen. "Sure, in theory it could have been one of the neighbors, but it's just as likely the perpetrator left through the back door and emerged here on Vuorimiehenkatu." Yusuf points at the enormous gray palace standing nearby. "In which case the security cameras from the Russian embassy would have caught him, but we haven't been able to get our hands on the tapes yet."

"Got it."

Jessica is lowering herself into the passenger seat when she sees Yusuf has taken a few steps toward the Flatiron Building.

"Goddamn it, what the hell is he doing here . . . ?"

"Who?"

Yusuf shuts the car door and starts striding purposefully toward a big man in jogging gear who is wearing a backpack.

"Where are you . . ."

Jessica realizes it's a futile attempt and decides to follow Yusuf. Yusuf has stopped to talk to the man, and she joins them a few seconds later.

"This is my colleague Jessica Niemi," Yusuf says.

The big man extends his left hand to Jessica. He must have immediately spotted her temporary disability. "Joonas Lamberg," he says in a serious tone.

Jessica silently conducts a quick analysis of his appearance: strong, with a massive jaw and sad, somehow lost eyes. The handshake is firm but isn't trying to prove anything.

"I'm sorry about your boss," Jessica says.

Lamberg nods lightly. "I didn't sleep a wink last night. I don't understand how I missed . . ." His empty gaze travels between the street and the building.

"Don't beat yourself up. You couldn't have seen the other door from your car," Yusuf says. Then he lights up a cigarette. "Is there something we can help you with?"

This inquiry is a polite version of *Why the fuck are you snooping around the crime scene?*

Lamberg seems to search for the right way to express his thoughts. "I'm trying to get an idea of the route . . ." He sounds somehow guarded. "I don't know. Somehow I want to figure out . . . or at least help the police figure out what happened last night because I failed at the job I was paid to do."

"The best thing would be to go home and keep your phone on. I'm sure we're going to need more information from you," Yusuf says.

Lamberg takes a step back as if shying from the cigarette smoke. He lets out a trembling sigh, then nods reluctantly. "OK. But find the asshole who did this to Zeta."

"Lamberg is a former police officer. SWAT," Yusuf says as he and Jessica walk back to the car.

"I guessed," Jessica says, and genuinely means it.

Something about Lamberg's übermasculine demeanor has piqued her interest. She recognizes her weakness, her tendency to be drawn to gruff, roguish men on the late side of middle age. A psychologist once suggested the source's being an unresolved relationship with her father, presumably a consequence of her father's premature and tragic demise.

"What the fuck was he doing here?"

"Maybe exactly what he said." Jessica opens the car door. "I thought you said he wasn't a suspect."

"Lamberg's involvement is highly unlikely," Yusuf says, "but theoretically possible, at least until we see the time stamps on the videos from the embassy."

"Maybe he's trying to form an understanding of what happened. He was Zetterborg's bodyguard, after all. And a police officer doesn't change his spots just because he starts working in the private sector," Jessica says, then climbs into the car.

The doors slam shut, and Yusuf looks tenderly at Jessica. "You're the smartest person I know. But you have a weak spot for guys like that."

"Shut up, Yusuf," Jessica snaps, and the Volkswagen Golf's small but spirited engine rumbles to life.

35

JESSICA WAVES GOOD-BYE and watches Yusuf speed off down Museo-katu; the taillights disappear behind a garbage truck idling at the corner of Cygnaeuksenkatu. Jessica squeezes the thick folder under her arm and tries to slide her fingers into the coat pocket containing her house keys.

I need your brains, Jessica. Promise me you'll at least take a look at this material.

Yusuf didn't sound desperate, but it's clear he wouldn't ask for help unless he truly felt he needed it.

There's no denying the visit to Zetterborg's apartment has sparked Jessica's professional curiosity, but she has decided to stick to her guns. Besides, going back to work now might mean that Hellu—ironically enough—would assign her to take over the investigation. And if that happened, Yusuf might lose credit for the groundwork he has so superbly laid. Yes, Yusuf is the one who asked her to reconsider her decision, but it's possible he wouldn't be that pleased with the potential consequences of Jessica's unexpected return.

Jessica heads toward her building, then realizes the man exiting is holding the door for her. She takes a few quick steps.

"Thank you," she says, and the man in the camel hair coat releases the handle and continues around the corner.

Suddenly Jessica realizes she's shivering.

You filmed this, Jessica.

Chills run through her body.

Jessica thinks about the man writhing on the ground, skin and clothes licked by flames. *It wasn't real.*

She walks toward the elevator, then stops. It's been less than a month since she started using this entrance, and she has met almost none of her neighbors. She doesn't participate in building association meetings herself; she is represented by a lawyer / asset manager with power of attorney. Only a couple neighbors know what she looks like, and the man in the camel hair coat isn't one of them.

Even so, he must have recognized her, because he started holding the door before he knew she meant to enter the building. She didn't even have her keys in her hand yet. And now Jessica remembers the phone call from last night. She doesn't believe in coincidence: everything is always connected.

Jessica backs up a few steps, then turns around.

She pushes open the door to the street and dashes to the corner. There's no sign of the man in the camel hair coat. The street is lined with parked cars he might have climbed into. But not one of the cars starts up, let alone pulls out of a parking space.

The deepening freeze makes the tiny bones in Jessica's smashed hand throb.

You're imagining things, Jessica. Someone just held the door for you . . . that's all.

But Jessica knows she's not imagining things. She knows that this time her paranoia is justified.

They're back.

36

It's nine a.m. and the business just opened. Yusuf and Nina step into the brightly lit shop, which is like traveling through time to decades past. It puts Yusuf in mind of his childhood, despite the fact that in reality the place is more like a toy store from the 1960s. The shelves are bursting with products that have no connection to smart technology or electronics in general. Heaps of colored markers, paints, and craft supplies; model airplanes, ships, race cars, and tanks. Miniature fantasy figures waiting for a coat of paint, and monsters that remind Yusuf of the board game HeroQuest and the ones he used to hoard on the windowsill in his bedroom. And last of all, hundreds of boxes of model train cars, which also chug along the miniature train track snaking across a big table. Yusuf has never been into trains, but the masterful miniature world created on the table—with its lawns, train stations, and tiny human figurines—is downright begging for closer examination.

"Am I going to be able to drag you out of here?" Nina says as she looks around.

Yusuf grunts. The sweet smell of paper and glue wafts through the air.

"Good morning," a male voice says somewhere behind the tall shelves.

Yusuf and Nina are separated from the shop owner by a wall of model Formula One cars. A 1993 McLaren MP 4/8, its iconic red-and-white coloring a throwback to childhood, catches Yusuf's eye. He sees a bit of green-and-yellow helmet in the cab. *Ayrton Senna.*

"Hi," Yusuf says, not sure whom to address his words to, until a man with red cheeks emerges from between the shelves. He has a thick waxed mustache and round John Lennon glasses.

"Sami Mäntylä," he says, extending a hand.

Yusuf takes it and thinks the only thing the guy is missing is a conductor's cap; in all other respects he could pass for a railroad man from the 1890s.

"Yusuf Pepple," Yusuf says. "And this is Nina Ruska." They both show their IDs.

The business is empty with the exception of one hunchbacked customer, who, in looks and body language, could be Rasmus Susikoski's brother.

"I just called," Yusuf says. "Do you have a minute?"

"Absolutely," Mäntylä says with an emphatic nod. He is the picture of an officious conductor.

"Quite a shop you have here," Yusuf says, finding genuine admiration in his voice.

"Thank you! You've never been in before?"

"No, unfortunately not," Yusuf says. Nina shakes her head.

"Oh dear. This is certainly a special place and well established to boot. We've been here since 1994."

"And you have enough customers?"

"But of course," Mäntylä says, stretching the words as if any other possibility is utterly absurd. "Hobby Sammy's customers are extremely loyal. Although much leisure-time activity has moved online, people still want real things, something they can touch. Something concrete to pass the time without staring at that ghastly blue light from dawn to dusk." Mäntylä circles around behind the counter. "Models are escapism, a very healthy sort."

"Glad to hear it." Nina lowers her hands to the counter. A poster of a large rail yard has been spread beneath the glass surface.

"How can I help you? Nothing has been stolen from us," Mäntylä says, revealing a row of exceptionally large and slightly crooked teeth beneath the whiskers.

"We're not here about a theft," Yusuf says.

"What, then?"

"We understand it's possible to order puzzles based on personal photographs here?"

Mäntylä nods.

"Could you explain how the ordering process works in practice?"

"It's easy. Although this shop looks traditional and we sell time-less products, that doesn't mean we don't make use of the latest technology."

Mäntylä turns his computer screen so Yusuf and Nina can see. He clicks the mouse and opens some sort of software.

"The customer sends me the image they want on their puzzle and the desired size, like so," Mäntylä says, selecting an image from his computer.

It's a photo of him with a large dog. A moment later, a mesh of fine lines appears over the image. On closer inspection, Yusuf and Nina can see that the lines follow the familiar puzzle pattern of little knobs and notches. Sami Mäntylä has just created a model of a puzzle.

"Voilà. I send the file to the supplier, and generally the puzzle arrives in the mail within one to two weeks."

"How much does it cost?" Nina says.

"Almost nothing these days . . . They have a company in Estonia they can use to saw the puzzle in a couple of minutes. I generally ask for something between fifty and a hundred euros, depending on the size and difficulty."

"And the difficulty is the same as the number of pieces?"

"Exactly. Now, the image itself could be difficult to make out, but that doesn't impact the price, of course."

Yusuf and Nina exchange glances.

"May I ask why you're interested in customized puzzles specifically?" Mäntylä asks.

Nina ignores the question. "How often do you get orders for puzzles?"

The distinctive row of teeth flashes, then quickly disappears behind the lush mustache. "Not too often, because the Internet is full of such services. When it comes to this product, our prices are probably not the most competitive. I'm to some extent an unnecessary middleman in this matter, although of course I don't go advertising that to my customers."

"I'm assuming you keep a record of all the orders on your computer?"

Mäntylä nods, and his mustache seems to droop an inch lower as his expression grows more serious.

Yusuf pulls his phone from his coat pocket and shows Mäntylä an image on the screen. "Did someone order this puzzle from you?"

Mäntylä leans across the counter and zooms in with his fingertips. Then he strokes his mustache and nods. "Yes, about a month ago. I thought: what a fun way to celebrate a new life."

Yusuf has the impulse to glance at Nina but decides it would be giving away too much. "Who ordered it?"

"Wait just a moment." Mäntylä takes hold of the mouse again. This time he turns the computer screen toward himself, as if he suddenly wants a little more privacy.

"Faust," he eventually says.

Yusuf snorts involuntarily. "Faust?"

"Yes."

"No other name?"

"It just reads 'Faust' here. Sort of like Tintin. Not even a phone number. I remember him vaguely. Very vaguely . . ."

"Could you describe him?" Nina says. "Height, hair color . . ."

Mäntylä's mouth turns down in a frown. "Maybe forty. Maybe

older. A little stout, not particularly short or tall. Darn it, I don't know what else to say. Rather ordinary-looking, I suppose . . ."

Yusuf has pulled out a small notepad and writes down Mäntylä's impressions.

"I can't say about the hair," Mäntylä continues. "As I recall, he was wearing a beanie and a thick scarf. I remember that because it wasn't particularly cold outside; as a matter of fact, it was very warm for the time of year."

"What else was he wearing?"

"Nothing particularly memorable. Maybe a black coat . . . This is certainly difficult." Mäntylä laughs, once again revealing his long teeth. They're like those of a cartoon rabbit. But then he abruptly falls serious.

Yusuf pulls a photo of Niklas Fischer from his pocket. "Could it have been this man?"

Mäntylä purses his lips in a way that reveals nothing. "Who is that?" he finally says.

"Does he look familiar?" Yusuf asks.

"I don't think so."

Yusuf feels like asking Mäntylä if he's a hundred percent sure but decides to drop it. He knows from experience that the average person has a nonexistent ability to remember faces they've seen unless the encounter is in some way memorable.

"There was something curious about him," Mäntylä continues. "As I remember, he barely spoke, gave his order on a piece of paper that had that name on it. Faust."

"On a piece of paper?" Nina says, glancing at Yusuf.

Yusuf knows what his colleague is thinking: the previous night, Sanni Karppinen told them her attacker didn't say anything. They decided Karppinen was in shock and forgot everything she heard, but apparently the guy spared his voice while shopping for puzzles too. The man named Faust would appear to be the perpetually silent sort.

"Yes," Mäntylä says distractedly. "He had written on a piece of paper that he wanted a two-thousand-piece puzzle."

"You said he didn't say much. . . . Did he say anything at all, or was he totally mute?"

Mäntylä appears to ponder the matter and strokes his whiskers. "Hmm. Maybe he didn't talk at all. But he clearly understood Finnish, because I told him he could pick up his order in a week's time."

"Do you still have that piece of paper?" Yusuf asks.

Mäntylä has already started rummaging through his drawers. But he settles for a shrug. "I don't think so. . . . I'm pretty sure he put the slip of paper back in his pocket when he left."

Yusuf waits patiently as Mäntylä feverishly eyes the counter and the area beneath it. But there's no sign of the piece of paper.

"Let us know immediately if it turns up."

Mäntylä nods emphatically. Then he delves into his computer screen again and frowns. "He paid for it in cash."

Yusuf nods at the half sphere peering from the ceiling. "What about the camera?"

"It records in one-week loops. He came in on December fifteenth to order the puzzle and picked it up a week later. Unfortunately I don't have the recordings from that period anymore."

"And you haven't seen this Faust since?"

Mäntylä shakes his head.

"All right," Yusuf says, slipping his phone and notepad back into his pocket. "Thanks for your help. Please let us know if you happen to see him again. Here at the shop or anywhere else."

Mäntylä nods absently without taking his eyes off his computer screen. As Yusuf and Nina head to the door, he starts talking again. "Just a moment. There's one more thing. . . ."

The detectives stop and turn around. "What?"

"I don't know if this matters, but this Faust bought something else during that same visit."

Yusuf returns to the counter, hands in his pockets. "What?"

"An Edding 8280 marker . . . five euros and ninety cents."

Yusuf glances at Nina. Maybe it's the marker he used to write the message on the back of the puzzle.

"A black marker?" Nina asks.

"Black? No, no . . . the Edding 8280 is a UV marker."

Yusuf feels his stomach lurch. "A UV marker? Do you mean—"

"A marker whose ink is only visible in ultraviolet light."

37

TWO BLUE BUSES accelerate past them as if they are competing in a race taking place in the roadway. A taxi stopped in the middle of the intersection with its hazard lights on is rewarded with a symphony of honking horns. Nina and Yusuf walk briskly toward the Golf parked at the corner of Annankatu. Yusuf listens to the phone ring for a while, then hangs up: Rasmus isn't answering. He checks to make sure his phone isn't on silent mode, then slips it back into his pocket, where his fingers graze the pack of cigarettes. He takes it in hand, then realizes it's too late to light up. The Golf is across the street, and it's unlikely Nina wants to spend a minute longer than necessary shivering in the biting wind.

"It's contradictory," Nina says. "The guy must have understood that if he ordered the puzzle online we'd be able to track him pretty easily through the credit card information. And yet . . ."

Yusuf finishes the thought: "It feels like he wanted us to track the purchase to Hobby Sammy."

"Yup," Nina says. "The puzzle was ordered and picked up so early that I wonder if he knew the security camera recordings wouldn't be stored longer than a month. However that happens."

"Exactly. Especially when you take into account the fact the killing itself was probably intended to be carried out on RealEst's fiftieth anniversary."

"Whatever it is we find with the UV light, he wants us to find it. Otherwise he would have bought that fucking pen somewhere else. He knew we'd see the marker purchase on the same receipt," Nina continues as they reach the car. Across the street, two meter maids are bustling around a van; they're wearing such heavy coveralls, you'd think the temperature was much lower than it actually is. "Rasse's not picking up?"

"No." Yusuf opens the car door, climbs in, and turns on the ignition. Nas' iconic rap classic "One Mic" mingles with the noise carrying from the street.

Writing names on my hollow tips, plotting shit.
Mad violence who I'm gon' body, this hood politics.

"Let's assume Faust didn't utter a word to Mäntylä when he ordered the puzzle," Nina says as she pulls her door shut. "I wonder if there's something about the guy's voice that's easily identifiable."

"I was just thinking the same thing."

"Because why else would anyone pretend to be mute if they're revealing their face in the same context?"

"It could be a dialect, accent, lisp, or why not a serious stutter? Something Faust assumed Mäntylä would remember and tell the police about."

An approaching car stops behind them with its turn signal on. Yusuf pulls the Golf into traffic and watches in the rearview mirror as the car parallel parks in the space he just vacated. Despite a huge increase in parking fees, there are fewer and fewer parking spaces in Helsinki every year.

"You're probably right." Nina sighs. "Where to now?"

"The Flatiron Building," Yusuf says, raising his phone to his ear again. "I'm going to ask Tanja to come there with a UV light."

Nina glances at Yusuf, a barely perceptible smile dancing across her face.

Yusuf notices. "What?"

"Tech Team Tanja? The one you were slobbering all over at the Christmas party?"

"Don't you start too."

"You want me to wait in the car so you guys can get your ultraviolet kicks—"

"Shove it, Nina," Yusuf says, and when Tanja answers the phone a moment later, he realizes the smile has spread to him too.

38

JESSICA STANDS IN the middle of her enormous living room, looking around uncertainly. She has circled her entire two-story apartment twice, searching for signs of intrusion. The image of the blond man who held the door for her is etched into her retinas. But everything seems to be in place; there is no detail that rouses feelings of suspicion in her.

There was no one here. The alarm was on.

But they're capable of anything.

Jessica clenches her fists and realizes they're shaking. She walks slowly up the spiral stairs to the second floor and enters the spacious bathroom with its elegant micro-concrete surfaces.

Jessica turns on the tap and adjusts the temperature of the water until it suits her: so hot it would no doubt feel unpleasant to most bathers. She loves the sensation of scorching water on her skin, the way it makes the sweat drip from her face.

She carefully removes the sling, strips off the sweatpants and sweatshirt she's wearing. Then T-shirt, socks, underwear. In the end, she stands naked at the bathroom mirror. She looks at her firm, well-proportioned breasts, toned arms, and finely boned face, to which a certain angularity lends a classic beauty. She has inherited her appearance from her actor mother.

Mom.

I don't know what's happening, Mom.

Jessica stares at her unclothed reflection, then shuts her eyes.

She needs guidance.

She is not prepared to continue alone.

She has had waking dreams at night for as long as she can remember, and years have passed since, despite their gruesomeness, they stopped being nightmares and became part of her everyday life. But what happened last night: she had never experienced anything of the sort before. That was a nightmare.

Jessica remembers looking through the black holes in the skull, the spots where her mother's eyes were before her body decomposed in her subterranean tomb.

Twenty-seven years.

Was her mother abandoning her now after all these years?

Jessica holds her breath and opens her eyes.

Come get in the water, sweetheart.

The bathtub is full. The water is no longer running from the tap.

Come get in the water.

Jessica turns around and lowers her hand into the bath. The water is crimson now.

She feels cold bones around her wrist. The white hand draws her tenderly, beckons for her to dip into the opaque water.

I know something's going on.

But her mother doesn't reply.

Jessica gingerly steps into the tub and lets herself sink in up to her neck. Black hair floats at her feet; it looks like a skim of seaweed on the water's surface.

Bubbles rise from below.

The man who was burned to death in Central Park is bothering me. . . .

Her mother's horrific face appears, yet still she doesn't speak.

Jessica closes her eyes again and wishes her mother would say something. Anything.

And then Jessica feels something crumble beneath her, give way. She gropes around the bottom of the tub and touches something sharp with her fingertips. She looks down and sees the crimson bathwater is flecked with tiny shards of white bone.

They are her mother's bones.

Jessica feels like she's suffocating. She opens her eyes and gasps for breath.

The water is clear again, but a delicate cloud of blood floats against the porcelain surface.

And then Jessica sees a face beneath the water. But this time it isn't her mother's; it's that of someone much older. Jessica would recognize that face anytime, anyplace. It's the face of pure evil.

Jessica screams.

The image of Camilla Adlerkreutz slowly sinks back into the crimson water, and then all is silent.

39

THE LARGE LIVING room that served as the scene of the industry magnate's murder looks different in the daylight, somehow less stately and mysterious. Once again Yusuf remembers why everything bad in detective novels and horror movies happens at night. The endless darkness opening up beyond the windows and the tableau lit by yellow ceiling lights create a threatening aura in a completely different way than a room bathed in sunlight. Not that anything exactly bathes in sunlight in Finland in January. The midwinter darkness is downright incapacitating.

Something about the old-fashioned and outdated apartment and its hallways reminds Yusuf of Stanley Kubrick's *The Shining*, the scene where six-year-old Danny rides a tricycle down the hallways of the eerie Overlook Hotel.

Things are creepier in the dark—that's just the way it is. Yusuf glances at the doorway leading to the kitchen and imagines how terrified Zetterborg must have been when he saw his attacker emerge from the gloom. Assuming, of course, the murderer came from the kitchen and the victim managed to notice before . . . well, before he took a massive knife to the chest.

"What are we looking for?" Tanja asks, pulling three ultraviolet lamps from her duffel bag.

"Good question," Yusuf says, taking the lamp Tanja hands him. "Nina and I think that whatever it is we're looking for, the perpetrator wants us to find it."

Nina clicks on her light and walks cautiously toward the grand piano, near the spot where Eliel Zetterborg's lifeless body lay the night before.

"It's possible he bought the marker for some totally different reason. Or that he just didn't think it all the way through, that it was an amateurish mistake," Tanja says.

"I think it would be an amateurish mistake not to take a look at this card." Yusuf pops a nicotine lozenge in his mouth. "You mind turning off the light?" These words are addressed to Tanja, who is standing next to the switch with her bag over her shoulder.

She does as asked, the ceiling light goes out, and the room and its furniture lose their golden glow. Light penetrates between the open curtains; the sun bobbing at the horizon has emerged from a thick blanket of clouds.

"We combed the living room with a UV yesterday," Tanja says.

"Yeah, I remember," Yusuf mumbles, turning on his lamp.

As Tanja noted the previous night, the apartment is incredibly tidy. The lid of the piano has been recently dusted, but complete or partial fingerprints are visible here and there, and also splatters that could have come from a sneeze. All sorts of samples were taken yesterday, but as of yet the laboratory hasn't come up with anything.

"Do you guys remember that movie *Seven*?" Nina says.

Yusuf pauses to think. "What about it?"

"One of the victims had his hand cut off, and the psychopath played by Kevin Spacey used it as a brush at the next crime scene."

Tanja shakes her shoulders as if the thought makes her shudder. "I remember."

Nina continues: "Then they found the words 'Help me' on the wall; they had been written with the severed hand. Was it behind some painting in the movie?"

Yusuf glances at the women in turn, then lets his gaze wander across the living room's numerous paintings. He remembers all too well the story Sissi Sarvilinna told him about the boating accident in the Gulf of Finland the night before and severed hands being carted around Greater Helsinki.

"No one's hand was cut off this time," Yusuf says. "We're probably looking for something the killer needed the UV marker he bought from the craft store to write."

"Let's hope so," Tanja says. "But if yours and Nina's suspicions are accurate, it's probably not a bad idea to take a look behind the paintings."

"OK," Yusuf says.

He illuminates the surfaces of the paintings and their gilt frames without finding anything. Maybe it's like Tanja said: maybe the marker bought from Hobby Sammy wasn't used in this apartment. Maybe the murderer bought it to draw stars on his bedroom ceiling. *Damn lunatics.* It's at moments like this that Yusuf wishes he had chosen some other profession, even that goddamned floorball career, which would probably be over by now anyway, at least if he smoked as much as he does....

Nina rouses him from his thoughts: "Look, Yusuf."

Yusuf turns to his colleague, who has directed her gaze at the floor. And then Yusuf sees it too: there's a faint blue glow on the wooden floorboards.

"What the hell . . . ?" Yusuf mutters to himself, takes a few considered steps, and stands there at Nina's side.

He looks at the two short lines and one long one drawn on the floor, which form a universal symbol: it's a sharp-tipped arrow pointing at the library.

40

YUSUF, NINA, AND Tanja advance, spellbound, toward Eliel Zetterborg's library. At the far side of the living room, near the doorway, there's a second arrow pointing in the same direction as the first.

The trio stops at the threshold of the library, at the spot where Tanja and Yusuf saw the puzzle dumped on the glass table the night before. Now the glass surface is bare.

"That's weird," Nina says. "Were the arrows drawn on the floor so we would notice the puzzle? Did Faust think we wouldn't think to put it together otherwise?"

"That doesn't make any sense." Yusuf scans the ceiling with his lamp, but there are no signs of more arrows. "It's your basic chicken-and-egg conundrum. We wouldn't have found those arrows without that fucking puzzle."

"Unless he assumed the apartment would be thoroughly combed with a UV light yesterday?"

"Somehow that's hard to believe. The guy knew we would trace the puzzle to Hobby Sammy and find the clue about the marker that way. The arrows must be pointing at something else . . . something we wouldn't have thought of otherwise," Yusuf says.

"Goddamn it," Tanja says softly, and scratches her head.

Nina walks around the room, waving the lamp randomly across the walls and furniture. "Is there something we're supposed to understand about the bookcase?"

All three of them slide their lamps across the spines of the books. Nothing.

"How much time did the perpetrator have," Tanja asks, "to build this weird escape room?"

"If we assume the guy got here at ten to six and Eliel Zetterborg arrived twenty-five minutes later, that would have been plenty of time," Yusuf says.

"Why the hell would anyone want to go to so much trouble?" Tanja asks.

"There are all sorts of crazies out there," Nina says.

Yusuf nods. Nina is right: their investigations over the past year alone have shown a twisted mind can come up with the strangest and sickest crimes. And if desired, toy with not only the victim, but also the detectives doing the investigating.

Yusuf is just glancing at his watch when he catches something out of the corner of his eye. The UV light has struck on something else: it's a new arrow, and it's drawn on the floor of the hallway leading from the library to the bedroom.

"OK, now this is getting exciting," he says, gesturing for Nina and Tanja to follow.

They advance warily toward the bedroom as if there might be someone in the apartment who could ambush them at any moment. It shouldn't be possible; the doors were sealed by the technical investigators. A moment before, Yusuf went to confirm the seal on the back door was still in place. Even so, he moves his light to his left hand and lowers the fingers of his right hand instinctively to his holster flap.

The arrows were gradually drawn more densely, as if grouped to foreshadow an approaching climax.

The trio steps into the bedroom, Yusuf at the lead. The wide bed is made, and everything looks untouched, just like the night before.

"The arrows point there." Nina indicates the antique dresser next to the nightstand. A big X has been drawn in UV marker on the top drawer. "X marks the spot. This guy loves clichés."

"Did you guys go through the drawers yesterday?" Yusuf asks. The glowing blue X is giving him goose bumps. He thinks about the severed hands again.

Tanja shakes her head.

Yusuf hands his flashlight to Nina and pulls his glove tighter as if the better fit will shield the drawer handle more effectively. Or maybe his fingers, actually. Suddenly it feels as if they ought to open the drawer some other way. Maybe its booby-trapped—maybe it is Yusuf's fate to have a bear trap break his wrist or a kitchen knife fly out at his forehead from the force of a tensed spring. Maybe there's an explosive somewhere that will be triggered by the opening of the drawer and kill them all. A trip wire. *Fuck.*

"What are you waiting for?" Nina says behind him.

"Step back," Yusuf says.

Nina is on the verge of offering some retort, but then decides to take Yusuf's suggestion. The suspicion of invisible danger has now spread to Nina and Tanja too.

Yusuf clenches his fists and takes hold of the small iron handle. He tugs it. His heart skips a beat, but nothing happens. No explosion, no snapping bones. His head is still there.

"What's in it?" Tanja says.

Yusuf pulls out the drawer and lowers it to the floor. The photograph at the bottom of the drawer sends shivers up his spine.

"Well, I'll be damned," he says, bringing the photograph closer to his eyes.

The black-and-white Polaroid is of three people in hunting gear. Their shotguns are strapped to their chests and the barrels peer over their shoulders.

Nina steps up to Yusuf's side and looks at the photograph. "Is that Eliel Zetterborg?"

"Yes, a few decades younger," Yusuf says softly.

It's hard to determine the identity of the others as their faces have been scratched until they are unrecognizable. It looks as if a middle-aged Zetterborg was posing in the photograph with faceless ghosts. And if you think about it, Zetterborg is a ghost now too.

41

1990

HJALMAR EK RAISES the breech of the shotgun toward the windows and peers into the chamber. White sky is visible at the muzzle end of the twin barrels welded together. The inner surface gleams beautifully; he has cleaned the barrels and wiped down the trigger mechanism that his father oiled for him the night before. Hjalmar closes the shotgun and carefully lowers it to the wooden table, next to the box of shells. The scents of fresh coffee and spruce logs crackling in the stove waft through the contemporary pine-log cabin.

Through the window, Hjalmar meets the stern gaze of his father, who is sitting outside at the fire. He instinctively turns away. *Here I am, stuck in the woods in the middle of nowhere.* At least the lodgings are tolerable: despite its ascetic furnishings, the one-story, two-bedroom cabin is perfectly comfortable. The walls are decorated with taxidermy: antlered heads and small mammals. Running water comes from the taps and electricity from the outlets. What more could a city kid who hates hunting hope for?

"Nice Parallelo," Axel says as he steps inside and pats Hjalmar on the shoulder.

Although the door is open no more than a few seconds, the biting freeze manages to slip in. Hjalmar feels its cold nip at his bare neck.

"Yeah." Hjalmar looks out the window again. The others are sitting at the fire out front.

Axel swings his own shotgun down from his back. It looks more modern than Hjalmar's.

Hjalmar takes a quick gulp of coffee. He doesn't know anything about firearms and has no interest in learning. The shotgun actually belongs to Hjalmar's father, Gunnar; Hjalmar just has a parallel permit for it. His father showed him the maintenance checks he just performed at home the night before. That's the sum total of his competence and knowledge.

Axel swings the shotgun onto his back again and trains his piercing gaze on Hjalmar. Maybe he's eyeing Hjalmar's shotgun, maybe Hjalmar himself; Hjalmar can't tell. In any event, the staring feels awkward, makes Hjalmar uneasy.

Nineteen-year-old Axel Zetterborg is two years older than Hjalmar and a much more seasoned hunter. Not that much would be required to make the claim: for Hjalmar, this weekend-long hare hunt is his first time hunting. In comparison, Axel has been running through the underbrush since he was a boy and, at least according to him, has brought down five moose, half a dozen deer, some wild boar, and even a bear once, in addition to countless hares. *Not to mention girls.* Axel, who speaks with an irritating self-confidence despite his high voice, is the son of Dad's boss, Eliel Zetterborg. Whereas the senior Zetterborg seems placid and even unassuming, his son, Axel, is a bigmouth and oppressively intense.

"You know what?" Axel says with a smarmy smile. "The hare hunt is sort of like the Super Bowl of hunting. . . . The sport itself isn't the most important event."

"It's not?" Hjalmar frowns, intrigued. "What is, then?"

"This is." Axel unzips one of the pockets of his green coat to reveal a bottle of Jägermeister. "The most important thing is putting on a good show! No one's going to bag any hares here. Oh, we always walk away with one or two, but that's just a bonus. A side dish."

A white-toothed grin spreads across Axel's face; his eyes retreat into thin furrows, and the laugh lines make his face beautiful and approachable. Hjalmar never smiles with his mouth open, because his slightly crooked buckteeth make him look like a cartoon character. To top it off, whereas Axel's jaw is square and manly, Hjalmar's face has a soft cast to it.

Hjalmar looks down at the tips of his boots, but Axel keeps staring at him. Axel seems to be observing him from a height, both figuratively and literally. And that's as it should be. As Hjalmar's father never fails to mention, Axel is the crown prince of Finnish industry. Hjalmar has heard it said on more than one occasion that Axel resembles the man who will one day rule Great Britain, Prince Charles, to an almost comical degree. Apparently there is more than one inspiration for Axel's nickname.

"We're going to go hard today. Hopefully your girl will be able to keep up." Axel nudges Hjalmar lightly in the chest. "Or what?"

"Yeah. For real," Hjalmar mumbles. He tries to flash a laddish smirk and apparently fails utterly.

"Right on," Axel says, pulls on a red beanie, and disappears through the door.

Hjalmar gazes out the window. A seemingly endless snowy spruce forest stretches beyond the dirt road. The fire where the others sit is burning inside the rim of a rusted tractor wheel bolted to a concrete pedestal. Hjalmar watches Axel join the men there. They're sitting on wooden benches covered with gray reindeer hides, roasting sausages. The semicircle is composed of the king of Finnish industry, Eliel Zetterborg; the company's attorney, Erik Raulo, and his son, Hans; and Hjalmar's father, Gunnar Ek, who is the longtime second-in-command at EZEM Pipes. A few yards away, a Finnish hound barks at the end of a lead tied around a tree. The dog is on loan from a neighboring farm and is named Simo, apparently after some famous sniper from the Winter War. That's the hunting party for the weekend. Six men, a hound named Simo—and of course Laura.

Laura. The most beautiful girl in the world and too good for Hjalmar by any measure, but whom Hjalmar has somehow managed to make his girlfriend. He and Laura attend the same high school, and she is two grades ahead of him. They've been dating since the beginning of the term, a little over a month.

Hjalmar hears the toilet flush and the tap run. A moment later, he feels Laura snuggle under his arm and catches a whiff of fresh deodorant. Fragrances are a violation of his father's instructions, because they frighten animals off. But Hjalmar would never in a million years say anything about that to Laura, and it's unlikely anyone else will either.

Laura presses her ear to Hjalmar's shoulder. "The water from the tap is ice-cold."

"Then the shower water will be too."

Laura laughs. "Shit."

"I know, right?" Hjalmar sees Laura is shaking something in her hand—a small rectangular piece of paper. "What's that?"

"You," Laura says, laughing again.

The Polaroid hasn't finished developing yet, but it's possible to make out a dark figure standing against a bright background.

"Did you take a candid picture of me?"

"Couldn't help it. You looked so mysterious standing there at the window."

Hjalmar forces a smile; Laura must have noticed something is off.

"What's wrong?" Laura says.

"Nothing."

"Come on, tell me."

Hjalmar glances out the window. The men sitting at the fire laugh at something. Someone just told a good story. He should be out there sitting with the others, but he has no interest in joining them.

"Maybe it would have been better if you'd stayed in Helsinki," he says, and plants a smooch on Laura's temple. Warmth spreads through his body, and blood rushes to his groin. Out at the fire, Axel flashes his broad smile again.

This is all going wrong.

42

HJALMAR PULLS HIS beanie down to further cover his ears. In Helsinki that morning, it was a few degrees below freezing and there was just a thin layer of snow. But here in central Finland, the snow in the woods is thigh deep and the temperature a good 10 degrees lower. Dad said snow is an important factor when you're hunting hare, because otherwise the animals are hard to track. And like his famous namesake, Simo the hound is in his element in snowy terrain.

"All right, is everybody here? Let's have a little briefing," Eliel Zetterborg says with a paternal smile.

Hjalmar has met his father's boss a few times before, and even though he always seems cheerful and mild off the clock, Hjalmar knows he's a demanding leader. Dad has spent very little time at home over the past few years, and Zetterborg calls the house even on Sundays, especially now that the ballyhooed merger of the century is approaching.

"To begin, I'd like to welcome Gunnar's son, Hjalmar, who is joining us for the first time, and above all this brave young woman." Zetterborg stands and takes a deep bow. "With her presence, she breaks decades of idiotic patriarchal tradition and brings much-appreciated female beauty to our hunting party."

Thudding smacks fill the air as gloved hands burst out in spontaneous applause. Hjalmar is embarrassed: not for himself, but for Laura's sake. The idea of Laura joining him on the hunting trip was originally meant as a joke, but after the game Laura announced she would accept the invitation (she actually called it a challenge), and Gunnar Ek couldn't back out.

If only Dad had said something, come up with some pretense for rescinding Laura's invitation at the last minute.

Besides, if what Axel said is true—if this is going to turn out to be more of a drinking trip than a bona fide hare hunt—bringing Laura along was a cardinal mistake.

"Thank you. And I apologize," Laura says with a soft laugh. "Thank you for having me. And I apologize for breaking decades of patriarchal tradition."

Eliel wags a finger at her. "It was a stupid tradition." Then he smiles tenderly and says: "No, in all seriousness, Laura, this is one hell of a refreshing change. You and Hjalle have your own room, and of course you two are welcome to retire whenever you get bored of the moldy campfire stories we old men—and younger men too, I suppose—like to tell."

Laura breaks out in her radiant smile. Hjalmar glances around and can't help but notice the men's lingering, penetrating glances, which they attempt to soften through forced smiles. With her blond hair and high cheekbones, Laura is incredibly beautiful; even beneath her loose winter wear, it's possible to make out her generous bust and firm butt.

Erik Raulo turns to the spitting fire and cracks a beer. By Hjalmar's count it's at least his third. Erik's son, Hans, who attends the same high school as Hjalmar and Laura, has hinted that his father has started drinking more and more of late. That the merger that's supposed to take place this spring has put enormous excess strain on him as well as on the entire upper management.

"I doubt I'll get tired of your stories," Laura says, seating herself on the hide-covered bench between Axel and Erik. "But if I'm one of the guys now, I could take one of the guys' drinks."

Erik Raulo hesitates.

Simo lets out a few shrill yelps, his eyes trained on the forest, where the hares await their reapers.

"It's fine. I'm already nineteen," Laura says with a laugh.

Erik reaches into the blue crate nestled in the snowbank, retrieves a beer, and opens it. He flashes a white smile that is both fatherly and somehow lewd.

"That's not what I meant. We've never carded the boys here either," Erik says, handing her the beer. They clink bottles. *Skål.*

"Thanks." Laura takes a long swig of beer. From the way she gestures, talks, and tosses back the beer, it's clear this isn't her first time.

Eliel Zetterborg smiles approvingly and lowers his gaze to the laminated map of the terrain.

"Super Bowl," Axel whispers.

Hjalmar doesn't hear what Axel says, but sees Axel has turned toward him. "What?"

"The show has begun," Axel says with a broad smile. "The Super Bowl."

Hjalmar feels a lump in his chest swell. Panic is welling up inside him. Not because he's afraid Laura won't be able to handle herself, but because their relationship is totally unbalanced in every way. Laura is far too beautiful and fun to be his girlfriend. Laura gets men—both young and old—to look at her in a certain way, and Hjalmar is sure she relishes it with every fiber of her being. That's how she is, an extremely open-minded free spirit who oozes a liberated sexuality and is open to the world and new encounters. According to Laura, she has had sex with five people before Hjalmar, but even so she has given Hjalmar plenty of time to prepare for their first time. Now and again Hjalmar shudders at the thought of so many boys having made love to his girlfriend, especially since he hasn't been able to yet. He wants Laura, yes, or at least he believes he does. But the desire doesn't appear when it should; he doesn't get the same sort of erection when he's looking at Laura's naked body as he does when he's satisfying himself in his own room on Puistokatu.

The situation has become untenable and agonizing. He's in a race against time, because if they don't do it before long, Laura is surely going to leave him or at least find herself a guy who can get it up. Then he'll be the same loser that he was throughout his adolescence again, and on top of that, he will have a new cross to bear: it won't be long before everyone knows about his inability to perform sexually.

A deep booming sound starts Hjalmar out of his reverie. Erik Raulo is blowing a curved hunting horn, with his cheeks puffed out. The others laugh. Eliel Zetterborg announces the hunt has begun.

Showtime.

43

IT'S FIVE TO noon, the brightest moment of the day. Hjalmar is sitting at the fire, smacking his ski gloves together. The frozen air makes his cheeks sting. Because there's only one hound, the group has decided to form two parties and take turns trying their luck in the woods. The first party is formed by the young men: Hjalmar, Hans, and Axel. But after an hour and a half of brisk stalking, they haven't caught so much as a glimpse of a hare.

When the three of them make it back to the fire, it's time for the grown men—Eliel, Erik, and Gunnar—to head into the forest, and they bring along Laura, whom Erik Raulo has jokingly named their unarmed military observer.

"Just like a pro," Axel says, glances discreetly around, and pulls a pack of cigarettes from his pocket. Hjalmar turns down Axel's offer, but Hans plucks one from the pack.

"You mean Laura?" Hjalmar asks as the match crackles in the fresh, frigid air.

Axel nods and sucks on the cigarette until the tip turns red.

"Pops doesn't like that I smoke," Axel says, changing the subject. He shakes out the match and tosses it in the fire. "He thinks smoking is a sign of weakness. Or any addiction, for the matter. He thinks you should be stronger."

"Are you hooked on these?" Hans says.

"Fuck no," Axel says confidently.

Hjalmar doesn't reply but can't help thinking Axel's remark about addiction was a nasty jab at Hans, whose father's alcohol problem appears to be a public secret among the management team. But Hans just shrugs and takes an uncertain drag of his cigarette.

The fire spits in crisp snaps. Hjalmar remembers his biology teacher saying spruce spits when it burns more than other types of wood because it releases its sap only at high temperatures, and then the sap pops. Or something like that.

"Well?" Axel abruptly asks Hjalmar as if expecting an answer to a question that hasn't been asked yet.

"What?"

"How is it?"

"How's what?"

Hjalmar knows perfectly well what Axel is getting at but hopes from the depths of his heart the subject will wither and die over the ensuing seconds.

"You guys have screwed, haven't you?"

"Of course," Hjalmar replies, and at some level, he doesn't even feel like he's lying—feels as if it has happened simply because the opportunity has been there. Which is how things are: Laura has expressed her desire to have sex with him. He could have Laura if he wanted to. If he were able to.

"So tell us about it," Axel says, white teeth flashing behind the smoking cigarette.

"I can't do that."

"Aha, a gentleman. I understand," Axel continues, and for a moment it seems as if Hjalmar's silence is reason enough to change the topic.

But then Hjalmar looks at Hans, who is staring at the fire. Hans has a barely perceptible smirk on his face. His mouth is neutral, but his eyes look like they're laughing.

Fuck. He knows. They all know.

"I was just wondering: you have a chick like that who everyone wishes they could have," Axel says. "Does that stress you out? Put pressure on you to perform?"

"No. Why would it?" Hjalmar says, unsure if his face flushed bright red or just the opposite, went as white as a sheet. Either way, his body is in fight-or-flight mode, and his heart is pounding under his layers of clothing.

"It can happen, you know, especially with hot chicks," Axel continues.

Hjalmar gives an unenthusiastic laugh. *How the hell do they know? Might Laura have said something to someone? Of course! Of course girls talk about these things with their friends. And then their friends tell their friends until it eventually reaches everyone's ears. Everyone's ears except his, that is. Now that he thinks about it, maybe it's happening at this very moment. The* circle *that began a month ago under the covers in Laura's bedroom is coming to a close at this fire in the worst possible way.*

"Speaking of stress," says Hans, who is sitting at the end of the bench. He flings his half-smoked cigarette to the embers smoldering beneath the flames, then burps into his fist and continues: "I think all of our dads are pretty much at the ends of their ropes."

Hjalmar doesn't know why Hans rescues him, but he gladly accepts the chance to change the topic of conversation. "Yup," he replies quickly as Axel shoots a doubtful look at Hans. "My dad's at work all the time."

"Big dreams don't come true on their own," Axel says mysteriously after a moment of silence. Loud caws carry from the tops of the nearby spruces. "That's what Dad always says. And he's totally right."

"Do you want to work for your dad's company someday?" Hans asks, although he must know the answer is self-evident.

"I already do," Axel says boastfully. He packs cigarette smoke into his cheek, then lets it ooze slowly from his nostrils. The icy air gives the smoke a thick, curiously liquid appearance. "After the merger goes through this spring, EZEM Pipes is going to be the biggest company in the field in Europe. I want to see it become the biggest in the world someday. And I'm going to see it. I'm going to make it happen."

Axel's words reverberate with inexplicable force; he speaks with determination and defiance. Hjalmar and Hans merely nod in silence. Axel appears to know what he's talking about, even though he's just studying for his springtime matriculation exams and hasn't worked a day in his life. But he's clearly already begun preparing for the future so he can take over the helm from his father someday.

Hjalmar doesn't know much about how the business world works, despite the fact that dinners at home would serve as an advanced course—on those occasional evenings when Dad makes it home early enough to eat, that is. Their dinner-table conversations are always about Dad's work: EZEM Pipes and the long-planned merger with some big West German component company. How they will swallow each other up in the near future and form a massive cluster called Realest or something. Sometimes Mom says she can't take it anymore: she's lonely, and the kids suffer from Gunnar's absence. Dad and Mom never argue, which makes the mood that much more oppressive. Getting their feelings out through a shouting match might do them good, pop the suppressed silence. But Mom and Dad always speak calmly. Always about Dad's work. They speak as if Hjalmar and his little sister aren't even there. No one asks Hjalmar what he makes of it all. Or what sorts of crises he's wrestling with himself.

"My pops relies on your dads. That's why they work so damn hard," Axel says. Now there's more warmth in his voice; it's as if he's talking to younger brothers who have paused to reflect upon the challenges of growing up.

Suddenly Hjalmar has the urge to tell them everything, tell them he might never be able to have sex with Laura—or any other girl, for that matter. That he wants to, but he might simply be incapable. He feels like spewing out all the things that keep him up at night. But

Hjalmar knows he never can. The secret will remain trapped inside him now and forever. It's possible, of course, that if he really concentrates on destroying the strange thoughts eating at him from the inside, his anxiety will fade. Maybe this is all something he has heard called a "phase" on television; apparently there's room for several during a young person's life. Maybe he can still be like everyone else someday. Maybe everything will work out.

"But to go back to what we were talking about before . . . ," Axel says, flicking his stub of a cigarette butt into the flames and turning back to Hjalmar.

Hjalmar clenches his beer bottle in his heavy glove. *Goddamn it, nothing is going to save me now.*

"I'm not—"

And then they hear it: the shot that rings out from the trees and echoes in the perfect stillness.

44

2020

AXEL ZETTERBORG'S LIVING room is jam-packed with hunting mementos. An enormous bearskin lies beneath the coffee table. Of the half dozen heads hung on the walls, Yusuf can identify a moose, a wild boar, and a white-tailed deer. The other, horned beasts look more exotic and must have been stalked in some remote corner of the world. Yusuf feels his stomach grumble. It's getting on to three o'clock, and he hasn't even had breakfast yet, let alone lunch. Seeing the taxidermic animals stimulates his hunger. Nina probably went to grab lunch at that new taco place, he reflects. He dropped her off at HQ a moment before.

"Well, that's weird," Axel says. He stares intently at the image on the tablet, then zooms in.

"Do you have even the slightest idea who the other two individuals in the photo might be?" Yusuf asks, taking a seat in the black leather armchair across from Axel. Despite its stark appearance, the chair is surprisingly comfortable—and presumably expensive as hell.

Yusuf looks around as Axel ponders his reply. The living room windows of the house in northwestern Kulosaari give onto the bay and Verkkosaari, which in the space of a few years has transformed from more or less undeveloped harbor into an urban neighborhood studded with three-hundred-foot high-rises.

Axel studies the photograph as if he is genuinely trying to recall anything of relevance. The corporate leader, who will be celebrating his fiftieth birthday soon, is in trim shape; his thick black hair is only slightly graying at the temples. He is tall but a little hunched: his neck thrusts forward even when he is seated.

Axel looks up from the tablet and shakes his head. "Dad hunted his whole life."

"Who with?"

Axel flashes his carefully practiced courtier's smile, which is presumably intended to telegraph that Yusuf has just said something amusing. "With everyone," he says, then quickly wipes the smile from his face. "The group changed over the years, but for Dad hunting was both an outlet and a stage where big business decisions were made. He hunted wild boar year-round. In the winter, it was birds and hare; in the autumn, deer and moose." He indicates the surrounding creatures with his eyes. "I went with him ever since I was a boy."

Yusuf silently drums his fingers on the arms of his chair. He is more than familiar with the hunting seasons for various types of game. He was born and raised in Söderkulla, and game was the only meat served at home. He twice cracked a canine biting into shotgun pellets that went unnoticed in hare meat. By summer, the moose stew always had a tinge of freezer burn. Yes, all of this is plenty familiar to him.

"Where did the hunts take place?" Yusuf asks.

"Usually at Ouninpohja, where we had some land. A good couple hundred kilometers from Helsinki toward Jyväskylä."

"Is that where the photograph was taken?"

Axel laughs joylessly. "It's impossible to say. All there is in the background is forest."

Yusuf nods a few times. He has stared at the photograph enough to know Axel is telling the truth. "Are you able to say how old your father is in that photograph? Fifty?"

"At most." Axel lowers his eyes back to the picture. "Maybe younger."

"Was it common to take Polaroids during the hunt?"

Axel shakes his head. "I don't think so. I don't remember ever seeing anything like this."

"But it's possible you were along on this trip?"

"Sure. I was almost always along." Axel traps his lower lip between his teeth. He does it constantly, perhaps to give the impression of thoughtfulness.

"So, lots of hunting trips were made to Ouninpohja every year, and the group changed frequently?" Yusuf says, hoping to prod Axel's memory.

"Yes." Axel hands the tablet to Yusuf as if he has stared at the picture long enough.

Yusuf looks at the image for a moment, then locks the screen and sees his reflection in its black surface. "You said major business decisions were made during these trips. So the top guys from RealEst participated?"

Alex nods. "Not always, but pretty often."

"Do you remember any names?"

"Listen. I don't want to be rude or seem uncooperative," Axel says, raising a hand. "Just the opposite, of course . . . If anyone wants to find the person who did this to Dad, it's me."

"But . . . ?"

"But over the course of my adolescence and adulthood, there have been dozens of leaders at RealEst, hundreds if you count middle management. And Dad would invite just about any of his employees as long as he saw them as worthy of the invitation. The hunts were a reward of sorts for a job well done, and an invitation was something a lot of people thought was worth angling for. So I can assure you the list of people who hunted with Dad is really long, and putting it together is no easy task."

"I understand."

Yusuf looks Axel in the eye. He doesn't necessarily disagree, but he's finding Axel's arrogant tone irritating. Besides, he doesn't care if the task is easy or hard; he wants to find out who murdered Eliel Zetterborg.

"Would your father have agreed to pose with someone farther down the ladder?" he then asks, gazing out the window again. The seaside property's substantial lawn looks gray.

"Sure. RealEst was never a particularly hierarchical or—how should I put it?—class-conscious company, like comparable Japanese companies or the German outfit we bought at the time. I've even seen pictures of Dad posing with factory workers."

"*Even* with factory workers?"

"I'm sure you know what I mean," Axel says, dismissing Yusuf's remark, and reaches over to the table for his coffee cup.

Yusuf shifts his gaze from the windows to the room. The house appears to be a few decades old and has been remodeled into a neat, comfortable home. The seaside windows aren't oversized, which gives the place a cozy feel, even though the total square footage of two stories is probably three or four thousand. The fact that Jessica could afford a house like this seems absurd.

"Oh, Dad knew how to be arrogant too. He called Joonas Lamberg his personal guard dog, for one. Not to his face, of course, but still. *My dog this, my dog that.*"

"Dogs are what we police officers are. Both former and present," Yusuf says drily.

Axel appears to regret his words. "Well, I never joined in that sort of talk," he says, folding his hands in his lap.

"I'm sure you understand why I'm asking these questions," Yusuf says. "It's important for us to find the two people who are in the photograph with your father."

Axel looks like he's rolling his tongue against the inside of his cheek. Then he gulps, and his face grows serious. "You have to find them because you're afraid something happened to them?"

"Has happened. Will happen. Or else this involves something only these two know about." Yusuf stands. "That's why I'm asking you to write down the names of all the people you remember seeing on the hunts over the years. And email the list to me. *As ASAP as possible.*"

Axel laughs. "For the whole forty years?"

"Whatever you think is best. But the focus is on the period when the photograph was presumably taken. Twenty or thirty years ago."

"Fine. I'll do what I can," Axel says. Suddenly he looks thoughtful.

"What is it?"

"Can I see that picture again?"

Yusuf turns on the screen and hands the tablet back to Axel.

"That watch," Axel says, pointing at the gold timepiece on his father's wrist.

"What about it?"

"It's a Vacheron Constantin Genève. Probably Dad's most prized possession. He wore it only on special occasions." Axel hands the tablet back to Yusuf. "It was locked in the safe at all other times."

Yusuf glances at the photo, then discreetly slips the tablet under his arm. The watch in question was removed from the dead man's wrist the night before, and it's waiting for the investigators in the evidence room at HQ, sealed in a transparent bag.

RealEst's fiftieth anniversary would no doubt have been considered a special occasion, but might the detail have some other significance too?

"Speaking of the safe," Yusuf says, "do you know the code?"

Axel erupts in glum laughter. "As I said before, absolutely not. It's an integrated super safe made by EZEM Pipes back in the day when the company still manufactured safes. The Fort Knox of Ullanlinna. That baby is so tough, you can't even blow her apart with dynamite."

Yusuf smiles, although what he's hearing isn't funny in the least.

"Are the rumors true?" Axel taps the carved lion head adorning his chair's arm. "Is Niklas Fischer suspected of murdering my father?"

Yusuf slips his hands in his pockets and studies the man with whom he seems to have nothing in common. Axel Zetterborg is a perfectly presentable, cultured man, but the delusion of his own superiority and an unpleasant emotional poverty simmer beneath the superficial friendliness. Damned spoiled narcissist.

"Send me that list as soon as you can," Yusuf says, and Axel raises his hand in a lazy salute.

45

NINA HEARS A clacking approach down the corridor, the consequence of Superintendent Helena Lappi's atypical choice of footwear. The low heels Hellu has on today boost the professional impression made by her formfitting pantsuit. She's dressed up for good cause; after a brief hiatus, she's spent a lot of time in the glare of the flashes again.

"Ruska," Hellu says, stopping at Nina's cubicle, "could I see you for a moment?" She nods toward her office.

Nina rises slowly from her chair and follows Hellu in the direction indicated.

Heads behind cubicle dividers turn as gazes follow the ominously advancing two-person parade.

"Close the door," Hellu says, and seats herself at her desk.

Nina obeys, and her eyes fix on a bobblehead Sauli Niinistö, president of Finland, its oversized head bobbing at the edge of the glass table. It's a new design element for Hellu, who usually respects authorities and appreciates a gray aesthetic.

"So, we got nothing from that second whisky glass?" Hellu says.

Nina shakes her head. "Just Eliel Zetterborg's own fingerprints."

Hellu shrugs. "Well, anything else would have been quite the lottery win."

During the moment of silence that follows, Nina starts wondering if Hellu didn't have anything more important to discuss. But then the superintendent opens a desk drawer.

"You asked me to dig up information on that child abduction," Hellu says, and passes a stapled stack of papers across the desk. Then she folds her hands and continues: "In December 2009, a man named Kenneth Guranov abducted a girl on her way to school and demanded a ransom of one hundred thousand euros from her parents. A small-time criminal known on the streets as Kangaroo."

"A fitting nickname," Nina says, sitting down across from Hellu.

"Tell me about it. In any case, the kidnapping was poorly planned and the police tracked down the suspect in no time. The decision was made, however, to pay the ransom first so the child could be brought to safety before the arrest. And then go in hard."

"But Kangaroo was killed during the SWAT strike?"

Hellu nods. "In the woodshed of a derelict house in Tattarisuo. In the report, Joonas Lamberg says he opened the door and saw a man sitting on a sofa, pointing a pistol at him. One lethal shot to the torso. An internal audit found that Lamberg did not act contrary to guidelines but fired in self-defense. Sometimes such use of force is justified, especially in SWAT assignments." After finishing, Hellu takes off her readers.

"OK."

"One thing worth noting here is that the girl's father was a member of the RealEst management team at the time." Hellu trains her gaze reflectively out the window.

"Really?" Nina says in surprise. "That's a strange coincidence—"

"Which isn't really a coincidence at all. I talked to an old friend at Security and Intelligence Services, and he told me it was the events at Tattarisuo that led to Lamberg becoming Eliel Zetterborg's personal driver and bodyguard. Apparently Zetterborg wanted a man protecting him who wouldn't hesitate to use force. And of course Lamberg had a material impact on the kidnapper of a daughter of a RealEst employee getting what he deserved."

"Sounds kind of . . . gangster. Sort of like Luca Brasi in *The Godfather*—"

"Either that, or this is exactly what it looks like. You can still talk to

Lamberg again, but the timing of the call to emergency services and the recording of that call support his account. I've also requested the CCTV tapes from the Russian embassy at Yusuf's request. I believe we'll have them in a couple of hours. If the footage shows Lamberg sitting in his car at the point when Zetterborg makes the call to emergency—"

Nina finishes the thought: "Lamberg can't have done it."

And the superintendent nods.

46

YUSUF COLLAPSES INTO the seat of the Golf and shuts the door. Fatigue is throbbing at his temples, but he can't quit now. Something inside him assures him that with each hour that passes they are closer to solving the case. On the other hand, the more time that passes since the commission of the crime, the harder it is to solve.

Yusuf has also been overwhelmed by the concern that the progress of the investigation is being decided not by Yusuf Pepple but by Eliel Zetterborg's murderer, who is somewhere out there, going by the name of Faust.

A puzzle left for the police to find, a UV marker, and a scratched photograph. Apparently this is some sort of cat-and-mouse game where the perp dribbles crumbs of information for the police and observes from his hiding spot as they scamper around gathering them up.

Damn it. Maybe they ought to be focusing their resources on everything except where the murderer wants them to look. It's unlikely the purpose of all these gimmicks is to lead the police to the guilty party; presumably it's to shuffle the pack.

But right now they don't have any other clues. Yusuf feels stupid. Lonely.

Anna.

Yusuf pulls his phone from his pocket and selects the number he learned by heart so long ago. He hears it ring a few times, and eventually Anna's voice comes on the line. It feels both foreign and more familiar than anything else in the world.

"Hi." Yusuf realizes his pulse has just accelerated. He turns the ignition and the engine starts up.

THE LAST GRUDGE 197

"Hey. Thanks for calling."

"I tried earlier. . . . I've been pretty slammed, and I just got a moment to try again."

"No worries," Anna says, and falls silent.

She doesn't ask anything about Yusuf's work. Maybe such questions belong in the past, but Yusuf would love to hear she's still interested in his everyday life. In him.

"You texted me last night, but apparently it's not anything urgent?"

An expectant silence.

"Anna?"

"Do you have time to meet?"

Yusuf doesn't know what to say. He feels like asking why she wants to meet all of a sudden after avoiding him for months. But the question feels somehow intrusive, impolite.

And because Anna knows Yusuf better than anyone else, she says: "You're wondering why."

"Yeah. It'd be nice but . . . I'm really slammed right now."

"OK. We don't have to."

Yusuf feels a lump in his throat. *Don't be a stranger.*

"But, so, was there something you—"

"Yes," Anna says without hesitating. Her voice sounds distant. "I wanted you to hear it from me, not Instagram or somewhere. . . ."

Yusuf rubs his Adam's apple to massage out the feeling of constriction.

"You have a new boyfriend," Yusuf says quickly, trying to seem nonchalant. "I kind of figured, since we haven't been in contact for a while."

Anna doesn't say anything.

This news is something Yusuf has already had time to work through in his head. As a matter of fact, it's an event that has been inevitable this whole time: of course Anna is moving on with her life, even though Yusuf is a little surprised she jumped into a serious relationship just a few months after their long-term relationship ended. It must be serious, since Anna wanted to discuss it on the phone with him.

"I'm happy for you," Yusuf says, and realizes he means it.

But something strange infects the silence that follows, like an unspoken apology that floats into the air, accompanied by a faint sigh from Anna.

"Yes, but there's something else too," she says.

Yusuf feels a pang in his heart. His free hand clenches the gear stick. His foot presses the brake pedal to the floor.

"Of course," Yusuf says, because there's no longer any doubt regarding what Anna is about to say.

Even so, the words that spill from Anna's lips crash into his consciousness like a right hook from a pro boxer.

"It all happened really fast. . . . I wanted to see you and tell you face-to-face. . . ."

The car's heater is humming unusually loudly. Yusuf's ears are burning. For a moment he thinks he's going to faint.

"Yusuf? Say something."

Yusuf mumbles a reply and sets the phone down.

A few minutes pass unnoticed, and when Yusuf finally stops crying, he can't remember the words that ended the call.

47

JAMI HARJULA WRAPS his fingers around the chin-up bar tensed across the break room doorway and does a few reps. One, two, three. A wide overhand grip. He probably won't be able to knock out more than a few clean ones in his current condition, so he decides to drop from the bar while he's still ahead.

Maybe if he forced himself to hit the gym at HQ even once a week or did a few chin-ups every time he got coffee, he could see serious results by summer. Would that be the solution to the problems at home? Train himself into trim shape like Yusuf and Nina. But that would require some tweaking of his diet too, and life is far too short.

"Excuse me," Rasmus' voice says behind him.

Harjula turns around, hands on his hips, and looks down at his much shorter colleague. The encounter fills him with a welcome sense of superiority. At least his situation isn't as bad as Rasmus', who has never been fit enough to pass the Police University fitness tests.

"Sure, Susikoski."

"You know about guns, right . . . ?" Rasmus begins.

Harjula's curiosity is immediately piqued. Yes, he does know his guns. As a matter of fact, he knows a surprising amount about anything and everything: cars, boats, motorcycles, guns. . . . Information technology, on the other hand, is like a train he should have jumped on twenty years ago in order to stay on board. Sometimes Harjula feels over-the-hill because he hasn't updated his technical competency to meet the demands of the new millennium.

"Yeah, I know a little about them," Harjula answers with a yawn.

Rasmus hands him a piece of paper, a printout of a photograph.

"Yusuf and Nina found this in a dresser in Zetterborg's bedroom. The perp had left the photo for the police to find."

"Look at that . . . ," Harjula whispers, running his huge thumb across the faces that have been scratched away. The photo reminds him of some suspense movie where an obsessive stalker shapes her reality by excising people who don't fit her agenda from photographs. *Bunny Boiler* or something like that.

"Yusuf says we need to find out the identities of the faceless men one way or another. And really the only clues are the hunting clothes visible in the photograph and—"

"The barrels of the firearms poking up behind their backs?"

"Yes."

Harjula turns around, pulls a chair from under the kitchen table, and sits down. He analyzes what he sees in typical Harjula fashion: long and hard.

"Well, in the first place, these are all shotguns," he eventually says. "That means they're either hunting birds or small game. And there's snow in the forest you can see in the background, which suggests it's a pheasant or capercaillie hunt. Fox, hare . . . something like that."

Rasmus has pulled out his notepad and is writing down what he hears. Actually, the situation is incredibly satisfying: for once, Rasmus needs Harjula's help, not vice versa. On the other hand, now that Rasmus has heard the brief lecture Harjula offered on the topic of interest, he will no doubt store the information in his gargantuan skull and never return to ask Harjula anything else.

"What else? Can you say anything specific about the shotguns?" Rasmus sounds like a reporter on the verge of a huge scoop.

"Wait. . . ."

Harjula brings the photograph closer to his eyes and his initial enthusiasm suddenly turns to frustration. The only element of Zetterborg's firearm—which presumably isn't even the most germane detail in this instance—that's visible is a bit of barrel. The shotgun barrels of the man standing to his right have partially vanished along with the face, and there's nothing Harjula can say about them with certainty except that the barrels are stacked vertically. The third individual's shotgun, on the other hand, is plenty visible, but Harjula is drawing a big fat blank.

"Goddamn it. . . . I've never seen a shotgun like that before."

"Really?" Rasmus says, rubbing salt into Harjula's wounds, probably unintentionally.

Harjula shakes his head and swallows his defeat. He has browsed through dozens of works on the topic and watched countless YouTube videos related to it, but the half-visible shotgun barrel isn't ringing any bells. In a lot of ways, it's completely unique.

"Send me a close-up of just this bit," Harjula says, pointing at the mystical firearm. "I'll ask my buddy who works at Sako. If he doesn't know what it is, then the guy in the picture designed and built it himself."

48

YUSUF STEPS OUT of the elevator on the fourth floor of police headquarters and walks slowly toward his workstation. The bomb Anna just dropped is still throbbing at his temples, and nausea has taken over his body. He raises his glazed eyes from the floor and sees his tall colleague rise from his chair and start walking toward him.

Hell no. Not now.

"Pepple," Jami Harjula says in a low voice, stopping in front of Yusuf, arms folded across his chest.

The guy's habit of calling his colleagues by their last names is really damn annoying: it's as if they are traveling back through time to their mandatory military service or some miserable reserve training.

Yusuf has no interest in dealing with this bullshit right now: the macho dynamics at HQ. Suddenly everything feels like a mistake. The direction of his life. The breakup with Anna. The solitude he himself chose. The career in law enforcement.

"Harjula," Yusuf snaps in irritation, immediately seeing it's not going to provoke the desired response. Harjula has always been Harjula. Yusuf probably should have called the guy Jami if he was trying to irritate him.

"Susikoski asked me to take a look at that photo. I have to admit, I didn't recognize any of the guns myself, but the barrel of the shotgun held by the guy on the left caught my attention."

"OK, did you find something out?" Yusuf says, dribbling himself some cold water from the drinking fountain. The back of his throat burns like someone rubbed it with sandpaper.

"Yup," Harjula says, and now Yusuf notices his colleague is a little worked up. "I showed the photo to a guy who knows guns, and it didn't take him long. . . ."

Harjula shows Yusuf a grainy enlargement of the shotgun's barrel.

"At first glance, it looks a little like a semiautomatic Remington 870, but it's actually something a lot rarer: it's a fully automatic twelve-caliber 7188 from the same manufacturer, and that's a gun not every kid has in his closet."

Yusuf can imagine a bit of foam in the corner of Harjula's mouth. This is Harjula in his element.

Nina's head rises behind the cubicle divider, and a moment later she is standing at Yusuf's side, listening to Harjula's rant.

"Are you ready for the climax?" Harjula says.

Yusuf swigs more water down his rough throat. "I am."

At least this will take my thoughts off Anna.

"The Remington 7188 is a self-loading shotgun the Americans' Navy SEALs originally used in the Vietnam War. Then they decided it was impractical, mostly because the recoil is insane and it doesn't tolerate mud and other shit without jamming—which makes it a pretty useless weapon if you're charging through the jungle. But a nice gun all the same. And extremely rare."

Yusuf shuts his eyes and tries to internalize the information spewing from Harjula's lips.

"So that will make it easier to find the owner—"

"I already found him." Harjula flashes a smile. "Two minutes before you walked in the door. Only one of this specific firearm was ever imported to Finland. It was registered back in 1984 to a man named Erik Raulo."

"Erik Raulo," Nina whispers softly, but the name isn't familiar.

"He's the former head of legal at RealEst," Harjula says, handing Yusuf a yellow slip of paper. "Here's the address and phone number. Seventy-five years old, a widower. Lives alone on the water in Munkkiniemi."

Yusuf looks at Nina, jaw hanging, and then at Harjula, who, without them realizing it, has apparently transformed into a team player.

49

"DID YOU ENTER the address into the navigator?" Yusuf asks Nina as he steers the Volkswagen Golf up the ramp and out of the underground garage. The revs rise before Yusuf pops it into second gear.

"Fifteen minutes."

"OK, call him again," Yusuf says, turning from Pasilanraitio onto Radiokatu.

Nina raises the phone to her ear and at the same time ensures Yusuf is headed in the right direction. They truly have no time to wait.

There isn't any music playing in the car just now. Yusuf drums his fingers against the steering wheel and hopes he'll hear Nina's voice. *This is Detective Nina Ruska from the Helsinki Police* and so on. That Erik Raulo will answer Nina's call and say he's fine.

But that doesn't happen.

Eventually Nina lowers the phone from her ear and shakes her head with a deep sigh.

Yusuf speeds through a yellow light and brings up a new number on his phone.

"Who are you calling?" Nina asks.

Yusuf doesn't reply; he gazes at the traffic slowing down up ahead at the Hartwall Arena and the hundreds of red taillights indicating congestion. It's not rush hour yet; it must be an accident or road construction that's cutting off one of the lanes.

And then Yusuf hears a man's voice on the line. "Axel Zetterborg here."

"Yusuf Pepple, police. We spoke an hour ago. . . ."

"Yes, I remember. I specifically saved your number."

"Do you know a man named Erik Raulo?"

For a few seconds, the line is silent. But something in the silence tells Yusuf that Axel isn't using the time to think back so much as to process the question.

"Of course," Axel says. "He's Dad's personal attorney. In principle retired but he still handles all of Dad's legal affairs. Or at least he did until yesterday."

"Did Erik Raulo ever go hunting with your father?"

"Yes. Countless times. As a matter of fact, I'm making that list right now and already wrote his name down here—"

"Could the man in the photograph be Raulo? The guy on the left?"

"I don't have the photo, but . . . I guess it could."

"When did you last hear from Raulo?"

Silence on the line again.

"You know, I can't say. He might have come by the office a few weeks ago. But he doesn't usually show up there; he works from home. He's not employed by RealEst anymore."

"A few weeks ago?"

"Yes . . ." There's a shift in Axel's voice. He seems to grasp the true purpose of the call. "Wait. You're not saying—"

"Axel, try to get in touch with Raulo. We're headed to Munkkiniemi to make sure he's OK. Call if you hear from him."

Yusuf hangs up, tosses the phone to the car's central console, and grips the wheel with both hands.

"Raulo is still Eliel Zetterborg's right-hand man, even though he hasn't worked for RealEst for a long time," Yusuf says. "I wonder if he thought to be cautious after what happened yesterday."

Nina doesn't reply. She ties back her hair in a ponytail and slips on her beanie. "Twelve minutes. Should we call it in?"

Soft profanity escapes Yusuf's lips and clots into one protracted curse.

"Go ahead. If we're lucky, the patrol will get there before us."

50

YUSUF PARKS ON the street at Munkkiniemenranta and looks at the yard sloping up gently to the large house. The blue lights of the police van in the paved drive lick the home's beige stucco walls.

Yusuf steps out of the Golf and starts briskly up the drive. The wind blowing off Laajalahti Bay snatches the hems of his undone coat and sets them flapping restlessly.

"The car's here," Yusuf shouts into the wind as he speeds up from a walk to a run.

Uniformed officers are waiting at the front door.

"Did you ring the doorbell?" Yusuf asks, because at first it's all he can think of. His pulse feels like it doubled during the few running steps he just took.

"Yup. We got here five minutes ago," one of the officers says.

"Goddamn it. . . ." Yusuf eyes the heavy wooden door. It would be possible to open it one way or another, but breaking a window is faster and a lesser evil to boot. Either way, it's a matter of life and death. "Wait here!"

Yusuf jogs along the wall of the house until he notices a chest-high window behind a bush. It's ajar. "We can climb in here!"

Yusuf doesn't wait for the officers standing at the front of the house. Yusuf grabs the window frame and pushes himself up. He balances there on his triceps, nudging the window with his forehead until it opens inward all the way.

"Hello? Erik Raulo!" Yusuf calls, and when there's no answer, he slides his torso through the window and lowers himself clumsily to a sideboard, knocking over half a dozen framed photographs in the process of getting to an upright position on the floor. He leans against his knees there in the kitchen and listens, but the house is silent.

"Police! Is there anyone home?"

Yusuf stands up straight and fumbles for his ID, pulls it out from under his shirt. Who knows? Maybe Erik Raulo, as a seasoned hunter, would fire his Navy SEAL shotgun first and ask questions later if he saw a black man in his living room.

"Police!" Yusuf calls out again, unsnapping his holster.

He hears Nina's voice outside the window behind him.

There are two pieces of burned toast on the kitchen counter, presumably the reason the window was open in the first place. Yusuf presses his finger to the charred surface of one of the slices: it's rock-hard and cold. There is no burned smell in the air, so some time has passed. Furthermore, the room is icy. And that's why he's sure there's something wrong: no one exiting the house would leave a window open in this weather. . . .

Yusuf!

"Meet me at the front door, Nina!" Yusuf calls out, warily crossing the living room to the entryway.

Yusuf sincerely hopes to find Erik Raulo unharmed, but on some level, he also hopes his suspicions are justified: if Raulo the lawyer ends up having nothing to do with the case, he could raise a hell of a shitstorm over Yusuf entering his home, even if the purpose of the spontaneous operation was to save his life.

Yusuf hears the wind whistling through the open window.

And then he sees a socked foot in the entryway, its toes pointed ominously upward.

Yusuf draws his gun and creeps toward the figure lying on the floor.

"Raulo?"

He bends over the man lying there and feels for a pulse even though he knows it's too late.

Someone shot Erik Raulo right through the heart.

51

THE HOUSE THAT stood eerily silent just an hour before has abruptly
come to life: the investigators in white protective gear call to mind the
TV series about the Chernobyl nuclear disaster. But instead of holding
radiation meters that hiss like rattlesnakes, these investigators are carrying sample-taking supplies: lights, brushes, bags, and powders.

Yusuf walks down the slope of Erik Raulo's front yard, an unsmoked
cigarette in his mouth, and seats himself on a stone wall. He engages
in a silent battle of wills, loses it, and lights the cigarette waiting between his lips. *What a fucking mess.*

A line of museum cars from the seventies slides past on the shore-
line road, the clatter of their motors drowning out all other sounds
and thoughts.

Two white vans are parked in Raulo's drive, having just disgorged
a slew of crime scene investigators.

"Two hatched eggs," Yusuf says softly when there's a break in the
growl of six- and eight-liter engines.

"What?"

Nina is standing behind Yusuf, and she circles around to sit at his
side.

"Those vans," Yusuf clarifies, not sure himself where the odd association came from.

Nina rolls her eyes, bewildered. "Right. Are you OK?"

"You mean, aside from the fact that I'm on the hook for solving two
high-profile murders that took place within twenty-four hours of each
other? And that all signs indicate there's one more to come?"

"Right. Aside from that fact. You've been acting a little weird ever since—"

"Anna's pregnant," Yusuf says, clipping the wings of Nina's guessing game.

He looks at the fiery tip of the cigarette he just lit, turns the cigarette in his fingers, and then flicks it in a handsome arc down to the street.

Everything has to change.

"Already?" Nina says, and immediately appears to regret it. "Sorry. I mean, assuming, that is—"

Yusuf bursts out in a joyless laugh and shakes his head. "The last time we saw each other was in October. It's probably some fucking Swedish-speaking banker. The guy's pecker spoke and whoops! Just like that—Anna's knocked up."

Nina lowers a hand to Yusuf's shoulder and gives it a firm squeeze. "Onward, Yusuf," she says. "It's the only way."

Yusuf looks at Nina. He might feel like talking more about it but knows it's not the right time. Besides, only total focus on the investigation is going to help him forget that Anna is about to start a family without him.

He nods, and Nina gives him a quick but affectionate hug.

The rattle of the museum cars has died.

"OK," Yusuf says, hands cupped in front of his mouth. "Do you agree we have a third body waiting for us somewhere? Or if not yet, then soon?"

"That's what it seems like," Nina says. She pats Yusuf on the back and stands.

Yusuf zips up his coat and pushes himself up and away from the cold wall, a little less spryly than Nina.

"First impressions?" Yusuf says, arms folded across his chest.

"Shot right through the heart," Nina says without thinking.

Yusuf nods. He noticed the exact same thing. "Yup. The heart is the common denominator. In other regards, a slightly different case. It looks as if the perpetrator approached the door with the gun in his hand, rang the bell, stepped inside, and shot Raulo. Straightforward. Cold."

Nina looks at Yusuf as if she isn't quick to agree. "What if we find another treasure map somewhere in there? Another puzzle and more UV scrawl . . ."

"We might. But I don't know where it would lead us. The tip-off about the other victims is in the photo we found at Muukalaiskatu. Of course the house will be thoroughly combed, but for some reason, I have the feeling that whereas there were all sorts of extraneous stuff involved in the big boss' murder . . ."

Nina completes the sentence: "Raulo's murder is just . . . a murder."

Yusuf nods. "Yup." Then he reaches into his pocket and pulls out a blue plastic box: two-milligram nicotine lozenges. He shakes the container until a white oval pill drops into his hand. Yusuf pops it into his mouth and uses his tongue to nudge it under his upper lip. *A healthier version of snuff.*

"I guess we'd better release Niklas Fischer," Nina says.

Yusuf nods. "Even if no proper alibi turns up for him for yesterday, he can't have a better one for today. There's no doubt this is all the work of one and the same killer."

"Unless Fischer had an accomplice."

"I don't know. We don't have anything concrete on Fischer, and speculation alone isn't enough of a reason to hold him."

Nina nods in silence and turns her gaze to the facade of Raulo's house. "There aren't any cameras here."

"Nope. The perp must have known that."

"In other words, he's been here before. He and Raulo were acquainted."

"Yup. And presumably Raulo recognized him too, because he opened the door even under the circumstances. I'm guessing Raulo knew to be on his guard after hearing last night's news. The techs say that judging by the blood spatter, Raulo was probably shot right where we found him. So it's unlikely the killer entered through the window as opposed to the front door. I just checked. There's a clear view from the kitchen to the door," Yusuf says.

"Does Raulo have any family?"

"A son, Hans Raulo. A trust-fund baby. Hellu sent someone to tell him the news. Apparently he's been at some boozy business meeting in the Mirror Room at the Kämp all morning. But maybe we'll find out something by talking to him—whether his father was threatened, for instance."

"OK . . ." Nina swears and rubs her forehead. "You think we might get lucky—might one of the neighbors have seen something? Did someone else's camera happen to cover Raulo's property? All of it or even partially?"

"We need to start asking right away."

"I'll handle it."

Nina pats Yusuf on the shoulder again and strides toward the front door, where the uniformed officers stand waiting.

Yusuf shuts his eyes and takes a moment to inhale the fresh air blowing off the sea. Then he taps out Rasmus' number. He hears the line ring once before the other man's soft voice answers.

"You heard the news, didn't you?" Yusuf asks.

"Yes."

"I know you've got your hands full, but could you please have a look at the base station data and see if anyone involved in the case was out here in Munkkiniemi this morning?"

52

NINA ENDS THE call as she strides toward the front door, where a woman in white protective gear is studying the lock.

The news about his father's death had already reached Hans Raulo, but the man at the other end of the line didn't sound particularly upset. As a matter of fact, the rumors of the boozy brunch-time meeting seem accurate, because Raulo sounded drunk on the phone. Nina arranged to see him downtown in a couple hours' time, but based on the brief call, she is relatively convinced the shocking news will not prompt Raulo to stopper the bottle. Just the opposite.

"We're going to head out," Nina says, trying to establish eye contact with the investigator fussing over the lock.

"Sounds good. It looks like this is going to take a while," the investigator replies. She has thick eyebrows and cauliflower ears, like a boxer.

"Is there anything worth mentioning at this point?" Nina asks.

"Well, as you guessed, the door hasn't been touched. The perp must have entered through an open door."

Nina glances at her watch. "What else?"

"There's one tiny detail that immediately caught my eye."

The investigator waves Nina in, and they step into the entryway, where Erik Raulo is still lying on the floor under a sheet.

"Do you see those elephants?" the investigator says.

Nina looks at the windowsill that the other woman is indicating. There are a dozen porcelain elephants there arranged in order of size, the littlest the size of a fingertip, the largest the size of a fist.

"This sounds pretty random, but an elephant is missing from the middle."

"So it seems." Nina walks over to the chain of tchotchkes. "But there could be a thousand explanations. . . ."

"Sure. It just caught my eye," the investigator says.

Nina uses her phone to snap a photo of the incomplete arrangement. "Let us know if you find anything similar in the house. If anything else seems to be missing."

"Of course."

Nina raises a hand in farewell and, after she steps out the door, hears her phone ring. She feels her senses heighten.

It's Tom. The Tinder date that finally led to something. Nina isn't sure what, but she's ready to find out. She sees Yusuf leaning against his car over on the street and tries to wipe the stupid grin from her face.

"Hey there."

"I saw the news yesterday. You guys must have your hands full," Tom says.

"We do," Nina says. "Thanks for yesterday. And sorry I had to head out so fast."

"Work is work. I was late myself."

"It was a pretty efficient thirty minutes, I have to say." Nina can no longer keep the smile from scurrying back onto her face.

"You have time to meet today?" Tom says.

A low bark echoes down the line.

Hush.

Nina laughs. "Where are you?"

"At home."

"There's a dog there?"

"Yeah. My ex's. I watch it now and again."

Nina feels a pang of jealousy. "OK, I didn't know that."

"There's a lot you don't know about me, which is why we should meet up today and pick up where we left off."

Nina lets out a weird laugh and shoots another glance at Yusuf, who has lit a cigarette while he's been waiting. "What if I don't like dogs?"

Tom chuckles. "You probably wouldn't like my ex either."

"Is that so?" Nina tucks her hair behind her ear. "Listen, I don't know what's going to happen today or how long this is going to take . . . but it would be nice to spend more than half an hour together."

"And without your handsome coworker bombing your phone while we're—"

"OK, OK. I'll call you."

Nina hangs up and feels her fingertips start to tingle.

53

THE TEMPERATURE HAS dropped a few degrees, and the condensation has crystallized into beautiful blooms of ice on the panes of glass.

Jessica opens the door and steps out. The incident in the tub is still haunting her; the sound of crushing bones echoes in her ears. She glances around before spotting Yusuf's ride on Töölönkatu.

At the same time, she sees a black car pull over at the far end of the street. Jessica has been extraordinarily cautious since the encounter with the man at the door to her building. And then there was the eerie phone call.

Caution is fine, but paranoia is something else.

Jessica ignores the thought that there's something suspicious about the black vehicle and makes her way to Yusuf's car. She can see from a distance that he's leaning back against the headrest, eyes shut. She walks up to the car, opens the passenger door, and climbs in. Elastinen's "Syljen" is playing on the radio.

I stood on the table and spat like an ace,
and they weren't ready, they laughed in my face.

"You hear that, Jessie?" Yusuf says softly, pointing at the radio.
"What?"
"*They weren't ready.* You get it? *They* weren't ready. It wasn't that he wasn't a hundred percent ready to do his thing. I dig that style. Not doubting yourself, believing in your vision so much that you don't care what anyone else thinks."

And then Yusuf's relaxed expression grows melancholy.

"I'm really sorry, Yusuf," Jessica says.

Fifteen minutes before, she received a text message from Yusuf asking her to come downstairs. The text message ended with the words I need you now if ever.

"I did everything in exactly the wrong order, Jessie. I was in a relationship when I should have been going out, screwing my brains out, having experiences. And then Anna and I called it off. I guess in part because I wanted to see other people. . . . The truth is, I don't want to see anyone else. It was some childish fucking illusion of the grass being greener on the other side. And now she's having a kid with someone else."

Jessica lowers her fingers to Yusuf's thigh and gives it a firm squeeze. "The first days are the worst, Yusuf. You'll be OK. You have to just keep pushing."

The words elicit a despairing laugh from Yusuf. "That's exactly what Nina said: keep moving forward. But it feels like I'm just going backward the whole time. Especially when I think things are progressing. I guess my point is," Yusuf says, looking out the driver's-side window, "I'm not ready to be investigative lead. I can't take the pressure, Jessie."

Jessica suddenly realizes Yusuf is crying.

"Maybe I could have if I hadn't heard this fucking news about Anna's baby. Holy fuck, what a pitiful loser I am."

Yusuf dries his tears on his sleeve.

Jessica finds herself feeling incredible empathy for the colleague and friend sitting at her side. It's at moments like this when you realize how much you care. Maybe in order to understand the depth of your affection for someone, you have to experience how easy it is to put yourself in their shoes now and again. Jessica feels Yusuf's pain in her own body, which tells her she cares about him a hell of a lot. Maybe even more than she cares about herself.

Guilt washes over Jessica: she realizes she has been selfish, bow-ing out of what might be the most important investigation of the year. She wanted to make a clean break from everything—her work, her coworkers—and focus on her own semilunatic detective game. She has always preached about the importance of being a team player, and now she has become the diva she was always afraid her incredible wealth would make her.

"You're neither one. You're neither pitiful nor a loser. We'll get through this together, just like you told me," Jessica says, pulling her phone from her pocket.

"Who are you calling?"

"Hellu. I'm going to join the team so you have more bodies."

Jessica raises the phone to her ear and gazes deep into Yusuf's brown eyes. They have always been beautiful, but the sadness and gratitude beaming simultaneously from them make them even more beautiful now.

WHEN JESSICA STEPS out of Yusuf's car a moment later, she notices the black car that caught her eye start up and drive off. The timing seems a little too coincidental. She considers running after it, but before she can act, it disappears around the corner.

54

WHERE'S THIS COMING from, Niemi? Well, welcome back to the team, then, but please don't change your mind again.

Hellu's words still pound at Jessica's temples. She opens the door to her apartment, deactivates the alarm, and strides across the living room to the large kitchen. She fishes a box of rose hip tea from the cupboard, fills the electric kettle, and turns it on with a click. This is the routine she performs every time she dives into a case. Laptop, papers, and bloodred tea that warms her whole body and gets her thoughts moving.

Yusuf is stressing over the responsibility he's been given, and it's clear that last summer's breakup is amping up the pressure. The breakup that Yusuf has clearly not processed yet. The rapid escalation of the gym ratting, the broad smile, the near-manic smoking: Jessica should have noticed the signs of burnout, been present, lent Yusuf her ear sooner. The law-enforcement authorities involved with society's underbelly—brutal murders and shocking circumstances—often collapse abruptly. As absurd as it is, the police are expected to tolerate all that grim garbage as if their job is like any other and they just happen to come across things that are a bit unfortunate now and again.

Jessica opens her laptop and lowers the folder Yusuf gave her to the table. Material gathered over the course of the day has been emailed to her: photographs, tech analyses, interrogation transcriptions.

Jessica remembers Yusuf's words: *You mind checking out Lamberg so we can cross his name off the list for good?*

Jessica clicks open a password-protected folder named *J. L.* The folder contains images and the transcript of last night's interrogation, as well as the report from internal audit and the verdict on the SWAT assignment that took place in 2009—the assignment that apparently resulted in Lamberg's being given the boot from special forces.

Kenneth Guranov . . . Kidnapping . . . RealEst . . . Child recovered unharmed . . . Suspected use of excessive force . . . Found to be groundless . . . The ransom money was never recovered.

Jessica studies the information intently for a couple of minutes, until the click from the kettle interrupts her.

She opens the recording from emergency dispatch, which Yusuf sent her a moment earlier, and listens to it twice. Classical piano music plays faintly in the background. Jessica shuts her eyes and tries to concentrate—does anything strike her as out of the ordinary?

Hello? What is your emergency? Can you hear me?

My chest . . . my chest . . . Kianto . . .

Jessica pauses the recording and enters the word Kianto into a search engine, but the only hits it brings up are related to the Finnish author Ilmari Kianto, who died half a century before.

Jessica pinches the bridge of her nose between her thumb and her forefinger. *Why the hell does Zetterborg mention Kianto? Does the author have anything to do with Mephistopheles? Faust . . . The devil's agent . . .*

No, that makes no sense.

Jessica types Kianto + Goethe into the search field, but the results don't reveal any link between the two authors, if one exists.

Jessica plays the recording again:

. . . are you having a heart attack?

A heart attack? I just walked in . . .

. . .

No, he's been stabbed in the chest with a steel blade . . .

Jessica browses to the report Sissi Sarvilinna typed out.

The trabeculae carneae in the left ventricle have been severed. . . .
The wound channel in the wall of the left ventricle is approximately
one centimeter wide and jagged. . . . The width and jaggedness of the
wound indicate the steel blade was withdrawn quickly. . . . At the
corresponding location in the wall of the left ventricle there is evidence of a plethoric change consistent with a recent infarction.

Eliel Zetterborg was doing poorly earlier in the day, which was presumably the result of a series of minor infarctions. But the cause of death
is irrefutably determined to be a knife blow to the heart.

Jessica's thoughts meander here and there. What about the watch
Yusuf mentioned? Eliel Zetterborg was wearing the watch in the old
photograph, and the pathologist removed this same watch from the
rigid wrist of his corpse the night before.

*Only on special occasions. Otherwise he always kept the watch in the
safe.*

Jessica massages her forehead with her fingers. Would Zetterborg
have put on the watch the morning of the company's fiftieth anniversary?

She enters 27 january + Eliel Zetterborg + press conference + kouvola into Google. The search engine brings up numerous
hits. Jessica clicks the first link, which is a *Helsingin Sanomat* article
about the events in Kouvola. But Zetterborg's wrist isn't visible in the
photo, so she keeps looking. Eventually she finds an image of Zetterborg sitting at a table in front of cameras, and he is raking his hair
back with his left hand. The wrist is bare.

*Eliel Zetterborg must have put on the watch after coming home that
evening. But so what?*

Damn it. Jessica is drawing a blank. There's no point following every possible clue. Now she has to divide her energies between two mysteries, solve them both—if there's anything to solve about the burned body in Central Park, that is.

Jessica rises from her chair and pours boiling water into her cup; the bag resting at the bottom imparts its flavor and color to the water.

She inhales the steam rising from it through her nostrils, goes back to the table, and clicks open an email Nina has sent the entire investigative team.

What the hell?

Confused, Jessica studies the photo of the little elephants arranged by size on a windowsill.

> Erik Raulo's home—observation. One of the statues, the size of a matchbox, appears to be missing.

Why does Nina think it's significant? On the other hand, in cases like this, anything might be.

Jessica closes her laptop and buries her face in her hands.

Concentrate. Let's start with Lamberg.

Jessica glances at the bottom of the television screen: three thirty-one p.m. According to Hellu, they should be getting the tapes from the Russian embassy before five. And as Hellu reminded her over the phone, if Lamberg was sitting in his car when the call to emergency services was made, he can be excluded from the list of suspects with certainty.

She will have time to talk to Lamberg before then.

Jessica opens the drawer next to the sink and lifts up the utensil holder. The bottom of the drawer is blanketed in yellow bills.

A cash stash. Every gangster has to have an escape plan, someone said in a movie whose title Jessica can't remember. And so do super-rich, law-abiding police officers who don't want to leave all their assets lying around in banks or securities accounts. Despite the fact that cash stuffed into a sock is perpetually devoured by the moth of economics: inflation.

Jessica takes eleven bills from the drawer, folds them neatly, and slips them into her pocket.

It's time to practice a little charity.

55

JOONAS LAMBERG'S ONE-BEDROOM apartment is located on the top floor of a three-story building at the corner of Valhallankatu and Linnankoskenkatu. The place is decorated with a minimalist simplicity, and Jessica has a hard time imagining any female has ever lived there.

She sits down on the worn leather sofa, and the muscular Lamberg lowers two cups of coffee to the table on a tray. The hoodie that would look like a sailboat sail on Jessica is pulled taut around his solid arms. His chest is big, but not as massive as that of a bodybuilder who swears by the bench press. Lamberg's physique speaks of explosive strength, but there's also an agility and refinement to it.

"Krav Maga?" Jessica says, pointing at the large picture hanging next to the glass balcony doors. In the framed photograph, Lamberg is posing on a wrestling mat in a white kimono, a tanned opponent of similar caliber trapped under his arm.

"Yup. It's my outlet. My escape. It also contributes to my professional competence," Lamberg says, pouring the coffee. "Milk?"

"No, thanks. Black."

Jessica nods her thanks. She rarely drinks coffee but has accepted the offer because she doubts Lamberg has rose hip tea in his cupboards.

For a moment, Lamberg looks like he's not going to sit. He eyes his own apartment as if he is scanning it—as if he wants to stay one step ahead of the detective on the couch. But ahead how?

"Sorry. I'm really nervous," Lamberg says, finally sitting down.

"That's understandable." Jessica takes a sip of her coffee. It tastes bitter and scorched.

"What did you want to talk about? I've already told everything I know twice. First to Pepple at the scene and then a second time at the station—"

"I'm not going to beat around the bush, Joonas," Jessica says. "I want to ask about your past. How you ended up working for Eliel Zetterborg."

Lamberg grunts, deflated. "You want to talk about the SWAT days."

He lifts his coffee to his lips. The little porcelain cup looks funny in the brawny Lamberg's mitt. It's as if the two of them are playing house, and he is sipping out of a tiny plastic cup.

Jessica nods. "We don't have any reason to doubt your story about what happened last night, especially since we know Zetterborg called emergency services before you entered the apartment."

"Jesus . . . ," Lamberg mutters under his breath. He shakes his head. "Eliel was my boss. My assignment. My profession. I can't believe you guys are even saying anything like that out loud. That I had something to do with him being stabbed."

"We just want to form a complete picture," Jessica says. "That's all."

"OK. Of course I'll do everything I can to help. For the reasons I just stated."

"Tell me in your own words what happened on December 5, 2009."

Lamberg smiles, but his eyes are sad.

"I'm sure you remember the date," Jessica suggests.

"Of course. I've often thought of it as some sort of finale. Basically, that night was the nail in the coffin of my SWAT career . . . and career as a police officer in general."

"Tell me about it."

"It's a simple story. A guy known as Kangaroo had abducted a first grader and was blackmailing her parents for a ransom. I think it was a hundred grand even. The kidnapping was never reported publicly so as not to put the girl's life needlessly at risk. The parents—or, I mean, the little girl's father—worked for the firm—"

"For RealEst?"

"Yeah. For the firm." Lamberg sounds as if this were self-evident.

Jessica can't help but think of the movie of the same name, a thriller starring Tom Cruise about an utterly corrupt legal firm.

"The parents paid the entire sum just in case, and the girl was returned in one piece. Then the asshole was tracked to Tattarisuo, where we were supposed to bring him in, along with the ransom that had been delivered that morning."

Jessica takes a sip of coffee. "'The asshole.'"

"What?"

"You called Kangaroo 'the asshole.' Did you take the case personally somehow?"

Lamberg wipes his face and looks reflective. Then he gulps as if to wash down the lump in his throat and nods.

"I guess I did. And that's why they smoked me out of the unit. You always have to keep your feelings out of your work. Nowadays they know how to talk about these things, even in the SWAT unit. . . . But back then, a culture of silence prevailed. Feelings were pushed down, and guys suffered for it. Everyone in slightly different ways, of course. We were expected to be made of stone, Gary Cooper or something."

"Why?"

"Why Gary Cooper?"

"No, why did you take it so personally?"

Lamberg laughs, clearly to himself. Then he turns serious. "I hate kiddie diddlers."

"Was . . . Kangaroo a pedophile?"

Lamberg trains his glazed eyes out the glass balcony doors. Then he nods. "He didn't have a record . . . because he never got caught. But I knew. I had heard from reliable sources that he abused kids. Motherfucking cocksucker."

Jessica sees Lamberg clench his fists. It wouldn't take a psychologist to detect a repressed rage that might have been channeled at a sexual predator he came across on the job.

"I thought the motive for the kidnapping was money?" Jessica says.

"It was. But I'm sure the shit got off on it, even just being able to keep the girl prisoner. The ransom money was sort of icing on the cake for him, I guess, but not the main point."

Jessica looks at Lamberg's rugged jaw, crooked nose, and eyes that have started to glisten.

"Did Kangaroo aim a firearm at you, Joonas?" Jessica says. "Or did you shoot him to punish him for all those other bad things?"

She's no longer sure if the incident that happened over a decade ago is in any way relevant to the present investigation. But even so, she is surprisingly curious about it. She knows perfectly well what it feels like to take justice into one's own hands. She's had personal experience with it herself, far too personal.

"With all due respect . . . I don't really get what this has to do with last night—," Lamberg says.

The statement is more than justified, and Jessica changes tactics. "When you quit the force," she says, lowering her cup to the table, "how was it you ended up working as Zetterborg's personal bodyguard?"

"Zetterborg found me, if that's what you're asking." Lamberg sighs and picks at a seam in the armchair's upholstery. "Zeta wanted someone with the balls to act. That's exactly how he put it, word for word. Of course it mattered that the kidnapped girl's father worked for the firm and word of the abductor's death reached all the way to the top."

Jessica shifts her gaze to Lamberg's thick fingers. It's curious that the Swedish-speaking industry magnate wanted a man to protect him who had a more gangsterlike approach than the typical risk-predicting bodyguard.

"The truth is probably somewhere there in the middle," Lamberg says after a moment. "That case is dead and buried . . . just like the guy himself. That prick had a gun in his hand. But I can honestly say his background and the stuff he did made my trigger finger itchy. I've spent plenty of time thinking about it." Lamberg takes his coffee cup in his paw and empties it with a quick tilt of the head. "But I don't have any regrets. What's done is done."

"I understand the money was never found," Jessica says.

"That's true. That's on me. He never had time to tell us where he'd hidden the cash."

Jessica crosses one leg over the other. Her freshly washed jeans feel tight.

"What happened to your hand?" Lamberg then says tenderly, as if the conversation they just had is nothing but a distant memory.

"Accident on the job."

"I understand. Happened to me too. I took a bullet once, a long time ago." Lamberg presses his forefinger to his kneecap. "It's a hell of a profession. Good thing the pay is so excellent."

"Tell me about it," Jessica says.

She looks Lamberg in the eye. Over the course of their ten-minute encounter, Jessica feels like she has succeeded in creating a pretty comprehensive picture of the man sitting across from her. Joonas Lamberg is a physically intimidating, psychologically damaged bruiser who upholds some sort of masculine code of honor and who committed some shenanigans the force apparently couldn't turn a blind eye to. A lone wolf. His eyes are more skittish than defiant. Everything about the big man's demeanor speaks of anxiety, and Jessica believes if anyone could benefit from a visit to a psychologist, it would be this guy.

"Doing evil to evildoers," she eventually says, letting her gaze slide across the room toward the kitchen. "Maybe by some measures it's right. Kind of the way two minus signs make a plus. I've seen it happen in my own life."

Jessica is instantly alarmed by her words and a little shocked by her quiet outburst. She has steered the conversation into dangerous waters.

But Lamberg doesn't cling to what she said, just flashes a broad smile of relief. "So you know what I'm talking about."

"Let's just say this conversation doesn't need to leave this apartment."

Lamberg nods, face beaming with gratitude.

Jessica rises from the couch and thanks Lamberg for the coffee. She glances at the time: four thirty p.m.

"Thanks, Joonas."

She extends her left hand, and Lamberg takes it with a slightly melancholy smile. Jessica is overwhelmed by the impression that a storm of emotions is raging beneath Lamberg's tough exterior: he probably regrets what he did, even though he won't admit it to anyone, even himself.

"There's one more thing," Lamberg says as Jessica is walking toward the door.

"What?"

"I was supposed to call Pepple, but I figured I'd go ahead and tell you since you're here." Lamberg is leaning against a white IKEA dresser, arms folded across his chest. "I read about another murder in Munkkiniemi in today's paper. Is it Erik Raulo?"

"I can't comment on—"

Lamberg waves dismissively. "I get it. But in any case . . . I know where Raulo lives and I put two and two together. . . . The boss asked me to deliver a message to Erik Raulo yesterday. An envelope."

"What was inside the envelope?"

Lamberg shrugs. "The message, I assume." His face grows thoughtful. "I didn't have time to deliver it, because . . . well, first Zeta went, and now apparently—"

"Do you still have the envelope?"

Lamberg nods. "I probably should have mentioned yesterday, but it slipped my mind in the chaos."

Jessica steps toward him. "Where is it?"

Lamberg wipes his nose on his cuff and opens one of the dresser drawers. A moment later, Jessica is handed a sealed white envelope.

"Didn't Eliel Zetterborg write the recipient's name on it?"

Lamberg raises a forefinger and taps it to his temple. "Not when he entrusted its delivery to me. Something sensitive, I'd guess. And personal."

"So you have no idea what the letter contains?"

Joonas Lamberg shakes his head.

56

JESSICA STEPS OUT of the building, the envelope in her breast pocket. She starts walking toward a taxi stand she spots a couple hundred feet away and glances back. For some reason, she wants to see whether Lamberg is watching her from the window. But there's no sign of him, and she realizes she's disappointed.

Her phone rings, and a broadly smiling face flashes on her screen.

"Jessica, where are you?" Yusuf's tired voice says after she presses the green icon.

"I just left Lamberg's place."

"OK, listen. . . . We got the tapes from the embassy. The time stamp on the video confirms Lamberg's story to a T."

Jessica finds herself feeling some sort of relief that the bodyguard can be permanently erased from the list of suspects.

"In other words, what was already extremely unlikely is impossible now," Yusuf says. "Did you find out anything new?"

"Maybe. Lamberg gave me a letter he was supposed to deliver to Erik Raulo," Jessica says, ripping open the envelope.

"A letter from Zetterborg for Erik Raulo?"

"Yup."

Jessica pulls out the piece of paper and unfolds it. Her eyes study the handwritten text. *Goddamn it, this changes everything.*

"This is really weird, Yusuf. . . ."

When Jessica looks up, she realizes a black car has pulled up next to her.

"What does it say, Jessica?" Yusuf says after a brief silence.

But Jessica has turned her gaze from the letter to the car window. "I'll call you back in a sec," she says in a low voice, and ends the call.

And then the tinted rear window of the car rolls down, and when Jessica sees the face of the person sitting there, she can't believe her eyes.

57

Axel Zetterborg is standing at the large window in his living room, gazing out to sea. Storm winds have raised swells in the bay. They crash into the shore and set the dock rocking on its pontoons.

"Is everything OK, Axel?"

Axel feels his wife's warm hand on his cheek. Alise has always been good at sensing his emotional state, especially in moments when everything is going to hell. And if there ever were such a moment, this is it.

"Erik Raulo's dead," Axel says, turning to Alise. He tries to look calm but is pretty sure he hasn't succeeded. Alise might be irritating sometimes, but she's not stupid.

Alise looks back at him, then raises her hand to her mouth in what is apparently the universal sign of horror. "Erik . . . What . . . what happened to Erik?"

"He was found murdered at home in Munkkiniemi."

"Oh my God!"

"Don't worry, Alise. Everything is going to be fine." Axel wraps his arms around his wife. His hands are shaking; he clenches his fists behind her back. "The police have a photograph the killer left in Dad's apartment. They showed it to me but I couldn't tell who the men in the picture were. Maybe if I'd realized one of them was Erik . . . maybe he'd still be alive."

"But are you—"

Axel shakes his head and releases Alise, then holds her for a moment longer in front of him, hands tenderly on her waist. His palms feel her hip bones through her sweater. "I'm not in the photo. It was from decades ago, and whatever's going on, it doesn't involve me. Or you."

Alise looks anything but convinced. She removes Axel's hands from her hips and wipes the corner of her eye. "But if you're sure this guy doesn't want to hurt us, why is there still a police car out in front of our house?"

"It's just a precaution. Think about it from the perspective of the factory closure. You never can tell what people will get into their heads at times like that."

Alise sighs and stands there at Axel's side. "What is wrong with this world?"

They gaze out at the billowing sea, which is separated from their luxurious home by a broad, gently sloping lawn.

The lights of the high-rises at Verkkosaari gleam on the opposite shore, and their own figures are reflected in the glass. Axel sees Alise's shocked face. How lucky he has been to share his life with a woman with a good heart, a woman like Alise. But all that luck could evaporate in an instant if she ever finds out about his nocturnal adventures. It might just be a matter of time before someone talks. One of those dozens of whores from whose naked asses he has snorted cocaine.

Yes. Cocaine. It has undeniably become quite the problem over the years. The paranoia that has crept into his life in the wake of Snow White has taken on wholly new forms recently: in the past few weeks in particular, Axel has had the strong sense that he is being followed.

"Axel!"

Alise's scream rouses him from his reverie. Axel turns from his reflection to his wife and sees that her face is frozen in fear.

"What is it?"

"There's someone down at the water!" Alise grabs Axel's wrist and takes a step backward.

Axel steps closer to the glass, shades his eyes with his palm to see out into the darkness, but it's hard to see the water from the home's illuminated interior. "Come on, there's not . . ."

But Alise has already bolted from the window. She climbs a few stairs, staggers in her panic, and finally flips off the living room lights.

And now Axel sees it too: a dark figure in the middle of their yard, only fifty feet from the house.

"What the hell?" he spits out before Alise lunges for the door and the police car parked outside.

He hears her scream hysterically for the police.

Shivers run through Axel's body as he watches the figure standing in the yard. For a moment, the two of them simply stare at each other, and all that stands between them are a large pane of glass and a 50-degree temperature difference. The figure raises a hand in greeting. And now Axel can see the figure is holding a phone as if he was video recording Axel through the window.

"Alise!" Axel yells in terror, and then he hears a dog barking and sees flashlight beams licking the yard.

But by the time the uniformed police and their dogs finally reach the back, the figure has vanished just as stealthily as it appeared. Axel pulls his phone from his pocket and realizes his hand is shaking.

Until now he thought he was imagining it all, thought he'd been seeing things, hoped his imagination was playing tricks on him. But now he realizes someone truly has been stalking him, following at his heels for weeks now.

What the fuck is going on?

58

YUSUF ENDS THE call and stifles an imminent coughing fit in his fist. His throat is dry and irritated, which is no doubt a result of the cigarettes he's been chain-smoking.

John Daly's "Hit It Hard" carries faintly from somewhere down the long hallway.

"Who was that?" Nina says. She's leaning against the corner of her desk, flipping through a thick stack of papers.

"Someone was creeping around Axel Zetterborg's property," Yusuf says, untwisting the cap of his water bottle. "Someone who was fast enough to slip into the yard in spite of the canine patrol posted outside the house."

"And evidently that someone didn't end up in the patrol's clutches?"

Yusuf shakes his head, bottle at his lips. He slowly gulps down half the bottle and caps it again. "The dog followed him down to the dock at Soutajankuja, where apparently he climbed over a metal fence and continued across the metro tracks on foot to the roadway and then disappeared," he says, and hacks, his voice raspy.

"Description?" Nina asks.

"Male, average build. The Zetterborgs didn't get a closer look; he was standing in the middle of the yard, holding up a phone. Probably filming the interior of the house with it."

"You think it's the same guy?"

"Who killed Zetterborg first and then Erik Raulo?" Yusuf shrugs, then whispers, barely audibly: "Faust."

"Yes."

"Maybe. Or then it's just some stalker who read the paper and went by to snoop . . . or some worker from the Kouvola factory who lost his job and wanted to give the prince a scare. How the fuck should I know?"

Nina lowers her papers to the desk and walks over to Yusuf, arms folded across her chest. "Somehow I get the sense that whoever was creeping around the yard is the guy we've been looking for this whole time. And that Axel Zetterborg is in serious danger."

"But then there's the photograph," Yusuf says, hears his voice is working, and continues. "Axel Zetterborg wasn't in it. In theory he could be lying, of course, or not remembering, but the guy in the picture has a totally different build from Axel."

Yusuf takes a printout from his desk and hands it to Nina. She stares at it for a moment, then slowly nods.

"What about the list of hunters Axel sent?" she asks.

"What about it?"

"Eliel Zetterborg was murdered yesterday. Erik Raulo was murdered today. By the same logic, a third person is going to suffer the same fate by tomorrow at the latest."

"Rasse has contacted most of them—all the ones who are still alive, that is; most of them are really old. They've all been warned to exercise extreme caution in case the triple-murder theory holds. But we don't have the resources to protect all of them."

Nina sighs. "Of course not."

"So something bad might be happening to any one of them at this very second while we're chatting about it here in the warmth and comfort of our offices."

YUSUF RUNS THE cold water over his hands and splashes it on his face. His heart is pounding furiously in his chest, and his whole body feels like it's in alarm mode. Not even a day in charge, and his body is suddenly overloaded. Nor did Anna's news make the burden any lighter, that's for sure.

Yusuf knows he was wrong thinking he wasn't ready to have a child. That he needed to see the world and have some adventures first. In this moment, the whole idea feels totally absurd.

The walls of the men's room feel like they're caving in on him. He has to get out of here fast.

"You have time for a meal today, Yusuf?"

Harjula is standing near the bathroom door as if he's been waiting there. His large eyes study Yusuf critically.

Yusuf shakes his wet hands and gives a glum laugh. His face is still wet, which must make it appear sweaty. "It looks like eating is a luxury a lead investigator can't afford."

The look on Harjula's face somehow speaks of paternal concern. It doesn't suit his typically smug face at all, although Harjula is apparently the father of two girls and must, therefore, be capable of empathy. But how the hell would Yusuf know?

"Horseshit," Harjula says. "A man has to eat. Let's go over to Tripla for a pint and grab a bite too."

"A pint? Now?" Yusuf says incredulously. It's a ridiculous thought. Before long, two corpses will be lying in Sissi Sarvilinna's cooler, and Harjula wants to go for a beer. To top it off, Harjula is probably the last guy Yusuf wants to spend time with over a pint. "No way in hell."

But Harjula doesn't relent; he sighs deeply and scratches his jaw with his long fingers. "Trust me, you need a half-hour break from all this. There's an army of investigators at Munkkiniemi, and they'll call if they need anything. You need to keep yourself in fighting form. It's kind of like what they say in the airplane: put on your own oxygen mask first before you help a child with theirs."

Yusuf hears Nina let out an amused whistle and turns to her. She has walked up to them at the restroom door without his noticing. To his horror, Yusuf discovers Nina has decided to join forces with the enemy.

"Actually, Harjula's right. Go eat. Grab some fresh air or maybe that beer," she says, tapping at her phone. "Then it continues. We'll keep the circus afloat in the meantime."

Yusuf opens his mouth to protest but finds he's too tired to wriggle out of this one.

W<small>HERE THE HELL</small> *have you been? Answer me!*

The man closes the door and locks it.

He hears the echoing, insistent knock but decides to ignore it. He shuts it out. This is one thing he knows how to do: focus only on what he sees before him.

He plugs the phone's charging cable into his computer.

`Synchronize.`

Do you hear me? Open this door!

The man slips on his headphones.

`Upload video.`

He takes off his wet beanie and opens the video editor on his iMac. Adds the material he just recorded to the footage stream. A stormy sea rages in the background of the clip.

Maybe he should have been smart and stayed hidden; maybe then he could have recorded a longer video. But this time he wanted to be seen, wanted to be noticed. For the first time, he has stepped out of the shadows.

The new video clip is only twenty seconds long.

That makes six minutes, all told.

JAMI HARJULA RAISES his beer to his lips, takes a long swig, then leaves the pint glass there to shield his mouth. Yusuf is gnawing on spicy chicken wings and looking around; the sports bar, part of an international chain, is a shrine to Boston athletics. It's packed with collectibles from legendary Boston teams. The Red Sox, the Bruins, the Celtics, and the New England Patriots are all represented. Yusuf's gaze comes to a stop on the renowned Red Sox hitter David Ortiz, whose photograph hangs at the end of their table. The baseball great, who quit the game in 2016, made an involuntary return to the headlines almost three years later, when he was shot in the back during a failed murder-for-hire scheme in his homeland of the Dominican Republic. The ironic thing about the case was that Ortiz wasn't the actual target of the attack. Wrong place at the wrong time, indeed.

"That sure did the trick," Harjula says, wiping sauce from the corner of his mouth.

"Yup."

Yusuf looks at the plate in front of him. When he thinks about the rest of the day's agenda, he isn't sure devouring medium-hot wings and curly fries on an upset stomach was such a good idea. His stomach's protests are no doubt audible all the way to Harjula's ears across the table.

As Yusuf is picking the last of the meat from the bone, he feels Harjula's eyes on him, evaluating him annoyingly.

"You know what, Yusuf? You actually have it pretty good right now. None of the responsibilities of civilian life . . . Aren't your folks in good shape too?"

Yusuf gazes at Harjula's long, narrow face and his lips moving behind the thick pint glass. The server arrives to clear their empty plates, then vanishes back into the kitchen.

"Yeah, they are," Yusuf replies reluctantly.

"When you get kids and all the stuff that goes along with it . . . everything just gets really damn hard."

Yusuf is about to reply, then realizes Harjula is just getting started.

Even so, a torturous number of seconds pass before Harjula is able to formulate his thoughts into words. Yusuf avoids eye contact by staring at the football-passing Tom Brady's white teeth.

"I'm not saying the kids themselves are so hard. My kids are the best thing that ever happened to me, as clichéd as it probably sounds to a *virile* single guy like you. I guess that's just the way it goes: the greatest happiness brings the greatest responsibility. Sometimes the responsibility is really damn heavy. And rips everything else to shreds."

Yusuf looks at Harjula in disbelief. After all the years he and Jami Harjula have worked together, it's surprising Harjula has suddenly lowered his guard and is talking to Yusuf as if they are somehow close. Or maybe it's a deliberate disclosure the guy has been holding in to spill to his shrink. Then Yusuf has an abrupt, unpleasant insight: he realizes the smart-assed Harjula, who is usually so cocky and overconfident, doesn't have any real friends, anyone he can share his feelings with over a beer.

"You're right, Harjula," Yusuf says, rubbing his knuckles. "I don't know anything about your situation or what it's like to be in your shoes. But I know you're not the only one who feels that way."

Harjula grunts ruefully. "I guess. I guess the world is full of unhappy parents," he says, drains his pint, then lowers it carefully to the middle of the cardboard coaster, as if the symmetry of the resulting white edges is the most consequential of his concerns.

"Is that what you are? Unhappy?" Yusuf says, and is alarmed by his words, which are in danger of leading this conversation with a man he hasn't ever particularly cared for to an even deeper level.

And then Harjula makes things worse by looking Yusuf in the eye. He crosses his long fingers on the table and lets out a profoundly deep sigh. Yusuf guesses that's all the answer he needs.

Yusuf feels his palms starting to sweat.

How the hell did I end up in this situation . . . ?

"Because I've always wondered what it is that actually makes us happy in the end. Healthy children, of course. It's another cliché but completely true. But if your worst fears don't come true, if nothing terrible happens to your children . . . is that really happiness or just gratitude? Nothing like the status quo, et cetera. Should you accept the way things are just because they could be a hell of a lot worse?"

"Good question," Yusuf says, glancing at his watch. He's going to have to think of some effective pretense for getting out of here soon.

He eyes the empty pint glasses in dread. He's sure Harjula is going to suggest they have another. That wasn't the deal. Yusuf needs an escape route, fast. What did it say in the letter Zetterborg wrote to Erik Raulo? And why hasn't Jessica called to report she's back at the station?

"Unhappy people . . . Take this Zetterborg, for instance," Harjula continues lazily. "One of the richest guys in Finland, but on television his face always looked tired and somehow jaded. I bet on some level the killer did him a favor."

"Don't ever say that in public, Harjula," Yusuf says semiseriously. "Folks will lose their confidence in law enforcement."

Harjula grunts wearily and directs his gaze out the window, where the snowflakes are dancing in the light of the streetlamps. He and Yusuf have been sitting there for only twenty-five minutes, but his laconic stream of self-pity already has Yusuf thinking he's going to die alone and miserable without the security of his family. Harjula is toxic company, even when you're also feeling blue and vulnerable. Maybe especially then.

But Yusuf knows that deep down, he's a softie, a humanist who has never enjoyed watching others suffer, no matter who is sitting across the table from him. He feels an involuntary compassion for his blow-hard colleague. It's plain without anything being said that Harjula needs some words of encouragement, a pat on the back, assurance that everything's going to be OK. Yusuf is going to have to be the bigger man, especially now that he's lead investigator on the case.

"Harjula, listen—"

"Happiness . . . it's a bitch."

Harjula's interruption instantly makes Yusuf regret his impulse toward empathy.

"I just heard some other filthy-rich bastard tried to ice himself this morning," Harjula continues absentmindedly. "They found him in his whirlpool tub on Tähtitorninkatu, with an empty prescription vial bobbing in the water. . . ."

Fast as lightning, Yusuf looks up from his watch. Something lurches in his stomach: either the spicy wing sauce or what Harjula just said. "What? What filthy-rich bastard?"

"I don't remember the name. Apparently he lives alone in a huge place in that building that was gutted a few years ago, the one that used to house a private tennis court and a YLE studio. After the remodel, the prices of those places soared to around one point five." Harjula shakes his head gravely, then glances over his shoulder, presumably to catch the server's attention. When there's no sign of her, he turns his massive chest back to Yusuf and continues: "He was lying there in luke-warm water, ready to check out. Texted his sister to come get the dog. He had some huge dog barking in there."

"What?" Harjula's final sentence has nudged Yusuf's thoughts into motion. "A big dog?" He sits up straighter. "What kind of dog?"

Harjula frowns with a tinge of the familiar smugness. "What do you mean, what kind of dog?"

"What kind of dog did he have?"

"How would I know what kind of dog it was? A big dog."

Yusuf leans across the table and meets his colleague's bewildered look.

"Were you asleep during the briefing or something?" Yusuf says excitedly, pulling his phone from his pocket. "The night of Zetterborg's murder, Joonas Lamberg told us about someone walking a dog who was standing there at the corner of the little park. And shouted something just as Lamberg stepped out of the car." Yusuf stands. "We talked about it last night; we were all there."

"Do you think—"

"Do I think?" Yusuf snaps in frustration. "Can we afford to think anything, huh? Afford not to take a look at this card?" Yusuf grabs his coat from the back of the chair. "A dog owner's suicide attempt a stone's throw from Zetterborg's apartment. How the fuck am I only finding out about this now?"

Jami lowers his dazed eyes to his empty glass. "Sorry. It didn't occur to me—"

"Fuck, Harjula. Where did you hear about this?"

"Holopainen from Narcotics."

"So is the guy alive?"

"That was my impression."

"Call Holopainen right now and get us all the info on that case. You and I are heading to the hospital to pay him a visit."

61

"Jump in, Jessica," a female voice says.

Jessica feels her breath catch. The wet street absorbs the dim light of the streetlamps, but she still recognizes the wizened, liver-spotted face. The sunken cheeks look as if they belong to the living dead, which is basically what this old woman is, a nightmarish memory from her previous life: someone who is supposed to be gone. If not dead, then at least somewhere far, far away.

Jessica's heart is galloping. Her entire body is screaming for her to turn and flee, to run for her life.

And yet as on so many occasions before, something within her resists.

It's not that simple. Nothing is.

Jessica shuts her eyes and wishes the car would disappear, and the old woman with it. But it doesn't.

A mild-mannered blond man has appeared at Jessica's side. She has seen him somewhere before. He opens the back door of the Mercedes, and Camilla Adlerkreutz makes room for Jessica by laboriously inching over into the neighboring seat.

"There's no point running, Jessica dear. Besides, you don't even want to."

"You . . . ," Jessica whispers. She tastes the salt of tears at the corner of her mouth.

Now Jessica realizes the man is the one she saw at the door to her building this morning.

Her heart is still hammering, but her mind is blank.

There's not a soul in the dark street; the streetlamps hanging over it dance in the wind. Jessica is alone, unarmed, and, with her arm in a sling, completely unable to defend herself.

Adlerkreutz flashes her simpering smile. "I went away for a moment. And I came back for your sake, because of what you did."

And then it all flashes past Jessica's eyes. *The car crash, the inheritances, the Niemis, Venice, Colombano, Erne, her mother's cold, gasping breath, the dozens of murder investigations, and last of all, Camilla Adlerkreutz and the witches.*

"I don't want to," Jessica says, and finds herself trembling.

Jessica knows she's stronger, knows that under no circumstances must she obey the old woman extending a bony hand from the depths of the car. But something about the world into which the old woman beckons Jessica exerts a pull on her. It's a place no one can escape, a place where all bad things must be faced.

Suddenly Jessica feels a push at her back, and she is steered roughly into the back seat. She has the impulse to shout, to shriek, but all that erupts from her throat is a dry rasp.

And then the world goes black.

62

YUSUF NERVOUSLY DRUMS his fingers against the dash and glances at his wrist to check the time. Harjula, who is sitting in the passenger seat, is on the phone and writing down what he hears in a little notebook.

"The guy's name is Hjalmar Ek, forty-seven years old," Harjula says when he finally lowers the phone from his ear. "According to the register at the Kennel Association, he owns a three-year-old apricot fawn English mastiff."

Yusuf sighs. "What the fuck is apricot fawn? Is that the same as beige?"

"How would I know?" Harjula says. "What color is apricot?"

"Google it."

Jami Harjula looks at Yusuf for a second, then starts tapping at his phone's screen with his massive fingers.

"Joonas Lamberg said last night that he didn't recognize the breed but the dog was big and beige," Yusuf says, pulling up to a crosswalk where an old couple with their rollators is waiting to cross.

"An English mastiff can easily weigh two hundred pounds," Harjula mumbles. "And Holopainen said the dog found at Hjalmar Ek's home was really damn huge."

"But is it beige?"

"Wait a sec."

"Isn't apricot the same as beige, or at least close?"

"Well, that's what it looks like. At least in the dark, I'd imagine."

"It has to be the same guy," Yusuf says, turns the wheel, and steps on the gas to circle around the old couple, who have only made it halfway across the intersection. "Anything else?"

"Unmarried . . . significant capital gains. No criminal record. That's it."

"OK, call Nina and ask her to go through anything she can get her hands on about the guy. There's no goddamn way it's a coincidence that he was seen shrieking a hundred yards from the crime scene just a moment before the murder. And then the same guy is found practically dead the next morning in his whirlpool tub," Yusuf says.

"On the other hand, if anyone has an alibi for the time of the murder, it's him," Harjula says, searching his contacts for Nina's number.

"Does and doesn't," Yusuf says. "He disappeared from view before Lamberg walked Zetterborg up to his door. Whoever it was who killed the big boss a moment later, he must have slipped in through the other entrance. He could have easily dropped his dog off at home and circled the block to Vuorimiehenkatu."

Harjula nods reluctantly and lifts his phone to his ear.

"And, Harjula . . . ," Yusuf continues even though he can already hear Nina's voice on the line.

"What?"

"We need to show Hjalmar Ek's passport photo to the owner of Hobby Sammy."

63

NINA RUSKA EXITS police headquarters through the side door. She zips up her coat, even though it's only thirty feet to the bus stop across the street. She's on the verge of running a few steps to beat a red delivery truck approaching the intersection, then changes her mind and waits.

I can't be in such a hurry that I'm going to risk getting hit by a truck.

A moment later, she opens the door of a dark blue Audi SQ5 and slides into the leather passenger seat.

She finds herself holding Tom's face in her hands and smiling when she feels his tongue against her teeth.

"I had to see you," Tom says when she finally pulls her lips away from his.

"I'm glad you did." Nina withdraws slowly to her seat. "But I'm really busy with work. And I probably will be tomorrow too."

"An hour. I'll bring you back here to this exact same place," Tom says.

Nina laughs. Tom's dark hair is curly, and his facial stubble is sliced by an old scar from an ice skate, or so he told her last time they met.

"Impossible," Nina says, pronouncing the word the French way.

Tom feigns over-the-top disappointment but has clearly accepted her answer. "OK."

"But thanks for coming by to see me."

"Tell me a little something about the case."

Tom turns on his hazard lights. A bus is approaching the stop.

Nina feels the heat in her cheeks as quickly as it appears there. "Why?"

"Of course I want to know if I need to be worried," Tom says playfully. "You remember how I told you we've been really slammed at work lately?"

Nina eyes Tom, trying to decide if he's serious. "Yes."

"We performed a due diligence check for the component company RealEst bought the day before yesterday. At the same time, we strongly recommended the closing of the Kouvola factory. I'm just thinking as the CEO of HCG I might also be in the hot seat if there's some serial killer on the loose who's going around murdering—"

"Are you serious?" Nina says, watching the bus zoom past.

They've known each other for only three weeks, and Nina hasn't fully understood what it is that Tom's consulting firm actually does. But she isn't bothered by whatever happened behind closed doors at HCG; she's bothered by the fact Tom might not have sped out to see her simply because he missed her.

Silence has fallen over the car. An explosives warning from a construction site intensifies and climaxes in a dull rumble.

Eventually, Tom laughs. "Of course not. Or, I mean, yeah, we handled the DD, but I came here to bring you back to my place in Punavuori."

Nina feels his lips against hers. She is overcome by relief, and once again the touch feels indescribably good.

"Come on."

"No."

Tom strokes Nina's hair and gives her a kiss on the forehead. "Once you get this investigation out of the way, there's someone I'd like you to meet. There's no rush."

Nina thinks she knows to whom Tom is referring, but the notion feels a little premature. "So you mean—"

"I know it's early. But life is short. Besides, he's a great guy. I'm sure you two will get along."

"It's been three weeks, Tom."

"He's a good boy. Or man, I guess. He's nineteen."

"Well, if you think it's a good idea . . ."

Tom's gaze shifts to the rearview mirror. Nina glances back and sees another bus approaching from the distance.

"I do. But take your time; think about it."

Tom pulls back to his seat and starts the car with a button on the dash. His expression is calm and loving.

"OK. As long as your ex isn't there. Your hairy friend can come."

Tom doesn't seem to immediately understand what Nina's talking about.

"The dog you're watching," she clarifies.

Tom bursts into laughter. "Exactly. Right. You can meet both boys at the same time."

NINA STANDS THERE watching the Audi speeding away to make room for the stopping bus. She can taste Tom's aftershave in her mouth and smell his hair in her nostrils. Her body is pulsating. She should have gone with him after all.

Now she has to get back to work.

She reads the text message Rasmus sent her a moment ago.

No phones belonging to anyone we're looking at were near Munkkiniemi at the time of Erik Raulo's murder.

She shoves her phone in her pocket and steps into the roadway. Then she sees Niklas Fischer standing across the street, apparently staring in her direction. When he spots Nina, he quickly looks down and saunters slowly away.

64

THE SHARP SMELL of disinfectant hangs in the air. Yusuf and Jami Harjula walk the hospital's long, sterile green-and-white corridor, where halfway down a bearded man in a white coat is leaning against a nurses' station. When they get within earshot, Yusuf realizes he's seen the doctor before.

"Hello," the doctor says, holding his small tablet computer to his stomach. "Alex Kuznetsov, chief physician."

"We've met before," Yusuf says, but there's no reaction to be read in Kuznetsov's impassive face. It's as neutral as a blank sheet of paper. And then Yusuf suddenly remembers: "A year ago, when we brought in the woman saved from the ice."

Kuznetsov concedes a slight nod. "Exactly. That was a rather unhappy case," he says, and raises his eyes to Harjula, who towers over both men and still appears to be ashamed it didn't occur to him to link Hjalmar Ek's suicide attempt to Zetterborg's murder.

Yusuf smoked a cigarette on the way to the car and popped a few pieces of salted licorice gum, but the smell of stale booze is still detectable. It must be coming from Harjula. Maybe the pint wasn't his first today.

"I was informed you would be visiting," Kuznetsov continues, scratching his coarse-looking beard. "But I don't quite grasp why detectives from the felony unit are coming to talk to a patient who overdosed on antidepressants. Do you suspect a crime of some sort has taken place?"

"There's not necessarily anything suspicious involved in the suicide attempt," Yusuf says, slipping his fingers into his pocket to retrieve a fresh piece of gum. Maybe he if chomps on the pungent gum, the doctor won't notice that Harjula stinks of booze. "But we're investigating a crime that took place in the vicinity, and we need to confirm a few things. Is it possible to talk to the patient now?"

Kuznetsov eyes the detectives. His expression speaks of skepticism or perhaps professional curiosity. "Is the name of the victim in this case you're investigating by any chance Eliel Zetterborg?"

"Unfortunately I can't give you any details," Yusuf says, and pops the piece of gum into his mouth.

"Oh, you can't, can't you?" Kuznetsov chuckles without so much as a flicker of a smile at the corners of his mouth. "So, based on this incomplete information, I'm supposed to decide whether I ought to let you see the patient. Shaky, I'd say. Very shaky indeed."

Yusuf looks at the doctor, the strip of thick neck visible under the stethoscope, the powerful arms. Now he remembers the head doctor, with his steady, self-satisfied voice, was anything but cooperative the last time too. Maybe a cop screwed his wife once or something. Yusuf is overwhelmed by the sudden temptation to ask Kuznetsov directly if that's the case.

Breathe. Don't say anything stupid or it's a wrap.

There's no point in arm wrestling with the doc who's the gatekeeper; it would serve only to further complicate things. And in the end, the chief physician is presumably just living by his professional ethics, which demand the patient's well-being take precedence over everything else.

"Fine," Yusuf says. "Between us, it's possible that the patient might have seen something related to the Eliel Zetterborg case while he was outside yesterday evening."

Kuznetsov's stony face looks jubilant, if detecting such emotions there is even possible. "Is that so?" he says, and activates his tablet with a quick finger swipe on the screen.

Yusuf nods.

"The patient had his stomach pumped this morning and under the circumstances is doing well. But I'm a little concerned about the heart. An overdose of tricyclics can easily lead to cardiac trouble. The patient's blood pressure is extremely low, and he is suffering from arrhythmia and conduction disorders, so under no circumstances must he suffer shock. The consequences could be fatal. Do you understand?"

"I understand," Yusuf says.

"But do you really understand?" Kuznetsov says with a satisfied smack of his lips—as if he is savoring the quip he just uttered—and adjusts his eyeglasses. "You have to treat him delicately."

"We will," Yusuf says, and points at the corridor questioningly.

"Well, maybe just this once. Room 319," Kuznetsov says. "A nurse is going by regularly to make sure he doesn't try to harm himself again. But right now it's unlikely he has the strength for such exertions."

"Thank you." Yusuf glares at the doctor as he steps past him, Harjula at his side.

They make it about fifteen feet down the green-and-white corridor before Yusuf hears the bearded doctor's patronizing voice again.

"Good luck. I hope one of you knows sign language."

Yusuf spins on his heels. The unpleasant sensation that they are yet again one step behind washes over him. "What do you mean?"

Kuznetsov flashes a gleefully malevolent smile, which he appears to have saved for this moment, the grand finale.

"The patient is unable to hear or speak."

65

YUSUF LEANS HIS hands against the windowsill and gazes out at the gray-washed neighborhood of Meilahti and its red-roofed apartment buildings, over which darkness drew its daily curtain some time ago. The light snowfall hasn't turned the ground white yet, and it looks as slippery and shimmery as a dolphin's back. The afternoon commute has begun, and an endless line of mud- and salt-grimed cars is striving westward on Tukholmankatu toward the Turku Expressway.

Yusuf and Harjula have settled in at the end of the corridor to wait for the sign language interpreter to arrive. Yusuf tried to call Jessica to report this latest twist in the case, but she didn't answer.

"How much longer?" Yusuf says, noting that his salted licorice gum has lost its flavor over the eternity of the past fifteen minutes. The interpreter was supposed to have been right there, but apparently the guy got caught up chatting—or signing—with someone.

Harjula shrugs and glances at the white clock on the wall. "He'll probably be here soon."

"Damn it," Yusuf says, stretches his stiff neck, and steps up to Harjula, who is standing next to the drinking fountain.

Farther down the corridor, two nurses are pushing a hospital bed toward the elevators. Faint crying can be heard coming from somewhere.

"Hjalmar Ek is our man. Faust," Yusuf says, hands on his hips. "The guy from Hobby Sammy said he came in to order a puzzle without saying a word. . . . He wrote down what he wanted on a piece of paper. It didn't occur to me before, but the reason he didn't talk was simply that he couldn't."

"Sanni Karppinen's story also matches," Harjula says.

"Exactly," Yusuf says, and looks at the number on the door: 319.

"As soon as the interpreter gets here, we need to . . ." Yusuf licks his dry lips before continuing. "Goddamn it, I don't know what the best strategy is. It's clear Ek ordered the puzzle and tied the cleaner to the bed, took the keys, stabbed Zetterborg with a knife. . . . We just need to get him to confess to everything without his heart giving out."

"What about Raulo?" Harjula says. "Ek texted his sister at nine fifty-five this morning. Would he have had time to go out to Munkkiniemi and shoot Raulo before the pangs of guilt set in and he tried to kill himself?"

"We'll get a more accurate time of death for Raulo later," Yusuf says. "But right now it looks like he was shot early this morning. That's indicated by the burned toast we found on the counter. You're the one who said the son said his dad ate breakfast at eight every day."

"So it all adds up," Harjula says.

Yusuf sees that Alex Kuznetsov has appeared at the nurses' station again and has trained his keen eyes on the police officers pacing restlessly at the end of the corridor.

"It's a weird way to try to kill yourself," Harjula says. "My understanding is that tricyclics are almost never prescribed anymore because the side effects are so severe. My mom took them for years, up to her dying day, even though her doctor kept trying to get her to switch to something newer."

Yusuf eyes his colleague, who has once again given something new and unexpected of himself. It's as if the purpose of this little tête-à-tête is to let Yusuf know why Harjula is the way he is and provide a human explanation for his sometimes intolerable behavior.

The thought of asking Harjula about his mother, maybe about her tragic battle with depression, crosses Yusuf's mind, but he decides not to venture down that path. This time, a few seconds of silence and an empathetic look will have to do.

"What do you think we can infer from that?" Yusuf asks.

"Well, I'm no expert, but if Ek had sought help recently for depression, I think we can assume he wouldn't have been prescribed tricyclics."

"And so . . ."

"And so I think he's been suffering from depression for years. Maybe decades. And in that case, maybe his medication wasn't updated at his own request."

Yusuf nods. The theory makes sense. Harjula is doing good work to compensate for choking earlier.

"Text that thought to Rasmus," Yusuf says. "And also that Ek is deaf and mute."

Harjula pulls his phone out of his coat pocket. "Of course, it's possible he wasn't depressed at all and got the medication somewhere else," he says as he taps out the text message.

"We won't have to guess for long," Yusuf says. "If we have probable cause to suspect Hjalmar Ek of Zetterborg's murder, the hospital will have to turn over his medical records."

"Or else he'll just tell us himself if we ever get in to talk to him."

And then they see a young man in white trousers and a red sweater emerge from the elevator and walk to the nurses' station. Kuznetsov turns and points in their direction.

"There's our interpreter," Yusuf says, and plucks the wad of gum from his tongue and wraps it in a bit of foil.

66

JESSICA OPENS HER eyes. Her mouth feels dry and her head aches ferociously.

The sight that gradually opens before her convinces her this is a dream—a ghastly memory welling up from the depths of her subconscious, forcing her to relive past horrors.

"I've missed you, Jessica," a harsh voice says.

Jessica tries to move but finds her wrists and ankles are tightly bound to the wooden chair where she sits. Her lip is split; she can taste blood. The hum at the ceiling must be from a fan or a heater.

She looks around and sees wavy concrete walls and a low ceiling. The space smells damp and musty. *Some sort of cellar.*

And then the old woman appears in Jessica's field of vision, led by a large man. Camilla Adlerkreutz has aged considerably since their last encounter; her gaze is weary and she has dark circles under her eyes.

"Do you ever regret it?"

"Regret what?" Jessica says. She knows her life is in immediate danger, but something deep inside orders her to remain calm. To listen to what the old devil has to say.

"Not joining us."

"I don't remember ever discussing the matter with you."

Camilla Adlerkreutz chuckles gently, then steps closer and grazes Jessica's cheek with her bony fingers. "There was no need, Jessica dear. I saw immediately you were not the one to carry on my story. You are too weak, just like your mother, who refused to join us. You were too weak then and you are too weak now. My successor must be strong of mind. At one time I thought it would be you. I hoped it would be, but ..."

Jessica focuses her eyes on the back wall and the red and yellow jars on the shelf there.

"Is that what your murderous cult was? Strong of mind?"

"It takes a strong will to change the world, Jessica." Camilla Adlerkreutz looks dissatisfied. "Not all of us have what it takes to spark the great revolution. Last winter our word spread across the world like quicksilver. It ignited a few flames here and there, but it did not achieve the sort of global conflagration I had hoped for: a series of ritual murders that would rouse the world from the corrupt torpor it's wallowing in."

"You're fucking crazy, Adlerkreutz." For some reason it pains Jessica to utter the words.

The old woman laughs drily. The veiny fingers gripping the head of her cane are trembling. Her life is coming to its end.

"You see it," Adlerkreutz says as if she's read Jessica's thoughts. "I am dying. Maybe tomorrow, maybe not for another month. But that's precisely why you and I are here in this room: we are going to settle accounts while we still can."

"Let me have it, then—"

Jessica's words are cut off by a fist punching into her diaphragm with incredible force. She gasps for breath, and bile sprays down the front of her coat.

67

ONE OF THE fluorescent tubes in the conference room has decided to rebel against its monotonous task and flickers restlessly.

Nina Ruska swipes her fingertips up the screen: gray and green speech bubbles flash before her eyes like a fast-forwarded movie. For some reason she has an obsessive need to find the message Tom sent that made her heart leap. The one that said something about *You're the kind of woman I'm in a hurry to get to know.* Or something like that. The two of them have exchanged hundreds of text messages during the course of their three-week relationship, which started off as a Tinder date, so tracking down this one message is tough. Especially since Nina doesn't remember how he phrased it, which would make it possible to use the search function. But she wants to read the message again right now, see the winking heart emojis at the end, and feel the emotional charge it carries. The message was somehow so honest and spontaneous; it might be the most beautiful thing anyone has said to her in ages—although the sentiment arrived in the form of a WhatsApp message.

She needs confirmation for her feelings, because doubt has been gnawing at her since Tom's pit stop. Maybe it's the way he talked about his work. Did the consultant jargon Tom spew open up a chasm between them? Or maybe the joke about the serial killer wasn't funny to Nina after all. Was it even a joke in the end? And is meeting Tom's adult son after dating for three weeks really a good idea?

Maybe that's exactly why Nina is looking for the old message now, because she senses something is off. Or maybe it's more that a three-week relationship isn't long enough for something to be off. Did Yusuf's calls last night really make Tom jealous, or does Nina just secretly wish they did?

"Nina?" Rasmus' voice cuts into Nina's thoughts, and she abruptly sets down her phone.

"How's it going, Rasse?"

"Sorry. Did I interrupt something?"

Nina shakes her head and feels slight shame at having dedicated two five-minute stints to analyzing her love life in the middle of an intense information search. First by going down to see Tom on the street and then by browsing through old text messages.

"No, you didn't." Nina turns to her computer.

"Have we heard from the hobby shop guy?"

"No." Nina glances at her watch. "I'll have to go over and talk to him if we don't hear from him soon. Yusuf said it's really important."

"OK." Rasmus massages his bald spot with two fingers. "This Hjalmar Ek is an interesting case."

"How so?"

"It's hard to draw any definitive conclusions without his medical records, but something clearly went awry at some point."

"What do you mean?"

"Born in 1973, raised in a Swedish-speaking home, has lived in southern Helsinki all his life: first with his parents in Etu-Töölö, then in Ullanlinna, and finally Eira up to 1991, when he became a legal adult. He moved into his own apartment almost right next door to his parents, then in 1999 to Kaivopuisto and eventually, two years ago, to Tähtitorninmäki. No income from work over that entire period; he has some capital gains but not enough to fund a lifestyle like that, not even close."

"So his parents have supported him his whole life? Or did he receive an inheritance?"

"Hjalmar Ek did receive an inheritance—or at least part of one—but not until 2009, when his father, Gunnar Ek, died. And from what I can tell, the father's estate was pretty substantial."

"You just said something went wrong. . . ."

"Right . . . Hjalmar Ek attended high school at Norsen but never graduated. I think that's pretty odd, considering his background. In comparison, his little sister graduated from the same high school and seems to have had an impressive career in business, while Hjalmar never got his graduation cap and never worked a day in his life." Rasmus scratches the corner of his mouth and continues: "Harjula texted me that he's unable to hear or speak and apparently has been on antidepressants for years. Sounds like he's had some challenges."

"Would it have been possible for a kid who can't hear or speak to attend Norsen in the late eighties?"

Rasmus shakes his head. "I'm not sure. We need to look into that. It's possible, of course, that high school was too much for him, and that's why he's depressed." He lets out a deflated sigh.

"What is it?"

"All this speculation is pointless until we get our hands on Ek's epicrisis."

"What about the parents? Did you find anything interesting there?"

Rasmus gnaws on his thumbnail for a moment. Then he lowers his laptop to the table, and his fingers begin flying across the keyboard.

"Gunnar Ek . . . Gunnar Ek . . . born 1944 . . ."

Nina studies Rasmus' look of concentration, and her thoughts wander off to Tom and his adult son again. To the fact that Tom's consultancy performed a due diligence for RealEst and recommended the closing of the Kouvola factory. That's quite a coincidence.

"Nina!" The excited squeal from Rasmus rouses Nina from her thoughts. "This just got wild. I found some old news stories. . . . Hjalmar's deceased father . . . Gunnar Ek . . ."

"What is it, Rasse?"

Nina feels the suspense spread to her fingertips over the course of the few seconds it takes Rasmus to work up the courage to open his mouth again.

"Gunnar Ek worked at RealEst for decades."

68

THE MAN IN the red turtleneck mumbled his name so softly that Yusuf didn't catch it. The interpreter, who is clearly under thirty, knocks on the door to the hospital room, then understands that maybe the gesture is unnecessary and tentatively cracks the door.

"It looks like he's awake," he says softly, and opens the door wide, allowing Yusuf and Harjula to pass him and enter.

Yusuf steps into the room and stops at a respectful distance from the hospital bed, where a feeble-looking man is lying under light blue covers. A cannula has been inserted into the back of the hand resting on the chest, and oxygen whiskers have been plugged into his nostrils.

Yusuf shoots a glance at Harjula, who stands at his side, arms folded across his chest like a bouncer.

Rasmus called just a moment ago to report the latest twist that links Hjalmar Ek's father to the industry magnate's murder last night. The link can be considered obvious enough that Yusuf has asked Hellu to send someone to the hospital to guard the suspect's door.

Hjalmar Ek is a slightly overweight man, around fifty, with a scraggly beard and a curving scar running from under his jaw to behind his ear. Yusuf cannot help but think that even though the scar is large enough to be visible, it would be relatively easy to hide if he wore a beanie and a scarf. Exactly the way the guy from Hobby Sammy said the customer who ordered the puzzle had been dressed, even though it hadn't been particularly cold outside.

The interpreter circles around them, then plants himself between the bed and the window, in a spot where it's possible for all parties to see and hear him at the same time.

"Would you please tell him we're from the police . . . ?" Yusuf stops when he sees the interpreter start to sign.

"Go ahead and talk," the interpreter says calmly. "I can keep up."

"Oh right," Yusuf says, embarrassed, and clears his throat with an audible cough. "We have a few questions for you related to last night and this morning."

The interpreter lowers his hands only a second after Yusuf stops talking, and it takes Yusuf a moment to collect his thoughts. The speed of the signing has caught him completely off guard. He looks back and forth between Hjalmar Ek lying in the bed and the interpreter, but nothing happens.

The interpreter signs at the patient again.

"He's not answering," he says.

Hjalmar Ek turns his tired eyes toward Yusuf but doesn't give the slightest indication of signing what he has to say—if he even plans to, that is.

"Tell the patient," Yusuf begins authoritatively, and takes a step closer to the bed, "that we have probable cause to suspect him of being involved in Eliel Zetterborg's death."

The interpreter obeys, but Ek's face doesn't so much as twitch.

Yusuf feels himself growing irritated. Instead of pity, he feels some sort of sprouting disgust for the figure reclining in the bed. He takes another step closer to emphasize his message but still speaks steadily, even though he knows Ek can't hear him. This time he directs his words at Ek, not the interpreter.

"Someone is going to be coming here soon to take your finger-prints and a DNA sample. Refusing will be viewed as supporting your culpability."

Hjalmar Ek doesn't turn his gaze to the interpreter, even though the latter has begun signing.

"He's not looking at you," Yusuf says. The situation has really started to piss him off, and it's audible in his voice, whether he likes it or not.

"He doesn't need to. I think he can read lips," the interpreter says, lowering his hands to his sides.

Yusuf pulls over a chair for himself and sits three feet away from the bed so his eyes and Ek's eyes are at the same height.

"Hjalmar Ek, nod if you understand me."

For a moment it seems as if Ek doesn't mean to reply, and Yusuf starts to wonder if he's all there after all. His blank eyes remind Yusuf of a salmon taken from the Sipoonjoki River. But then the eyelids close, the little muscles around them tense, and the face suddenly looks sad.

Ek nods and opens his eyes with effort.

"Good. Thank you," Yusuf says.

The interpreter has become aware of his superfluousness and holds his hands behind his back. Meanwhile, Harjula hasn't budged during the past few minutes; he stands there like a bronze statue.

"The interpreter is here so you can tell us what you know about what happened last night, OK?"

Hjalmar Ek nods again, but his eyes are wandering around the room.

"I know you aren't doing very well, but the sooner we get everything we need, the sooner you can get back to recuperating. We don't want to bother you any longer than necessary. All we want is the truth. Now, I'm going to ask a few questions I need you to answer. Nod or shake your head."

At that moment, the door opens behind them and Alex Kuznetsov steps in, tablet under his arm. Goddamned bloodsucker. Yusuf sees the doctor shut the door behind him and lean against it. Yusuf decides to ignore the chief physician and turns back to Hjalmar Ek.

"Were you walking your dog in Ullanpuistikko around six last night?"

Ek looks Yusuf in the eye and nods.

Yusuf feels adrenaline surge through his veins. They're getting somewhere. "Did you order a puzzle from Hobby Sammy using the name Faust?"

Ek shuts his eyes for a few seconds.

The only sound in the room is the hum of the devices monitoring Ek's vitals.

Yusuf holds his breath. His heart has started pounding in his chest.

Eventually Ek nods. A tear trickles down his cheek.

"Good. This is going really well. Did you force your way into Eliel Zetterborg's cleaner's apartment, tie her to her bed, and take the key to Zetterborg's home?" And now that he sees the man's pain-distorted face up close, Yusuf realizes his anger has turned to pity.

Ek nods and blinks his moist eyes.

"Were you in Eliel Zetterborg's home last night? Did you kill Eliel Zetterborg?"

Ek's exhaustion-numbed face twists up tearfully.

"Just answer this last question. Then it's over, Hjalmar."

The weeping gradually escalates, then turns to uncontrollable sobbing.

"That's enough," Kuznetsov says curtly. "We had a deal that you would under no circumstances upset the patient!"

Yusuf hears the chief physician move behind him and tell the interpreter to leave. Harjula, who hasn't said a single word since he set foot in the room, does his part and starts offering a cocktail of explanations about how important it is to finish the interrogation and gets a frosty response from the chief physician.

"Did you hear me, Hjalmar? I want the truth," Yusuf continues even though he feels Kuznetsov's fingers on his shoulder. They're like the talons of a ravenous vulture. "Did you kill him?" Yusuf asks again.

"Don't you understand Finnish?" Kuznetsov snaps when Yusuf shakes off his hand.

Call security. At this rate these idiots are going to kill the patient. . . .

The interpreter slips out of the room, alarmed. Ek is now weeping uncontrollably.

The situation is escalating into a conflict between the police and the hospital staff, and at the center of it all is a patient who has caused himself serious harm, whose head Yusuf wants to see moving one more time, in one direction or the other.

Kuznetsov grabs Yusuf's shoulder again, this time more firmly. "This is about the patient's heart, which is—"

"Get your fucking hand off me," Yusuf says, and springs to his feet so fast that the chief doctor is startled and takes a few backward steps toward the door.

All the stress that has accumulated during the last twenty-four hours erupts in one slow sentence. "Do—not—touch—me," Yusuf says between gritted teeth. His brain is working at full steam to restrain the impulses that occur to him. He feels like slamming Kuznetsov into the door and knocking the wind out of him.

Kuznetsov looks frightened; apparently he didn't expect this sort of aggression from a police officer.

Yusuf raises a finger. "Stay there."

Then he leans down again, with his face close to Ek's. "Tell me, Hjalmar. Was it you?"

He can smell Ek's perspiration.

Ek shuts his eyes, pinches the lids into tight lines, and when he opens them again, they tell the answer.

"No," Ek says, mangling the long vowel with his mouth open too wide, as if he is speaking for the first time in years, which apparently is the case.

Yusuf nods quickly and takes Ek gently by the hand. "Good, Hjalmar. I believe you. Who did it?" Yusuf says, offering Ek a pen and his notepad.

But Ek makes no sign of reaching for them.

Yusuf glances at the bedside monitor: the patient's pulse has clearly accelerated.

"Who was it, Hjalmar? Write the name here," Yusuf whispers, and at that moment the door opens and two big men rush in, whose touch isn't as gentle as the chief physician's.

But before Yusuf lets himself be led out by the security guards, he casts one last look at the patient, who is crying inconsolably in his bed and hasn't answered the most important question of all.

69

"WHAT PART OF what I said about the patient's heart didn't you understand?" Alex Kuznetsov hisses, cheeks blazing with rage.

Yusuf looks into the agitated doctor's eyes; he can hear Harjula explaining to the security guards that they're police officers investigating a murder.

"I'm sorry I lost my temper," Yusuf says, raising his hands in a truce.

He isn't genuinely sorry—just the opposite as a matter of fact—but a conflict with the physician attending to Ek is truly not going to make it any easier to get the medical records or arrange the next interrogation. And that's why Yusuf has to shift gears into diplomacy.

"Too late, Pepple. I'm going to report you," Kuznetsov says, turning up his nose. "You disobeyed my instructions and risked the patient's health. In addition, you behaved threateningly toward the staff. Never in my career have I seen such behavior within the walls of this hospital, especially from a representative of law enforcement."

Yusuf clenches his fists; his temples are pulsing with rage. Anna is lurking in his frontal lobe, along with the lion-maned stallion wrapping his arms around her pregnant belly. "I'm really sorry."

Kuznetsov starts tapping away furiously at his tablet, muttering about the unbelievable indifference of the police.

"Come on. I said I'm sorry," Yusuf says.

"And I said it's too late."

"Listen, Kuznetsov," Yusuf says, fingers pressed to his forehead.

"Don't turn this into some sort of crusade. You want to save people here, and I'm trying to do the same thing outside this hospital. We have reason to believe that whoever took Eliel Zetterborg's life can do it again. That's why we have to get more information as quickly as possible. At least one life is on the line!"

Alex Kuznetsov raises his incensed gaze from his tablet and eyes Yusuf probingly.

The elevators halfway down the corridor open, and two patients in beds are pushed out.

"I don't know how much you just overheard . . . ," Yusuf says, now in an intentionally low voice. He picked up this trick in a course on negotiating skills: leaning in toward the other party and lowering your voice to give them the illusion of confidential information and complete trust. Yusuf just isn't sure if such tricks are any use on the vigilant chief physician. "The patient just admitted he aided someone in carrying out the murder of Eliel Zetterborg."

"As I recall, his answer wasn't quite that direct."

"Ek admitted to having taken action that made it possible to break into Zetterborg's home. In addition, he bought something that was later found at the crime scene. The only thing he denied being involved in was the killing itself." Yusuf is getting the sense confiding in Kuznetsov is the only way to move forward.

"Regardless, the patient was far too shocked for you to continue," Kuznetsov eventually says.

"I understand. But I hope you understand we have to find out the name of the guilty party. And the man in that room knows it," Yusuf says, pointing firmly at the closed door.

Kuznetsov takes a deep breath. "And you truly believe someone else's life is in danger?"

"There is absolutely no doubt."

"I was serious about what I said about the patient's heart. It can give out from emotional strain, and if that happens, you won't have anything."

"All we want is the name," Yusuf says.

Kuznetsov closes the cover of his tablet. "Fine. Sixty minutes."

"What?" Yusuf exclaims in surprise.

"You can continue questioning him in an hour." Kuznetsov nods at Harjula. "And he's going to do it."

Yusuf is about to protest but then raises his hands to indicate he accepts the terms. "Wonderful. Thank you."

"Remember that I will call off the session immediately if the patient's heart rate rises too high," Kuznetsov says drily, and directs one of the security guards to stand outside Hjalmar Ek's door. "And I'm still going to report you. Truly vulgar behavior."

At the same moment the elevator doors open, and a big man in jeans and a blazer walks toward them. Yusuf and Harjula look on as he stops outside the door to room 319 without saying a word. This has to be the guy Security and Intelligence Services sent. It's a funny sight: one guard on either side of the door as if the room is Checkpoint Charlie.

Yusuf's phone rings. "Hey, Nina!"

"We've been going through Gunnar Ek's history. He played a significant role at Zetterborg's company for decades."

"So he's dead?"

"Yup. Years ago. Which in a way supports the theory that he could be the third man in the photograph. I guess the idea here is that all of them are dead now, not so much how and when it happened," Nina says.

"I need to show the picture to Hjalmar. We'll be able to talk to him in an hour at the earliest, if then," Yusuf says.

For a moment there's silence on the line. Yusuf hears furious tapping in the background and Rasmus' unintelligible voice.

"What if . . . ," Nina then says. "What if I talked to Hjalmar's sister, Smilla, who found her brother in the bathtub? She might have something interesting to tell us."

Yusuf wishes Nina luck and hangs up.

He can sense his pulse in his ears.

Jessica.

Why hasn't he heard from Jessica?

70

1990

HJALMAR CURLS HIS toes inside his rubber boots; even with the wool socks, they're almost numb. He probably ought to go in and warm up for a bit, but the shot that rang out nearby has piqued his curiosity. Axel stands, takes a few steps toward the forest, and pricks up his ears for any other sounds carrying from its depths.

Then unintelligible shouts echo from the woods, and before Hjalmar has time to be truly alarmed that something awful has happened, the shouting mingles with squeals of exhilaration and laughter. The cries sound like those from a baseball game after a home run: they ring with elation, encouragement, and team spirit. And then it breaks through the other voices: Laura's bright whoop.

"They got a hare," Axel says, laughing and smacking his gloved hands together. "They got a fucking hare!"

"That was fast," Hans remarks. He tosses a log on the fire, where the brightly burning flames have faded to smoldering embers.

Hjalmar remembers what Axel said earlier in the cabin: this hunting trip isn't about the hares—they aren't the main event. Nonetheless, the party led by Eliel Zetterborg—which includes Laura—has bagged a hare. For some reason, Hjalmar is sure such rapid success is only going to even further intensify the urge to celebrate.

"You want one? Huh?"

Hjalmar feels a nudge at his shoulder and turns to see a beer at the end of Hans' extended arm.

"Umm, yeah. Thanks," Hjalmar says, clumsily opening the can with a forefinger encased in a fat ski glove.

Hans tosses a second can to Axel, who snatches it effortlessly from the air without taking an unnecessary side step.

"I think that's a record," Axel says, propping a foot against a big rock.

The trees carry the quartet's laughter all the way to the fire.

"Will they try to get another one?" Hans asks.

"Nah, they're headed this way," Axel replies self-confidently.

Peals of Laura's bright laughter again, this time closer. To Hjalmar's ears the sound is both beautiful and unpleasant: he has never made Laura laugh that way, at least not so uninhibitedly—as if she is able to release the steam compressed inside her only in the company of middle-aged men.

"What did I say?" Axel growls, takes a step backward toward the fire, and lights another cigarette. "Here they come."

Hans stands to get a better view of the figures that gradually appear from the forest's eaves. There's a squawk of louder laughter; Eliel Zetterborg is saying something, overjoyed, and Simo is romping at their legs, barking animatedly.

"You boys are never going to guess what just happened," Zetterborg shouts, moving aside a large spruce bough and knocking the snow from his boots against the packed surface of the plowed road.

"That was the fastest kill I've ever—," Axel says as Gunnar Ek and Erik Raulo emerge from the branches.

Only none of the men are carrying a dead hare, bird, or any other game.

"Where is . . . ?"

And then Laura steps onto the road from the deep snow, a white animal tossed over her back as if it is a luxurious collar from Grünstein's. In her other hand she dangles a shotgun, its barrel crusted white from brushing against the snow.

"Gentlemen," Zetterborg says, raising his hands to present Laura.

She is beaming, and the eyes above her red cheeks are twinkling with delight.

"Hell no," Axel says, bursting into incredulous laughter. "Are you saying—"

"Laura came, saw, and killed," Eliel Zetterborg says, and the men erupt in thunderous applause.

71

HJALMAR CHECKS HIS wrist for the time and realizes it's only five p.m. It seems like an eternity has passed since darkness fell around the fire.

He is appalled to discover Axel's predictions have come true. He is disgusted by the middle-aged men's raucous, drunken laughter, the hungry eyes licking Laura's body. But Laura seems amused by it all, and she appears to be having a great time.

Too great.

We'll discuss that some other time, Erik.

Hjalmar hears Eliel Zetterborg's ponderous voice from the cabin door. The adults stepped inside for a moment to go over something work related, but now they emerge, apparently meaning to return to the fire. Hjalmar turns to look at the small circle standing on the porch. Hjalmar's father is trying to light his pipe with little success; the box of matches falls to the ground.

"I'm just vexed you aren't considering my opinion. If you push this thing through too fast, the merger isn't an opportunity; it's a threat, plain and simple," Erik Raulo says, apparently thinking he's speaking softly enough that the young people sitting at the fire can't hear him. His speech is a little slurred, but his tone is resolute.

"As I said, Erik, this is neither the time nor the place. And when it comes to your shares, there's a clause in the articles of incorporation that clearly states how different classes of shares are treated. You were the one who drafted the damn document in the first place. There shouldn't be any surprises here," Eliel Zetterborg replies.

A bright light burns above the porch; Hjalmar can see the men's faces are grim.

"Fine, Eliel. We'll discuss this later. It's just sometimes—"

"It's just sometimes what?"

"I get the sense you don't value my opinion."

"Nonsense, Erik. Listen to this man, Gunnar. Now calm yourself, my good man, and let's have a drink."

"Exactly," Gunnar Ek chimes in like the miserable crony he is.

At that moment, Hjalmar is ashamed of his father, who appears to have zero will of his own. Hjalmar glances at Laura, Axel, and Hans, who are sitting across the campfire, but they don't seem to hear the men's conversation.

"Besides . . . ," Gunnar says. "I might have a little surprise for everyone."

"A surprise? Oh for goodness' sake." Zetterborg chuckles without taking take his eyes off Raulo.

Raulo nods and flashes a reluctant smile. Zetterborg squeezes his shoulders, shakes him with a gentle playfulness.

"OK," Raulo finally says.

A moment later, the trio sits down at the fire with the young people and the mood normalizes. Whatever that just was, it doesn't appear to have had any lingering effects.

The log Axel flings to the fire sends up sparks that look like a swarm of fireflies taking off in flight. Hjalmar lets his gaze travel across the men sitting on the reindeer hides. He can clearly see the smiles, the laugh wrinkles under the eyes; he can tell whom they're looking at. He can see the little looks containing a message encoded in microexpressions. *Now, that's an ass I'd like to screw.*

Of course no one says so out loud; the forced joviality hanging in the air is sustained by Hjalmar's presence alone. Even Gunnar, his father, having tossed back enough shots, has joined in the leering and the sleazy jokes.

"What's wrong, honey?" Laura's moist voice tickles Hjalmar's ear. She has somehow appeared on Hjalmar's lap and wrapped her arms around him. "Aren't you proud of your little bunny killer?"

"Of course," Hjalmar says, and receives a kiss on the mouth. Laura tastes of Jägermeister and cigarettes.

"I might come again sometime," Laura says, gently tugging on Hjalmar's earlobe. "As a matter of fact, I'd like to come today," she whispers, sending Hjalmar's heart galloping in his chest.

Hjalmar hears the men reminiscing about a trip to Saaremaa in the late seventies to hunt wild boar—the trip where everyone was so drunk, no one so much as spotted any animals—but he knows the attention is at least halfway on them: on him, the worst hunter in the world, and on beautiful Laura, who has surprised the whole group by shooting a hare on her first try.

"Did you hear me? Do you think maybe tonight is the night?" Laura whispers, giving Hjalmar a pointed look.

"Yeah," Hjalmar whispers hoarsely.

He knows he's lying. He can already tell it's not going to work out here in the woods, in a place where they have no privacy. They do have their own room in the cabin, but its paper-thin walls wouldn't block out any noises. Instead of Laura's moaning, everyone would hear hushed curses and excuses, the agonized admission that tonight wasn't the night after all.

"Let's get really drunk and then we'll do it," Laura whispers.

"Yeah," Hjalmar says again, trying to produce a smile.

He feels uncomfortable; Laura's bottom is pressing awkwardly against his nonexistent thigh muscle.

"Thanks for inviting me," Laura says, stroking Hjalmar's cheek. "I love you."

The utterance leaves Hjalmar's lips spontaneously; it's like a pail of water used to try to douse an uncontrolled fire. He truly means it: he loves Laura. He feels the emotion deeply; it's the desire to hold the other person close, own them, to be the only person in the whole world for them. And the fact that his inability to physically love Laura is ruining everything only makes him love her twice as hard.

Laura smiles broadly, revealing her beautiful white teeth, and pinches Hjalmar's nose.

"You're cute," she says, and climbs off his knee.

Hjalmar is overcome by dread that he and Laura have just orbited the moon and turned back toward Earth, and from here on out, it's all going to be downhill.

He is roused from his reverie by his father's voice; it's coming from the cars parked near the cabin.

"Ladies and gentlemen of the hunt," Gunnar Ek says, clearly intoxicated, "could I have your attention for a moment?"

"Oh yes, the surprise. What has that Gunnar come up with now?" Eliel says as he uncorks a vodka bottle.

Erik Raulo takes the bottle and pours shots into little birch-bark cups.

The trunk of the Mercedes whooshes shut.

Hjalmar watches his father; a wooden box has appeared in Gunnar's arms.

"What they say about Vegas goes for Ouninpohja too. What happens at the cabin stays at the cabin," Gunnar says, lowering the crate to the cabin's porch.

"What do you have there? Bring it here!" Eliel says.

Hjalmar's father turns toward the fire, and the tall, sparking flames illuminate his euphoric face. "No. These little babies don't do well with campfires," he says. A deep laugh wells up from his chest.

Hjalmar is stunned; he has no idea what his dad has transported to central Finland in his trunk. But he can hear the roar rise around him and understands everyone else is blown away.

"Where the hell did you get those? You old devil, you."

72

HJALMAR JAMS HIS fingers firmly into his ears, but the boom from the forest's edge is still deafening. In the beam of light trained on the trees, he sees shuddering branches and the cloud of snow sent up by the explosion drifting slowly back to the road.

"Goddamn!" Axel exclaims enthusiastically as he climbs out from behind a big rock and begins hopping around on one foot like a lunatic.

The rest of the group is situated at a safe distance, near the fire.

"Tell us, Gunnar," Eliel Zetterborg says, lowering a hand to Hjalmar's father's shoulder, "where the heck did you find those?"

Hjalmar sees the proud look on his father's face; he has succeeded once again in making an indelible impression on his boss. Hjalmar has heard people talking about Dad as the Gunman, Crazy Gunnar, who does his work well and is never predictable, always amusing company to boot.

"You can never tell anyone about this; we're talking about a felony firearms offense," Gunnar says with a chuckle, then takes a swig from the whisky bottle.

"Tell us," Eliel says.

A little farther from the cabin, the plastered Axel and Hans are jumping around in excitement like little boys.

"I have a buddy who's career military, works at Parolannummi. They were left over from a shooting camp . . . had originally been marked as used. The captain found them in the trench after the rest of the gear had been packed up. So he loaded them in his trunk. Said he meant to take them to the garrison, but as it turns out, he didn't."

Gunnar shoots a quick glance at his son as if to make sure Hjalmar understands the spirit of the game. *Never speak to anyone about this.*

"There's the perfect amount in the box; one for each," Gunnar continues, stumbling into an uncontrolled sidestep.

Eliel laughs and pats Gunnar on the back. "You damn son of a gun. Always full of surprises."

"I just hope none of the neighbors call the cops. Those things are terribly loud," Erik Raulo says.

But Eliel Zetterborg shakes his head. "It's a good fifteen miles from here to the nearest farm. Let's just go ahead and have our fun now and that's the end of the discussion."

The perfect amount. One for each.

Hjalmar feels his heart racing. He doesn't want to fire a shotgun, let alone hold a hand grenade.

Laura drains another birch-bark cup, then stumbles over to the jubilant Axel. They embrace wildly, as if celebrating a goal on the soccer pitch.

"What do you think, son?" Gunnar says. Hjalmar's father has turned to Hjalmar; his speech has grown soft; his eyes look tired. "Did you want to throw yours next? Or are you too chicken?"

"Umm . . ."

"Just as I thought. Well, well, looks like he is," Hjalmar's father says with malicious glee. A mischievous smile spreads across his face.

"Well, we're not going to force anyone," Eliel Zetterborg says as the gang of three younger people crosses the spotlight and sits, laughing, at the fire.

Laura leans against Axel, whinnying uncontrollably. Axel seems to whisper something in her ear, and then they both look at Hjalmar.

Hjalmar feels a wave of nausea tear through his insides.

"All right, who's going to throw next?" Gunnar says, crowning the question with a raucous, rollicking laugh that wells up from deep in his belly.

Hjalmar glances at his father. At this moment, he hates the drunken pig who is partially responsible for this farce. Laura should never have come. Not because she can't hold her own. Just the opposite: because she's taken to it like a duck to water—hanging off Axel like a leech, laughing at his jokes.

Hjalmar feels like a fool.

"Hjalle?" his father asks as if to raise the humiliation to the next level.

"I don't really . . ."

The look of disappointment on his father's face does nothing to encourage Hjalmar. Three incredibly long seconds pass.

"Well, hey, I'll go," Laura says suddenly.

Hjalmar sinks deeper into his gloom, somewhere no one can see, and where, as a result, it's always safe.

The group claps and cheers.

Gunnar hands Laura a grenade and offers inebriated instructions on how to remove the pin and how she should squat down behind a rock right after she hurls the grenade.

"Looks like Laura just pulled on the pants in that relationship," Hans says, and everyone bursts into laughter.

It's laughter that in some other place and time might sound well-meaning, but on this dark winter evening in the woods, its impact is downright paralyzing.

73

2020

JESSICA FEELS COLD concrete against her cheek. The hum at the ceiling has stopped.

She doesn't know how much time has passed, but the pain gnawing at her stomach and ribs has intensified. The goon who was helping Adlerkreutz punched her numerous times all over her body, everywhere except her face.

Suddenly Jessica feels the room spin. She retches and realizes she's sitting upright in the chair again.

"You caused all of it, Jessica," Adlerkreutz says.

The old woman has walked up and now stands in front of Jessica, supporting herself with her cane. There is no sign of the man, but Jessica knows a blow could fall at any moment. She feels her muscles tense and gasps in pain.

"You caused your family's death. It was you, not your mother," Adlerkreutz continues.

"Mom was driving—"

"Your mother was driving, yes. But what made her do it, Jessica dear?"

"Mom was sick . . . ," Jessica whispers. The cellar's musty air tickles her nostrils.

"There you go again. Sick. You see it as a sickness. I've always said a mind like your mother's—and why not yours?—is a gift. Not a sickness. But unfortunately neither one of you was ever prepared to admit it."

"What the hell is it that you want?" Jessica says, and spits blood to the floor.

"You are going to disappear today, Jessica. But that's really of no interest. What's more interesting is what is going to happen outside after you disappear."

"What are you—"

"I don't understand how you managed to talk your way out of it, Jessica. You were supposed to be fired and labeled insane, because that's how you see yourself. Insane."

"Go to hell."

"No, Jessica. You're the one who is going to hell. Don't you understand? What you did was unforgivable. You ruined everything. You and your mother before you. I wanted to change the world, but you decided to interfere with my plans. You destroyed all I had built. And now it's too late to start over. I'm too old, too sick."

"I never thought I'd say this, but hearing you now makes me smile."

Camilla Adlerkreutz chuckles softly. "You won't be able to worm your way out of this predicament."

She snaps her fingers, and the man appears in Jessica's field of vision. "Henrik is going to kill you today, Jessica. After that, information about your illness will be leaked to the media. In addition, it will be conclusively demonstrated that you murdered and burned a man in Central Park on Christmas Eve."

Jessica feels her stomach lurch as if these words have finally rattled her awake.

"Henrik dropped by your place today and left a rather incriminating video recording of the murder in Central Park. In addition, the security camera from the stable and the fitness app on your phone confirm you were in the vicinity at the time of the killing. What sort of person lights a homeless drunk on fire? And to top it off, films it all?"

"No one is going to believe it," Jessica whispers. "You're not going to get away with this."

"Wrong, Jessica dear. You forget the papers your superior decided to ignore can easily be delivered to the police again. This time they will understand your delusions have compelled you to commit terrible crimes. You went on to kill your colleagues: Yusuf, Nina, and the rest. People will wonder why you killed those you loved. And in the end, you decided to disappear like dust in the wind."

"No . . ." Jessica's words turn to a yelp when the man forcefully pulls her hair.

"Exactly, Jessica. You're a murderer, and you will face punishment generally spared the mentally ill. Do you see now? You ruined everything, and you'll suffer for your mistake. How is it you refused to see the greatness of my plan? After all, it would have given a purpose to your pathetic little existence."

"Please, Camilla, you don't need to involve anyone else in this—"

"Oh, they're already involved. Every last one of them. And it's only because you, Jessica, chose the wrong path. For all of you."

74

NINA RUSKA WATCHES the skillfully twirling girls, who take one another's hands to create a streamlined three-row formation and then break off again on their own, following precise choreography. Skate blades slice into the surface of the ice, their low-pitched scrapes bouncing from the arena's towering walls. "Another Day of Sun" from *La La Land* is playing from the speakers.

Nina crosses the rubber mat puddled with melted ice and sees a middle-aged woman at the bench leaning against the boards. She's wearing a black sweatsuit and a black-and-white-striped beanie with a pom-pom. The profile reveals a sculptured, attractive face. Chestnut brown hair spills out from the beanie to her shoulders; a black whistle hangs around her neck.

When she reaches the woman, Nina asks: "Smilla Ek?"

"Yes." The woman turns to Nina and stands up straight. She is somewhat shorter than Nina, and the deep-set brown eyes are large and mournful.

Nina extends a hand. "Nina Ruska, police."

Ek takes off her fingerless gloves and shakes Nina's hand. She looks like she wants to answer Nina's frank smile but can't seem to find it within her. Then she turns to the ice, blows the whistle, and calls out to her team.

"Sorry, girls. There's something I have to deal with here. Let's take it from the top."

She presses the screen of her iPad, and the music blaring in the background stops, only to start over again from the beginning.

"I'm usually on the ice with the girls," Ek explains in a vaguely defensive tone as if concerned her coaching from the sidelines is giving Nina the wrong impression of her methods. "I spent the entire day at the hospital with Hjalle. . . . But the doctor said he needs rest, and there wasn't much I could do for him there. I didn't want to cancel this practice. . . . I'm just so incredibly furious with Hjalle. Worried but at the same time really damn angry he would go and do something like that . . ."

"I understand," Nina says, unzipping her coat a bit. It's cold inside the arena, but her formfitting down parka feels suffocating.

"I'm assuming it's him you wanted to talk about? Hjalle? That's what he goes by in the family," Ek continues, now more calmly.

"I see." Nina gestures for Ek to take a seat. "I'm sorry you have to answer our questions in the middle of this mess."

"That's all right. But I don't exactly understand why the police are investigating a suicide attempt. . . ."

Nina scratches her eyebrow. "We have cause to believe your brother's suicide attempt is in one way or another related to a crime that took place in the vicinity yesterday."

"What crime?"

Nina deliberates whether to tell the truth and concludes that Ek deserves to hear it. "The murder of Eliel Zetterborg."

"How . . . how on earth would that be possible?"

Ek doesn't look surprised per se, but the tenderness vanishes from her eyes. She stares at Nina like a blank-faced wax doll.

"It's likely he knows something," Nina says. "Unfortunately that's all I can tell you."

"Do you suspect Hjalle—"

"As I said, it's more a question of what he possibly knows as opposed to what he might have done."

Ek hangs her head and gazes at the floor. "I've been following the news," she says, absentmindedly adjusting the sleeve of her sweatsuit. "I understand Hjalle chose an unusual time to attempt suicide again. Somehow I thought it couldn't be a coincidence."

"Again?"

"Poor choice of words. To my knowledge, he hasn't ever truly attempted it before, despite all the times he has talked about it."

Nina nods and takes a breath. "I understand. This is the sort of information we're very interested in: Hjalmar's history."

Ek gives a joyless laugh. "There's more than enough history there for one family." She sits on the bench, knees pressed tightly together. "If you really want to know what happened to Hjalle way back when, I'm not the right person to tell you, although I'm not sure there's anyone else left."

"I know this is hard, but—"

"It's not that I don't want to tell you, but the whole thing is a mystery of sorts to me as well."

Nina seats herself at an appropriate distance from Ek. The wooden bench feels aggressively cold through her thin denim jeans.

"Let's start from childhood. Tell me what you know," Nina says as a unified front of a dozen girls glides past, arm in arm. Nina finds the sight incredibly beautiful.

"Hjalle was a cheerful child. Smart and photogenic. Good at school. He was two years older than me, so my memories of that time are pretty shaky. But that's how I remember him, always positive." Ek wipes her nose on the back of her hand. "But then something happened . . . when Hjalle was maybe about fourteen or fifteen. . . . I suppose you could say that for some reason, adolescence was an extremely difficult time in Hjalle's life. He started brooding, became gloomy, as if the world that adulthood offered and that he'd been anticipating for so long didn't live up to his expectations." Ek shakes her head, lost in thought. "Poetic, huh? I didn't come up with it myself," she says, lowering her head again. "I remember this one school psychologist saying something like that, and it stuck with me. I don't think Hjalle was in any way unusual in that regard. I've come across the phenomenon in my own teenagers and with other girls, even if no one else I know has reacted to that stage of life as dramatically as Hjalle."

"Was there something in particular that happened then?" Nina asks.

Ek shakes her head. "Dad was always at work, but he had been during our entire childhood, so there was no change in circumstances at home. And yet it started seeming to all of us that Hjalle was suddenly depressed, wandering around in a fog. On the surface, things were pretty good: we had everything we could have wanted, and even though Dad wasn't home much, he was never particularly distant or, you know . . . domineering or violent or anything like that. Hjalle made it into Norsen without any trouble and did pretty well in high school, if not as well as he had before. I remember Mom asking him why he wasn't getting perfect grades on his tests anymore or even top grades."

"Did Hjalmar feel pressure to do well at school?"

"No. Or some, of course; probably the normal amount. We were certainly encouraged to do well, but as I said, we weren't pressured, and perfection wasn't expected of us the way it was of some of my friends or here at the arena. Something else was clearly going on." Ek smiles as if she's caught hold of some warm memory. "He also had a very beautiful girlfriend. I believe a lot of his classmates were envious of him because of her."

"In high school?"

"Yes."

"But Hjalmar already seemed depressed before?"

"Before he met Laura? Yes, I guess her name was Laura."

"So the relationship with this Laura didn't do anything to mitigate Hjalmar's problems?"

"I don't think so, at least nothing worth mentioning. Besides, as I recall, I didn't particularly care for Laura."

"Why not?"

"It's hard to explain, especially since three decades have passed since then. And I was only fifteen or so myself at the time. But I remember thinking Laura was too bubbly somehow, too hungry for attention. They were a pretty odd couple: a beautiful, vibrant girl and my moody, apathetic brother. On top of that, Laura was a couple years older than Hjalle, which at that age is rather unusual. For a girl in twelfth grade to date a boy in tenth. I couldn't help but think . . ."

A moment of silence ensues, during which Ek's eyes are nailed to the formations gliding across the surface of the ice.

"Think what?" Nina probes tentatively.

"That Laura wasn't really dating Hjalle, that it was more like she was dating Hjalmar Ivar Ek, a rich boy from Eira who had extensive social networks. It feels bad saying this, but at that time our family represented a certain social status at our high school. Our family had strong ties to Finnish industry and the small world of the Swedish-speaking elite, if you understand what I'm saying."

"Did Laura come from a different world, then?"

Ek nods. "Somehow you could sense even then that the relation-ship wasn't going to end well. And since Hjalle was already a glum kid, I was afraid a doomed relationship would just make my brother's situation worse."

"And is that what happened?"

"Much worse than I could have ever imagined. But first there was the accident."

Nina presses her fingers against the wooden surface of the bench. "The accident?"

"I'll never forget that night," Ek says, and Nina can't help but notice the other woman's eyes grow moist. "The night he lost his hearing."

Ek blinks to hold back tears, then continues: "That morning, Hjal-mar left for a hare hunt organized by Dad's boss . . . by Eliel Zetterborg, somewhere a couple hours' drive from Helsinki. Our dad was there and so was Eliel's son and the firm's lawyer and his son." Ek appears to hold her breath. "And Laura."

"Laura was along on this hunt?"

"Yes. And that's when it happened. Hjalle found a grenade in the woods. . . . Apparently it exploded near him. Of course the silver lining was he didn't die."

"But your brother lost his hearing?"

"And got those horrible scars on his face."

The song playing from the speakers ends, and the silence that falls over the arena is broken by the sounds of skates scraping against ice.

Ek rises to her feet, quickly dries her eyes, and leans against the boards. "Thanks, girls. That's it for today. I'll be in the locker room in just a minute."

The girls clap and glide on soft kicks toward the door, which Ek has just opened. She and Nina wait patiently for the skaters to pass on their way to the locker room. Nina answers the occasional greetings she receives from the girls with a smile.

When the locker room door at the end of the hallway closes, Ek turns back around and folds her arms across her chest. "Since then, Hjalle's life has gone completely downhill. He was so depressed for so long that we were afraid he'd take his life. He basically just lay in bed, staring at the ceiling. Hjalle lost his hearing, and stopped talking to people as a result. I suppose it's difficult when you suddenly can't hear your own voice . . . but it took a long time before he agreed to go to see a therapist or even a sign language teacher. He prolonged his recovery, even though the rest of the family had already started learning so we could communicate with him. Goddamn, I hated Hjalle for that. I thought he was acting really selfishly, even though he was the one who suffered most from the whole tragedy. It was a hell of a heavy time for all of us."

"And that's why he never graduated from high school?"

Ek nods. "The little positivity Hjalle still possessed vanished with the accident. After that, he was never able to do anything that required any effort."

"What about Laura?"

"I said I didn't care for Laura, and it's true. But I never blamed her for not wanting to become a nurse at the age of eighteen. I told Hjalle over and over . . . I wrote it to him on a piece of paper . . . that he needed to help others help him. Otherwise recovery wouldn't be possible. But I suppose it's easy for someone who's severely depressed and physically disabled to turn into a bottomless black hole . . . a burden there's no way anyone could have the strength to carry."

Nina lowers her gaze to the black rubber mat, where the slush that traveled into the bench area with the girls' skates has melted into little puddles.

"My brother grew severely depressed after that hunting trip, and he's been medicated ever since. There have been stints when he's been fine, but in between there have been plenty of times when I've been really concerned about his welfare. I suppose in some ways it's ironic that money, which generally means freedom, became his prison. If Hjalle had been forced to exert even the tiniest effort to support himself, it's possible he would have gotten a better grip on normal life. Met people, maybe found love, even had kids. But what happened thirty years ago not only wounded him physically but somehow crushed his desire to be part of normal society."

"I'm sorry, Smilla. I feel for your family, even in retrospect," Nina says. She has come across countless sad lives over the course of her work, but for some reason, Smilla's story strikes her as incredibly touching.

Then Nina rises from the bench and slips her hands into the pockets of her down coat. The time has come to lead the conversation out of the comfort zone.

"Unfortunately, I have to ask: do you know if your brother harbored any sort of grudge against Eliel Zetterborg?"

Ek's demeanor instantly becomes guarded. "You said this is about what my brother might know . . . so is he a suspect after all?"

"The matter stands just as I expressed it earlier. But I'll still ask you to answer the question. Did Hjalmar have any reason to nurse particular bitterness for Eliel Zetterborg?"

"Have you considered the possibility that Hjalle was simply so shocked by yesterday's killing that he downed his pills in despair?" Ek replies, voice quavering.

"Of course," Nina says. "But does that sound believable to you? Did Hjalmar have any dealings with his father's former boss over the intervening years? Were they so close that the incident would have been such a shock to your brother?"

Ek shuts her eyes, appears to consider her answer for a moment, then shakes her head. "No," she admits reluctantly. "To my knowledge, they never saw each other again after that hunting trip."

Pounding music can be heard coming from the locker room.

"What about you? How well did you know Eliel Zetterborg?"

Ek looks surprised. "I mean, I knew him. My father worked at RealEst until 2005 when he retired as CEO. I saw Eliel countless times at various parties and Dad's work-related affairs."

"What about Eliel's son, Axel?"

"Axel went to the same school as us, and he graduated in the spring of 1990, a few months after Hjalmar's accident. Since then, I've bumped into him occasionally at the affairs I just mentioned."

"Were the two of you friends?"

"Absolutely not. I was only in eighth grade at the time."

Nina lets out an imperceptible sigh and looks up at the arena's ceiling, which is supported by long, sturdy steel beams. Team jerseys and championship pennants dangle among the bright lights.

"I'm not intentionally avoiding your questions," Ek says. "I understand that what happened during the hunt was an unlucky accident . . . the sum of a chain of unfortunate events. But I can't for the life of me imagine why Hjalle would blame Eliel Zetterborg for it, and even if he did . . . even if he wanted to hurt Zetterborg for some reason, why would he wait three decades to commit such an appalling act?"

"I understand." Nina extends her hand to Ek. "Thank you."

She has already turned on her heels when something Ek said a moment before scurries back into her mind.

"Sorry. One more thing," Nina says, reflecting that the expression is from some classic police show, maybe *Columbo*. "You said the firm's attorney was present the night of the accident, along with his son?"

"Yes."

"Do you remember the attorney's name?"

"Of course. Erik Raulo. His son, Hans, went to high school with us too."

NINA STEPS OUT through the arena doors and catches a whiff of cigarette smoke. The girls hanging around the smoking area are about the same age as the teenagers Smilla Ek coaches. Nina shoots them a disapproving look and lifts her phone to her ear.

It's not long before she hears Yusuf's voice at the other end of the line.

"Hey, I just left the ice arena," she says, waiting at the crosswalk as a blue city bus zooms past without stopping.

"How did it go?" Yusuf's voice sounds tense. "We're waiting to get in to talk to Hjalmar Ek. He's fucking asleep, and this doctor loves throwing his weight around, says we can't wake him up—"

"It was an interesting chat. I believe we can say with certainty the third man in the photograph is Gunnar Ek," Nina says, unlocking her car. "I'm a hundred percent convinced this whole thing leads back to an accident that took place during a hunting trip in 1990."

"OK," Yusuf says, intrigued. "What accident?"

"A grenade found in the woods exploded in Hjalmar's hand."

"A grenade? What the hell?"

"It's an unusual case, I have to say. There were four teenagers on the hunt, and three middle-aged men. Eliel Zetterborg, Erik Raulo—"

"Both murdered . . ."

Yusuf's interjection prompts a brief pause from Nina.

"Yup. And the third one was Gunnar Ek, Hjalmar's father. They all worked at RealEst."

"But what makes you think this is all related to that?" Yusuf asks.

"Hjalmar lost his hearing as a result. I'm positive he's been holding a grudge against Zetterborg as the guy who arranged the hunt ever since. And now he finally decided to get his revenge."

"OK," Yusuf says. "Call Rasse and ask him to look into the incident. In the meantime, I'll put some pressure on the head physician: we need to get our hands on Hjalmar Ek's epicrisis."

"Sounds good."

Nina opens the car door, and as she climbs in, she notices a text from Tom.

I slipped something in your pocket. =)

Don't open it until I tell you to, OK?

Nina reaches into her coat pocket and pulls out a tiny package wrapped with a pretty yellow ribbon.

75

RASMUS UNTWISTS THE cap of his energy drink and swears silently when he gets some of the sugary liquid on his fingers. He lifts the bottle to his lips and tanks up on chemicals in a flavor the brain registers as strawberry purely thanks to the label.

"Susikoski," Hellu says, shutting the door to the room Rasmus has been assigned.

A moment earlier, Rasmus visited the archives to look for documents not yet touched by the digitalization project that will continue far into the future. He photographed the documents, climbed back upstairs to his own unit, and plopped down at his desk with his drink in hopes of being allowed to do his work in peace for once, without bosses or colleagues constantly inquiring as to his progress.

"I guess you're the only one on the team who isn't in the field." Hellu wraps her fingers around Rasmus' bottle and raises it to eye level. Her nails are painted dark blue.

"Yeah."

"You go through a lot of this junk." Hellu lowers the bottle to the table and rubs her sticky hands together. "Ugh."

"I'm just reviewing the incident that resulted in Hjalmar Ek losing his hearing thirty years ago."

"Yusuf mentioned it on the phone. He seems to think Ek is the man we're looking for." Hellu seats herself across from Rasmus. Her phone bursts out ringing, and she discreetly silences it. "Just think. The breakthrough is so close. As long as the guy opens his mouth."

"Or in this case, moves his fingers," Rasmus adds, managing to sound too clever by half.

"I suppose. Is there anything in the reports?"

Rasmus shakes his head. There's a lot of material, and it's too soon to draw any conclusions. "It was an extremely unusual accident. Hjalmar Ek found a hand grenade in the woods at night, and it exploded in his hand. The explosion damaged his inner ear and caused injuries to the face and neck. The appropriate investigations took place—the explosive found in the woods was a concussion grenade used by the Defence Forces."

"Right, they don't send out fragments; the grenade's effectiveness is based on blast pressure."

Rasmus can't help but think his boss wants to show off what she picked up during her voluntary military service. "Right."

For his part, Rasmus has never been near a garrison; he did civilian service instead of military service and spent it archiving files. His knowledge of weapons is based on years of experience with the Call of Duty games, where he has irrefutably developed into a beast of a super soldier.

"An ambulance was called, but it took over an hour to reach the location. None of the people at the cabin were in any shape to drive the victim to the nearest hospital."

"And this delay presumably exacerbated the damage to his hearing?" Hellu asks.

"It's plausible."

"Could there be a motive there for decades of ill will? That the adults were too drunk to drive Ek for medical care?"

Rasmus isn't convinced, and Hellu doesn't appear to be expecting a reply in the affirmative. "The police talked to everyone present the night of the accident. The story seems consistent in all respects. They drank and partied. Hjalmar went into the woods at night, maybe to do his business, and found a grenade on the ground."

Hellu chuckles. "And was so drunk he took out the pin?"

"Yes," Rasmus says expressionlessly, flipping through the papers in front of him. "He must have. I doubt the grenade would have exploded if he hadn't."

"And was the source of the grenade ever discovered?"

Rasmus shakes his head. "None of the garrisons had reported missing ammunition. As a result of the incident, detachments were ordered to conduct a full inventory, but there wasn't a single grenade missing in the entire country."

"If you consider how seriously the Defence Forces and the police take any ordnance disappearing during drills, it's unlikely the grenade was left behind by a camp for new recruits."

"I guess. Besides, no combat exercises have ever been held there, or anywhere in the vicinity, for that matter."

Hellu glances at her phone, which is ringing for a second time during the conversation. She silences it again and leans across the table toward Rasmus.

"What about the young people? Who was there, aside from Hjalmar?"

"Axel Zetterborg, Hans Raulo . . . They're the sons of the victims in our investigations."

"I got that."

"The fourth one was Laura Karolainen, Hjalmar's girlfriend at the time."

"Bringing a girlfriend along on a hare hunt." Hellu chuckles, as if the thought is completely absurd. "Hans Raulo has been interrogated once today, but would it be a good idea for someone to probe him a little about what happened during that hunting trip?"

Rasmus nods. "I'm sure it would be."

"Could you make sure that happens? I need to run upstairs again," Hellu says, adjusting her short hair into a more authoritative attitude.

Rasmus mutters something in response and stares at a photocopy of Laura Karolainen's passport.

What an incredibly gorgeous young woman.

76

THE MAN STARES at the video recording playing on the screen.

Some of the material was filmed with a handheld camera. Some is from news clips found online, from red-carpet interviews or the couches of morning television.

He pauses the footage intermittently, tries to capture Axel Zetterborg's face at the correct angle. And there it is: the unusually clear and recognizable crescent of laugh wrinkles that makes the smile so unique. The hairline that dips when he frowns. The relaxed, drowsy eyes he rolls as if they are more critical to communication than speech is.

He stops the video, shuts his eyes, and holds in his tears.

He needs more material to make the video complete, whole. And who knows? Maybe a few pictures of himself too: by intercutting the photos quickly, it's possible to create the illusion of the two of them being in the same image.

If he were only a better editor, it might be possible to combine—

He hears a knock.

Open the door! I want to talk to you!

Damn it. Never a moment's peace.

Open this door right—

He feels rage flare up inside him. He rolls his chair away from the desk and dashes to the door. Walks past his mother, who is standing there, grabs his coat, and opens the front door.

Hey, where do you think you're going?

He steps into the stairwell, hears the door thunk shut behind him, his mother's demanding voice from inside. He stares at the door sealed by the police, the one that reads ZETTERBORG on the mail slot.

Then he starts running down the stairs, around and around, and the tearful voice echoing in the corridor does not slow him down.

It's all fake. A big fat lie.

77

YUSUF GRABS A *Tech World* from the table, realizes it's a few years old, and tosses it back to the stack of magazines. He has tried calling Jessica five times and sent two text messages, but she has vanished like dust in the wind.

He lowers his phone from his ear and turns on the speaker, which broadcasts the monotone ring at the other end of the line.

He and Jami Harjula are still sitting near the windows at the end of the corridor, where it feels like they've already spent half the day.

"She's still not answering?" Harjula asks, glancing at his watch. He has passed the long minutes mostly cracking his knuckles.

"No. Last I heard from her she had just left Lamberg's place," Yusuf says.

"You think something happened to her?"

"Fuck. I don't know. But—"

Yusuf abruptly stops talking and shifts his intense gaze to Harjula. "But what?"

"She said Lamberg gave her a letter Zetterborg had told him to deliver to Erik Raulo. And that she would tell me more once she got to HQ."

"If Jessica was already on her way to HQ at that point, she should have been there a long time ago," Harjula says.

"Yup. Damn it. But I don't think . . ."

"Lamberg would have done anything stupid?" Harjula suggests.

Yusuf isn't sure if the words sound frightening because the same thought just occurred to him.

But if Jessica already made it out of Lamberg's apartment . . . No, it doesn't make any sense. If Lamberg wanted to harm Jessica for some incomprehensible reason, he wouldn't have let her leave his home. And why would Lamberg do anything of the sort? He was already removed from the list of suspects.

Yusuf lets out a heavy sigh. The stress has caused some sort of alarm reaction in his body, and the cold sweat will not relent.

He glances up and down the corridor, but there's no sign of the hospital's bearded authority.

"Listen, Harjula . . . Kuznetsov said I won't have any business in Ek's room anymore."

"Yeah, I guess he did."

"Could you handle it? Squeeze Ek for the information on who . . . or on whose behalf he did it all? Without making his heart stop."

"Of course," Harjula replies without hesitation.

"Are you sure?"

"Do you think I'm not capable or something?"

"No, but this whole heap of shit is my responsibility now. I have to make sure I can count on you!"

Harjula calmly rises from his chair and stands in front of Yusuf. "I understand I made a mistake earlier when I didn't immediately connect Hjalmar Ek's suicide attempt to this case. But I'm awake now, and you can trust me."

Yusuf tries to look convinced, but apparently doesn't completely succeed.

"Besides," Harjula continues, "you just said it yourself: the doctor was clear that I was the only one who would be handling the interrogation. You're not even going to be allowed in there."

Yusuf looks his colleague in the eye, then silences the ringtone echoing from his phone.

Where the hell is Jessica?

And suddenly something Jessica said earlier today creeps into his mind.

Christmas Eve. The witches. Camilla Adlerkreutz.

Jessica was afraid something was going on.

At the moment, Yusuf was so focused on bringing Jessica on board the investigation that he settled for saying what he thought she wanted to hear. *We'll sort this out together, Jessie. Everything's going to be fine.* Now Yusuf can see that maybe he didn't take Jessica's words seriously, that he found her stories far-fetched.

But suddenly it all seems possible.

Jessica might think of herself as crazy, but she definitely isn't. Not that way, making stuff up in her head. How could he have been so damn selfish . . . ?

Yusuf knows he has to make sure Jessica is OK. Despite the fact he has two unsolved murders on his plate.

"Thanks, Harjula. Call me right away when you find something out," Yusuf says, and starts walking toward the elevators. A moment later, the walk turns into a run.

78

RASMUS STARES AT the reports strewn across his desk and rubs his stiff neck. After all these years of sitting hunched over his desk, it's odd that his neck is starting to bother him only now.

Tanja knocks on the door to indicate her presence and steps in.

"This is becoming a habit," Tanja says, "me bothering you."

"That's all right," Rasmus replies. "I enjoy the company."

Tanja sits down across from Rasmus. "Is there anything new?"

"I was just having a look at an accident that took place in early 1990, which resulted in our prime suspect being disabled."

"Who's that?"

Rasmus looks up from his papers and pauses to reflect whether it's appropriate to share this information with a crime scene investigator, albeit one who is friendly, cute, and for all practical purposes part of the investigative team.

"Hjalmar Ek," he says without further hesitation.

"Who's that?"

So the crime scene investigator hasn't heard about the latest dramatic twists in the case. Rasmus immediately regrets having revealed Ek's name to Tanja, but it's too late to shut up now. "A guy who tried to kill himself in Ullanlinna today. It's a long story. . . ."

"OK. Do you need any help?"

Rasmus shakes his head. "No . . . or actually I'm not sure. This is quite a slog."

Tanja grabs a paper cup, pumps coffee into it from the dispenser, slides it over to Rasmus.

"I already drank two liters of Euro Shopper," he says.

"Good. It's going to be a long night."

"Probably. Was anything interesting found at Erik Raulo's home?"

Tanja shakes her head. "A slew of samples that we sent to the lab. No clear indication of the perp."

"Darn it."

"The only thing that struck me was a little porcelain elephant missing from the windowsill."

Rasmus looks confused.

"There were these porcelain elephants arranged in a line by size. It looked like one was missing: the third one from the left." Tanja laughs wearily. "It probably has nothing to do with this."

"Well, you can never be sure." Rasmus sighs.

"What exactly is it you're looking for in these papers?" Tanja says, flashing her cute smile. She is relentless.

"A woman named Laura Karolainen." Rasmus' fingers return to the keyboard. "She disappeared without a trace in 1990."

There's a knock at the door. The young man assigned that morning to help Rasmus has appeared in the doorway. The baby of the investigative team is named Lionel.

"Am I bothering you, Rasse?"

"Not at all."

"You asked me to look into the names of the owners and residents of the building on Muukalaiskatu. Here's the list." Lionel steps into the room and lowers a printout of an Excel worksheet in front of Rasmus. Lionel is younger than Rasmus and very handsome.

Rasmus notices him exchanging discreet glances with Tanja. "Thanks."

"I did what you asked and compared the list to the people who were questioned last night. There's only one case where the information wasn't a complete match."

Rasmus adjusts his glasses and picks up the printout. "Which one?"

"The owner of number eleven is different from the person who was questioned. It's the apartment across from Zetterborg's."

"A renter?"

Lionel shakes his head. "No, the flat is owned by Felix Salo. But the police spoke to his mother. Rea Salo is on the books in Stockholm. According to the report, she said she heard a shout from Zetterborg's apartment—"

Rasmus raises a hand to interrupt. "Wait. So at the time of Zetterborg's death, the mother was visiting her son?"

"Well, based on her official residence, that's what it looks like, but there's no mention of that in the report."

Rasmus scratches his bald head and shoots a quick glance at Tanja, but she doesn't seem to join in his befuddlement. "So at the time of Zetterborg's murder, there was someone next door who doesn't officially live in the building?"

"Yes."

Rasmus shuts his eyes and thinks. There's nothing strange about a mother visiting her son. But why didn't Rea Salo mention she doesn't live in the building? It's something the police would find out before long in any event.

"There's one more thing that stuck out when I looked into it," Lionel continues. "Felix Salo is thirty years old but has a guardian. The guardian is his mother, Rea Salo."

"Why does Felix Salo need a guardian?" Rasmus asks even though he's a lawyer by training and more than familiar with the laws and regulations regarding guardianship. In practice, a guardian can be ordered for anyone who isn't able to look after their own interests—such as property—due to old age or illness.

"I don't know. I haven't gotten that far yet."

"OK. Thank you," Rasmus says, and Lionel quietly exits the room.

Tanja eyes Rasmus, intrigued. "You look thoughtful."

Rasmus doesn't reply. He swipes his finger across the printout, then brings up the system the authorities use to view people's personal information. He enters Rea Salo's personal identification number in the search field.

"What is it?" Tanja asks.

"Bingo," Rasmus whispers, and feels the itch spread from his scalp to his back.

79

Nina steps into the restaurant, where the dated decor is reminiscent of the smoke-ingrained seventies and business lunches that lasted all afternoon. The place is perfectly clean, but the white tablecloths and servers in collared shirts and dress trousers cannot hide the fact that half the customers are there to consume alcohol, not the five-course menu. Nina walks up to the bar. The bartender, who is drying a pint glass with a dishrag, looks at her as if he can tell she's a police officer and knows without asking whom she's looking for.

"Can I help you?" he says nonetheless.

Nina glances at the dining room from end to end but doesn't see anyone matching the description she's been given. "I'm looking for—"

The bartender cuts her off. "Hans? He said you'd be coming." He lowers the pint glass behind the counter and nods toward the stairs. "I'll show you the way."

Nina follows the bartender up the narrow spiral staircase. To her surprise, there are almost as many tables up top as down below. There aren't many customers, however, only a trio of men sitting near the windows, tossing back shots.

Salonen's damn bachelor party . . . Food was good, though. Who did the catering, again?

The bartender indicates the table, and Nina strides toward the men. Their drunken jabbering stops dead in its tracks.

Nina casts a quick glance at the three men and instantly recognizes the type. High-income drunks: their eyes have the blank glaze of alcoholics, but the clothes and nicely cut hair indicate a healthy balance in their bank accounts. It's an equation Nina is more than familiar with, having once dated an NHL player whose career had just ended and whose life went to pot in the cross pressures of meaninglessness, too much free time, and enough money to last him for the rest of his life.

"Damn, that's a strong-looking woman," one of the men says, and smiles, impressed. He's bearded, middle-aged, and wearing a dress shirt.

"Knock it off," says one of the other men, whom Nina recognizes as Hans Raulo. "I have a meeting."

Nina doesn't know how long the men have been sitting there, but judging by the filthy tablecloth and the level of inebriation, the meeting that began in the Kämp's Mirror Room has continued at an intense pace despite the sad news.

"A meeting, huh?" the bearded guy says, then wipes his mouth and grabs the coat hanging from the back of his chair. "Come on, Poksa, let's go for a smoke."

Hans Raulo's drinking buddies stand, politely wish Nina a pleasant day, and weave their way to the spiral stairs, steep enough to prove the duo's end.

"Please have a seat," Hans Raulo says and holds out his hand. "Hans."

"Nina Ruska."

"OK. Goddamn it." Raulo holds his hands at his eyes for a second. "I'm pretty sauced, if you know what I mean. . . . This day. I guess we probably would have gotten drunk anyway, but the news about Dad . . ."

"My condolences."

Raulo waves dismissively. "Thanks; it hasn't really hit yet. I don't know if it's a good idea to drink after getting news like that, but I can't take it sober either," he says seriously. "This might look strange, me sitting here with those guys. Us drinking and laughing. But like I said . . ."

"I'm not one to tell anyone how they should process their grief. Or their shock—whichever it is." Nina scans the table for a spot that isn't fouled by food or red wine so she can set down her leather gloves.

In the meantime, Raulo splashes vodka into a shot glass and tosses it back.

Nina watches the Adam's apple move at the unshaven throat like an elevator. Raulo's stubble is surprisingly gray, considering he isn't even fifty yet.

"Erik, my father . . . the big lawyer," Hans says in a voice presumably intended to imitate his father. "We haven't been in touch for a long time. I already told you guys everything I know. In other words, basically nothing."

"This is about something else." Nina leans back in her chair. "What do you know about a man named Hjalmar Ek?"

The look on Hans Raulo's face turns simultaneously grim and surprised. "About Hjalle?"

"Yes."

"I haven't seen him in ages. Or, I mean, he lives over on Tähtitorn-inmäki. I've seen him walking his dog a few times when I've been at the patio of the Sea Horse or the Central. But I haven't really talked to him since . . . since high school. How so? What does Hjalle have to do with this?"

"Am I wrong in assuming the last time the two of you spoke—I mean, the way you and I are speaking here now—was the fifth of February 1990? In other words, almost exactly thirty years ago?"

"Um . . . ," Hans stammers, and reaches for his water glass.

At least Nina hopes it's water and not a full glass of vodka. Otherwise they won't be continuing this conversation until tomorrow at the earliest.

She continues: "Because according to the information I have, Hjalle lost his hearing that night and hasn't been capable of verbal communication since. You were there. At the hare hunt in Ouninpohja. When the accident happened."

"Yes, I was. I don't think I've ever denied that, have I?"

Nina shakes her head. "No, you haven't. But we have reason to believe that the deaths of both Eliel Zetterborg and your father are somehow related to that trip."

"But . . . how is that possible? I mean, do you guys think Hjalle did it . . . ?"

"Why would you ask that, Hans? Did Hjalmar have some reason to be bitter? Angry?"

Raulo drains his water in a single swig, then glances over Nina's shoulder, presumably to establish eye contact with the server. "Listen, my father was fucking killed today and I need to calm down a little first. . . ."

"I understand. But if we think that the events of the last twenty-four hours somehow culminate in that hunting trip, then we need to talk to you too, and take our time doing it. At the station. The older generation from that trip is no longer with us: your father tragically died today and Eliel Zetterborg yesterday. Gunnar Ek years ago, of cancer. We know Laura Karolainen was also there, and that she later moved to Sweden." Nina feels a little disgusted with herself for playing games with the man across from her, who looks perfectly presentable and harmless in his navy blue V-neck. But she ignores her reaction. "And Hjalmar. We're talking to him. We don't know where Laura is at the moment, and Axel told us . . . well, that there was nothing to tell about the trip. That Hjalmar found a grenade in the woods and that it exploded in his hand. End of story."

"So why don't you believe—"

"Because there's something fishy about the story." Nina leans across the table, and her nostrils are assaulted by the ethanol fumes rising from the half-empty glasses. "You were just boys then, Hans. How old were you? Seventeen? Maybe something happened there you weren't capable of understanding yet. Something that has had far-reaching consequences. Whatever happened there, if it was a crime, the statute of limitations has no doubt passed. One of the three of you is going to start talking soon. Or else Laura will, once we find her. But my advice to you is, you be the first to open your mouth."

Raulo twirls his water glass in his fingers and suddenly looks scared.

The speakers aren't on upstairs, but music carries faintly from downstairs.

Nina knows she doesn't have any weapons to use against Hans if he refuses to tell what really happened during the accident. In a moment, she will be making room for the sots returning from their smoke, and Hans will be able to continue numbing his brain until he passes out, head to the tablecloth, which was presumably white a few hours ago.

"Thirty years," Hans says enigmatically, and Nina feels adrenaline surge through her veins. "We agreed back then . . . that we wouldn't talk about it. And in the end, the truth didn't diverge so much from the story."

"In what way did it diverge? What happened to Hjalmar?"

Hans Raulo looks at Nina like a whipped dog. There's sadness in his eyes, and not an ounce of hope that tomorrow will be any better than today.

"OK. I'll tell you. But first I need a little more courage."

80

1990

I'm going to bed, Laura.

   Already?

   Are you going to—

   I'm going to hang out and party a little longer. I'll come crawl in next to you soon, honeybun.

Hjalmar presses his face to the pillow and tries to stifle the tears streaming from his eyes. It's midnight, and he has retreated alone to the room he wishes Laura were lying in too.

For a couple hours now, he has been sleeping or listening to the bursts of laughter carrying in from outside, the drunken slurring, and he was woken up once when someone from the group fired a shotgun, to the others' applause.

   The hare hunt. The Super Bowl. Indeed.

Even before the trip, Hjalmar knew his place in the group's pecking order: he is perfectly aware of being the weakest link in the ecosystem, Gunnar Ek's insecure son who shies from guns, booze, and dirty stories. But counter to his hopes, Laura's presence hasn't softened the macho vibe of the trip or helped Hjalmar feel less like an outsider. Things haven't gotten as wild as Axel threatened; as a matter of fact, they have gotten way more out of hand. The grenades Dad brought, combined with the incessant drinking, have pitched things to a totally new level of recklessness.

His grenade is still in the wooden box on the porch.

Maybe Axel and Laura will throw it into the woods together tonight.

Hjalmar tries to take a deep breath.

Tomorrow they'll be heading home, and he'll be able to spend time alone with Laura in the evening.

He needs to calm down, forget all the pressures of the outside world, and confront Laura's beautiful naked body.

A normal reaction. You don't even have to think about it. A normal reaction. Normal.

Hjalmar knows he's far from normal. He's a freak. A weirdo who needs treatment as soon as possible.

They were queers, Hjalle. You know, people become gay when they're trying to protest the natural order of things. Being queer is like giving the finger to the norms we all live by.

Hjalmar reflects on the words his father uttered in the agonizingly hot sauna, a beer in his hand. And Hjalmar has pondered the possibility that he doesn't get turned on when he sees a naked woman simply because he's gay. But no, he knows deep down that's not it; it's something totally different. He has gotten caught up in a cycle from which there is maybe no return to normalcy. He thinks about his father, his mother, and his little sister, who will hopefully never have to experience the hell he has been wallowing in his entire adolescence.

As the hours gradually pass, Hjalmar registers that the voices carrying in from outside have faded, maybe because the others have come in one by one and passed out on their sleeping pads, maybe because in the darkness he has, without realizing it, fallen into a torpor somewhere between sleep and waking.

Maybe tomorrow things will be better.

81

HJALMAR WAKES UP, sits up in his bed. He's breathing heavily and remembers having a horrible nightmare: he was standing naked in a snowbank, shotgun in hand, as urine ran down his leg and everyone laughed.

He shakes off the thought and glances at his watch: it's almost two thirty in the morning, and Laura still hasn't crawled in next to him.

Then he hears it again, the sound that presumably woke him a moment earlier. A low moan; it's coming from the other side of the bedroom door, from the main room.

Hjalmar tries to listen, but all he hears are snores rumbling from somewhere.

He rubs his eyes, then thinks about the terrible dream he just had and tries to make sense of exactly what happened in it.

He hears the moan again, and this time Hjalmar can also make out Laura's soft voice barely carrying through the closed door. He climbs quietly out of bed with the blanket around his shoulders, reaches for the door handle, and warily pushes the door open.

The voices are clearer now and mingle with the crackle from the wood-burning stove.

Hjalmar steps across the threshold; his gait is unsteady. He had a few beers and a shot over the course of the evening, and he doesn't feel like himself.

He sees his father and Erik Raulo slumbering on the floor on their sleeping pads. Eliel Zetterborg must be sleeping, as is his right, in the cabin's other bedroom.

Hans Raulo is slumped in a weird position on a reindeer hide, still in his coat and boots. He looks dead.

Hjalmar creeps quietly past the stove.

He hears another moan, a louder one.

He hears Axel Zetterborg's slurred speech. He hears Laura shush him, tell him to be quiet.

Hjalmar stands there in the middle of the living room and watches Laura's beautiful body bathed in the fire's yellow glow. Beneath her thighs, he sees abs that contract every time Laura moves her hips.

"You're so fucking hot—"

"Shhh, you idiot . . . ," Laura says, but Axel cuts her off by lifting his backside off the floor, provoking more moans from her.

Hjalmar isn't sure how long he stands there watching these two beautiful, naturally capable young people make love without any inhibitions. Listening to Laura's and Axel's breathing intensify. Despite his inner turmoil, he doesn't berate himself for being stupid or naive—he knew all along that this was how it would end.

One of the men sleeping on the floor stops snoring and smacks his lips in his sleep.

And then it washes over him, at a slight lag: a blind fury caused not only by the horrible deed, but by the humiliating way it's being done.

Laura's moans grow louder, and she drops her head back. Her blond hair hangs over Axel's knees.

Hjalmar feels hatred shudder through his body.

He has the urge to grab the old ax hanging from the wall and sink it into Laura's head. And then move on to Axel.

But something inside him compels him to continue standing there as if he is relishing his own invisibility.

Hjalmar just waits and watches as the couple advances toward a drunken climax, which, judging by their accelerating movements, isn't far off.

And when Laura finally lowers her quivering, sweat-sheened body to Axel's, Hjalmar knows she's ready. He knows it despite never having seen Laura orgasm.

"I'm too drunk to nut," Axel whispers, and Laura laughs softly.

Hjalmar's shaking has turned to silent weeping. He just stands there, mouth gaping, crying.

The humiliation is too great.

There's no way he can run from the situation; after all, they're in the middle of the woods and it's deadly cold outside.

But there's no way he can stay inside the cabin. He would rather die.

Hjalmar shuts his eyes, and before he has had time to decide his next move, he hears Laura's startled voice coming from the floor in front of the stove.

"Hjalle! What the fuck?"

"Goddamn it . . . we were just . . ."

Hjalle doesn't reply. His thoughts have shifted to the box of grenades on the porch.

He hasn't thrown his yet.

82

HJALMAR KICKS OPEN the sticky door and steps out onto the porch. The frigid concrete and the thin layer of snow fallen on it make his bare soles tingle.

Inside, Laura is calling his name.

He hears Axel say something and laugh. Then the door shuts behind him, leaving him alone in the freezing night.

It's a terrible thought. But in the midst of his emotional turmoil, Hjalmar understands that if there's ever a time he needs to stop thinking, this is it. It's the endless ruminating and overanalyzing that have brought him to this point, driven him into a corner, thrown him into a chasm from which he will never be able to climb out on his own.

The grenade is ice-cold, and its touch against his fingertips seems to quench the thirst of his perspiring skin.

Hjalmar walks down the stairs and passes the grenade from one hand to the other. It feels surprisingly light, like an icy apple.

There's something biblical about the moment.

The door opens behind him. "Hjalmar!"

Laura's voice isn't regretful, more inebriated and embarrassed.

Hjalmar turns and raises his hand; his fingers are wrapped around the explosive.

"Holy shit . . . ," Axel exclaims in fright. He has pulled on sweatpants and appeared at Laura's side; the yellow glow from inside casts shadows across his naked torso. "Papa! Hjalle has a grenade!"

The lump in Hjalle's chest has grown; it's like a gigantic clump of Play-Doh he gobbled down. He has no plan. No escape. Primed by absolute humiliation, he has become a walking bomb—literally.

"Wake up! Hjalle's freaking out and he has a grenade!" Axel shouts, pulling Laura back inside by the arm.

And then Hjalmar understands that even the deadly explosive in his hand hasn't convinced Axel to take him seriously. He's a joke, even when he could blow up the whole cabin and a bunch off assholes with it if he wanted.

He pulls the pin.

He has never held anything in his hand even remotely reminiscent of a grenade but remembers the instructions his father gave earlier that evening: as long as the lever is pressed down, the grenade won't go off.

I could wait until someone opens the door, toss in a grenade, and put an end to this humiliation.

He's standing in freezing temperatures in his nightshirt but doesn't feel the cold.

He is numb.

Eventually, after several long seconds pass, Eliel Zetterborg opens the door. He seems groggy.

"Hjalmar, vad fan . . . ?"

Hjalmar is sobbing.

"Did you remove the pin, damn it . . . ?" Eliel asks.

Now Axel and Laura reappear in the doorway behind Eliel.

Hjalmar looks at Eliel's lips but can't hear the words they're forming.

He has grasped that hurling the grenade into the cabin wouldn't solve anything. It would only make things worse.

Hjalmar, throw that as far as you can into the woods!

What a fucking lunatic.

Wake Gunnar up!

Wake him up, goddamn it. This is an emergency!

Come inside, Hjalle. I'm sorry.

Let's call the police.

Silence! That's not going to do any good.

Then Hjalmar casts one final glance at Laura, the most beautiful person on the face of the earth. Just a moment ago she was still his, but the inevitable has happened. For a long time now, Hjalmar has known he has wanted the impossible, has anticipated the coming of the end. Tried to navigate toward a solution that was never in sight.

Hjalmar turns around and walks toward the forest. His toes are numb from the cold.

Now he's shivering. His sweaty T-shirt feels like it has frozen to his back.

What the hell is he doing?

Someone follow him!

Fuck no. He has a goddamned grenade.

Hjalmar hears the voices fade. No one has come after him.

He steps into knee-deep snow and lumbers, straining and shivering, farther into the woods.

He stops amid the tall pines and looks back.

He is not going to miss this unjust world.

HJALMAR CRACKS HIS shaking fingers and releases the lever.

But the instant after the decision, he is full of regret.

Of fear.

His grip on the grenade slips, and he manages to take a few steps toward the cabin.

Hjalmar catches Laura's words: *He's coming back!*

They are the last thing he later recalls hearing.

He remembers nothing of the blast.

There is only pain, which eases for a moment, only to return more horrific than ever.

83

2020

Nina looks at Hans Raulo, who has lowered his eyes to his drink and holds them firmly there.

Loud laughter echoes from the stairs, and a moment later, Nina sees the duo returning from their extended cigarette break.

"Not yet. Sorry, guys," Raulo says, hand raised. "I'll be down soon. Get yourselves something on my tab."

The men vanish down the staircase without protest.

"But why—"

"Don't you get it?" For the first time, Raulo seems a little aggressive, and his words spew through gritted teeth. "This was going to be the merger of all time. Historic on a Finnish scale. That spring, EZEM Pipes bought a majority stake in some German technology company, and the result was RealEst, the second-largest company in Finnish history, right after the Nokia of the early 2000s. Do you think Eliel Zetterborg was about to step out in front of the cameras and give an interview where he revealed the company's upper management was guilty of felony firearms violations and causing grievous bodily injury to a boy?"

"But how didn't the story leak to the media? After all, Hjalmar—"

Raulo bangs his fist against the table. "You're not understanding me. I'm sure they wished Hjalle would die . . . everyone except maybe Hjalle's dad. Although things were damn frosty between Hjalle and his dad too. It was an insanely delicate situation, and even though they were three sheets to the wind, they all knew it. We were kicked up and out of our sleeping bags. . . . That's when I woke up. There was a land-line in the cabin, and Eliel called an ambulance. But it took the ambu-lance a hell of a long time to get out there to the middle of the woods, and no one was close to being in any shape to drive. Especially Hjalle himself. He was so badly injured, he couldn't do anything but shout. Fuck, I will never forget the way he shouted. I suppose the fact that he couldn't hear himself shouting just made it worse."

"And so, while you were waiting for the ambulance, the men agreed on the next steps?"

Raulo nods. "Eliel dictated what everyone should tell the police in that emphatic tone of his. That Hjalmar had found a grenade in the woods and had been foolish enough to fuss with it. That as long as everyone stuck to the story, the police would have no reason to suspect its authenticity. And that Eliel would use all his influence to make sure the accident—that's what it was already being called that night—wasn't written about in the press."

"And everyone agreed?"

A cryptic smile forms on Raulo's lips. "I'm assuming you never met Eliel Zetterborg face-to-face. Holy hell, he was a scary guy back in his prime. Not necessarily intimidating physically but all the more au-thoritative for it. He forced the fathers to swear to him that their sons would stick to the story. A little like Don Corleone giving an order to his capos, who pass it on to their soldiers. Gunnar was promised that his son would be taken care of and that everyone would receive a mas-sive bonus as long as the merger didn't fall through. For a little while there, it seemed to me Gunnar was more worried about the merger than whether his son survived until the ambulance arrived."

A shudder of disgust runs through Nina. "OK. What happened next?"

"The biggest question mark was Laura. Eliel didn't have any sort of hold over her. And although it wasn't long before it came out that Laura had caused the whole scandal through her callous actions, Eliel was concerned about her sticking to the story." Raulo pours a shot down his throat and grimaces in pleasure. "Now, you have to take into account that the situation was truly chaotic. Hjalle was on the floor, screaming, his face a pulpy mass. There was blood everywhere. . . . Jägermeister pumping through everyone's veins. It was downright frightening how sharply Eliel was able to think at that level of intoxication."

"How was it resolved?"

"Eliel tore into Axel. Said it was all his fault. Then he turned to Laura and asked if she understood what had just been agreed. Laura nodded, and that was that. I don't know about the others, but at least I was scared as hell."

"The ambulance took Hjalmar to the hospital?"

"Yup. The police showed up at the same time as the ambulance. Everyone stuck to the story. The empty grenade crate was burned in the campfire before the authorities arrived."

"But what about Hjalmar?"

Nina sees her phone ringing on the table. It's Yusuf, but Nina doesn't want to interrupt Raulo's story. She feels like they are just coming to something major, so she silences the call.

"Right, how did they make sure Hjalle would keep his mouth shut? I know he was bitter at everyone in the group. Apparently Eliel swore Hjalle's father to handle it: Gunnar must have somehow managed to talk his kid into staying mum." Raulo tosses back the remnants of a gin and tonic he spied at the edge of the table and takes a few seconds to chomp on the ice that makes its way into his mouth.

"Maybe the truth was too embarrassing for Hjalle himself. Think about it from your perspective: would you rather be the victim of an accident or a cuck who tried to kill himself with a grenade?"

"Is that what Hjalle is in your eyes?" Nina's cold tone wipes the sad smile from Hans' face. "A cuckold?"

"What Laura and Axel did that night . . . while Hjalle was sleeping in the next room. That's a humiliation no one hopes they will ever have to deal with. But the worst was still to come."

Nina sits up straighter. "What do you mean?"

"What I'm about to tell you now is based on rumor, not fact. But I don't think there's any doubt about it."

"About what?"

"Axel knocked Laura up. Either that night at the cabin or later. I'm not sure. But the one thing that was sure is Laura was suddenly pregnant. So now there was another potential scandal that spring before the merger. The deal was anything but certain, so Eliel Zetterborg tried to pressure Laura into having an abortion. When she wouldn't agree to it, he paid Laura's mother a considerable sum to handle it some other way."

"In what way?"

Apparently Nina is unable to hide her shock, because suddenly Raulo seems more empathetic. "They didn't force Laura to abort her child," he says with a soft chuckle. "But we didn't see Laura at school anymore. The rumor was she moved abroad with her mom."

"But wasn't Laura legally an adult?"

"Exactly. I think all parties were paid such substantial sums, there was no need to stay in Helsinki."

The outraged Nina glances at her phone, which is flashing on the table again. "Sorry. I have to take this." She stands and walks toward the rear of the dining room, phone at her ear.

Yusuf sounds like he's out of breath: "Where are you, Nina?"

"I'm talking to Erik Raulo's son. . . . I just learned something really crazy. Laura Karolainen—"

Yusuf cuts her off. "Yup! Rasmus tracked her down."

"What?"

"Listen, Nina. Jessica is missing. My head feels like it's going to explode. You need to head to Muukalaiskatu right now. Hellu is already on her way with a few patrols!"

"To Muukalaiskatu?"

"Laura Karolainen recently returned to Finland under a different name—"

Nina connects the dots before Yusuf can finish his sentence. And suddenly it all makes sense.

Rea Salo and Laura Karolainen are the same woman.

84

THE ELEVATOR DOORS open, and Yusuf runs across the hospital's expansive lobby toward the front doors. What Nina just told him on the phone makes the pieces fall into place. The murderer must have been aware of Eliel Zetterborg's fondness of literature; he must have been someone who knew the guy, at least to some extent. *Faust and Mephistopheles.* Yusuf remembers Jessica's words from that morning: had Zetterborg sold his soul and paid for it with his life? Or was he Mephistopheles, the devil's agent? Or maybe the devil was RealEst, the company Zetterborg was prepared to do anything to protect.

But something about the setup is still unclear. Why did Laura Karolainen leave a riddle in the apartment if Zetterborg was supposed to die that same night? Why go to so much trouble: the puzzle, the treasure map, the Polaroid? Were the clues meant for the police after all? And if they were, why did she want them to find her tracks?

Yusuf steps through the doors and rubs his eyes: the space where he parked his car a little over ninety minutes ago is empty.

What the hell?

Yusuf dashes off, wondering if it's possible he misremembers the spot where he left the car. . . . *No, this is absolutely where I parked. Right in front of the main doors.* Yusuf shifts his gaze down to the street and sees the headlights of the Volkswagen Golf. The car appears to be standing at a height of three feet and reversing toward the intersection.

"Hey! Goddamn it!" Yusuf shouts, sprinting after it.

He catches a glimpse of the tow truck signaling right and turning lazily out of the hospital lot.

"Motherfucking fucking goddamn," Yusuf says, giving up. There's no way he's going to catch up to the tow truck on foot.

He glances back and sees the no-parking sign.

He forgot to set the police insignia in the windshield for the meter maids to see.

Yusuf looks at his watch.

Jessica.

There's no time to lose. Laura Karolainen will be brought in right away. In the meantime, he has to look for Jessica.

Yusuf looks up and spots a taxi pulling onto the ramp. He will begin his search at Joonas Lamberg's place.

85

YUSUF HOLDS HIS gun at the ready and hammers on the door as if he is trying to break it down.

The door pops open; Yusuf feels his arm being wrenched and finds himself on the hardwood floor. The gun flies from his grasp, and fingers wrap around his throat.

"Hey!" Yusuf gasps, pounding the floor with his hand.

The grip eases and the pressure around his throat relents. For a moment the room spins like a carousel; then Yusuf is pulled to his feet.

"Sorry. I didn't realize . . ."

Yusuf looks around for his gun and sees it in the hand of the powerful, agile man standing in front of him.

Joonas Lamberg just took him at the front door and is now holding his service weapon. *Nice job, Yusuf. Real tough fucking SWAT guy.*

"Sorry. I couldn't see through the peephole properly. I saw the gun and—"

"Hand it over," Yusuf says, irritated.

Lamberg does. "I didn't realize it was you."

"I guess not. I thought you were going to strangle me, damn it!" Yusuf slides the gun into its holster and strides into the apartment.

"Old habits die hard. Krav Maga—"

"I don't have time for this bullshit right now. Where's Jessica?" Yusuf is pacing Lamberg's living room like a caged animal. "Where is she?"

"You can't just force your way in here, damn it, and—"

"I don't care! Do you know where Jessica Niemi is?" Yusuf shouts.

Now he steps right up to Lamberg, despite knowing he might find himself with his cheek to the tatami again in no time flat.

THE LAST GRUDGE 331

Lamberg looks confused and shrugs. "Um . . . she was here like an hour ago."

"Was? Did she say anything about where—"

"Why would she have said anything to me? But—"

"But what?"

"I happened to be watching from the window when she left the building, and I saw a car pull up next to her."

Yusuf looks at Lamberg probingly. His powerful jaw is chewing gum.

"A taxi?" Yusuf asks, letting his breathing settle.

"Didn't have the cheese on top, if that's what you mean. But it could have been a taxi. Black Benz. Maybe one of the better—"

"Fuck!" Yusuf shouts, running his hand over his shaved head.

"There was something weird about it."

"What? Weird about what?"

"Your colleague stopped, was staring and chatting. . . . Yeah, no, it wasn't a taxi, because someone unrolled the rear-passenger window—"

"Did she get in?"

"I don't know. . . . My phone rang just then and I didn't hang around to watch."

"OK. OK. OK." Yusuf shuts his eyes. His phone rings in his pocket, then stops. *Two unanswered calls—Nina.* But right now Yusuf's brain is focused on processing Jessica's situation. He can't help but think something horrible has happened to his friend. "What the hell car could it have been . . . ?"

"I assume you want the license plate number?" Lamberg says.

Yusuf feels hope spark inside him. "Huh? Did you write down the license plate?"

"Nope. Twenty-five years in the field." Lamberg taps his temple with his forefinger and flashes a proud smile. "You learn to memorize things."

86

FELIX SALO ADJUSTS the brightness of the video. He has gathered less material than he meant to, but he's still satisfied with the result. For the background music, he chose songs he thinks they might have listened to if they could have only spent time together. If Mom hadn't moved to Sweden when she was expecting Felix. He's not sure he's ever going to be able to forgive Mom for that.

The twenty-minute video begins with Will Smith's "Just the Two of Us," which features lyrics and samples from the Grover Washington song. In it, Will Smith raps about his son and how the two of them will face the world together: *Just me and you against the world.*

Felix has decided to add a short clip from the stairwell at the very beginning. First comes Trey Smith saying: *Now, Dad, this is a very sensitive subject.* Then the melody begins. And before long there's humming in the background and the drums kick in.

Just then, Mom bursts in through the door he forgot to lock. "Felix!"

"What?"

Mom takes Felix by the shoulders and urgently whirls his gaming chair around. Felix takes off his headphones.

Mom's eyes are teary and panicked.

"What's wrong?" Felix says, but Mom can't get a word out.

Now Felix hears the noise again. It's an insistent knocking coming from the front door.

Will Smith's rapping is blasting quietly from the headphones Felix has lowered to his neck.

"What's happening, Mom?"

"They're coming to take me away."

"Who?" Felix says.

"The police."

Felix hears the front door open.

Then to my knees, and I begged the Lord please
Let me be a good daddy, all he needs.

"Everything's going to be fine," Mom says, kneeling before Felix. Tears stream down her red cheeks. Her lacquered nails dig into the backs of his hands.

And at that moment, a group of armed men enter. Barked orders fill the room. *Police! Put your hands where I can see them!*

"Don't fight back," Mom says, raising her hands.

Felix follows her example.

He has the urge to turn around and take one last glance at the figure on the screen.

Maybe he will never meet him face-to-face now.

Maybe it will all be over now.

87

JAMI HARJULA STANDS next to the hospital bed, looking at the frail figure weeping inconsolably. He hears Kuznetsov's words behind him: once again, it's time to stop. It doesn't matter anymore; Harjula would have quit anyway. The story Hjalmar Ek told through the interpreter has rendered Harjula speechless, and he would be useless at questioning now. It's the story of an impossible love, insecurity, humiliation, and exploitation that picked up again after all these years. She came back to Finland and wrapped Hjalmar around her little finger once more. Spoke of revenge, of how Eliel Zetterborg served as the devil's agent once upon a time and bought the silence of both of them. Of how it was now time for payback, in the literal sense of the word. Of how they would frighten Zetterborg into paying more, of how they would keep him on his toes even in his old age. She had convinced Hjalmar that if he did his part, helped her avenge that stinging wrong they had both experienced so long ago, perhaps they could be together again. Give the relationship another chance without any of the pressure to perform entailed in youth.

Harjula is at a loss for words in the face of all the weak-willed, gullible Ek has been through. Some sort of altruistic attachment compelled him to dance to whatever tune she played. She convinced him to stoop to a crime that under normal circumstances he probably never would have even been able to imagine: forcing his way into the cleaner's home and tying her to her bed.

Of course, it's possible Ek is lying, but Harjula doesn't think so. It all adds up: the poor, lonely, manipulated bastard didn't know that Eliel

Zetterborg was going to be murdered. When he read about it the next morning, he was so shocked, he tried to take his own life.

Laura Karolainen played her cards in such a way that the trail would lead directly to Ek. She relied on his not talking. Or—and a cold wave washes over Harjula—on his committing suicide before the police found him.

Harjula opens the door, heads toward the elevators, and hears Ek's crying gradually fade and soon die completely.

But something still feels off. Harjula doesn't doubt Ek's story, but why would Karolainen have gone to so much trouble to lay the groundwork for the extortion if she meant to murder Zetterborg? The puzzle, the arrows, the photograph—were they all for the police after all? Were the details bread crumbs meant to lead the authorities to Ek's door?

At that instant his phone rings. It's Nina. She sounds agitated.

"Hey, the big wheels are turning and I can't get ahold of Yusuf. No one can!"

Harjula presses the button for the elevator. "What's wrong?"

"Salo . . . or Karolainen . . . or whatever the fuck her name is has been brought in."

Harjula feels his pulse start to race. He studies himself in the large mirror inside the elevator and decides the stubble actually suits him. Maybe Sini will be into it too.

"But that means we're close to wrapping this up."

"We also brought in Salo's grown autistic son."

"Who's doing the questioning?"

"I don't know! I don't have any experience with an interrogation like this, and Jessica isn't picking up either. . . ."

"OK, Nina. I'll be at the station soon. Keep it together until I get there."

88

YUSUF IS SITTING in an armchair in Lamberg's living room, eyes glued to the framed photos that advertise his host's martial arts fascination.

"Great. Thanks a lot."

He lowers the phone from his ear. His hand is shaking in excitement. He has just discovered that the 2014 Mercedes-Benz S350 is owned by Helsinki Luxury Car Service, which rents premium cars.

Yusuf mutters the name of the company, Googles its contact information, and clicks the link to call.

After a few rings, a chipper male voice answers. The rush of traffic is audible in the background.

"Yusuf Pepple from the Helsinki Police Department . . ."

"What can I do for you?"

"I urgently need information about a car that was rented from you."

"Well . . . we don't give out any information over the phone."

"This is a police matter."

"Then I'm afraid you're going to have to handle it through the official channels. I have no way of knowing who is calling and if the person on the line is actually—"

"Listen. There's a life on the line," Yusuf says sternly, and sees that Lamberg has raised his hand across the room.

"I understand," the man says. "But we have a clear policy regarding—"

Yusuf cuts him off: "I want to talk to your boss." The phone seems to be slipping from his sweaty grip.

"I am the boss. Owner, CEO, and one of the drivers. It's not an *easy* business."

"Goddamn it!"

Lamberg is waving his hand.

Yusuf presses his finger to the speaker. "What?" he snaps at Lamberg.

"Is that Helsinki Luxury Car Service?"

"Yeah. Why?"

"I know the owner. RealEst rented cars from them all the time. . . ."

Yusuf stares at Lamberg as if trying to shut him up with his glare alone, but an instant later understands that they need to turn over all cards now. He stands, strides over to Lamberg, and hands him the phone.

"We need to know who rented the car," Yusuf says. His voice is determined, authoritative.

Lamberg nods and walks into the kitchen, phone at his ear. "Hey, Joonas Lamberg here . . ."

Actually is a police officer . . . a missing woman . . . There's no time to waste.

Yusuf suddenly feels dead tired. He doesn't have it in him to keep track of all the threads. He knows Hellu is wondering why he isn't at the station questioning Laura Karolainen, but he doesn't want to call Hellu now. Worst-case scenario, she will tell Yusuf just to focus on the murder investigation and say she knew they shouldn't bring Jessica on board.

"Thanks, Late. Thanks a lot." Lamberg ends the call and returns to the living room.

"So?"

"The car was rented to the Bättre Morgondag Hospital, and it was signed for by a man named Henrik Borg."

Yusuf feels pain shoot through him, from the back of his head to his fingertips.

"Bättre Morgondag?" he says. He can hear his voice quavering.

Joonas Lamberg nods.

Now Yusuf knows he was right. No, Jessica was right; it took Yusuf far too long to realize the threat was real.

Bättre Morgondag. Camilla Adlerkreutz. Yusuf sees himself lying helplessly on the floor, at the mercy of those goddamned lunatics, the unconscious Nina at his side. How the fuck did he let Jessica start digging on her own?

"Thanks."

He taps out a text message to information. A few seconds later, Henrik Borg's phone number and home address arrive in a text message. He lives in the suburb of Soukka, across the Espoo city line.

"Fucking fucking fuck . . ." Yusuf wipes the sweat from his brow.

Where else would they take Jessica except someone's house? So they could do their thing without being disturbed . . .

Yusuf slips the phone into his pocket and lurches toward the door.

"Are you sending someone there?" Lamberg asks.

It's not really any of Lamberg's business; it's been ten years since he was a police officer, and even then his list of merits was questionable to say the least.

"Yes," Yusuf says regardless. "I need a taxi now."

"A taxi?"

"It's a long story."

Lamberg grabs his coat from the back of a chair and opens his front door. "I've already been pulled into this thing, Pepple. I may as well give you a ride."

Yusuf looks at him, confused.

"You're in a hurry and I still have a Maybach down there on the street. That six-liter baby will get you there before SWAT team."

89

JAMI HARJULA IS sitting in the conference room. He folds his hands on the varnished tabletop.

Nina has seated herself at his left and Rasmus is at his right.

The mood is expectant. The serigraph on the wall is a little askew, although Harjula could have sworn it was level earlier that day. Someone must have bumped it when getting up from the table.

And then the door opens and in walks Hellu, with the uniformed Jukka Ruuskanen, chief of the Helsinki Police, in her wake.

All three investigators stand, but Ruuskanen puts a stop to the obsequiousness with a wave of his hand. "Have a seat."

Ruuskanen is Hellu's age, a sly-looking man with blond hair receding a little at the brow. The glint of playfulness in his eyes makes him a charismatic and well-liked leader.

"Where are Jessica Niemi and Yusuf Pepple?" he asks as he and Hellu seat themselves across the table.

The three investigators exchange glances as if seeking refuge in one another.

Eventually, Jami Harjula clears his throat. "We don't know."

"What do you mean, you don't know?" Hellu asks.

"The last time I saw Yusuf was at the hospital . . . before he . . ."

"Before he what?" Hellu says, and there's not the slightest doubt she's revving up her tone to give the chief the impression of a tough, forceful boss.

"Yusuf went to look for Jessica."

Hellu's eyes go wide, and Harjula notices red splotches appearing at her throat. She lets out a nervous laugh. "To look for Jessica?"

"What exactly is going on here, Lappi?" Ruuskanen says. He has turned to Hellu, who as superintendent is responsible for her subordinates' actions.

"That's a question I don't have the answer to at this moment. But you can be sure I'll find out." Hellu sits up straighter. "They've been out of contact for some reason, but—"

"Good, because I didn't come here to play hide-and-seek," Ruuskanen continues neutrally. "We have more important things to do. I understand you have apprehended a suspect, and I'd like to hold a press conference as soon as possible. We don't need the missing lead investigator or even Superhero Niemi for that, but before our press liaison contacts the media, I want to know if we can consider the case solved."

"Nina, could you please brief us?" Hellu says calmly, shifting her bottle of mineral water back and forth across the table.

"I'd be happy to."

Nina reveals the biceps bulging under the sleeves of her taut T-shirt, and Harjula can't help but reflect that he has ended up in the middle of some unspoken contest for supremacy being fought in body language.

"Rea Salo—the former Laura Karolainen—has admitted to entering Eliel Zetterborg's apartment last night. In preparation for this act, she received assistance from a man named Hjalmar Ek, who also confessed to his role in the incident. Salo left both a puzzle and a photograph at the scene . . . and of course the UV arrows and other—"

"Did Salo kill Eliel Zetterborg? And Erik Raulo?" Ruuskanen interrupts, fingertips pressed firmly together.

"Rea Salo denies committing the murders. But she claims to know who did it."

Ruuskanen bursts out in laughter, and Hellu joins in at a brief lag. Then Ruuskanen's laughter dies as if it hit a brick wall. "So who is it?"

"Salo wants to cut a deal. We haven't had time to question—"

"A deal? This isn't some fucking episode of *NYPD Blue*. Why hasn't she been interrogated properly yet?"

Harjula glances around nervously. "We were going to, but then Hellu called this meeting together," he says before grasping he just threw his boss under the bus.

Chief Ruuskanen shakes his head, an enigmatic smile still smoldering on his face. He turns to Hellu. "Do you think maybe the interrogation might have been more important than this fucking meeting?"

He stands, dusts the sleeves of his uniform, then leans across the table with his hands on the back of his chair. "We know it couldn't have been anyone else. And we know that we don't even need a confession in this instance. I'm going to call Superintendent Lappi in one hour. By then, I want to be able to serve the media dinner on a silver platter."

Ruuskanen tromps to the door and out, and silence falls over the room.

"As you all can see, Ruuskanen is rather worked up. The interrogations need to start as soon as possible," Hellu says after catching her breath. "Is there anything else interesting I ought to be aware of?"

Rasmus looks as if he is brooding on a secret; he has removed his glasses and is now cleaning the lenses with a gray cloth.

Hellu crosses her legs. "Rasmus?"

"According to the bank's records, Hjalmar Ek withdrew thirty-five thousand euros in cash from his account yesterday morning. I find that curious, considering he later tried to commit suicide." Rasmus places his glasses on his nose and looks up from the table.

"But didn't he decide to kill himself only after he found out Zetterborg was murdered?" Hellu says. "He withdrew the money yesterday morning."

"True. But still, why did Hjalmar Ek need thirty-five thousand euros in cash?" Rasmus asks.

"Presumably Rea Salo asked him for money. And Ek agreed, just like he did to everything else Salo wanted."

"We'll have to ask Salo herself," Nina says emphatically.

"Exactly. Goddamn it, what the hell is that damn Yusuf—" Hellu's eruption is cut off by the sound of her phone ringing. "Speak of the devil."

Hellu answers and her lips soundlessly form Yusuf's name. His agitated voice carries from Hellu's phone into the conference room.

Jessica . . . Adlerkreutz . . . Hurry!

90

YUSUF IS THROWN back against the leather seat as the 530 HP V12 purrs at his feet. Joonas Lamberg steers the car onto the Turku Expressway and floors it. Yusuf feels the acceleration tingling in his gut.

"What if they didn't drive to Soukka after all?" Lamberg says, glancing over at Yusuf.

"There's an APB out for the vehicle throughout the region. One patrol is headed to the hospital on Bulevardi and another one is headed to the house on Kulosaari where Adlerkreutz lived before she disappeared last winter."

"But the SWAT team is headed to Soukka?"

"Yup," Yusuf says. "Shooting in the dark. I'm sure Adlerkreutz isn't taking any unnecessary chances this time. On the other hand, they don't know we have the car's license plate number."

Lamberg gives Yusuf a questioning look, but Yusuf has no intention of diving any more deeply into the history of what's going on. The ritual murders of a year ago got plenty of column space in the press; one of the homicides even ended up on Instagram Live, where it spread like wildfire. And yet few people know who was behind the crimes. The majority of Adlerkreutz's accomplices vanished as if the earth had swallowed them up, and no more was reported to the public than was absolutely necessary.

"It's a pretty big coincidence, actually," Yusuf says.

"What?"

"You catching the license plate number. Otherwise we wouldn't have anything," Yusuf says, then falls silent as a new thought pops into his mind.

Coincidence.

Yusuf doesn't believe in coincidences.

The events of the last twenty-four hours and the stress they've produced have clearly impacted his judgment. He dashed out of the hospital, left Harjula to handle the most important interrogation in the case, and took a taxi straight to Lamberg's front door, brandishing his weapon. *What do I actually know about Joonas Lamberg? This guy has been a possible suspect this whole time. . . . Do the CCTV recordings from the Russian embassy really prove he can't be a murderer?*

"I know," Lamberg says, and pulls into the right lane between cars putting along at the speed limit. "Tireless observation of the environment is an old ingrained habit that turns out to be useful now and again."

The thought won't leave Yusuf in peace. He is dying for a cigarette. *Why was Lamberg watching Jessica from the window in the first place? Is it even possible to see the license plate number of a car stopped on the street from his apartment? What about the rental agency where Lamberg just happens to know the owner?*

Another punishing acceleration glues Yusuf to his seat. He's headed to Henrik Borg's house with a man who more than conveniently offered to drop him in his dead boss' ride.

Have I walked into a trap? It wouldn't be the first time. Can Adlerkreutz still have enough influence to plan something this complicated? Are Zetterborg's and Raulo's murders somehow entwined with what's happening to Jessica?

Or maybe Lamberg has plans of his own. Maybe there is no Henrik Borg.

Yusuf glances at the square-jawed man out of the corner of his eye. "You gave Jessica Niemi a letter."

"Yes."

"And you don't know what it said?"

Lamberg shakes his head. "I didn't open it."

Yusuf nods. He tries to remember what Jessica said before she got off the phone. *That's weird . . .* or something like that.

And then Yusuf's phone rings. It's the SWAT team commander.

"Pepple, we'll be at the destination in thirteen minutes."

Yusuf glances at his watch. He and Lamberg will beat the SWAT team there.

I need to calm down. As long as the SWAT team is coming to the same address, I have nothing to worry about.

91

NINA RUSKA HAS sped from a walk to a jog and briskly pushes open the conference room door. Rasmus is standing in front of the screen, arms folded across his chest. Harjula is talking agitatedly into his phone.

Nina addresses her question to Rasmus. "Any news?"

"They suspect Jessica was taken to a house in Soukka. There's a pretty big arsenal on its way there now, but . . ."

"But what?"

"There are no guarantees Jessica is actually there, of course."

Rasmus' words give Nina goose bumps. She props her ankle against the back of a chair and stretches her hamstrings. Suddenly her whole body feels stiff as hell.

She and Jessica aren't the best of friends, but even so, the abduction of one of her colleagues brings her emotions to the surface.

"Where's Hellu?"

"I don't know. Maybe in her office."

"The Rea Salo interrogation can wait. She's not going anywhere."

Nina tries to take a deep breath. She thinks about the little package in her pocket, which Tom still hasn't given her permission to open.

"We should be out in the field. All of us," Rasmus says. He crooks his fingers nervously, a mannerism the usually placid investigator is rarely seen performing.

"I agree," Nina says. "I'll go look for Hellu."

92

JOONAS LAMBERG STOPS the car at a T intersection. The sign erected at the side of the road indicates the street is a dead end.

"Number fifteen is right up there at the end of the road, at the edge of the woods," Lamberg says, eyes on the navigator on the dash.

Yusuf glances at his watch—it will be at least nine minutes before the SWAT team gets there. The knowledge that Jessica might die at any moment pounds at Yusuf's temples, leaving no room for other thoughts. He will have to discover immediately whether Jessica was brought here. If the house is empty, the special forces can quickly be directed elsewhere. But where?

"Drive a little closer."

"I wouldn't recommend it," Lamberg says in a bored voice. "Who knows what will happen if they spot the car?"

Yusuf is on the verge of protesting but then reasons the former special forces officer knows what he's talking about. It's best to approach the target on foot. If everything is as it seems.

If I could only be sure.

"There's no sign of the rental Benz," Yusuf says, pulling his gun from his belt.

"Maybe it's parked between the house and the woods," Lamberg offers.

Yusuf draws a breath and looks at his watch again. Time seems to have stopped. "I'm going to go take a look."

Lamberg grabs him firmly by the arm. "Are you crazy? We don't know how many people are in there. They could be armed and . . . ," he says, appearing surprised by his own words.

Yusuf eyes Lamberg probingly. It's not at all clear if the guy is a bird, a fish, or something in between. It's possible Joonas Lamberg is part of Adlerkreutz's incessantly spinning machine and that the whole point of the scheme is to catch Yusuf in the same trap Jessica is already in. But Adlerkreutz has perhaps not counted on the SWAT team arriving soon and finishing off what Yusuf may have time to start. He will never be able to forgive himself if he learns Jessica lost her life during those few minutes he spent in a warm car only a few hundred yards away, waiting for the cavalry to show up.

"You get fired from the SWAT unit, Joonas?" Yusuf yanks himself free of the man's grip.

"Maybe."

"Well, you're going to have a chance to say hi to your old buddies soon. But you don't think they're going to let you in on the action again, do you?"

Joonas Lamberg looks at Yusuf, perplexed, but then seems to catch the curveball Yusuf just tossed him. "I don't even have a gun, goddamn it!"

"What does a big man like you need a gun for?" Yusuf says drily as he opens his door. "Krav Maga and so on and so forth, right?"

He loads his pistol and starts jogging toward the yellow wooden house at the end of the road. Yusuf hears the car door shut behind him.

Come hell or high water.

93

YUSUF ADVANCES ALONG the evergreen hedge lining the lot next to the yellow house. He glances back and sees Joonas Lamberg creeping along about thirty feet behind him. If Lamberg turns out to be a traitor, Yusuf will shoot the guy himself.

Yusuf squats in the cover of the trees and glances at the wooden house a stone's throw away. The yellow paint is peeling; the yard is untended and overgrown.

"I'll go around back," Yusuf hears a voice whisper behind him.

"Maybe this isn't such a good—"

"Trust me, bro."

Lamberg nudges Yusuf in the shoulder, then speeds past him at a hunch, fists clenched like a boxer preparing for his first round. The large man's swift, rolling gait is surprisingly soundless.

Yusuf holds his gun at the ready and dashes across the yard to the shelter of an old woodshed. He leans against the wall, catching his breath, and dares a glance around the corner a few seconds later. And then his heart skips a beat. At the end of a narrow gravel drive behind the derelict house gleams a perfectly waxed black Mercedes.

I'm coming, Jessica.

Yusuf establishes eye contact with Lamberg, who is crouched across the yard. He points at the car, even though he knows Lamberg can't see behind the house.

Yusuf settles for swinging his fist over his head and pointing at the house.

Let's go.

For a fleeting moment, Yusuf wonders if maybe they should wait for the professional strike squad to arrive after all. What if Jessica is killed because their raid is anything but well planned?

Yusuf turns to Lamberg, but the other man has already disappeared.

Fuck. Too late to back out now.

Yusuf walks toward the front door, gun raised, and is just about to climb the stairs to the porch when he sees something behind the Mercedes, at the edge of the woods.

An old cellar dug into the ground.

Jessica may have been carried straight from the car into the cellar. Yusuf runs to the car and crouches at the rear doors.

He listens for a moment but all he can hear is the cawing of crows mingling with the rush of the wind. The leaves that fell last autumn have frozen to the grass like a brown carpet.

Lamberg must be inside the house by now.

Yusuf disengages his weapon's safety and warily approaches the door to the cellar.

His heart is galloping in his chest.

He sees impressions in the frost: one large pair of shoes, and maybe two smaller ones.

Jessica has been frog-marched into the cellar.

Maybe he should wait for Lamberg to catch up with him.

Jessica . . .

But Yusuf doesn't stop moving; he continues slowly toward the door.

Coincidence. License plate. Trap. If Jessica's life is in danger, if she's already dead . . . then none of it matters anymore. Anna, the child. The family I didn't realize I wanted. The mistakes. The regret.

He hears voices carrying from the ground.

He lowers his fingers to the handle of the heavy-looking door. It's ajar.

Is this how I want to die?

Yusuf yanks the door open in a powerful movement, then grips his weapon with both hands.

And when his eyes grow accustomed to the gloom, he sees something that is both a relief and monstrous.

94

THE LIGHT BULB hanging from the ceiling offers its wan light to the absurd scene in the cellar.

Jessica is alive. But that state of affairs is in danger of changing very quickly.

An old woman is holding a large shard of glass at Jessica's throat. The frail figure looks as if she may leave this world at any moment. Adlerkreutz's bluish face resembles an angular piece of furniture over which a thin, unironed sheet has been draped. The eyes peering out from their deep sockets are red. Black gums are revealed behind the quivering lips.

"I'll kill her," the old woman says in her wheezing voice.

Yusuf adjusts his grip on the pistol and straightens his arms to aim. *It's all happening again. They really have come back.*

Camilla Adlerkreutz is a calm, single-minded psychopath who managed to play the sweet old lady for a good long while last winter.

But now her gaze displays no trace of the self-control that once made it chilling. She is clearly afraid: like an angry and underfed bloodhound that has been driven into a corner. Yusuf has succeeded in catching that damned inhuman creature off guard. He could emerge the victor.

"Put down the glass," Yusuf says, and takes a step deeper into the cellar.

Jessica is bound to a wooden chair and appears to be in some sort of state of shock: her body is shaking uncontrollably, and she's not making a sound, but her chest is rising furiously as if she is gasping for breath.

"I spared you too," Adlerkreutz says, and then Yusuf sees the shard of glass press into Jessica's throat and puncture the skin.

The wound isn't deep, but Yusuf feels rage well up inside him when he sees the pumping blood spill to Jessica's pale skin.

"Take it easy," Yusuf says.

Adlerkreutz is clearly feeble but doubtless capable of ending Jessica's life with one firm movement of her hand. Yusuf stares at the shard of glass. He should just pull the trigger. *Do it, Yusuf. What the fuck are you waiting for?*

"I spared you. We could have killed all of you there in that basement. But we were merciful," Adlerkreutz says as if she has read Yusuf's thoughts.

Yusuf is burning with the impulse to argue. To say that nine dead isn't a sign of mercy but sadism and mental illness. Even if Adlerkreutz really did leave the three of them alive: Jessica, Yusuf, and Nina.

"I'm going to count to three," Yusuf says. "This can all still end well."

Sweat is pouring down his back. The gun feels slippery in his hand.

What the hell happened to Lamberg?

A faint ripping sound carries from the street, which if he's lucky means the SWAT vehicles have pulled up to the intersection next to the Maybach. But their arrival isn't going to resolve the stalemate; it might even escalate it into a bloodbath.

Shoot, Yusuf. Shoot the crazy old bitch, damn it.

Just then Yusuf sees Jessica's lips forming silent words.

It takes him an instant too long to read the message there. *Behind you.*

And then Yusuf feels cold metal at the back of his head.

It's all over.

THE ARMORED VEHICLES stop at the T intersection, and a squad of SWAT officers in full tactical gear spills out from them. Squad commander Roni Kerman jumps from the car, lets out the dog panting at the end of its leash, and watches as some of the special forces officers begin securing the intersection.

"That's not something you see every day," one of the men says to Kerman, pointing at the Maybach parked at the side of the road.

"You have to be fucking kidding me," Kerman whispers, wrapping the dog's lead tighter.

The custom luxury vehicle in question isn't a common mode of transportation around these parts. There's only one man Kerman can think of who he knows drives one.

One unit ready.

Two unit ready.

The messages crackle from the radio.

Kerman rogers them as he circles the Maybach. There's a piece of paper on the dash, behind the windshield.

Hi, boys. We got tired of waiting and went in. —Joonas

"What the fuck is going on here?" Kerman says under his breath.

YUSUF DOESN'T DROP his weapon. He waits for the man behind him to make his next move. Urge him to give up, hit him with the butt of his gun, shoot.

The familiar smirk has spread across Camilla Adlerkreutz's face. *Damn it, I should have listened to my instincts.*

"Henrik isn't much of a shot, perhaps," Adlerkreutz says softly, "but I don't think even he would miss at that distance."

"Henrik?" Yusuf feels hope flare up inside him. *So it's not Lamberg.*

He looks at Jessica, bound to her chair, her sad face and the black streaks the tears have painted there. Here they are once again, he and Jessica, *royally screwed.* In a situation where there are no easy solutions if any exist at all.

And yet there's no other place Yusuf would rather be at this moment.

He grips his gun. He feels the barrel press more firmly against the back of his head. Hears the man's words. *Drop the gun.*

Yusuf's thoughts start spinning. Suddenly his focus isn't on the gun drilling into the back of his head; his mind is frantically searching for some way to escape.

Anna. Anna is having a child with another man. Anna, whom Yusuf has loved all these years. Anna, his love for whom has gradually morphed into a comfortable affection. The shift was mutual and served as an impetus for the final split. There shouldn't be anything ambiguous about it anymore.

Yusuf doesn't even want a child. Not yet. Maybe never.

The driving reason for the split was specifically to prevent Yusuf from waking up one day and realizing he was trapped unhappily in family life, mourning everything he has never experienced or lived, grieving the cards he has never turned over. Why is he longing for a life he doesn't want when having it is still possible? He feels his eyes grow moist, not from sadness but anger.

He sees Adlerkreutz's smile and the trickle of blood dripping down Jessica's throat.

He understands he never would have entered the cellar for anyone but Jessica. No one is ever going to hurt Jessica.

Yusuf raises the barrel of his gun and trains his sights on Camilla Adlerkreutz.

"Drop the gun or you die. And then the girl will die too."

Yusuf isn't going to obey. They will probably both die anyway.

But Adlerkreutz is not going to get Jessica. Ever.

I'm sorry I didn't listen to you, Jessie.

Jessica's sad eyes say she understands Yusuf's decision. She has accepted it.

Do it, Yusuf.

Suddenly the barrel of the gun slips from his neck, and he hears a pop, like someone stepping on a dry branch. Then he feels a bump at the back of his knee as a man drops at his feet.

Yusuf hears the man's inconsolable shrieks and Lamberg's words behind him.

"I said you could trust me, bro."

Yusuf doesn't lower his gaze from Adlerkreutz. She looks desperate. She raises the hand holding the shard and presses Jessica's head to her chest.

Yusuf catches a final glance of the wizened face before he pulls the trigger. Two times. Three times. The head snaps ferociously backward, and the frail creature is hurled against the cellar wall, where she collapses to the floor in an unnatural position, like a rag doll stuffed with cotton.

Yusuf drops to his knees and gasps for breath.

The pressure is released from his body in long, shuddering sighs. He hears someone kick in the doors of the yellow wooden house. And then he feels Lamberg's hand on his shoulder.

We did it.

97

JESSICA CLIMBS ONTO the vast back seat of the luxury vehicle and straightens her legs. It feels absurd to be sitting on the seat industry magnate Eliel Zetterborg used to travel on before his death. She shuts her eyes and lets out a long, deep breath.

The door on the other side opens, and Yusuf clambers into the seat next to her.

A stylish central console, complete with cup holders, rests between the seats. The car smells like new leather and a citrusy air freshener.

"Headquarters, please," Yusuf says.

Lamberg's eyes smile in the rearview mirror. The engine starts up and the car nudges into motion considerably more calmly than it did an hour earlier when they left Lamberg's apartment.

"It was fun sitting up front, but the back seat is what makes this car," Yusuf says.

Lamberg chuckles. "You're right. Enjoy the ride." He turns the country music playing on the radio up a notch.

"What's going to happen to the car now?"

"I don't know. I'll take it to the garage tomorrow, where it will eventually become part of the boss' estate. Why? You interested in buying it?"

"I might have to work a couple more years first," Yusuf says, shooting a pointed look at Jessica.

For a moment, Jessica regrets having told Yusuf about her fortune.

"How are the injuries?" Yusuf asks, touching her arm.

"I'll live. The medics said it didn't seem like there were any ribs broken," she says, then trains her gaze out the window.

Lamberg turns the car around, and the three of them see the SWAT team climbing back into their vehicles. No one was found in the house, and right now it seems as if Adlerkreutz truly managed to lure only one follower to join her last crusade: Henrik Borg, whose femur Lamberg just crushed with one sharp kick. Apparently the rest deserted her when forced to flee the country. In the end, leading a group of such people proved a difficult task.

"Speaking of money," Jessica says, and pain shoots through her side, "I think I left an envelope at your place, Lamberg."

"Really?"

"Yup. On the shelf in the entryway. It has two grand in it. I was going to make a contribution to charity."

Yusuf glances at Jessica. He seems impressed.

"Well, it's still there, then. I'll get it back to you as soon as possible," Lamberg says.

"Thanks." Jessica looks at Yusuf. "Thanks to both of you."

The engine roars elegantly as Lamberg races through an intersection and onto the ramp leading to the highway. Jessica looks at Yusuf and takes him by the hand. Her beloved colleague has just pulled the trigger and taken a life for the first time in his law-enforcement career. Jessica knows Yusuf well enough to know that processing this isn't going to be completely unproblematic for him.

"You did the right thing, Yusuf. You saved me."

Yusuf grunts almost shyly and shakes his head.

Jessica shoves her hand awkwardly into the breast pocket of her coat and pulls out a sheet of paper folded in two.

"Here it is," Jessica says softly and hands the letter to Yusuf.

Yusuf takes the piece of paper and reads it carefully.

"Goddamn it. There's a motive here for both murders," he whispers a second later.

Jessica nods. "Exactly. We need to bring this guy in ASAP."

98

THE SUPERINTENDENT'S GAZE exudes something, the existence of which Jessica was not previously aware. Hellu is looking at her with a maternal pride. They are standing face-to-face in the open-plan office at HQ at a closer proximity than ever before.

Yusuf is sitting on a table next to them, swinging his legs.

"Are you sure you want to do this now?" Hellu asks Jessica.

"Absolutely," Jessica replies. "Or what do you say, Yusuf?"

Yusuf nods.

Jessica has put on a high-necked sweater that hides the stitches and big bandage on her neck. Despite all that has transpired, she insisted on continuing immediately with the case, and Hellu didn't want to get in her way. The clock is ticking, and they need to wrap up the interrogations. The case is, for all practical purposes, solved; only a confession is lacking.

"Should we go?" Jessica says, and twisting her torso makes her grimace in pain. She feels like she's been run over by a truck.

She and Yusuf start heading toward the interrogation rooms.

"Listen, Niemi," Hellu says.

"What?"

"I'm so happy that . . . I was truly shocked by this episode," Hellu stammers. "It's wonderful that you're both safe."

Jessica grunts. "Thanks. The credit goes to Yusuf," she says, giving his shoulder a nudge.

"Hey, this crew always has one another's back," Yusuf says. "Jessica would have done the same for me."

Hellu looks at the two of them tenderly, like a proud mother or teacher. The moment is so syrupy, it's almost embarrassing.

"And then there's this letter. . . ." Hellu waves the sheet of paper in her hand.

"I know. And it never would have seen the light of day if . . . if Yusuf hadn't kept his wits about him," Jessica says.

"Where did they find the bastard?" Yusuf asks.

"At home. He wasn't expecting the police to show up."

Jessica nods in satisfaction, and she and Yusuf look each other in the eye.

Then Jessica starts walking toward the room where Rea Salo is already waiting.

99

JESSICA FILLS THE glasses with water and slides one across the table to Rea Salo. Then she takes two pain relievers from her pocket, washes them down, and turns on the recorder.

"OK, Rea," Jessica says, "in your own words, let's go back to yesterday evening at five fifty p.m. What happened?"

Rea Salo sits, slumped in her chair, hands in her lap, and stares at her glass. "I already told you."

"One more time. Go ahead."

THE NIGHT BEFORE, FIVE FIFTY P.M.

Rea starts and spins around. Felix has appeared out of nowhere.

She looks at her son standing before her in the entryway, hands hidden in the sleeves of his sweatshirt. He is crying.

"Go watch TV, Felix," Rea says firmly as she glances at her watch.

It's almost ten till. She has to act immediately; otherwise she won't have time to prepare everything before Eliel Zetterborg gets home. It took over half an hour to calm Felix, and in the end, he went to his room to watch a Marvel movie with his headphones on. But now her son has popped out of bed like a jack-in-the-box and followed his mother to the front door.

Her fingers, which are gripping a canvas bag, are instantly sweaty. "Mom needs to run a couple of quick errands."

"I'll come with you." The toes of Felix's right foot draw restless circles on the floor.

"No, Felix," Rea says, more tenderly. She walks up to the son who towers over her and gives him a hug. "Wait here. Everything's fine."

"Where are you going?"

"To run some errands, Felix. I'll be right back."

"I—I—I have a funny feeling . . . ," Felix says, rubbing his neck with both hands.

"There's no reason to be worried. Go watch your movie now."

Rea glances at her wrist again. This is taking far too long. The cleaner has been tied up in her apartment for hours. She has assured Hjalmar she will call the police to leave an anonymous tip about the woman's plight as soon as everything is in place. There's no need for the woman to suffer more than necessary. Felix hangs his head in dejection. "OK."

REA OPENS ELIEL Zetterborg's door. She has the blue plastic fob she has seen the cleaner use to deactivate the alarm system at the ready. She hears the beeps, feels a rising panic during the few long seconds it takes her to wave the fob at the right place on the alarm unit. The time counts down across the LCD screen: eighteen, seventeen, sixteen . . . and then the beeps stop. Rea casts one last glance into the empty stairwell and shuts the door behind her.

So far, so good.

She is alone in Eliel Zetterborg's home.

How damn absurd and amazing.

She has made all the preparations. She left her home in stocking feet so she wouldn't accidentally leave any shoe prints or make any unnecessary noise. She also left her phone at home, in the bathroom medicine cabinet on the Vuorimiehenkatu side of the apartment.

Rea scans Eliel Zetterborg's stately home, impressed by the beautifully finished furniture, the chandelier that glitters in the gloom, the valuable art hanging on the walls.

Concentrate. First things first: open the window.

Hjalmar has been standing outside in the cold with his dog for half an hour now. It is past time to signal to him that things are going according to plan, if slightly behind schedule. Felix's agitation delayed her departure by ten minutes. Rea crosses the living room to the window facing the Russian embassy and the little park to its right. Hjalmar is standing there at the foot of the stairs, at the park's edge, in his puffy red coat. The enormous dog sits at his side.

Rea waits until Hjalmar looks up and sees her. Then she raises a hand, and he touches his beanie. Just as they agreed. The signal has been given.

Hjalmar's task is simple: when Eliel Zetterborg pulls up to his building in his car, Hjalmar is supposed to shout so Rea has time to gather up her things, reactivate the alarm, and return to her apartment before Zetterborg and his bodyguard make it up to the sixth floor. Then she will simply toss the cleaner's keys out the window into the bushes below.

Rea reaches for the brass window pull. Just as in her home across the hall, this window opens inward. Rea takes the photograph of a woman that's in her way and moves it to the next windowsill over. The wind's murmur immediately intensifies, and for a moment, Rea wonders whether she will hear Hjalmar's signal in this weather. Maybe she won't even have to hear it. She just needs to be fast enough.

REA LOOKS AT the photograph of the three hunters. It was taken with her own Polaroid camera almost thirty years before. Those damned hypocritical bastards forced her to move to Sweden and raise the child on her own. When Eliel finds the photograph, he will immediately understand its significance: Rea is going to make his life a living hell until she gets what she wants.

Rea draws an X on the top drawer of the bureau with the UV marker and places the photograph inside, right side up. She hopes

Eliel won't find it until after he has finished the puzzle, but ultimately it makes no difference. She could have slipped the Polaroid through Eliel's mail slot, but she wants to scare him. And presumably there's nothing as unsettling as the thought of someone creeping around your home, going through your belongings, leaving things behind.

I want to see you sweat, you old shit.

Besides, based on the description the cleaner will give them, the police—if Eliel Zetterborg decides to get the authorities involved, that is—will be looking for a middle-aged man. Involving poor Hjalmar in her scheme felt unavoidable, and it wasn't difficult to coax him into complying.

Rea assured Hjalmar that what happened thirty years ago was merely an alcohol-fueled onetime mistake and that the love the two of them shared was genuine. She is sure if Hjalmar is caught, he will never talk. Not because he can't, but because his loyalty to Rea is unshakable.

Rea shuts the drawer and glances at her watch: 6:08. It's time to get out of there, turn on the alarm, and sneak back to her apartment across the way. She has been fast and already finished her preparations; Hjalmar has yet to shout to warn her that the car has arrived, and she has only a few minutes before Zetterborg and his driver reach the apartment.

What was that?

Rea hears the front door open. Her heart starts galloping furiously. Panicking, she dives under the bed.

What the hell?

She didn't hear Hjalmar shout. He would never disappoint her, not at such a critical moment. Is it possible his signal was drowned out by the howling wind?

100

YUSUF SHOOTS A discreet glance at the video camera recording the interrogation and slips off his hoodie.

His arm muscles are aching from the stress of today's altercation.

He has pulled the trigger and killed for the first time in his life.

An old woman. He knows it will take a moment for the reality to sink in.

Which is good, because he has no time for feelings right now.

"You know Rea is in the next room over, spilling her guts."

Yusuf lights a cigarette. Normally he'd ask the person he's interrogating if they mind if he smokes. Not because he's worried about their exposure to secondhand smoke, but for the sole purpose of creating trust between him and the person sitting across from him.

But right now that doesn't interest Yusuf in the least. They have more than enough evidence.

"OK. Can I have one?"

Yusuf slides the pack of Marlboros and the lighter across the table. "Help yourself. As long as we can get down to business."

"OK," Axel Zetterborg says, his voice trembling the tiniest bit.

THE NIGHT BEFORE, 6:07 P.M.

Axel Zetterborg opens the door to the apartment and raises a finger to deactivate the alarm, but it's not beeping.

For a moment he just stands there, listening.

Strange.

Joonas Lamberg has spoken sternly with Axel's father about the need to leave the alarm on not only when he exits the apartment but also when he's at home. But apparently his father, who usually takes such advice to heart, has forgotten to activate the alarm on his way out the door.

An unpleasant feeling washes over Axel: maybe he hasn't stepped into an empty apartment after all; maybe there's someone lurking in the darkness. He leans against the wall and shuts his eyes as if trying to sensitize his hearing to the extreme.

But no sounds carry from the dark apartment other than the wail of the wind outside. Now that Axel thinks about it, he has never heard the wind as loudly at his father's place as he does right now.

Axel slips off his dress shoes, takes them in his left hand, and taps in the code for the alarm system. *Home mode.* If Dad comes home right now, Axel will hear him and have time to slip out the back, just like in his youth when he brought his friends or girls over to party at the apartment.

Axel crosses the entryway in his socks. The wooden floor creaks under his feet.

He looks around and stops to listen.

He has the impulse to call out, but something prevents him. Of course there's no one in the apartment; the lock on the door was fine and the lights are out.

And then Axel understands where the sound of the wind is coming from: one of the living room windows is ajar.

What the hell?

Dad would never keep the windows open in the wintertime.

Something's up.

Axel tiptoes quietly toward the window but stops in the middle of the living room. He doesn't want anyone seeing him from the street.

He glances at his watch. It's ten past six; he doesn't have much time. He ought to be at the restaurant. The others must be waiting there by now.

A tram clanks past down below as Axel crosses the living room to the kitchen and on to the bedroom. He stops at the foot of the bed.

There's no sign of anything suspicious.

Axel casts one last glance around the bedroom and then moves on to Dad's study, which is located between the bedroom and the kitchen.

He sees the bottle of ink and the pen on the desk as well as a sheaf of blank stationery emblazoned at the top with the RealEst logo and contact information. A desk calendar, yellow Post-its, and a magnetic paper clip holder have been arranged tidily on the left side of the desk, where a rubber stamp and its ink also stand. Dad is extremely old-fashioned in his ingrained habits: he still writes his personal letters by hand and stamps the family crest at the top of each sheet of paper. He seals the envelope with red wax as if it is royal correspondence containing state secrets.

Shoes still in hand, Axel walks over to the desk and opens the middle drawer.

Bingo.

Axel reaches for the envelope. It is sealed and stamped, just as he assumed.

REA SALO IS lying under Eliel Zetterborg's bed, holding her breath. He came home, and somehow Hjalmar wasn't able to warn her.

Damn it all to hell, I shouldn't have relied on that deaf bumbler for anything.

Rea thinks through what's going to happen next. The old man is probably not going to think to look under the bed, even if he sees someone has been inside the apartment. He might notice the open window and find the puzzle pieces on the table in the library. And if he does, he'll immediately call his bodyguard and then the police and . . .

Damn it, damn it . . . I have got to get out of here without making any noise. And fast.

Maybe Zetterborg will take a shower or go back out. If he does, it will be easy for Rea to sneak back to her own apartment. But it is far more likely that all hell will break loose before an opportunity opens up for her to slip out.

She listens to the hardwood floor creaking beneath footfalls.

A moment later she sees black socks on the bedroom carpet.

Rea holds her breath.

There's none of an old man's stiffness in the way the feet move.

They don't belong to Eliel Zetterborg; they belong to someone younger.

The fat metal marker is getting sweaty in her palm. If Rea makes the slightest peep, whoever is in the room will hear it and look under the bed. Panic washes over her.

Just when she feels an irresistible need to draw oxygen into her lungs, the black socks turn and disappear through the doorway, into the next room.

Rea sighs in relief, but she knows the coast isn't clear yet.

Who the hell is creeping around Eliel Zetterborg's apartment? And are they going to leave before the owner returns?

And then Rea hears what she has been expecting all along: Hjalmar's croak sounds almost comical carrying from the park. It reminds her of a bird of prey spotting a victim as it soars through a canyon.

Under other circumstances, Rea would laugh. Not just because the cry sounds like an animal's, but because Hjalmar agreed to Rea's lunatic scheme in the first place.

But she's not laughing now. Just the opposite.

AXEL JUMPS. SOME sort of bestial squawk carries in through the open window facing the little park. The window bangs in a current of air, and then all is quiet again.

He glances back, burning with desire to walk to the window and see what's going on outside, but the letter transfixes him.

He turns over the envelope and sees the address written there in a tidy hand.

Erik Raulo, Esq.
Munkkiniemenranta 42
00330 Helsinki

Axel stares at the envelope as if it is the world's most valuable treasure and it conceals ancient secrets within. Then he reaches for the letter opener and slices into the envelope without further ado. The heavy stationery folded neatly in half rustles in his hands, and for a moment, Axel just eyes the rows of flawless characters drawn in his father's steady hand. Eventually, he shifts his eyes to the first sentence of the letter and begins to read.

Dear Erik,

It is with a heavy heart that I have decided to at long last take concrete steps regarding the distribution of my estate.

We all live for our children in a way. I suppose it is our primary task in life. Anne-Marie succeeded particularly well at it, even though she did so without knowing the truth—I protected her from it until the end. Since her passing, however, I have begun to question my motives, and now it seems to me there is no one left who needs protecting.

It is my wish that, upon receiving this letter, you undertake without delay to put in place the measures you have with such discretion (and tact) prepared and transfer my assets in their entirety (the controlling interest in RealEst, my real estate, as well as the investments in my Nordea Private Bank securities account) to a trust and out of the reach of my son, Axel Olav Ruben Zetterborg.

Even if my son is never called to task for his lifestyle and his mistakes, I believe that in taking this action I may be able to teach him a final lesson. A lesson I should have taught him long ago. A lesson that would have made him a better man. But one I left untaught because it would have broken Anne-Marie's heart.

The so-called period of deliberation you urged me to take has dragged on without convincing me to change my mind. On the contrary, it has served only to confirm my decision.

Respectfully, your old friend
Eliel W. Zetterborg

Helsinki, January 28, 2020

"Here it is," Yusuf says, tossing the letter across the table to Axel Zetterborg. "Your father made two copies of it."

"No . . . this has to be the same one I . . . ," Axel says, then takes a drag of his cigarette.

"No, Axel. You took the original. You thought it was the only copy."

"But—"

"We'll come back to that in a moment. Tell me the rest of the story," Yusuf says, rolling out the tip of his cigarette in the porcelain ashtray.

THE NIGHT BEFORE, SIX FOURTEEN P.M.

Axel feels a crushing pressure at the corner of his eye, and the shoes drop from his hand. He takes the letter in both hands. The tremor in his fingers that began gradually has intensified. He feels like ripping the letter into a thousand pieces.

The fucking asshole.

Tears start streaming down his cheeks.

And then he hears the floor creak in the living room. *What the hell . . . ?*

Axel wipes his tears on his sleeve and strides toward the living room, the letter in his fist.

I'm sure I heard footfalls!

He's on the verge of rushing out of the apartment before remembering his shoes fell to the floor of the study. He listens to hear if the sounds he just heard are repeated, but the howl of the wind drowns out everything. He steps over to the window and pulls it shut without looking down at the street.

And just as he makes it back to the archway between the living room and the kitchen, he hears his father's voice in the stairwell. And the door opens.

AXEL SLIPS BACK into the study.

"Will you be all right?"

"Yes, thank you. I'll see you downstairs in a minute."

The front door shuts and the alarm is deactivated.

Axel stands in the middle of his father's study, breathing heavily.

The letter burning in his fist is like a timed explosive that has by no means been defused.

How the hell could you, Dad . . . ?

For a moment, Axel feels like a little boy again, like the gangly, insecure seven-year-old who wanted his father to pick him up and sit him in his lap. Hug him. Tell Axel he's proud of him. Stand at the edge of the pitch, arms folded across his chest, and nod encouragingly whenever Axel takes possession of the ball, tackles an opponent, scores a goal, or achieves anything else requiring effort.

But his father doesn't hug, and he isn't proud. He never has been.

Dad didn't send Laura and her baby away to protect Axel, but to protect the impending merger.

Of his father's two children, RealEst is the one he loves best.

Asshole . . .

Axel hears his father's footsteps shuffle slowly into the living room. Then music Axel knows all too well starts coming from the speakers. It's the tune his cousin played at his mother's funeral three years ago. His father thinks it's the most beautiful piece of music ever composed.

J. S. Bach. Axel bursts into silent tears. *Mom wouldn't have let Dad do this. Of course not. That's why Dad is doing it now, on the firm's fiftieth anniversary. Now that Mom isn't around to stop him anymore.*

That bastard is listening to his favorite music even though he knows he just signed his son's social death sentence.

Axel stifles his crying on his sleeve and lets out a few trembling gasps.

The letter is dated the day before yesterday.

Why didn't he send it yet? Maybe he's had second thoughts.

Axel takes a deep breath and walks slowly toward the kitchen, the letter in his fist.

ELIEL ZETTERBORG'S HEART skips a beat. It's an automatic reaction to the sound he just heard again. Now it's coming from the other side of the wall, from the kitchen. A low dragging that ends in an abrupt thunk. *A kitchen drawer.*

A cold wave climbs Eliel's spine to his neck.

He grabs his phone, uses speed dial to bring up Joonas' number.

Now he hears the footsteps more clearly.

And then Eliel sees it, the figure emerging calmly from the dark kitchen. The phone slips from his grasp and falls between his feet.

"*Hej, papa,*" the voice says, and it takes Eliel a few seconds to grasp that the face distorted by sadness, the quivering lips, belong to his son.

"Axel, what the hell . . . ?"

Eliel looks at his son and immediately understands something is seriously awry. Instead of walking up to Axel and embracing his shocked son, he instinctively steps back. Something about the boy is giving him goose bumps.

And then he sees the paper in his son's hand, the dark blue letters that stand out against the white background, and the family crest from the stamp on his desk.

"Axel, did you break into my home?" Eliel says, surprising himself with the sternness of his tone.

Now he understands Axel has read the letter, but he doesn't feel the need to explain its contents. His hands are shaking with anger.

"I have a key, Dad. You didn't forget that, did you?"

Eliel finds himself clenching his fists. "And that gives you the right to sneak into my home and read my private correspondence?"

A faint smile flashes across Axel's face. "Is that what it is, Dad? Private correspondence? Because at first glance it seems like it impacts me too."

Axel's eyes are bloodshot and his bottom lip is trembling, but the words that spew from his lips sound chillingly calm.

"This is inappropriate behavior, Axel. What exactly is it you want?"

"An explanation," Axel says, turning his eyes to the letter.

Eliel feels like roaring, ordering Axel out of his home. Or retrieving the phone from the floor and asking Joonas to throw the boy out like the bum he is. That's why Joonas is there, to keep trespassers at bay. And despite their blood kinship, at this moment, that's exactly what Axel is: a trespasser.

But something about the music playing in the background makes him remember a time the three of them were still a family, and Anne-Marie's presence compelled him to sweep his son's debauchery under the rug. How he was convinced Axel's mother would forgive the boy

THE LAST GRUDGE 375

everything, and so he was forced to be the bigger person too. Anne-Marie was the glue that held the three of them together.

"I'm sorry, Axel," Eliel eventually says, takes a tumbler from the cabinet, and pours a splash of Macallan into it. But Axel refuses the glass Eliel holds out to him.

"You're sorry?"

"I'm not taking away what you already have, Axel. And you have more than enough."

"More than enough? I've dedicated my whole life to RealEst. . . ."

An unintentional laugh escapes Eliel's mouth. He lowers the glass rejected by his son to the piano lid. "You've dedicated your whole life to it? No, Axel. I have. It's my baby."

Axel looks deep into his eyes. "Your baby? Your only child?"

Eliel feels a pang; his son is right. RealEst has always been the most important thing in his life; he would probably be more willing to give up fatherhood than to travel back to his youth and rewrite his history without his company.

"Are you drunk, Axel?"

His son doesn't appear to hear the question. Axel has lowered his eyes to the letter again and is flapping the hand holding it as if trying to exorcise the words from the page.

"Who knows about this?"

Eliel swallows the lump in his throat. The time has come to face the facts, and it's only fair to be honest with Axel. Tell the truth as it stands.

"Only Erik. He and I have agreed he has permission to bring up the past if you contest the will." Eliel takes a step closer to his son. "I sincerely hope you do not go down that path, Axel."

"Laura Karolainen was a climber and an opportunist who wanted money and attention," Axel says. "I didn't rape her, Dad. I didn't rape her, even though she claimed I did."

"There's no way for me to know that," Eliel says softly.

"So you decided to believe that slut instead of your own son." Axel wipes his eyes on his sleeve.

Eliel sighs deeply. "What happened back then is ultimately immaterial, Axel. You've lived a life of depravity and soullessness in any event. All the drugs and prostitutes—"

Eliel stops midsentence. Suddenly he realizes Axel is holding something behind his back. And in that instant, Eliel is overtaken by the impression that he shouldn't have answered Axel's last question. Shouldn't have told him how easy it would be to annul the plan laid out on paper.

"Axel—"

"You know what? I really wish you would die right now . . . you old piece-of-shit bastard! The firm has always come first. The firm, the firm, the firm. And the little that was left over . . . you gave it to Mom! Do you hear me, you crusty old fuck? I wish you would just hurry up and die, damn it!"

And then Eliel feels a sharp, paralyzing pain in his chest. He tries to cry out but isn't sure anything emerges from his gaping mouth. And somewhere in the back of his mind, Eliel can't help but picture a just lathed metal cylinder, sparks flying like fireflies, rings of steel being soldered together while a cigarette hangs from the corner of his mouth. Picture how proud Anne-Marie would have been of him tonight, upon the firm reaching this incredible milestone. And perhaps Anne-Marie would understand that Eliel's failure as a father didn't go unpunished after all. That everything went just as it was supposed to. How Anne-Marie would tell him she loved him. Maybe he could hear the words from her lips. Tonight.

Then the Siciliano ends and all that remains is the scratch of the needle against vinyl.

Can you see me yet, darling? Soon it will be just you and me. We shall live as the dead. And all that lives shall be dead to us.

101

Rea Salo holds her cup in both hands as if she asked for coffee merely to keep her hands warm. Jessica makes herself comfortable and glances at the camera, where the red light is burning beneath the lens.

"Then I heard the door open," Rea continues tearfully. "I had just crawled out from under the bed and was standing there in the corner. I heard the entire conversation. I saw Axel. . . . And when I finally dared to move, I ran across the living room and took a quick look at Eliel. He was sprawled on the floor next to the piano—"

"So you didn't do anything to help the victim? Or call an ambulance?" Jessica says drily, folding her arms across her chest.

Salo looks at Jessica as if the question was both completely logical and utterly absurd. "He looked dead. . . . I saw the knife lying on the floor next to the body. . . ."

"Even so, it would have been impossible for you to determine whether Eliel Zetterborg was dead or not. And now we know he was alive. And even managed to place a call to emergency services only a moment after you left the apartment."

"Yes, but . . . ," Salo says, training her glassy eyes on Jessica, "what would it have looked like if I had called the police? I wasn't supposed to be there. . . . No one would have believed me if I'd said that there was a third person in the apartment, that Eliel Zetterborg was murdered by his own son."

Jessica folds her hands on the table. "So you're saying you heard their entire conversation?"

Salo nods. "They weren't that far away. I was standing in the next room, in the corner of the library."

"But you saw for certain that the man was Axel Zetterborg? You recognized him even after thirty years?"

"I've seen pictures of him in the press, of course. . . . Besides, his identity was revealed during the conversation: Eliel addressed him by name a couple times—"

"I need to get it on tape again, Rea. Did you see Axel Zetterborg's face?"

Salo appears to consider her answer, then takes her first sip of the coffee, which must have cooled to the point of being undrinkable. "I did," she says, lips hovering above the rim of her cup. "I'm a hundred percent certain it was Axel Zetterborg. He had a large knife in his hand. I have no doubt."

Jessica pinches her lips firmly and decides that now would be as good a time as any to take a little break. A brief status check that will give Salo a moment to catch her breath.

But before that, she suddenly asks: "Why did you ask Hjalmar Ek for money?"

Salo starts. "What do you mean?"

"You asked Hjalmar to withdraw a large sum of cash. Why?"

"I didn't. . . . I don't know anything about that."

Salo looks surprised, but Jessica can't tell if she's lying. Until now Rea Salo has told her story without grumbling and provided straightforward answers to all questions. Which doesn't mean, of course, that everything to come out of her mouth is the truth.

The sum withdrawn from Hjalmar Ek's account is large enough that it's hard to believe it has nothing to do with the case. On the other hand, the knowledge of what the money was used for would do nothing to change Salo's and Zetterborg's present circumstances. Some explanation for the money will turn up before long.

"If you saw Axel Zetterborg holding a knife in the apartment, why didn't you tip off the police?"

"But then I would have had to admit I was there."

"Not necessarily. You could have lied and said you looked through the peephole."

"If I'd become a key witness to such a serious crime, I know the police would have looked into my background. You would have discovered my connection to the case in no time flat and questioned my testimony."

Jessica shuts her eyes. Salo's right.

"Besides . . . ," Salo says, and blows her nose into a white handkerchief.

"Besides what?"

"I'm scared to death of Axel. I wouldn't have dared . . ."

"Why?"

"He's the root of all this evil. He raped me all those years ago."

"Why didn't you report the rape to the police?"

"You know the answer to that. They bought my silence. Forced me to move to Sweden to have the baby."

Jessica eyes Salo at length. She's an unscrupulous and clearly unstable woman. It wouldn't be much of a stretch for her to have made up the rape story back then to strengthen her hand and get more money out of the Zetterborgs.

"OK, so you're afraid of Axel. But you're talking to us now."

"Of course. Otherwise I'd be your only suspect."

"Exactly. So you could have just as easily made all of this up."

Salo looks flustered but not the slightest bit more guilty.

"I don't know, Rea. Laura. Rea. The whole puzzle thing with the Polaroid and everything seems totally crazy. It's a miracle you were able to convince Hjalmar to go along with it."

"It's not just about the money," Salo says, voice trembling. "I wanted to scare that old bastard. If I'd just asked for money, he would have paid up and slept too well at night. I wanted him to lie there awake in his home, knowing I'd been there. That his memento-filled refuge had been desecrated. And that his torment wasn't over."

Jessica shakes her head. "What do you think, Rea: would Hjalmar have ever given the police your name?"

"No," Salo replies softly, "he wouldn't have."

"Which is exactly why he was the perfect accomplice for you. Hjalmar is still in love with you. And you used him cruelly."

Salo doesn't say anything, but the way she lowers her eyes says more than any verbal response could.

Jessica rubs her face. The pain gnawing at her body mingles with an enervating exhaustion. Despite the arrests, the outcome of the case is anything but clear-cut. Aside from Salo's account and the letter, there's nothing to put Axel at the scene of the crime. And Salo has plenty of reasons to lie, because otherwise, as she herself said, she's the only suspect. It's her word against his.

Jessica is just about to turn off the video camera when there's a knock at the door. Nina enters the interrogation room, muscular hands at her waist.

"Could you come here for a moment, Jessie?"

Jessica shuts the door behind her and walks over to the table, where a frightened, confused-looking man sits on the other side. Felix looks like a child whose unsullied mind is imprisoned in the body of an adult man.

"What is it?" Jessica says, hands on her hips.

Nina points at the iPhone on the table. "I believe we have everything we need here.

"Felix," she continues gently as if waking him from sleep.

And when his bleary eyes turn from his hands to Nina, Jessica can see "sleep" isn't necessarily a wholly inaccurate word for Felix's dazed state right now.

"What?"

"Could you please show us the video you just showed me again?" Nina says.

Jessica knows the phone is evidence and officially in police custody, but she also grasps that Nina doesn't have to intimidate Felix to get what she wants.

Felix rubs his curly black hair. In the room's wan light, somehow cornered and with his back hunched, Felix is the spitting image of his father.

Felix fiddles with his phone, then slides it across the table to Nina. Jessica gasps in pain as she leans over Nina's shoulder.

Nina presses Play.

At first Jessica isn't sure what she's looking at. The edges of the image are blurry, and the shapes emerging from the dimness seem strangely curved. Then she understands the sudden movement in the middle of the image is an elevator gate opening. She sees a dark figure standing at a wood door. The camera's automatic focus zeroes in on the figure, and the contours sharpen.

"Wait a minute. Was this filmed through a peephole?" Jessica asks.

"Yup." Nina looks pointedly at Jessica. "Felix shot it from his apartment with his phone."

"But—"

"Wait," Nina says, indicating the screen.

Jessica shoots a quick glance at Felix, who is restlessly twiddling his earlobe.

Then Felix's excited voice can be heard over the clink of keys.

Daddy.

The figure in the stairwell appears to freeze. He must have heard Felix's voice through the door. Or he imagines he heard something.

The figure turns toward the camera, and not even the dim light of the stairwell can conceal the identity of the man at Eliel Zetterborg's door. The nervous-looking Axel Zetterborg stands there like an alert dog, listening for sounds from the apartment opposite. Then he spins on his heels and opens his father's front door.

Jessica stands up straight. "And the time is visible in the file information?"

"Yup, six oh seven p.m. It can also be confirmed by the metadata, which makes this completely watertight evidence. Axel Zetterborg was there at the exact moment Rea Salo claims he was."

Jessica isn't fully able to conceal her jubilation, despite understanding Axel Zetterborg's fate has just been sealed by a son who is unlikely to understand the consequences of his actions. Felix doesn't actually know his father. He has grown to adulthood in a dreamworld of sorts, developing a fixation on Axel—not only because Axel is his biological father, but because he hopes someday to get the affection and warmth he craves from Axel.

Jessica wipes the elation from her face and looks at Felix. "Thank you, Felix. You did the right thing."

"What's going to happen to Daddy now?"

"It's likely he's guilty of homicide."

"So he killed Grandpa?"

Jessica lowers her chin slightly. She didn't think about it from that perspective. "That's right."

"Is my dad going to jail?"

Jessica sighs and tries to come up with a single good reason to lie to Felix. But there isn't one. "Yes. But that means your mom will probably be released."

"Would you please wait here for a moment, Felix?" Nina says.

She gestures for Jessica to follow her out into the corridor, where she shuts the door and folds her arms across her chest. "This is all we need, isn't it?"

Jessica answers in a low voice: "Rea Salo's version of the evening's events is credible. The conversation Salo claims to have overheard jibes with Axel's likely reaction upon reading the letter. Axel has a motive, and he was demonstrably at the scene at the time the murder was committed. His guilt is also supported by the fact that the perp found the kitchen knife used as the murder weapon so easily. It's been pointed out numerous times that the murderer wouldn't have found the knife if he didn't know where to look." Jessica glances over her shoulder at the room where Rea Salo sits nursing a cold coffee. "Plus Salo would have never gone to so much trouble only to kill Zetterborg before her little game had begun. Now she's not going to get a cent. And Eliel Zetterborg is never going to experience a single sleepless night in his apartment."

Nina and Jessica exchange thoughtful glances, perhaps a few seconds longer than either intended. For a spilt second, it seems the old grudges have vanished and the hatchet has finally been buried.

"Good," Nina says. A tentative smile spreads across her face. "We caught him."

"You'd better fucking believe we did."

Suddenly there's a loud crash from the interrogation room.

Jessica grabs the door handle and dashes in. She and Nina see the legs of the wooden chair crunch into the shattered cell phone over and over. Tiny components fly around the room.

"No! Felix!" Jessica cries, rushing over to restrain him.

Felix manages to elbow smash his phone a few times before Jessica can push him up against the wall.

"Nina! Tell me we didn't just lose our one piece of watertight evidence!" Jessica cries, eyeing the object that was a phone a moment ago and is now in pieces strewn across the floor.

Nina looks more sad than shocked.

"I'm sorry, Felix," she says, pulling her phone out of her pocket. "Just to be sure, I sent your video to myself with WhatsApp."

102

AXEL ZETTERBORG'S SPINE is arched and his torso rests on his hands. Eventually he looks up from the table. His eyes are bloodshot. His hands are shaking.

"The only thing we don't know yet, Axel, is how you knew to look for the letter in your father's apartment that night," Yusuf says.

The cigarette from which Axel has yet to take so much as a drag is tilted into the ashtray on the table.

"I was walking into my father's office that morning when I happened to hear"—Axel's voice is quavering, and he pauses before continuing—"Dad talking on the phone . . . with Erik Raulo, I guess. He said he had written the letter now, with a heavy heart. That it took backbone to write it and sending it would take twice as much. But that it was too late to back down."

Axel falls silent and takes the cigarette he lit a moment ago between his fingers. He studies it absentmindedly as if he doesn't know which end to put in his mouth.

"But how did you know the letter your father mentioned was about you?"

"It wasn't just that phone call. Dad never liked me. I was always on my toes, worried he would do something like that: cut me out. Try to disinherit me. Leave me without any share in what was the most important thing in the world to me: the firm." He taps the ash from the cigarette and takes a few short drags. "I knocked on the door and stepped into his office. I asked if everything was all right. Dad looked startled, said everything was fine. But the way he looked at me said more than a thousand words. It said that from that moment on, I was something other than his son. Something completely other than the person who would carry on his legacy . . ."

"And so you decided to conduct your own search."

"It was a spontaneous idea. I'd parked and was about to go into the restaurant when I decided to head over to Dad's instead. I had to see it with my own eyes, Dad's betrayal. Just pop by the apartment. In, out. Maybe I would find the letter and my suspicions would be confirmed. And it turned out that all my fears were justified."

"And so you killed your father," Yusuf says.

Suddenly Axel looks completely lost. "I don't remember anything about that moment," he says inconsolably. "I've never been so angry in my life. . . . I saw red. On an impulse, I grabbed a knife from the kitchen drawer. I still don't get what was going through my head." Axel shakes his head. "I guess it was some sort of defense mechanism. . . ."

"The knife? Against your unarmed father?"

Axel's face twists up in grief. "It sounds crazy, but . . ."

"Axel," Yusuf says, "we've been through this several times now, and now you just need to tell us the whole truth. I don't want to hear any more stories about blacking out and panicking. There was a brief argument and you stabbed your father in the heart with a knife. You fled the scene, called your father a couple of times to create the illusion that you didn't know why it was taking him so long to get ready for the firm's fiftieth anniversary party. Then you called Lamberg. All the information and the times match. We have an eyewitness statement as well as video footage that incontrovertibly proves you were present in the apartment. The data from cell phone towers indicates you were moving up and down the block at the time. There is no scenario in which you will not be convicted of this homicide!"

Yusuf steadily raises his voice and finds his final words emerge more vehemently than intended.

The tears stream down Axel's cheeks. "I don't remember how it—"

"You said it yourself. You heard your father talking to Erik Raulo, and presumably no one else knew about the letter or its contents. That's the reason you went to Raulo's home the next morning and killed him too, so no one would know about your father's will and things could continue as before."

"No . . ."

"You found the letter but remembered Raulo knew about the plan anyway. That's why you had to kill him too, just to be safe. What you didn't know was that there was a copy of the letter, and your father had given it to his bodyguard to deliver. Raulo died in vain."

Yusuf eyes the figure sobbing against the table in a state of utter helplessness.

"I never could have killed Dad. . . . I thought it was a heart attack." Axel rubs the left side of his chest with his fingers as if demonstrating heart pain.

Yusuf glances at his watch and stands. "If there's one word I'd use to describe all this, it would be 'sad.' Really damn sad."

And then he exits the room.

103

"HAVE A SEAT, Yusuf," Hellu says, and closes the blinds to keep the sun's rays from penetrating the room.

It is in many ways dramatically appropriate that, the day after the arrests, the sun has dawned in a cloudless sky and the morning is the most beautiful in weeks.

Hellu coughs into her fist a few times, then settles into her ergonomic wonder chair. For a moment, the superintendent simply eyes Yusuf critically, like a boss on *The Apprentice* about to fire a contestant who performed poorly on an assignment. Eventually she opens a drawer and sets two stemmed glasses down on the table. Yusuf looks on in surprise as a sweating bottle of champagne appears from behind Hellu's computer screen.

The smile Hellu has intentionally held in during the past few minutes spreads across her face. "Bravo, Yusuf."

She wraps her fingers around the cork and effortlessly pops it off.

"Well, thank you. . . . This is . . ."

"I have to admit, I was a little nervous making you lead investigator. Not because I didn't trust you; just the opposite. But the fact is, it was a new situation for you."

"Thanks for showing confidence in me," Yusuf says.

His boss' praise feels incredibly good. He is tired, and the stress that has been ravaging his body for the past thirty-six hours will finally be released when the glass of bubbly is in his hand.

"The case was solved in a day, for all intents and purposes," Hellu says, "which is quite the accomplishment, considering Rea Salo spent months planning her puzzle prank."

"I'm happy to accept your compliments," Yusuf says as Hellu hands him a glass filled to the brim. "But there was also a lot of luck involved."

"Luck is one of the ingredients of success. It's like salt. Without it, cooking is a disaster, but I've never seen anyone eat salt alone."

"That's a good metaphor," Yusuf says, amused, and tosses back half the glass. The cold sparkling wine tastes of summer, sun, and victory. "Did you just come up with that?"

"Goddamn it, Yusuf," Hellu responds playfully. "I guess I did. Maybe I'm in the wrong field. Maybe I should be a poet, philosopher, or . . ."

"A thinker?"

Hellu laughs and takes a sip from her glass. "Yes, a thinker would be an amazing profession."

They sit in their comfortable chairs, enjoying the moment, the champagne, and the fact that the success has no doubt just made working together in the future easier.

And then their faces grow serious. They both know the case isn't in the bag yet.

"Axel hasn't confessed to the killing," Yusuf says.

Hellu shrugs. "Remember, a confession is only one piece of evidence among others."

Yusuf swirls the champagne in his glass. "Then, of course, there's the right not to incriminate yourself."

Hellu grunts wryly. "Right you are. On the one hand, you can't punish a suspect for not contributing to proving his own culpability, but on the other, a confession might result in a less severe sentence. So it's a stick masquerading as a carrot. The whole right not to incriminate oneself is a total crock—off the record."

Yusuf glances at his watch. "Interesting perspective."

"In the Zetterborg case, we have a perfectly valid motive as well as watertight proof that Axel Zetterborg was in the apartment at the time of the killing. There's a clear motive for Erik Raulo's murder as well, and then there's the ballistics report. The Smith and Wesson pistol belonged to Eliel Zetterborg, and it was easy for Axel to get his hands on it. In all likelihood he took it from his father's apartment the night of the murder. At this point, the confession is only of cosmetic significance," Hellu says.

"I suppose." Yusuf nods and drains his glass.

Hellu raises the bottle, and Yusuf doesn't refuse a refill, even though he's so tired from lack of sleep that the first glass went straight to his head. He could drink the entire bottle. Then he's going to go home to get some sleep. They won't be needing him at the station until tomorrow.

"It's just, I was thinking . . ."

"Thinking what?"

"Somehow it bothers me that Axel's culpability in the murder of his father is supported by Rea Salo's statement specifically. She's clearly an unstable narcissist who used Hjalmar Ek. We have evidence that both Salo and Axel were in the apartment, but in theory Axel could have exited first, after which Salo could have killed the victim."

Suddenly Hellu looks serious. "Yusuf, don't complicate things. Axel took the knife from the kitchen and sank it into his father's heart. Salo's plan was to blackmail Eliel Zetterborg. Why would she kill the golden goose?"

"To silence him? Maybe he saw her, and she had to—"

"Zetterborg was supposed to know who was blackmailing him. I'm assuming that was the whole point of the treasure map."

"But Rea didn't want Zetterborg to recognize her, right? Then he would have known she was living with her son next door and—"

"Yusuf," Hellu interrupts emphatically, "Rea Salo did not shoot

Erik Raulo. She has an alibi: she was at home that morning and demonstrably in Teams contact with a party in Sweden."

Yusuf sighs. He eyes the bubbles rising from the bottom of the glass to the surface, then drains the glass in a single swig and stands.

"Thank you, Hellu. I appreciate your confidence. I really mean that."

104

Yusuf walks toward the unit's workstations, hands in his pockets. He is exhausted but happy.

Deep down, he feels a tinge of pride that he's not completely satisfied with the results of the investigation. Maybe his tendency to hedge is a good trait in a lead investigator after all. The quip-dishing Watson has become a perfection-seeking Holmes. But there's not much to be done anymore: the baton will be passed to the prosecutor, and the fates of Axel Zetterborg and Rea Salo will be transferred into other hands.

Yusuf looks at Jami Harjula, who is on his phone at his desk, head rising higher than the others. Yusuf's opinion of the guy has done a one-eighty over the course of the brief investigation. Yusuf has seen the flip side, come to understand the arrogance and cockiness mask insecurity and distress. Harjula isn't a jerk; he's just lost: an underpaid policeman wrestling with middle age and limping along in a dying marriage for the children's sake, and who on top of everything else has been overshadowed by those with more social skills. He's in a spiral he'll need a breakdown or perhaps professional help to pull out of. Or at least a divorce.

Yusuf's eyes seek out Nina, who is standing at the drinking fountain. Her muscular hand is holding a phone, her fingers whiz across the screen, and the smile on her face stretches from ear to ear. She looks like she's in love, and if anyone deserves happiness, it's Nina. Yusuf hopes with all his heart the guy doesn't turn out to be a creep like the past two. You'd be hard-pressed to find a person sweeter than Nina.

"Congratulations."

Yusuf is roused from his reverie by Tanja's voice. She has soundlessly appeared behind him, an open bottle of Coke in her hand.

"Same to you," Yusuf says. The dopamine surge stimulated by the champagne he drank in Hellu's office puts a smile on his face more quickly than may be wise. Or . . . who cares? *Knock it off with the overanalyzing already.* "I thought you went home."

"So did I."

"Huh?"

Tanja winks enigmatically. "Hey, Yusuf, do you know if Rasmus is single?"

"Rasmus?" Yusuf says slowly, and immediately regrets his tone. Why is he trying to hold down a guy they all really like? "I mean, I'm not sure. Yeah, he is."

"You're not sure but he is?"

"I guess he lives . . . Umm, yeah, I don't think he's seeing anyone at the moment."

"At the moment?" Tanja reveals her disarming smile and takes a swig of Coke.

"Why do you ask?"

Tanja doesn't immediately reply. She twists the cap back on the bottle with exaggerated slowness, then looks back up at Yusuf. "I have a friend who would probably be crazy about him. She's got this thing about taking care of people, if you know what I mean."

"I'm not sure I do, but—"

"Should we all go out tomorrow night? The four of us. Kind of like on a double date."

Yusuf glances at the workstations and sees the bald head peering over the cubicle divider. He isn't sure what's going on with Tanja, but Rasmus can't afford to lose this opportunity at any price.

Then he thinks about Anna and the baby she's having with Bradley Cooper.

And suddenly it all feels remote and unimportant. He can almost hear the shackles snap.

"Um . . . yeah. Sure. That would be fun," Yusuf says, then bursts into happy laughter out of sheer surprise.

105

THE INEVITABLE AFTERNOON darkness has once again snatched up the palatial Etu-Töölö apartment in its embrace. The wall clock in the kitchen ticks, indicating the hour.

Jessica is sitting at the end of the table, staring out the window. She had been intending to take a hot bath, to shut her eyes and try to peer into the other reality. To see if it truly is all over, if she is finally free now that Adlerkreutz is dead. No more waking up in the middle of the night, no more feeling her mother's hand on her shoulder. But does she want it all to end? She has been traveling between two worlds so long that she ultimately isn't sure she can live without both of them, without the shadow and the light.

But Jessica hasn't filled the bath, because she cannot tear herself away from the interrogation recordings.

Something about the whole thing stinks. That's what Yusuf said. And Jessica agrees one hundred percent.

She starts playing the video over again.

The screen is filled with Axel Zetterborg's angular face. The delicate neck between tensed shoulders carries a head crowned with black hair. Zetterborg is handsome and charismatic in his own way, sort of like a fiftyish Prince Charles, after whom he was nicknamed. The eyes are alert and lively. He speaks clearly, and the voice is soft. With its unsophisticated angles and faded colors, the recording reminds her of some movie's making-of documentary that includes footage of the actors' screen tests.

It's unlikely Axel Zetterborg would land a single role based on the video, unless the producers were specifically looking for utter despair and confusion. The man on the tape is anything but self-confident and charismatic. He looks like he's afraid of everything around him: the interrogator, the gray walls enveloping him, the approaching night he will spend in a holding cell. Most of all, however, he probably fears for his future, which he has flushed down the toilet by murdering his father. *Allegedly.*

Jessica sits up straighter and groans. Her ribs hurt like the devil, and even tiny movements are painful.

She rewinds to the beginning of the recording.

I've never been so angry in my life. . . .

I saw red. On an impulse, I grabbed the knife from the kitchen drawer.

I still don't get what was going through my head. . . .

Axel Zetterborg stumbles through his answers to Yusuf's questions. It seems as if he genuinely doesn't remember what happened in the apartment. Of course, it's possible he's an extraordinary actor.

Jessica understands perfectly well why Yusuf is dissatisfied with the material the investigative team has put together. Zetterborg is not going to confess, which in and of itself is not a catastrophe—a conviction will probably be secured even without a confession. But the more Jessica watches the video, the stronger her sense grows that something just doesn't add up.

She opens a folder on her computer that contains over a hundred images of the victim's apartment.

Living room: *The safe is closed. No one knows the combination.*

Entryway: *Books on the floor.*

Library: *Posters on the wall.* Silver from Across the Border. Under Your Skin. The Lapua Bride. *Director: Mikko Niskanen.*

Damn it. Jessica feels like she's scratching a match against the side of the box but can't get it to light.

She Googles Mikko Niskanen and brings up the Wikipedia article about the director.

Films . . .
Eight Deadly Shots (1972), *Pagliacci* (1973), *Small-holders* (1973)

And then . . .
The cursor stops on a made-for-TV movie filmed in 1974.
Wait a second. . . .
Jessica gapes at the screen.

Kianto

Jessica feels her pulse start racing.
She rewinds the recording to the beginning and watches it again.
I never could have killed Dad. . . . I thought it was a heart attack.
Jessica pauses the recording and looks at Axel Zetterborg's hand, which he has pressed to his chest. The fingers are clenched over the left pec.
The sudden insight cracks like a whip.
Goddamn it.
Jessica brings up the video footage Felix Salo shot through the peep-hole. In the grainy video, the figure stops, glances at the camera, and then opens the door. Before the door shuts, the camera captures a couple seconds of the apartment's dim entryway.
On the entryway floor, she sees a blotch of bright yellow.

106

NINA APPLIES A bit of gloss to her lips and casts a quick glance in the oval mirror. Tom's bathroom is surprisingly spacious and swanky. She didn't have occasion to use his bathroom the day before yesterday when they crossed the threshold and beelined for the bed and made love until Nina received word of Zetterborg's murder. It seems absurd to think the homicide happened only a moment before—

"What's keeping you?"

Tom's voice is coming from the other side of the door.

Nina smiles. "I'll be right out."

"I'm going to pop over to the restaurant downstairs for some ice."

Nina laughs. "OK."

She hears the front door open and unlocks the bathroom door. Her bare feet step onto gleaming parquet. Tom's generous, luxurious, stylishly decorated home is located in one of the best spots in town: its windows face Dianapuisto and the steeples of St. John's Church beyond.

Tom lives in a totally different world from the one she lives in.

Might the chasm between the worlds form a hurdle in the relationship?

Nina reaches for her stemmed glass and shakes off the doubt. She stands in front of a wall hung with a half dozen black-and-white photographs. One of them is of Tom with a young boy who has an arm thrown over the neck of a huge dog. Nina lets her fingertips graze the frame. The boy looks just like his father.

Nina is roused when an incoming text pings on her phone. She glances at the door and retrieves it from the table.

The message is from Tom.

You can open your present now.

Nina frowns.

She's followed Tom's instructions and hasn't opened the package he slipped into her pocket the day before.

She walks into the entryway and notices the front door is ajar. She can hear footsteps in the stairwell.

Nina slips her hand into her coat pocket, fishes out the pretty little gift box. And just then she is overcome by the curious sensation that she knows exactly what it contains.

107

JESSICA SITS DOWN on the bench, and the square-jawed man smiles tenderly at her.

"Warm evening," Joonas Lamberg says, crossing his legs.

"It sure is," Jessica replies. "If you weren't familiar with the realities of February, you could even say it felt like spring today."

Lamberg laughs good-naturedly. "Let's come back to that in two months' time."

Despite the cold weather, he isn't wearing gloves. Jessica looks at his rough fingertips; the tiny cracks in them are almost black. This has always been Jessica's thing, looking at people's hands. They say more about a man than a thousand words: have they lain for decades on a keyboard, or have their fingers clenched the grips of tools or weapons? She has studied countless hands and fingers over the course of her life, some of which she has permitted to wrap around her waist, sink into her hair, stroke her cheek, thrust inside her. Lower around her neck.

Their touch has sent her soaring to the heights but also plummeting down.

Joonas Lamberg's hands are safe and straightforward. They have no doubt seen more than enough life for one person.

"Thanks again for the other day. You and Yusuf saved my life," Jessica says.

Lamberg grunts and looks up at the branches of the leafless trees. "No big deal. But I think I was kind of in the wrong place; my former colleagues didn't seem too happy to find me going rogue there. We'll see if I'll be charged with something. . . ."

Jessica shakes her head. "You were helping a police officer. You saved one."

A wordless moment passes. The sound of a church bell carries from somewhere.

"I've been thinking a lot about what you said earlier. That by doing bad you can accomplish something good. At least by some calculation," Lamberg says.

"Are you still talking about Kangaroo? I thought we agreed that whatever we said about that would stay within the walls of your apartment."

Lamberg chuckles and zips up the imaginary zipper running across his mouth.

"And I remember you said the experience wasn't completely foreign to you. Can I ask what you meant by that?" Lamberg asks tentatively, and fails at not sounding intrusive.

Jessica sweeps a strand of black hair from her brow and shoves it under her beanie. "Not right now."

"Not now? But someday?"

"We'll see," Jessica says.

Lamberg folds his hands and leans back, relaxed. On this clear evening, the view from Tähtitorninmäki hill toward the brightly lit Market Square is downright breathtaking.

"The envelope . . . ," Jessica says.

"Right." Lamberg laughs and slips his hand into his breast pocket. "Did the orphans miss their money?" He hands the envelope to Jessica.

"No. I'm going to drop the money off at the organization this evening."

The corners of Lamberg's mouth turn down in an exaggerated frown. "So you're not going to stay for a little while?"

"Not this time."

"Maybe some other time?"

Jessica flashes a mysterious smile and removes the stack of bills from the envelope. Eyes it quickly, crumples up the envelope, and jams the bills into her wallet.

"Making sure it's all there?" Lamberg says with a laugh.

Jessica shuts her eyes and draws her lungs full of the biting frozen air. She gazes at the lights of Katajanokka, which are flickering under the bright starry sky.

"What were you thinking of doing now that you're unemployed? Taking a sabbatical?" Jessica eventually asks as she slips the wallet into her coat pocket.

"I don't think I can afford to yet. Unfortunately."

"Oh really? I was just thinking . . ." Jessica's voice trails off.

Lamberg laughs, then frowns. "You were just thinking what?"

"That you bought a one-way ticket. That doesn't sound like a week-long vacation."

Lamberg's face instantly darkens.

"To Málaga, right?" Jessica says.

"What are you—"

"If I had to guess, I'd put my money on Joonas Lamberg never setting foot in Finland again. If you board that plane, that is."

Lamberg scooches a few inches away and turns his torso toward Jessica. The mouth above the square jaw is searching for words, but the lips are glued shut.

"But I don't think that's going to happen," Jessica continues, "because you're going to be doing a lot of time for murder. Maybe life."

Lamberg laughs incredulously. "For murder? What the heck are you . . . You know the Kangaroo case is closed and . . ."

Jessica glances at her watch, then looks sternly at Lamberg. "I'm not talking about Kangaroo anymore, Lamberg. I'm talking about how you murdered Eliel Zetterborg."

108

SUDDENLY THE MOOD is charged as if lightning has struck. Something happens behind Lamberg's eyes that makes his face freeze in a stony impassiveness.

"We police have wondered this whole time how it would be possible for this setup to so powerfully combine such precise planning with a certain spontaneity," Jessica says. "And just a little while ago, it seemed as if it was all an incredible coincidence: that two people had broken into Zetterborg's apartment at the same time, for completely different reasons and without each other's knowledge. That would have solved the entire mystery. It was both a long-planned scheme and, on the other hand, a spontaneous homicide committed in the heat of the moment. And you as Zetterborg's bodyguard didn't have the slightest clue about either one."

"I didn't! How can you even—"

"But neither of those people killed Eliel Zetterborg."

"What makes you think—"

"Listen. Axel Zetterborg arrives early at the restaurant and decides to visit his father's apartment, which is only a block away. He searches for the letter and finds it. After reading the letter, Axel is taken over by a fit of passion. He feels the letter is the worst possible betrayal that a father can commit against his son. And then Dad suddenly appears as if by magic. Not sure himself why, Axel takes a knife from the kitchen. He is simply out of his head with rage—and Axel is known to have a tendency toward this sort of behavior: impulsive and reckless.

"And so Axel and Eliel have a fierce exchange, and the old man's heart can't take it. Maybe Eliel spots the knife in Axel's hand. In any event, Eliel has had heart trouble for a long time and medicated it with aspirin, and now he falls to the floor, lifeless. Axel panics, drops the knife and the letter to the floor, and flees the apartment through the back door. After he makes it out, Axel initially intends to call an ambulance but quickly reasons that he can't. He wasn't supposed to have been in his father's apartment. And then there's the knife that's lying on the floor. And the letter! No, Axel thinks his father has probably died from the attack, and in that chaotic moment maybe even hopes he has. Instead of calling emergency services, he calls his father twice in order to have some sort of alibi, however weak, and a reason to make a concerned call to you. So the agitation you hear in Axel's voice is completely genuine, and you bound up the stairs to your boss' apartment. In the meantime, Eliel has recovered sufficiently to have called for an ambulance himself. But he's too weak to tell the operator what's happening, and a moment later he loses consciousness again. It can be heard clearly on the recording how you ring the doorbell, knock, and then finally step in. You see Zetterborg there on the floor and the kitchen knife lying nearby. Maybe the cell phone in your boss' hand. But what you don't immediately realize is that he's on the line with emergency services. You probably have no idea what happened in the apartment, but the scene looks chaotic. You assume of course that Zetterborg was stabbed and is now dead.

"But what you didn't fail to notice was the open safe in the living room wall. The one where your filthy-rich boss keeps everything of value that doesn't fit in his securities accounts at the bank. A rainy-day stash that surprisingly many wealthy people have. You tell yourself you can call emergency services after you've taken yourself a little souvenir. You grab a fat stack of cash, and when you turn to look, to your surprise Eliel is conscious again and staring at you. 'Kianto,' he manages to say."

Joonas Lamberg shakes his head and looks simultaneously offended and amused.

"*Kianto* . . . You can hear it on the recording," Jessica continues. "We thought long and hard about what it meant, but it was only when I realized that Eliel loved Mikko Niskanen's films that we figured it out. *Kianto—Bite the Hand That Feeds You* from 1974. It was the only word the old man managed to say as he was dying. I immediately knew it was you: Eliel's dog. The nickname had carried to your ears too, which is probably one reason you didn't think much of the guy."

"Horseshit," Joonas Lamberg says, and stands.

"Wait," Jessica says. "I'm not finished yet. Let's go back to that moment. Arms weighed down with your loot, you walk over to Eliel, who is struggling for his life. You understand your opportunistic theft will come out if Eliel recovers. You look at the knife and wonder what exactly happened to him. What if you stabbed him again, this time so he will be sure to die? No—then you might be suspected as the perp. Damn. But you notice the phone in Eliel's hand. You see he's connected to emergency dispatch. At first you freak out, but after you pause to think, you see the opportunity this presents. You can see from the screen that the call has already lasted six minutes. Eliel encountered an attacker armed with a knife in his apartment and called emergency services. Axel called you five minutes before and asked you to run upstairs. It's audible on the recording when you ring the doorbell and knock. You enter and call out for Zetterborg. And it's not until a minute later, when you *finally* find your boss stabbed on the floor, that you grab the phone and give the address. I know one of the security cameras on the block will reveal to the police not only the fact that someone fled the scene, but also that you were still sitting in the front seat of the Maybach when the emergency call was originally placed. In other words, you have a watertight alibi. There's no way you could have been the assailant."

"You've got some balls," Lamberg says.

"You calmly and coolly report to emergency dispatch that someone has been *stabbed in the chest with a steel blade* . . . although in reality, the knife hadn't even touched Zetterborg yet at this point. Which explains how Zetterborg held on as long as he did after the knife had supposedly pierced his heart. Well, he didn't hold on. As a matter of fact, Zetterborg died almost immediately of the wound he received. It's just that it was inflicted six minutes later than we originally assumed. I can imagine the dread Zetterborg felt when he heard your words and understood your intentions. In theory, it would be possible to hear the blade sink into his heart in the background of the emergency call, while you hold your huge hand over the victim's mouth to stifle his death rattle. Of course some of the sounds are drowned out by the piano music playing in the background."

"This is some shaky guesswork," Lamberg says.

"Then Axel returns to the apartment. On the recordings from the embassy's CCTV cameras, you can see him run up to the door to the building and unlock it with his own key. Axel is shocked, but you don't let him contaminate the scene. In reality, Axel returned to look for the letter he left at his father's side in his panic."

Joonas Lamberg shuts his eyes and breathes deeply through his nose.

"But there is no letter on the floor, because you have it. I'm not sure at what stage you read the letter, but after you read it, you understand it will steer suspicions in Axel's direction."

"Listen, if that were true and I really found the letter, why wouldn't I have turned it over to the police right away and had Axel sent straight to prison?"

"That's a question that can be answered only by someone who knows the nature of your soul. The letter was another opportunity. You shoved it in your breast pocket for later use. It was your get-out-of-jail-free card just in case, in spite of everything, suspicions fell on you. On the other hand, maybe Axel knew you had the letter. Maybe you'd be able to fleece Axel for some cash before you flew to Málaga to live out your retirement days. But first you had to take care of Erik Raulo, because why would Axel Zetterborg have left the only person who knew about the letter alive?"

"I could have just said I saw Axel fleeing the scene while I was sitting in the car. . . ."

"You know yourself that's not true. The cameras you thought would prove your innocence saw the same thing you did sitting in your car. Whoever the killer was, they must have run out the back door and through the gate to the street. There's no way you could have seen Axel leave."

"Is that it?" Lamberg says with a mocking smile. "Is that the best you can do?"

"Opportunistic kleptomania," Jessica says. "It's a relatively rare impulse control disorder, but you clearly suffer from it. My suspicions were roused when you said the ransom money paid to Kangaroo was never found. And the only person who knew the location of the money just happened to take a bullet to the skull. Kangaroo wasn't a pedophile; I checked with the vice unit, and there was never any mention of it. The theory is also supported by the fact that Erik Raulo's killer simply had to take something from the house immediately after committing the homicide. Literally anything. A little porcelain elephant was chosen as the spoil; the police weren't supposed to be able to deduce anything from its disappearance, if they even noticed. You're a smart man, so maybe you either hid the elephant or got rid of it already, but I wouldn't be surprised if it was found during a search of your apartment."

"You're crazy."

"I wanted confirmation for this hypothesis, so I left an envelope in your apartment containing eleven two-hundred-euro bills. And just as I suspected, you returned only ten. Why did you dare to do that? Because I mentioned in the car that the envelope contained two thousand euros. And if you're prepared to take a risk like that over such a small sum, it's not hard to figure out human life doesn't weigh much in the equation when the stakes rise."

Joonas Lamberg looks around. The park is far from empty: there are families and people walking their dogs, and that's exactly why Jessica has chosen this public spot for their meeting.

"Would you like me to continue?" Jessica says.

"Be my guest," Lamberg says, trying to feign amusement.

"Eliel Zetterborg always sealed his letters with red wax. But the letter you gave me was sealed in a white envelope. You made up a story according to which Eliel never wrote names on envelopes, which wasn't true, of course. And when you couldn't think of a safe way to blackmail Axel, you decided to settle for the money you stole from Eliel and handed the envelope to me."

"You listen here, Jessica Niemi," Lamberg says, leaning in closer.

Jessica's pulse is pounding in her ears, but she tries to look calm and relaxed.

"If I nicked Zeta's money from the safe, how the hell did I carry it out of that apartment? In my pockets?"

"We're just coming to that. My colleague was right the whole time to wonder why there was a stack of books on the floor. The cleaner didn't misremember; they really were waiting there in a yellow bag to be returned to the library. So, after you've pulled the knife out of your boss' chest and seen him die, you immediately start to think how to get the money past the authorities. You remember the bag in the entryway, grab it, and stuff the money in it. On a whim, you take the pistol from the safe before you press the door shut. But what then? You can't go out into the stairwell with the bag. There's the embassy camera. Maybe one of the neighbors will peek out their door. And the police might check the Maybach; maybe it will be confiscated right away. If you throw the bag out the window to Vuorimiehenkatu, someone— a police officer or a bystander—will find it before you have time to come back for it. Well, of course you've been inside Zetterborg's apartment dozens of times, made coffee, and read the paper in the kitchen. Your eyes have no doubt struck upon the hatch above the sink: the trash chute, no longer in use. So it was possible for you to wait for the police to arrive and walk down to the car with them without anyone even theoretically suspecting you of theft. You came to the station to tell your story, after which you were allowed to go. The next morning you jogged from your home to Ullanlinna, where Yusuf and I happened to run into you. A moment before, you had entered the basement, which has its entrance on the Vuorimiehenkatu side of the building. You played angst ridden, distressed that you had done your work poorly. The truth was, you had something in your backpack that at that point no one even knew was missing and maybe never would, because Eliel Zetterborg was the only one who knew the code to the safe. And even if someone realized it was missing, no one would have ever thought to look for it in the basement."

Joonas Lamberg shuts his eyes.

"I've squashed only assholes. Kangaroo was an asshole, OK: maybe not a pedophile, but a kidnapper just the same. Zetterborg, a real fucking asshole. Same for Raulo. You I like, but maybe I can make an exception. Take your life—even though I just helped save it."

"Here? With all these people around?"

"You know I could snap your neck without anyone even noticing," Lamberg says calmly. "I don't need a weapon to kill."

"Right. Krav Maga. A demonstration of professional competence, or how did you put it?" Jessica speaks calmly, but her instincts are screaming at her to get out of there. Once again, she has deliberately put herself in harm's way, although she has a loaded pistol under her coat and civilian-disguised colleagues will rush to her aid in seconds if the situation so requires.

"Or I can let you go and we forget this chat. Your word against mine, right?" Lamberg laughs. "We both know that tinfoil-hat theory of yours isn't going to go through in court. Remember, I attended the same police college courses you did."

Jessica looks for a moment at Lamberg, whose eyes are no longer melancholy at all. Just the opposite: they blaze with pure rage.

"Maybe it won't. But there's something you still don't know. Your apartment is being searched by half a dozen police officers as we speak, and I bet they'll find—well, if not that porcelain elephant, then at least the contents of the yellow plastic bag." As Jessica speaks, Lamberg's hands clench into fists.

Suddenly Lamberg rises from his bench and starts walking briskly down the icy path. Jessica pulls out her gun and aims it at his back. Her right hand, which is holding the weapon, feels awkward, her trigger finger stiff.

"Joonas Lamberg, you are under arrest for two homicides!"

Lamberg turns around, face red with rage. "Fucking whore!" Instead of making the slightest sign of giving in, he starts walking toward the armed Jessica.

"I'll shoot," Jessica says, and the pain from hooking her finger spikes all the way to her wrist. Her entire body is on fire.

"Go ahead and shoot, goddamn it. I'm going to wring your fucking—"

Jessica's heart skips a beat.

Lamberg is within two yards of her before a shot rings out. Then another.

People shriek; strolling turns to running.

Two civilian police sprint up, pistols in hand.

Jessica gasps for breath.

Lamberg falls to his knees before her.

It's over.

NINA SITS UP and listens to the man at her side snoring. She came to the conclusion long ago that there's no such thing as a perfect life. There are only moments that brush up against perfection, with room sometimes for longer quiet spells in between. This evening has been truly perfect, and she wishes it will never end. She and Tom live in different worlds, and that's a fact. But suddenly that feels like an opportunity, not a threat. The necklace dangles from her hooked fingers. And it too is perfect.

THE HUM OF the electric kettle grows louder until a faint click kills it.

"What made you realize it was Lamberg all along?" Yusuf says, sitting down at the table.

Jessica's enormous kitchen is bathed in the soft light Jessica set with the dimmer a moment before.

"I was sitting at that table in the darkness. That's when I always think most clearly," Jessica says, pouring boiling water into the cups. She hands one to Yusuf, then sits down next to him.

The muted flat-screen television is showing the news about the latest twists in the case. An image of Joonas Lamberg's face flashes across the screen.

"Actually, it all started when I realized Axel couldn't have done it."

"What made you realize that?"

"It was more of a hunch than certainty. I watched the videotape of you questioning him. He was talking about a heart attack and put his hand here." Jessica places her hand on top of her left breast. "To the left. Too far left. And a little too high. In reality, the heart is in the middle of the chest, tilted a little to the left. That's where the myth comes from that the heart is located under the left breast, and most people seem to believe it."

Yusuf whistles, impressed.

"Zetterborg was stabbed straight in the heart. And Erik Raulo was shot there. And so was Kangaroo in 2009. The killer knew where the human heart is located and understood how to take someone's life as efficiently as possible. Axel Zetterborg is a douche but he's not a killer."

"You're so fucking good."

Jessica rakes her hands through her hair and ties it back. "Yusuf, you just saved me from certain death. You're the one here who's fucking good."

"I got help from Lamberg," Yusuf says.

"So should I have been grateful?"

Yusuf shakes his head.

Jessica knows the question will never leave her in peace. Joonas Lamberg will come to her in her dreams, just like everyone else with whom she has stared death in the face.

"What about the money thing? How did you come up with that?"

"I thought there was something strange about the Kangaroo case. About the ransom never having been found. And that Lamberg wasn't liked by his fellows in the SWAT unit. In groups like that, the only way to be unpopular is by being dishonest or going rogue. I thought I'd play the good old Poirot trick on him to reveal opportunism and dishonesty. The fact that Lamberg took one of the bills simply because he happened to have the opportunity confirmed my suspicions."

"The good old Poirot trick? Have you played it on me too?"

"Maybe you'd remember if I had. Maybe not."

Yusuf smiles and stretches his arms. Jessica leans in toward him.

"Listen, Yusuf. There's still one more favor I need from you."

"What?"

"And you'll either do it or you won't. But I'll be really offended if you refuse."

"Tell me. What's this favor?"

"When you go to HQ and Hellu asks how suspicions ultimately landed on Joonas Lamberg, I want you to take the credit. You did such amazing work as lead investigator that it would be wrong if you didn't—"

"But, Jessica . . . I can't, damn it. . . ."

"Like I said, you decide. But I'm asking you."

"Holy hell. Of course you should get the credit for solving the case. Earlier today we didn't have a clue as to who—"

"Yusuf," Jessica says softly, and presses her finger to Yusuf's mouth, "shut the fuck up."

Yusuf looks her dead in the eye. Jessica can feel his lips against her finger, the warm breath surging from his nostrils against her palm.

Jessica slowly lowers her finger, but Yusuf's eyes don't follow it; they remain firmly locked on hers. The two of them are leaning toward each other, sitting so close that Jessica can see the pores around Yusuf's nose and the finer-than-fine veins in his eyes.

"OK," Yusuf eventually says. "If that's the way you want it."

Jessica breaks the spell by coughing into her fist and standing. She walks over to the sink and begins scouring the cup with a dish brush as if trying to come up with some activity to distract herself.

She dries the teacup, puts it in the cupboard, and then turns to look at Yusuf, who has risen from his chair.

"I guess we could celebrate somehow . . . watch a crappy movie or something," Jessica suggests.

But Yusuf shoots her an apologetic look. "I'm actually busy tonight."

"Oh, you are? OK."

"Yup."

"A date?"

"Something like that."

"With that CSI?" Jessica says. For some reason, it's hard to conjure up a teasing smirk.

"Yeah, and . . . it's a long story. I'll tell you sometime."

A MOMENT LATER, the front door closes, and Jessica is left standing alone in her huge entry hall.

She listens to the sounds carrying from the stairwell: the metallic thunk of the elevator gate and the whir of the elevator car's cables. Soon Yusuf will open the door to the street and speed off in his Golf to his date with pretty Tanja.

Good for you, Yusuf.

But something about it all feels off.

Jessica can still open the door and call out to Yusuf. Or phone him and . . .

Say what?

She doesn't know what she should say. Or wants to say. Or if there will even be anything to say.

Yusuf is the only one who knows the truth about her: her apartment, her money. Yusuf knows Jessica, and she believes she knows Yusuf.

And now he's on his way to meet Tanja, whom he probably doesn't know at all yet.

And maybe that's the way it's supposed to go: there's something beautiful about new beginnings. The excitement of novelty and the illusion of perfection that Yusuf will never have a chance to experience if they ever—

No.

Don't even go there.

The vast apartment radiates emptiness, as it always does. But for some reason, there's a finality to Yusuf's departure today. Jessica knows deep down that the recent days, in all their horror, have put something irreversible into motion.

She squeezes her eyes shut.

She never has to ask.

All she has to do is wait, and her mother will return. Lower a hand to her shoulder. Comfort her.

Jessica wants to be the little girl whom her mother lifts into her lap. Whom her father tucks in. Whom Toffe admires and looks up to.

Mom?

Jessica waits, hopes. But she doesn't feel the hand on her shoulder.

Mom, please.

Nothing happens. She doesn't hear the rustle of a gown's hems anywhere.

A tear rolls over Jessica's cheekbone and finds an as-yet-untraveled route across her skin, follows it over her jaw and down to her throat.

I need darkness.

Jessica turns off the lights, steps over to the window, and closes the curtains. And then to the second window, and the third, until the large living room is almost pitch-black.

She never has to ask. That's the way it has always been.

Mom! Jessica now says, and her sobbing makes her stammer.

She would give anything to see the crushed, bloody pulp of her mother's face again, the shattered cheekbones, the limbs contorted into unnatural positions.

Her mother's rigid gait, which projects something abominable.

Mom!

Mom! Mom!

Jessica finds herself shouting at the top of her lungs, but instead of her mother, what appears is pain: the unbearable neuralgia that radiates from her neck to her fingers and all the way to her toes knocks her to the floor.

She is used to pain; it has been her companion since childhood. Even so, she has never tasted the absolute solitude that punches into her awareness on this February afternoon.

The dead have deserted her.

Does this new loneliness mean everything's going to get worse? Or could this be the first step toward healing?

RASMUS SUSIKOSKI RUBS the moisturizer furiously between his palms, then spreads it over his scalp. The ointment, which smells of tar, cost dozens of euros, but the pharmaceutical assistant said it would relieve inflammation and get rid of dandruff. Rasmus has already smeared on several layers, but his scalp looks as awful as ever.

Fourth time's the charm.

Rasmus exhales a deep, trembling sigh and studies his reflection in his computer monitor. There is no mirror in his room, so the integrated webcam is going to have to play the part.

You look nice.

Despite his lack of experience, Rasmus has always kept his ears open and knows perfectly well that it's not sexy to be insecure. And that's exactly what he is. Not sexy, just *really darn* insecure. Why on earth would anyone want to go on a date with him? Is this some cruel joke? Rasmus has plenty of experience with those, although in recent years he has managed to avoid the worst humiliations.

But Yusuf assured him Tanja's friend is interested in him. Rasmus asked three times if the friend had actually seen his picture, and each time Yusuf answered in the affirmative. Rasmus trusts Yusuf, knows Yusuf wouldn't put him in an awkward situation, at least not intentionally.

Rasmus wipes the excess ointment on a dirty T-shirt and realizes his hands are shaking.

He has changed shirts three times and ultimately gone back to his original plan: an ironed white dress shirt and a light blue sweater that won't show dandruff. Or will show it but not as obviously.

As long as you feel good in it. That's what Yusuf told him.

Let's have a fun evening. No stress.

It's easy for Yusuf—with his perfect smile, six-pack, and angelic face—to not stress.

Rasmus glances at his wrist to check the time. Half an hour to go.

It will take him three minutes to walk to the bus stop, where he will wait for maybe two, and then the bus will take thirteen minutes to reach Kaisaniemi. From there, a five-minute walk to the restaurant.

He has time to change his shirt. Or should he ask Yusuf's opinion?

"Rasse."

Rasmus emerges from his reverie to see father in the bedroom doorway. Normally Rasmus would have heard the knock, but apparently he is far too worked up. Either that or Dad didn't knock.

"We're leaving in fifteen minutes," Dad says.

Rasmus' heart skips a beat. "Fifteen minutes . . . Where?"

Dad sighs as if the question alone is the greatest of betrayals. "Grandma's birthday."

"I thought it was tomorrow."

"No, it's today. Look, you're already dressed for it."

"I wasn't getting ready for that. I . . . I have other plans."

"You?" The way his father says the word hurts. "What plans?"

Rasmus knows he can lie and say he has to work. This is the first evening in several that he's been home. But lying to his parents is something he simply isn't programmed to do.

"I'm meeting friends."

"Listen." Dad shuts the door behind him and steps into the room. "Grandma is turning ninety and is expecting to see you. What friend can be more important than that? It might be Grandma's last birthday. Her last decade, at least."

"But . . ."

"I think it's best if you reschedule your plans, don't you? Besides, you have to drive because Mom and I had a little red wine."

Rasmus feels like he's going to explode with frustration.

Dad lowers his hand to Rasmus' shoulder, just like he has for the past thirty-four years.

Rasmus burns with the desire to wrench free of Dad's tender touch. Tell him to go screw himself.

Rage that the desiccated mummy who trained spotlights on Russian bombers during World War II doesn't even realize who visits her at the assisted-living facility in hopes of a little inheritance. He burns with desire to pack his favorite games and collectibles and finally look for an apartment of his own and live his own life. Just like any other normal thirty-four-year-old . . .

"We'll see you downstairs soon. Why don't you change into that black shirt? That one is a little threadbare," Dad says, and leaves the room.

Rasmus stares at his reflection in the computer monitor: The face above the threadbare light blue sweater. Thick glasses. A monk's haircut and a bald spot the expensive ointment has made even angrier than before.

Maybe it's better this way.

Maybe Mom and Dad have just saved him from certain humiliation.

Rasmus gulps to get rid of the lump stuck in his throat.

It's time to cut the cord.

112

HELENA LAPPI STRETCHES the fingers of her left hand; they feel stiff in the pinch of the tight glove. *The glove is supposed to be tight*—that's what the damn pro said. Hellu adjusts her grip, and her feet take teeny steps as the body searches for the perfect stance.

The head of the driver rises back slowly and pauses before Hellu swings the club through the ball into the air. There's a thud as the ball falls into the gap between the net and the backstop, and Hellu glances at her computer screen. 332 feet with a seven iron. Apply more force to the shaft. Damn it. She's going to have to put in a ton of work before she dares to fly to Portugal with Hanna to tour some of the best greens in the world. She doesn't want her wife to be ashamed of her.

Hellu sees a shadow fall across the driving range mat.

"Take a wider stance," Yusuf says.

Apparently Hellu has been holding her breath this whole time, because now the air evacuates her lungs in one long exhale.

"Are your tips worth taking?" Hellu says, shoving her driver into the bag.

"I spent my childhood at the Nevas course," Yusuf says seriously as he unzips his coat.

"OK. I didn't even know you play."

"Childhood was a while ago."

Hellu takes a sip from her bottle of mineral water. "Did you come to hit too?"

Yusuf shakes his head.

Hellu can tell from his body language that he has come to confess.

"It was Jessica," he says, sitting on the bench behind the mat. "Jessica is the one who realized it was Lamberg."

Hellu swirls the mineral water in her mouth before swallowing it, then gives an enigmatic smile. "I guessed." She sits down next to Yusuf. "And I'm not saying you couldn't have solved it just the same, but . . . well, somehow it had Jessica's handprint on it. I respect the fact that you came to me and told me the truth, though. It won't be held against you; I can promise you that."

"I couldn't have taken the credit for something—"

Hellu cuts Yusuf off with a dismissive wave. "Yusuf, now I know the truth. But let's keep this between you and me. Jessica doesn't need to know that I know."

"OK."

Hellu can see Yusuf feels bad. He clearly doesn't like going behind Jessica's back—despite the fact that his confession has raised Jessica's stock in the boss' eyes. Yusuf probably promised not to say anything and in violating his promise has betrayed his friend's trust. The fact that Jessica insisted her colleague take the credit also says a lot about Jessica. Hellu feels like her respect for the aloof detective sergeant grows by the day.

She decides to change the focus of the conversation. "Salo and Zetterborg junior were released to await trial."

"I figured. The charges weren't that serious in the end."

"I know. In a way, I wish both of them could be charged with more."

"Tell me about it." Yusuf glances at his watch. "The world is an unfair place."

Hellu tosses her empty bottle into her bag and eyes Yusuf. Something about the way he's acting indicates more surprises are in store. "What is it now?"

"Speaking of unfairness, there's something else," he says listlessly.

"What?"

"I received word from the hospital fifteen minutes ago that Hjal-mar Ek is dead."

Hellu's heart skips a beat. "What? How . . . ?"

"He slit his wrists in the bathroom. I don't know what he used. He left a handwritten note saying it's worse to live with a murder on your conscience than to nurse an eternal grudge."

Hellu shuts her eyes. For a moment, all she can hear is the hum of the HVAC equipment and the thunk of a clubhead; an old man is hit-ting farther off.

"But the hospital was supposed to look after him. . . ."

"Sure. But if someone really wants to ice themselves, what the fuck can you do about it in the end?"

"But what about the note? Hjalmar didn't kill anyone. . . ." Hellu's voice trails off. "Or did he?"

Yusuf shrugs. "I don't get it. If Hjalmar really killed someone at some point, the victim's identity is going to remain an eternal mystery to us. At least there was no indication of anything of the sort during any of the interrogations."

Hellu unclenches her gloved fist. The white leather at the base of the thumb is stained black from the worn rubber of her grip.

Yusuf glances at his watch.

"Plans for the evening?" Hellu asks.

"Yeah." Yusuf grunts. "We're going out to eat . . . or actually I'm going out to eat. . . . Whatever. See you at the press conference in the morning."

"Thank you, Yusuf."

Yusuf rises from the bench and disappears through the driving range exit without another word.

Hellu turns to the backstop: a beautiful fairway has been painted on it, with the water hazards gleaming bright blue and sand traps as golden as the beaches of a tropical island. A white fireball blazes from a sky shaded in different tints of blue, which binds the landscape into a single soul-stirring whole. Hellu places her fingers at the sides of her forehead to block the ugly white concrete walls from her field of vision, along with the tacky halogen lights that illuminate the place. For a moment, she can pretend she's sitting at one of the Algarve's countless golf courses, which are where she and Hanna will be playing this summer. Sun, self-care, golf, and stress-free love.

The trip has set her back a small fortune. She means to board that plane if it kills her.

She shuts her eyes and hopes she'll be able to forget her work and its grimness for the duration of her two-week vacation.

There's not much more she can hope for from life.

But right now, with her eyes closed, Hellu sees an image of a lifeless man sprawled on the floor of a hospital bathroom—a man who, despite his privileged start in life, turned out to be anything but successful and loved.

It's worse to live with a murder on your conscience than to nurse an eternal grudge.

The trip. A small fortune.

No one has ever said fun is free, and it's true there can always be more money. But killing someone over it is something Hellu will never understand.

Hellu thinks about the money Lamberg took from his boss' apartment. Two hundred thousand euros in five-hundred-euro bills. Four hundred bills packed in a yellow plastic shopping bag.

The motive for terrible deeds seems so often to be money.

Money. Hot money. Cash.

But why did Hjalmar Ek withdraw so much cash?

The world is an unfair place.

Holy hell!

The insight zaps into her awareness like a lightning bolt shooting up her club.

It's a thought that has never even remotely occurred to anyone yet.

Hellu flies to her golf bag and fumbles in the side pocket for her phone.

Hurry!

Yusuf is sure to have Axel Zetterborg's number saved on his phone. Hopefully it won't be too late.

113

Axel Zetterborg steps out of the car and zips up his coat. He sees the woman standing on the sand, smoking and gazing out to sea. Her blond hair is tossed in the brisk wind. She is still damn gorgeous.

"Hey," Axel says, slamming the car door shut.

"Hey to you too."

Axel walks thirty feet toward the woman and stops at a safe distance, hands in his pockets. For a moment the two of them eye each other, probing intensely. It would be impossible for an outsider to grasp anything about the nature of their relationship. There is no longing in the piercing gazes, at best some sort of twisted satisfaction in the reunion.

"Rea Salo?" Axel says, a faint enigmatic smile forming on his lips.

"I had to come up with something," the woman says with a shake of her head. "Your father would have remembered my name."

"You're all grown-up."

"I'm not sure I can say the same for you," Rea says. "There you go again, ready to screw people's lives away."

"Screw, maybe. But what the fuck were those rape accusations back then?"

Rea grunts drily. "Nothing ventured, nothing gained."

"You're one sick bitch." Axel shakes his head. "When was the last time we saw each other?"

"Is something wrong with your memory? Two days ago, inside your father's apartment, although I guess you didn't see me."

Axel laughs mirthlessly and looks out to sea. A large passenger ship sails in the distance.

"I guess we were at the wrong place at the wrong time, Laura. Kudos to the detectives for their thorough police work; otherwise both of us might be in prison for life."

Rea tosses her cigarette butt into the sea. "We might still end up in prison, Axel. Trespassing, inciting assault, abandonment . . ."

Axel nods slightly and rocks between his heels and the balls of his feet.

The ironically affectionate foreplay is over. The warm-up, the small talk. Time to get down to business.

"What the hell do you want, Laura? You already got everything you needed," Axel said. "I don't understand why you came back."

"You don't?"

"I bet you could have gotten more money if you'd just asked—"

"I asked. I sent your father plenty of emails. He didn't reply to a single one. And then I understood how damned disrespectfully I'd been treated all those years ago. Like some cheap whore you knocked up and was sent abroad, out of sight."

Axel laughs and shoves his hands into his pockets. "Well, if we're being honest, I guess technically that's what you were."

Now Rea looks at him in a different way; hatred burns in her eyes.

Axel takes a few steps toward her. "Let's knock it off with the nonsense. The old man did quite a number on me. I'm not going to inherit the kingdom. And I don't have much left to split with you or any other gold diggers. So why don't you pack your bags and get the fuck out of here?"

Rea pinches her eyes shut, presumably to prevent the tear ducts from opening. "Felix wants to meet you."

"Felix? That creep who secretly filmed me—"

"Felix is your son!"

Axel bursts out in rollicking, incredulous laughter. "Felix or whatever the fuck nutjob . . . he's not my son. He never was and never will be. Get that through your head and that freak's life will be easier too."

A tear falls to Rea's cheek and disappears surprisingly quickly in the icy wind.

"You're a monster—a spoiled brat and a monster."

"No, Laura. We're both monsters. I think that's already been made plain."

"If that's what you think . . . why the hell did you ask me to meet you here?" Rea retorts, incensed.

In that second, time seems to stop.

Their eyes freeze on each other. Axel feels his stomach lurch. The wind picks up.

He has the urge to say something, to argue, but the unexpected realization prompted by Laura's question has stopped him in his tracks.

It was Laura who asked to meet, not the other way around.

"Why?" Rea asks again, but she stops talking when she sees the perplexed look on Axel's face.

"Did you get a text message?" Axel says.

"Yes! You're the one who sent it to me. . . . Axel?"

The taut tarps outside the warehouse pop and snap in the gusts.

"Axel?" Rea says.

Axel takes a wary step backward and looks around. And in that instant, Rea appears to understand too.

Axel turns on his heels and starts walking toward his car. He scans his surroundings frantically. Thirty feet.

He sees the ladder leading to the roof of the metal warehouse. The movement at the top.

And then he hears it: the long, reedy wail that is like a brisk whistling wind.

The dark, wet landscape with yellow streetlamps sprinkling their light unevenly abruptly turns pitch-black. Axel no longer sees anything; he feels a light pressure at his forehead, a slight pain, and notes a fleeting taste of iron. Then nothing.

———

L'Étranger looks through the scope as the curly-haired man slumps to the asphalt, as if the bullet severed the noose from which a corpse hung. The woman is shrieking in terror. L'Étranger loads another round into the barrel, quickly shifts the scope, a little too quickly, and manages only to wound the woman. He will finish her off at close distance.

He slips down the ladder nimbly, like a firefighter roused by an alarm.

He drops to the asphalt as soundlessly as a ghost and steps toward the hysterically weeping woman. Blood is pumping from the temple of the man sprawled on the asphalt.

A beautiful hit, if I do say so myself.

The woman tries to crawl away, but L'Étranger grabs her blood-spattered hair and turns her face toward him. Strands of blond hair coil around his gloved fingers.

She begs for mercy. Finnish sounds strange even when the person speaking it isn't in mortal danger, let alone now, when the words are panicked. L'Étranger presses the barrel to the woman's forehead. Not gently but as painfully as possible.

"No one is going to hear you scream, least of all the person who sent me."

He can tell from the woman's expression that she doesn't speak French. Otherwise she would probably have time to register the meaning of the words before the bullet sends part of her brain flying to the gravel sloping toward the sea.

And then silence. L'Étranger glances around. The harbor is deserted. The faint shots were drowned out by the crash of the waves. The thirty-five-thousand-euro assignment has been completed; his ship will leave in two hours.

His thoughts have returned to the dissertation, which has been lent fresh perspective and inspiration by these days in Helsinki. He doesn't know why he was sent to do this job, and he doesn't need to know. He knows nothing about the decades-long grudge there was no diluting, even with all the seas and raindrops in the world. But maybe L'Étranger could have benefited from a brief conversation with his client: perhaps the motive would have deepened his understanding of the meaninglessness of existence.

THANK YOU

Friends and family—thank you for your patience!

Editorial Manager Petra Maisonen and the team from Tammi: Outi, Jaakko, Timo T., Johanna, Miguel, Reetta, Markko, V-P, and Timo J.

Elina Ahlbäck Literary Agency: Elina, Linda, Toomas, and Ebba

Michelle Vega at Berkley

Jon Elek at Welbeck

Rhea Lyons and Josh Getzler at HG Literary

Kristian London

Professor Antti Sajantila

Harri Gustafsberg

Mika Niemi

Teemu Kaarniemi

THE
LAST
GRUDGE

MAX SEECK

READERS GUIDE

QUESTIONS FOR DISCUSSION

1. The relationships between fathers and sons figure prominently in *The Last Grudge*. What effects do their relationships with their fathers have on Axel and Hjalmar? How have their lives been altered by their fathers?

2. After Yusuf is made lead investigator on the Zetterborg case, what challenges does he face in his new role? Have you ever been intimidated by a new opportunity? How did you handle it?

3. Yusuf experiences personal turmoil throughout the book. How does his personal life affect his work? How do you feel about the realization he comes to regarding his ex-girlfriend?

4. How do you feel about Jessica's decision to take herself off the Zetterborg case? Do you think she let Yusuf down?

5. Jessica's relationship with her mother is extremely complicated. Do you think Jessica needs her mother in her life? Do you think she loves her?

6. As the book progresses, the frequency and nature of Jessica's interactions with her mother change. How do these changes affect Jessica? How has her relationship with her mother shaped who she is?

7. Do you agree with how Zetterborg handles Axel in regard to his company? Is he justified in his decision?

8. Both Nina and Rasmus are important contributors to the investigation. How do they use their skills to help? How do their respective pasts affect the new relationships that spark for each of them as the case unfolds?

9. Yusuf and Jessica are more than coworkers; they are close friends as well. What challenges does their friendship face throughout the book? What strengthens their bond? Does anything weaken it?

10. Helsinki is a character in its own right. Are there any spots you would like to visit in the city and throughout Finland?

Photo by Marek Sabogal

International and *New York Times* bestselling author **Max Seeck** writes novels and screenplays full-time. His accolades include the Finnish Whodunnit Society's Debut Thriller of the Year Award 2016 and the Storytel audiobook award for Best Crime Novel for *The Witch Hunter*, known internationally as *The Faithful Reader*. An avid reader of Nordic noir for personal pleasure, he listens to film scores as he writes. Max lives with his wife and children near Helsinki.

CONNECT ONLINE

MaxSeeck.com/books

🐦 MaxSeeck
📷 MaxSeeck
f MaxSeeck

Ready to find
your next great read?

Let us help.

Visit prh.com/nextread

Penguin
Random
House